Nightmares
In
Dixie

When night falls over the American South, stories loom out of the landscape. Everything hints at legend: the scream of a train whistle across Kentucky, the roar of hot-rodders streaking through the Florida Everglades. French Quarter voodoo seems a little less laughable than it did in broad daylight. On Dixie byways the kudzu vine twines a little thicker; what sinister life might it be hiding?

This is the darker side of the Southern imagination, and from all thirteen Southern states comes *Nightmares in Dixie* —stories of fantasy, suspense, and horror by some of America's best writers, including John D. MacDonald, Cornell Woolrich, and Ted White. In this book the South's hot weather takes on a chill . . . read it, and shiver.

NIGHTMARES IN DIXIE

THIRTEEN HORROR TALES FROM THE AMERICAN SOUTH

EDITED BY:
FRANK MCSHERRY, JR.
CHARLES G. WAUGH &
MARTIN HARRY GREENBERG

August House / Little Rock
PUBLISHERS

Published by August House, Inc.,
P.O. Box 3223, Little Rock, Arkansas,
501-663-7300.

Printed in the United States of America
10 9 8 7 6 5 4 3 2 1

LIBRARY OF CONGRESS CATALOGING-IN-PUBLICATION DATA

Nightmares In Dixie.
1. Horror tales, American—Southern States. 2. Southern States—Fiction.
I. McSherry, Frank D.   II. Waugh, Charles.   III. Greenberg, Martin
Harry.
PS648.H6N53   1987   813'.0872'083275   87-1009
ISBN 0-87483-034-6
ISBN 0-87483-035-5 (pbk.)

First Edition, 1987

Cover design by Byron Taylor
Typography by Lettergraphics, Little Rock, Arkansas
Design direction by Ted Parkhurst

This book is printed on archival-quality paper which meets the
guidelines for performance and durability of the Committee on
Production Guidelines for Book Longevity of the Council on
Library Resources.

AUGUST HOUSE, INC.   PUBLISHERS   LITTLE ROCK

Acknowledgments

"Beyond the Cleft" by Tom Reamy, copyright © 1974 by Tom Reamy and copyright © 1979 by the Estate of Tom Reamy, is reprinted here by permission of the copyright holder's agent, Virginia Kidd.

"Coven" by Manly Wade Wellman, copyright © 1942 by Weird Tales Ltd., is reprinted here by permission of Karl Edward Wagner, literary executor for Manly Wade Wellman.

"Cry Havoc" by Davis Grubb, copyright © 1976 by Davis Grubb, is reprinted here by permission of Kirby McCauley, Ltd.

"Dark Melody of Madness" by Cornell Woolrich, copyright © 1935 by Cornell Woolrich, is reprinted here by permission of the agents for the author's estate, the Scott Meredith Literary Agency, Inc., 845 Third Avenue, New York, NY 10022.

"Fast-Train Ike" by Jesse Stuart is reprinted here by permission of the Jesse Stuart Foundation, Judy B. Thomas, Chair, P.O. Box 391, Ashland, KY 40292.

"The Fireplace" by Henry S. Whitehead, copyright © 1925 by Weird Tales Ltd., is reprinted here by permission of the agents for the author's estate, the Scott Meredith Literary Agency, Inc., 845 Third Avenue, New York, NY 10022.

"The Legend of Joe Lee" by John D. MacDonald, copyright © 1964 by John D. MacDonald, is reprinted here by permission of John D. MacDonald, Inc.

"The Night of the Piasa" by J. C. Green & George W. Proctor, copyright © 1986 by J. C. Green and George W. Proctor, first appeared in *Nightmares,* edited by Charles L. Grant, in 1979.

"Only Yesterday" by Ted White, copyright © 1969 by Ultimate Publishing Company, Inc., for *Amazing Stories,* is reprinted here by permission of the author.

"Ooze" by Anthony M. Rud, copyright © 1923 by Rural Publications Ltd., is reprinted here by permission of Weird Tales Ltd.

"The Wait" by Kit Reed, copyright © 1958 by Kit Reed, is reprinted here by permission of Brandt & Brandt Literary Agents, Inc.

"Where the Summer Ends" by Karl Edward Wagner, copyright © 1980 by Karl Edward Wagner for *Dark Forces,* is reprinted here by permission of the author.

CONTENTS

INTRODUCTION

"Then I wish I was in Dixie,
Hooray, hooray!
In Dixie's land I'll take my stand,
To live or die in Dixie!"

—*D.D. Emmett*

You're holding horror in your hand like a black rose.

Little dolls that kill…old, forgotten gods that can inflict a terrifying vengeance…ghosts that walk at night by the mighty Mississippi…a visitor from a future of horrifying destruction…They're all gathered here, nightmares out of Dixie, in this, the first anthology of tales of the supernatural South. In fact, you might even call this book a confederacy of monsters.

What and where is Dixie?

To most of us, Dixie means the Confederacy, the romantic dream of the Lost Cause. "A land of cotton and cavaliers," as the famous film put it, "a civilization now gone with the wind."

The term conjures up a romantic picture out of the past, a white-pillared mansion candlelit at night, waltz music flowing like a river in spring, sensuous as the odor of magnolias. Inside we can see lovely women in ball gowns, a swirl of red and gold, dancing in the arms of gallant gentlemen. Voices float outward, charming and flirtatious, in the soft southern accent, "the banter," F. Scott Fitzgerald wrote in "The Dance," "which presumed every girl to be infinitely…attractive, and every man to have been secretly and hopelessly in love with every girl present...'We like to die laughin'"..."said he was fixin' to shoot him without he stayed away.' The girls "clared to heaven'; the men 'took oath' on inconsequential statements. 'How come you nearly about forgot to come by for me—' and the incessant Honey, Honey, Honey, Honey, until the word seemed to roll like a genial liquid from heart to heart."

Until the waltz music fades, first into a mutter of drums, and then, beyond the horizon, into the rumble of guns...

Now the nightmare begins—for all the charm, all the luxury, is based on the evil of slavery.

But the South is more than the eleven states of the Confederacy. It includes, for example, West Virginia, part of Virginia until Fort Sumter was fired upon and the Civil War began, and it seceded from its own state; and Kentucky and Tennessee, border states that almost joined the southern side.

For the South was a way of life, as much as a region; a culture as much as a country. It was a brilliant society at first; the roll call of the Founding Fathers is resonant with southern names: Thomas Jefferson, Virginian, scientist, author of the Declaration of Independence; George Washington, Virginian, who led the ragtag, bobtail amateur American army to victory over Lord Cornwallis's polished professionals and made that independence stick; James Madison, Virginian, major architect of the Constitution and the Bill of Rights, the New World's heart and soul. For our first century, two-thirds of our presidents were southerners (half from Virginia alone). Nor does it reflect any discredit on New England and the middle states to say that the South contributed more than its share, intellectually, politically, militarily, to the leadership of the new nation.

But southern society had a fatal flaw. It was a society based on family. If you were one of the Carters, Lees, or Randolphs, all doors, all political and business posts, were open to you, a suitable suitor for any lady in the land. If not, the highest places were automatically closed to you. It was a British-based society, the *ancien régime* in America, that excluded the very people who—like the military genius Nathan Bedford Forrest—might have saved it.

Naturally, the ambitious went north. Brains, energy, capital, accumulated in the North, where a new, American (not imitation European) society was being built, one where a person's worth was based on his actions and not on his ancestors. When the Civil War came, the South, not surprisingly, went down into the nightmare of a tragic and bloody defeat.

But the South of today is different. With the Civil War and Jim

Crow behind, the South is growing into a new, high-tech society. When humanity first rocketed into interplanetary space, it did so from a base in Florida, guided by a headquarters in Texas.

There are then three Dixies—colonial, Civil War, and high-tech. What nightmares will such societies have?

See for yourself.

There are thirteen nightmares here, one for each state of Dixie. Dark visions, these, by such authors as John D. MacDonald, the best-selling mystery writer; Jesse Stuart, one of the nation's best regional writers; Karl Edward Wagner, a psychiatrist whose knowledge of the abysses of the mind gives his tales a terror of solid conviction; and William Gilmore Simms, full-grown when Madison was president, one of whose works Poe himself called the best ghost story he'd ever read.

Most of the authors are southern born and bred. Each tale tells something of the state it's set in, from the mountains of Tennessee to the sand dunes of Florida and the bluegrass of Kentucky, its people, climate, and customs, be they voodoo, duelling, or Mardi Gras. Even a bit of the future is covered—for who knows what terrors are lying in wait for us down that road of time we are moving down?

These nightmares concern us all. For this is not merely a regional anthology. These stories are set, not only in the South, but in the dark heart of man, the same eternally from ancient Egypt to tomorrow on the dark side of the Moon.

Frank D. McSherry Jr.

Ooze

Anthony M. Rud

I

In the heart of a second-growth piney-woods jungle of southern Alabama, a region sparsely settled by backwoods blacks and Cajans—that queer, half-wild people descended from Acadian exiles of the middle eighteenth century—stands a strange, enormous ruin.

Interminable trailers of Cherokee rose, white-laden during a single month of spring, have climbed the heights of its three remaining walls. Palmetto fans rise knee high above the base. A dozen scattered live oaks, now belying their nomenclature because of choking tufts of gray, Spanish moss and two-foot circlets of mistletoe parasite which have stripped bare of foliage the gnarled, knotted limbs, lean fantastic beards against the crumbling brick.

Immediately beyond, where the ground becomes soggier and lower—dropping away hopelessly into the tangle of dogwood, holly, poison sumac and pitcher plants that is Moccasin Swamp—undergrowth of ti-ti and annis has formed a protecting wall impenetrable to all save the furtive ones. Some few outcasts utilize the stinking depths of that sinister swamp, distilling "shinny" of "pure cawn" liquor for illicit trade.

Tradition states that this is the case, at least—a tradition which antedates that of the premature ruin by many decades. I believe it, for during evenings intervening between investigations of the awesome spot I often was approached as a possible customer by woodbillies who could not fathom how anyone dared venture near without plenteous fortification of liquid courage.

I know "shinny," therefore I did not purchase it for personal consumption. A dozen times I bought a quart or two, merely to establish credit among the Cajans, pouring away the vile stuff immediately into the sodden ground. It seemed then that only through filtration and condensation of their dozens of weird tales regarding "Daid House" could I arrive at understanding of the mystery and weight of horror hanging about the place.

Certain it is that out of all the superstitious cautioning, head-wagging and whispered nonsensities I obtained only two indisputable facts. The first was that no money, and no supporting battery of ten-gauge shotguns loaded with chilled shot, could induce either Cajan or darky of the region to approach within five hundred yards of that flowering wall! The second fact I shall dwell upon later.

Perhaps it would be as well, as I am only a mouthpiece in this chronicle, to relate in brief why I came to Alabama on this mission.

I am a scribbler of general fact articles, no fiction writer as was Lee Cranmer—though doubtless the confession is superfluous. Lee was my roommate during college days. I knew his family well, admiring John Corliss Cranmer even more that I admired the son and friend— and almost as much as Peggy Breede whom Lee married. Peggy liked me, but that was all. I cherish sanctified memory of her for just that much, as no other woman before or since has granted this gangling dyspeptic even a hint of joyous and sorrowful intimacy.

Work kept me to the city. Lee, on the other hand, coming of wealthy family—and, from the first, earning from his short stories and novel royalties more than I wrested from editorial coffers— needed no anchorage. He and Peggy honeymooned a four-month trip to Alaska, visited Honolulu the next winter, fished for salmon on Cain's River, New Brunswick, and generally enjoyed the outdoors at all seasons.

They kept an apartment in Wilmette, near Chicago, yet, during the few spring and fall seasons they were "home," both preferred to rent a suite at one of the country clubs to which Lee belonged. I suppose they spent thrice or five times the amount Lee actually earned, yet for my part I only honored that the two should find such great happiness in life and still accomplish artistic triumph.

They were honest, zestful young Americans, the type—and pretty nearly the *only* type—two million dollars cannot spoil. John Corliss Cranmer, father of Lee, though as different from his boy as a microscope is different from a painting by Remington, was even further from being dollar-conscious. He lived in a world bounded only by the widening horizon of biological science—and his love for the two who would carry on that Cranmer name.

Many a time I used to wonder how it could be that as gentle, cleansouled and lovable a gentleman as John Corliss Cranmer could have ventured so far into scientific research without attaining small-caliber atheism. Few do. He believed both in God and humankind. To accuse him of murdering his boy and the girl wife who had come to be loved as the mother of baby Elsie—as well as blood and flesh of his own family—was a gruesome, terrible absurdity! Yes, even when John Corliss Cranmer was declared unmistakably insane!

Lacking a relative in the world, baby Elsie was given to me—and the middle-aged couple who had accompanied the three as servants about half of the known world. Elsie would be Peggy over again. I worshiped her, knowing that if my stewardship of her interests could make of her a woman of Peggy's loveliness and worth I should not have lived in vain. And at four Elsie stretched out her arms to me after a vain attempt to jerk out the bobbed tail of Lord Dick, my tolerant old Airedale—and called me "papa."

I felt a deep-down choking...yes, those strangely long black lashes some day might droop in fun or coquetry, but now baby Elsie held a wistful, trusting seriousness in depths of ultramarine eyes—that same seriousness which only Lee had brought to Peggy.

Responsibility in one instant become double. That she might come to love me as more than foster parent was my dearest wish. Still, through selfishness I could not rob her of rightful heritage; she must know in after years. And the tale that I would tell her must not be the horrible suspicion which had been bandied about in common talk!

I went to Alabama, leaving Elsie in the competent hands of Mrs. Daniels and her husband, who had helped care for her since birth.

In my possession, prior to the trip, were the scant facts known to authorities at the time of John Corliss Cranmer's escape and disappearance. They were incredible enough.

For conducting biological research upon forms of protozoan life, John Corliss Cranmer had hit upon this region of Alabama. Near a great swamp teeming with microscopic organisms, and situated in a semitropical belt where freezing weather rarely intruded to harden the bogs, the spot seemed ideal for his purpose.

Through Mobile he could secure supplies daily by truck. The isolation suited him. With only an octoroon man to act as chef, houseman and valet for the times he entertained visitors, he brought down scientific apparatus, occupying temporary quarters in the village of Burdett's Corners while his woods house was in process of construction.

By all accounts the Lodge, as he termed it, was a substantial affair of eight or nine rooms, built of logs and planed lumber bought at Oak Grove. Lee and Peggy were expected to spend a portion of each year with him; quail, wild turkey and deer abounded, which fact made such a vacation certain to please the pair. At other times all save four rooms were closed.

This was in 1907, the year of Lee's marriage. Six years later when I came down, no sign of a house remained except certain mangled and rotting timbers projecting from viscid soil—or what seemed like soil. And a twelve-foot wall of brick had been built to enclose the house completely! One portion of this had fallen *inward!*

II

I wasted weeks of time first, interviewing officials of the police department at Mobile, the town marshals and county sheriffs of Washington and Mobile counties, and officials of the psychopathic hospital from which Cranmer made his escape.

In substance the story was one of baseless homicidal mania. Cranmer the elder had been away until late fall, attending two scientific conferences in the North, and then going abroad to compare certain of his findings with those of a Dr. Gemmler of Prague University. Unfortunately, Gemmler was assassinated by a religious fanatic shortly afterward. The fanatic voiced virulent objection to all Mendelian research as blasphemous. This was his only defense. He was hanged.

Search of Gemmler's notes and effects revealed nothing save an immense amount of laboratory data on *karyokinesis*—the process of chromosome arrangement occurring in first growing cells of higher animal embryos. Apparently Cranmer had hoped to develop some similarities, or point out differences between hereditary factors occurring in lower forms of life and those half-demonstrated in the cat and monkey. The authorities had found nothing that helped me. Cranmer had gone crazy; was that not sufficient explanation?

Perhaps it was for them, but not for me—and Elsie.

But to the slim basis of fact I was able to unearth:

No one wondered when a fortnight passed without appearance of any person from the Lodge. Why should anyone worry? A provision salesman in Mobile called up twice, but failed to complete the connection. He merely shrugged. The Cranmers had gone away somewhere on a trip. In a week, a month, a year they would be back. Meanwhile he lost commissions, but what of it? He had no responsibility for those queer nuts up there in the piney-woods. Crazy? Of course! Why should any guy with millions to spend shut himself up among the Cajans and draw microscope-enlarged notebook pictures of—what the salesman called—"germs"?

A stir was aroused at the end of the fortnight, but the commotion confined itself to building circles. Twenty carloads of building brick, fifty bricklayers, and a quarter-acre of fine-meshed wire—the sort used for screening off pens of rodents and small marsupials in a zoological garden—were ordered, *damn expense, hurry!* by an unshaved, tattered man who identified himself with difficulty as John Corliss Cranmer.

He looked strange, even then. A certified check for the total amount, given in advance, and another check of absurd size slung toward a labor *entrepreneur,* silenced objection, however. These millionaires were apt to be flighty. When they wanted something they wanted it at tap of the bell. Well, why not drag down the big profits? A poorer man would have been jacked up in a day. Cranmer's fluid gold bathed him in immunity to criticism.

The encircling wall was built, and roofed with wire netting which drooped about the squat-pitch of the Lodge. Curious inquiries of workmen went unanswered until the final day.

Then Cranmer, a strange, intense apparition who showed himself more shabby than a quay derelict, assembled every man jack of the workmen. In one hand he grasped a wad of blue slips—fifty-six of them. In the other he held a Luger automatic.

"I offer each man a thousand dollars for *silence!*" he announced. "As an alternative—*death!* You know little. Will all of you consent to swear upon your honor that nothing which has occurred here will be mentioned elsewhere? By this I mean *absolute* silence! You will not come back here to investigate anything. You will not tell your wives. You will not open your mouths even upon the witness stand in case you are called! My price is one thousand apiece.

"In case one of you betrays me *I give you my word that this man shall die!* I am rich. I can hire men to do murder. Well, what do you say?"

The men glanced apprehensively about. The threatening Luger decided them. To a man they accepted the blue slips—and, save for one

16

witness who lost all sense of fear and morality in drink, none of the fifty-six has broken his pledge, as far as I know. That one bricklayer died later in delirium tremens.

It might have been different had not John Corliss Cranmer escaped.

III

They found him the first time, mouthing meaningless phrases concerning an amoeba—one of the tiny forms of protoplasmic life he was known to have studied. Also he leaped into a hysteria of self-accusation. He had murdered two innocent people! The tragedy was his crime. He had drowned them in ooze! Ah, God!

Unfortunately for all concerned, Cranmer, dazed and indubitably stark insane, chose to perform a strange travesty on fishing four miles to the west of his lodge—on the further border of Moccasin Swamp. His clothing had been torn to shreds, his hat was gone, and he was coated from head to foot with gluey mire. It was far from strange that the good folk of Shanksville, who never had glimpsed the eccentric millionaire, failed to associate him with Cranmer.

They took him in, searched his pockets—finding no sign save an inordinate sum of money—and then put him under medical care. Two precious weeks elapsed before Dr. Quirk reluctantly acknowledged that he could do nothing more for this patient, and notified the proper authorities.

Then much more time was wasted. Hot April and half of still hotter May passed by before the loose ends were connected. Then it did little good to know that this raving unfortunate was Cranmer, or that the two persons of whom he shouted in disconnected delirium actually had disappeared. Alienists absolved him of responsibility. He was confined in a cell reserved for the violent.

Meanwhile, strange things occurred back at the Lodge—which now, for good and sufficient reason, was becoming known to dwellers of the woods as Dead House. Until one of the walls fell in, however, there had been no chance to see—unless one possessed the temerity to climb either one of the tall live oaks, or mount the barrier itself. No doors or opening of any sort had been placed in that hastily contructed wall!

By the time the western side of the wall fell, not a native for miles around but feared the spot far more than even the bottomless, snake-infested bogs which lay to west and north.

The single statement was all John Corliss Cranmer ever gave to the world. It proved sufficient. An immediate search was instituted. It showed that less than three weeks before the day of initial reckoning, his son and Peggy had come to visit him for the second time that winter—leaving Elsie in company of the Daniels pair. They had rented a pair of Gordons for quail hunting, and had gone out. That was the last anyone had seen of them.

The backwoods Negro who glimpsed them stalking a covey behind their two pointing dogs had known no more—even when sweated through twelve hours of third degree. Certain suspicious circumstances (having to do only with his regular pursuit of "shinny" transportation) had caused him to fall under suspicion at first. He was dropped.

Two days later the scientist himself was apprehended—a gibbering idiot who sloughed his pole—holding on to the baited hook—into a marsh where nothing save moccasins, an errant alligator, or amphibian life could have been snared.

His mind was three-quarters dead. Cranmer then was in the state of the dope fiend who rouses to a sitting position to ask seriously how many Bolshevists were killed by Julius Caesar before he was stabbed by Brutus, or why it was that Roller canaries sang only on Wednesday evenings. He knew that tragedy of the most sinister sort had stalked through his life—but little more, at first.

Later the police obtained that one statement that he had murdered two human beings, but never could means or motive be established. Official guess as to the means was no more than wild conjecture; it mentioned enticing the victims to the noisome depths of Moccasin Swamp, there to let them flounder and sink.

The two were his son and daughter-in-law, Lee and Peggy!

IV

By feigning coma—then awakening with suddenness to assault three attendants with incredible ferocity and strength—John Corliss Cranmer escaped from Elizabeth Ritter Hospital.

How he hid, how he managed to traverse sixty-odd intervening miles and still balk detection, remains a minor mystery to be explained only by the assumption that maniacal cunning sufficed to outwit saner intellects.

Traverse those miles he did, though until I was fortunate enough to uncover evidence to this effect, it was supposed generally that he had made his escape as stowaway on one of the banana boats, or had buried himself in some portion of the nearer woods where he was unknown. The truth ought to be welcome to householders of Shanksville, Burdett's Corners and vicinage—those excusably prudent ones who to this day keep loaded shotguns handy and barricade their doors at nightfall.

The first ten days of my investigation may be touched upon in brief. I made headquarters in Burdett's Corners, and drove out each morning, carrying lunch and returning for my grits and piney-woods pork or mutton before nightfall. My first plan had been to camp out at the edge of the swamp, for opportunity to enjoy the outdoors comes rarely in my direction. Yet after one cursory examination of the premises, I abandoned the idea. I did not *want* to camp alone there. And I am less superstitious than a real estate agent.

It was, perhaps, psychic warning: more probably the queer, faint, salt odor as of fish left to decay, which hung about the ruin, made too unpleasant an impression upon my olfactory sense. I experienced a distinct chill every time the lengthening shadows caught me near Dead House.

The smell impressed me. In newspaper reports of the case one ingenious explanation had been worked out. To the rear of the spot where Dead House had stood—inside the wall—was a swampy hollow circular in shape. Only a little real mud lay in the bottom of the bowl-like depression now, but one reporter on the staff of *The Mobile Register* guessed that during the tenancy of the lodge it had been a fishpool. Drying up of the water had killed the fish, who now permeated the remnant of mud with this foul odor.

The possibility that Cranmer had needed to keep fresh fish at hand for some of his experiments silenced the natural objection that in a country where every stream holds gar, pike, bass, catfish and many other edible varieties, no one would dream of stocking a stagnant puddle.

After tramping about the enclosure, testing the queerly brittle, desiccated top stratum of earth within and speculating concerning the possible purpose of the wall, I cut off a long limb of chinaberry and probed the mud. One fragment of fish spine would confirm the guess of that imaginative reporter.

I found nothing resembling a piscal skeleton, but established several facts. First, this mud crater had definite bottom only three or four feet below the surface of remaining ooze. Second, the fishy stench become stronger as I stirred. Third, at one time the mud, water, or whatever had comprised the balance of content, had reached the rim of the bowl. The last showed by certain marks plain enough when the crusty, two-inch stratum of upper coating was broken away. It was puzzling.

The nature of that thin, desiccated effluvium which seemed to cover everything even to the lower foot or two of brick, came in for next inspection. It was strange stuff, unlike any earth I ever had seen, though undoubtedly some form of scum drained in from the swamp at the time of river floods or cloudbursts (which in this section are common enough in spring and fall). It crumbled beneath the fingers. When I walked over it, the stuff crunched hollowly. In fainter degree it possesed the fishy odor also.

I took some samples where it lay thickest upon the ground, and also a few where there seemed to be no more than a depth of a sheet of paper. Later I would have a laboratory analysis made.

Apart from any possible bearing the stuff might have upon the disappearance of my three friends, I felt the tug of article interest—that wonder over anything strange or seemingly inexplicable which lends the hunt for fact a certain glamor and romance all its own. To myself I was going to have to explain sooner or later just why this layer covered the entire space within the walls and was not perceptible *anywhere* outside! The enigma could wait, however—or so I decided.

Far more interesting were the traces of violence apparent on wall and what once had been a house. The latter seemed to have been ripped from its foundations by a giant hand, crushed out of semblance to a dwelling, and then cast in fragments about the base of wall—mainly on the south side, where heaps of twisted, broken timbers lay in profusion. On the opposite side there had been such heaps once, but now only charred sticks, coated with that gray-black, omnipresent coat of desiccation, remained. These piles of charcoal had been sifted and examined most carefully by the authorities, as one theory had been advanced that Cranmer had burned the bodies of his victims. Yet no sign whatever of human remains was discovered.

The fire, however, pointed out one odd fact which controverted the reconstructions made by detectives months before. The latter, suggesting the dried scum to have drained in from the swamp, believed that the house timbers had floated out to the sides of the wall—there to arrange themselves in a series of piles! The absurdity of such a theory showed even more plainly in the fact that *if* the scum had filtered through in such a flood, the timbers most certainly had been dragged into piles *previously!* Some had burned—*and the scum coated their charred surfaces!*

What had been the force which had torn the lodge to bits as if in spiteful fury? Why had the parts of the wreckage been burned, the rest to escape?

Right here I felt was the keynote to the mystery, yet I could imagine no explanation. That John Corliss Cranmer himself—physically sound, yet a man who for decades had led a sedentary life—could have accomplished such a destruction, unaided, was difficult to believe.

V

I turned my attention to the wall, hoping for evidence which might suggest another theory.

That wall had been an example of the worst snide construction. Though little more than a year old, the parts left standing showed evidence that they had begun to decay the day the last brick was laid. The mortar had fallen from the interstices. Here and there a brick had cracked and dropped out. Fibrils of the climbing vines had penetrated crevices, working for early destruction.

And one side already had fallen.

It was here that the first glimmering suspicion of the terrible truth was forced upon me. The scattered bricks, even those which had rolled inward toward the gaping foundation ledge, *had not been coated with scum!* This was curious, yet it could be explained by surmise that the flood itself had undermined this weakest portion of the wall. I cleared away a mass of brick from the spot on which the structure had stood; to my surprise I found it exceptionally firm! Hard red clay lay beneath! The flood conception was faulty; only some great force, exerted from inside or outside, could have wreaked such destruction.

When careful measurement, analysis and deduction convinced me—mainly from the fact that the lowermost layers of brick all had fallen *outward,* while the upper portions toppled *in*—I began to link up this mysterious and horrific force with the one which had rent the Lodge asunder. It looked as though a typhoon or gigantic centrifuge had needed elbow room in ripping down the wooden structure.

But I got nowhere with the theory, though in ordinary affairs I am called a man of too great imaginative tendencies. No less than three editors have cautioned me on this point. Perhaps it was the narrowing influence of great personal sympathy—yes, and love. I make no excuses, though beyond a dim understanding that some terrific, implacable force must have made this spot his playground, I ended my ninth day of note-taking and investigation almost as much in the dark as I had been while a thousand miles away in Chicago.

Then I started among the darkies and Cajans. A whole day I listened to yarns of the days which preceded Cranmer's escape from Elizabeth Ritter Hospital—days in which furtive men sniffed poisoned air for miles around Dead House, finding the odor intolerable. Days in which it seemed none possessed nerve enough to approach close. Days when the most fanciful tales of medieval superstitions were spun. These tales I shall not give; the truth is incredible enough.

At noon upon the eleventh day I chanced upon Rori Pailleron, a Cajan—and one of the least prepossessing of all with whom I had come in contact. "Chanced" perhaps is a bad word. I had listed every dweller of the woods within a five-mile radius. Rori was sixteenth on my list. I went to him only after interviewing all four of the Crabiers and two whole families of Pichons. And Rori regarded me with the utmost suspicion until I made him a present of the two quarts of "shinny" purchased of the Pichons.

Because long practice has perfected me in the technique of seeming to drink another man's awful liquor—no, I'm not an absolute prohibitionist; fine wine or twelve-year-in-cask Bourbon whiskey arouses my definite interest—I fooled Pailleron from the start. I shall omit preliminaries, and leap to the first admission from him that he knew more concerning Dead House and its former inmates than any of the other darkies or Cajans roundabout.

"...But I ain't talkin'. *Sacre!* If I should open my gab, what might fly out? It is for keeping silent, y'r damn right!..."

I agreed. He was a wise man—educated to some extent in the queer schools and churches maintained exclusively by Cajans in the depths of the woods, yet naive withal.

We drank. And I never had to ask another leading question. The liquor made him want to interest me; and the only extraordinary topic in this whole neck of the woods was the Dead House.

Three-quarters of a pint of acrid, nauseous fluid, and he hinted darkly. A pint, and he told me something I scarcely could believe. Another half-pint...But I shall give his confession in condensed form.

He had known Joe Sibley, the octoroon chef, houseman and valet who served Cranmer. Through Joe, Rori had furnished certain indispensables in way of food to the Cranmer household. At first, these salable articles had been exclusively vegetable—white and yellow turnip, sweet potatoes, corn and beans—but later, *meat!*

Yes, meat especially—whole lambs, slaughtered and quartered, the coarsest variety of piney-woods pork and beef, all in immense quantity!

VI

In December of the fatal winter, Lee and his wife stopped down at the Lodge for ten days or thereabouts.

They were en route to Cuba at the time, intending to be away five or six weeks. Their original plan had been only to wait over a day or so in the piney-woods, but something caused an amendment to the scheme.

The two dallied. Lee seemed to have become vastly absorbed in something—so much absorbed that it was only when Peggy insisted upon continuing their trip that he could tear himself away.

It was during those ten days that he began buying meat. Meager bits of it at first—a rabbit, a pair of squirrels, or perhaps a few quail beyond the number he and Peggy shot. Rori furnished the game, thinking nothing of it except that Lee paid double prices—and insisted upon keeping the purchases secret from other members of the household.

"I'm putting it across on the Governor, Rori!" he said once with a wink. "Going to give him the shock of his life. So you mustn't let on, even to Joe, about what I want you to do. Maybe it won't work out, but if it does...! Dad'll have the scientific world at his feet! He doesn't blow his own horn anywhere near enough, you know."

Rori didn't know. Hadn't a suspicion what Lee was talking about. Still, if this rich, young idiot wanted to pay him a half dollar in good silver coin for a quail that anyone—himself included—could knock down with a five-cent shell, Rori was well satisfied to keep his mouth shut. Each evening he brought some of the small game. And each day Lee Cranmer seemed to have use for an additional quail or so...

When he was ready to leave for Cuba, Lee came forward with the strangest of propositions. He fairly whispered his vehemence and desire for secrecy! He would tell Rori, and would pay the Cajan five hundred dollars—half in advance, and half at the end of five weeks when Lee himself would return from Cuba—provided Rori agreed to adhere absolutely to a certain secret program! The money was more than a fortune to Rori; it was undreamt-of affluence. The Cajan acceded.

"He wuz tellin' me then how the ol' man had raised some kind of pet," Rori confided, "an' wanted to get shet of it. So he give it to Lee,

23

tellin' him to kill it, but Lee was sot on foolin' him. W'at I ask yer is, w'at kind of a pet is it w'at lives down in a mud sink an' *eats a couple hawgs every night?*"

I couldn't imagine, so I pressed him for further details. Here at last was something which sounded like a clue!

He really knew too little. The agreement with Lee provided that if Rori carried out the provisions exactly, he should be paid extra and at his exorbitant scale of all additional outlay, when Lee returned.

The young man gave him a daily schedule which Rori showed. Each evening he was to procure, slaughter and cut up a definite—and growing—amount of meat. Every item was checked, and I saw that they ran from five pounds up to *forty!*

"What in heaven's name did you do with it?" I demanded, excited now and pouring him an additional drink for fear caution might return to him.

"Took it through the bushes in back an' slung it in the mud sink there! An' suthin' come up an' drug it down!"

"A gator?"

"*Diable!* How should I know? It was dark. I wouldn't go close." He shuddered, and the fingers which lifted his glass shook as with sudden chill. "Mebbe you'd of done it, huh? Not *me*, though! The young fellah tole me to sling it in, an' I slung it.

"A couple times I come around in the light, but there wasn't nuthin' there you could see. Jes' mud, an' some water. Mebbe the thing didn't come out in daytimes…"

"Perhaps not," I agreed, straining every mental resource to imagine what Lee's sinister pet could have been. "But you said something about *two hogs a day?* What did you mean by that? This paper, proof enough that you're telling the truth so far, states that on the thirty-fifth day you were to throw forty pounds of meat—any kind—into the sink. Two hogs, even the piney-woods variety, weigh a lot more than forty pounds!"

"Them was after—after he come back!"

From this point onward, Rori's tale became more and more enmeshed in the vagaries induced by bad liquor. His tongue thickened. I shall give his story without attempt to reproduce further verbal barbarities, or the occasional prodding I had to give in order to keep him from maundering into foolish jargon.

Lee had paid munificently. His only objection to the manner in which Rori had carried out his orders was that the orders themselves had been deficient. The pet, he said, had grown enormously. It was hungry, ravenous. Lee himself had supplemented the fare with huge pails of scraps from the kitchen.

From that day Lee purchased from Rori whole sheep and hogs! The Cajan continued to bring the carcasses at nightfall, but no longer did Lee permit him to approach the pool. The young man appeared chronically excited. He had a tremendous secret—one the extent of which even his father did not guess, and one which would astonish the world! Only a week or two more and he would spring it. First he would have to arrange certain data.

Then came the day when everyone disappeared from Dead House. Rori came around several times, but concluded that all of the occupants had folded tents and departed—doubtless taking their mysterious "pet" along. Only when he saw from a distance Joe, the octoroon servant, returning along the road on foot toward the Lodge, did his slow mental processes begin to ferment. That afternoon Rori visited the strange place for the next to last time.

He did not go to the Lodge himself—and there were reasons. While still some hundreds of yards away from the place a terrible, sustained screaming reached his ears! It was faint, yet unmistakably the voice of Joe! Throwing a pair of number two shells into the breech of his shotgun, Rori hurried on, taking his usual path through the brush at the back.

He saw—and as he told me, even "shinny" drunkenness fled his chattering tones—Joe, the octoroon. Aye, he stood in the yard, far from the pool into which Rori had thrown the carcasses—*and Joe could not move!*

Rori failed to explain in full, but *something,* a slimy, amorphous something, which glistened in the sunlight, already engulfed the man to his shoulders! Breath was cut off. Joe's contorted face writhed with horror and beginning suffocation. One hand—all that was free of the rest of him!—beat feebly upon the rubbery, translucent thing that was engulfing his body!

Then Joe sank from sight...

VII

Five days of liquored indulgence passed before Rori, along in his shaky cabin, convinced himself that he had seen a phantasy born of alcohol. He came back the last time—to find a high wall of brick surrounding the Lodge, and including the pool of mud into which he had thrown the meat!

While he hesitated, circling the place without discovering an opening—which he would not have dared to use, even had he found it—a crashing, tearing of timbers, and persistent sound of awesome destruction came from within. He swung himself into one of the oaks near the wall. And he was just in time to see the last supporting stanchions of the Lodge give way *outward!*

The whole structure came apart. The roof fell in—yet seemed to move after it had fallen! Logs of wall deserted layers of plywood in the grasp of the shearing machine!

That was all. Soddenly intoxicated now, Rori mumbled more phrases, giving me the idea that on another day when he became sober once more, he might add to his statements, but I—numbed to the soul—scarcely cared. If that which he related was true, what nightmare of madness must have been consummated here!

I could vision some things now which concerned Lee and Peggy, horrible things. Only remembrance of Elsie kept me faced forward in the search—for now it seemed almost that the handiwork of a mad-man must be preferred to what Rori claimed to have seen! What had been that sinister, translucent thing? That glistening thing which jumped upward about a man, smothering, engulfing?

Queerly enough, though such a theory as came most easily to mind now would have outraged reason in me if suggested concerning total strangers, I asked myself only what details of Rori's revelation had been exaggerated by fright and fumes of liquor. And as I sat on the creaking bench in his cabin, staring unseeing as he lurched down to the floor, fumbling with a lock box of green tin which lay under his cot, and muttering, the answer to all my questions lay within reach!

It was not until next day, however, that I made the discovery. Heavy of heart I had reexamined the spot where the Lodge had stood, then made my way to the Cajan's cabin again, seeking sober confirmation of what he had told me during intoxication.

In imagining that such a spree for Rori would be ended by a single night, however, I was mistaken. He lay sprawled almost as I had left him. Only two factors were changed. No "shinny" was left—and lying open, with its miscellaneous contents strewed about, was the tin box. Rori somehow had managed to open it with the tiny key still clutched in his hand.

Concern for his safety alone was what made me notice the box. It was a receptacle for small fishing tackle of the sort carried here and there by any sportsman. Tangles of Dowagiac minnows, spool hooks ranging in size to silver-backed number eights; three reels still carrying line of different weights, spinners, casting plus, wobblers, floating baits, were spilled out upon the rough plank flooring where they might snag Rori badly if he rolled. I gathered them, intending to save him an accident.

With the miscellaneous assortment in my hands, however, I stopped dead. Something had caught my eye—something lying flush with the bottom of the lock box! I stared, and then swiftly tossed the hooks and other impediments upon the table. What I had glimpsed there in the box was a loose-leaf notebook of the sort used for recording laboratory data! And Rori scarcely could read, let alone *write!*

Feverishly, a riot of recognition, surmise, hope and fear bubbling in my brain, I grabbed the book and threw it open. At once I knew that this was the end. The pages were scribbled in pencil, but the handwriting was that precise chirography I knew as belonging to John Corliss Cranmer, the scientist!

> Could he not have obeyed my instructions! Oh, God! This...

These were the words at top of the first page which met my eye.

Because knowledge of the circumstances, the relation of which I pried out of the reluctant Rori only some days later when I had him in Mobile as a police witness for the sake of my friend's vindication, is necessary to understanding, I shall interpolate.

Rori had not told me everything. On his late visit to the vicinage of Dead House he saw more. A crouching figure, seated Turk fashion on top of the wall, appeared to be writing industriously. Rori recognized the man as Cranmer, yet did not hail him. He had no opportunity.

Just as the Cajan came near, Cranmer rose, thrust the notebook, which had rested across his knees, into the box. Then he turned, tossed outside the wall both the locked box and a ribbon to which was attached the key.

Then his arms raised toward heavens. For five seconds he seemed to invoke the mercy of Power beyond all of man's scientific prying. And finally he leaped, *inside...!*

Rori did not climb to investigate. He knew that directly below this portion of wall lay the mud sink into which he had thrown the chunks of meat!

VIII

This is a true transcription of the statement I inscribed, telling the sequence of actual events at Dead House. The original of the statement now lies in the archives of the detective department.

Cranmer's notebook, though written in a precise hand, yet betrayed the man's insanity by incoherence and frequent repetitions. My statement has been accepted now, both by alienists and by detectives who had entertained different theories in respect to the case. It quashes the noisome hints and suspicions regarding three of the finest Americans who ever lived—and also one queer supposition dealing with supposed criminal tendencies in poor Joe, the octoroon.

John Corliss Cranmer *went* insane for sufficient cause!

As readers of popular fiction know well, Lee Cranmer's *forte* was the writing of what is called—among fellows in the craft—the pseudo-scientific story. In plain words, this means a yarn, based upon solid fact in the field of astronomy, chemistry, anthropology or whatnot, which carries to logical conclusion improved theories of men who devote their lives to searching out further nadirs of fact.

In certain fashion these men are allies of science. Often they visualize something which has not been imagined even by the best of men from whom they secure data, thus opening new horizons of possibility. In a large way Jules Verne was one of these men in his day; Lee Cranmer bade fair to carry on the work in worthy fashion—work taken up for a period by an Englishman named Wells, but abandoned for stories of a different—and, in my humble opinion, less absorbing—type.

Lee wrote three novels, all published, which dealt with such subjects—two of the three secured from his own father's labors, and the other speculating upon the discovery and possible uses of interatomic energy. Upon John Corliss Cranmer's return from Prague that fatal winter, the father informed Lee that a greater subject than any with which the young man had dealt now could be tapped.

Cranmer, senior, had devised a way in which the limiting factors in protozoic life and *growth,* could be nullified; in time, and with cooperation of biologists who specialized upon *karyokinesis* and embryology of higher forms, he hoped—to put the theory in pragmatic terms—to be able to grow swine the size of elephants, quail or woodcock with breasts from which a hundredweight of white meat could be cut away, and steers whose dehorned heads might butt at the third story of a skyscraper!

Such result would revolutionize the methods of food supply, of course. It also would hold out hope for all undersized specimens of humanity—provided only that if factors inhibiting growth could be deleted, some methods of stopping gianthood also could be developed.

Cranmer the elder, through use of an undescribed (in the notebook) growth medium of which one constituent was agar-agar, and the use of radium emanations, had succeeded in bringing about apparently unrestricted growth in the paramoecium protozoan, certain of the vegetable growths (among which were bacteria), and in the amorphous cell of protoplasm known as the amoeba—the last a single cell containing only nucleolus, nucleus, and a space known as the contractile vacuole which somehow aided in throwing off particles impossible to assimilate directly. This point may be remembered in respect to the piles of lumber left near the outside walls surrounding Dead House!

When Lee Cranmer and his wife came south to visit, John Corliss Cranmer showed his son an amoeba—normally an organism visible under low-power microscope—which he had absolved from natural growth inhibitions. This amoeba, a rubbery, amorphous mass of protoplasm, was of the size then of a large beef liver. It could have been held in two cupped hands, placed side by side.

"How large could it grow?" asked Lee, wide-eyed and interested.

"So far as I know," answered his father, "there is *no* limit—now! It might, if it got food enough, grow to be as big as the Masonic Temple!

"But take it out and kill it. Destroy the organism utterly—burning the fragments—else there is no telling what might happen. The amoeba, as I have explained, reproduces by simple division. Any fragment remaining might be dangerous."

Lee took the rubbery, translucent giant cell—but he did not obey orders. Instead of destroying it as his father had directed, Lee thought out a plan. Suppose he should grow this organism to tremendous size? Suppose, when the tale of his father's accomplishment were spread, an amoeba of many tons weight could be shown in evidence? Lee, of somewhat sensational cast of mind, determined instantly to keep secret the fact that he was not destroying the organism, but encouraging its further growth. Thought of possible peril never crossed his mind.

He arranged to have the thing fed—allowing for normal increase of size in an abnormal thing. It fooled him only by growing much more rapidly. When he came back from Cuba the amoeba practically filled the whole of the mud sink hollow. He had to give it much greater supplies...

The giant cell came to absorb as much as two hogs in a single day. During daylight, while hunger still was appeased, it never emerged, however. That remained for the time that it could secure no more food near at hand to satisfy its ravenous and increasing appetite.

Only instinct for the sensational kept Lee from telling Peggy, his wife, all about the matter. Lee hoped to spring a *coup* which would immortalize his father, and surprise his wife terrifically. Therefore, he kept his own counsel—and made bargains with the Cajan, Rori, who supplied food daily for the shapeless monster of the pool.

The tragedy itself came suddenly and unexpectedly. Peggy, feeding the two Gordon setters that Lee and she used for quail hunting, was in the Lodge yard before sunset. She romped alone, as Lee himself was dressing.

Of a sudden her screams cut the still air! Without her knowledge, ten-foot *pseudopods*—those flowing tentacles of protoplasm sent forth by the sinister occupant of the pool—slid out and around her putteed ankles.

For a moment she did not understand. Then, at first suspicion of the horrid truth, her cries rent the air. Lee, at that time struggling to lace a pair of high shoes, straightened, paled, and grabbed a revolver as he dashed out.

In another room a scientist, absorbed in his note-taking, glanced up, frowned, and then—recognizing the voice—shed his white gown and came out. He was too late to do aught but gasp with horror.

In the yard Peggy was half engulfed in a squamous, rubbery something which at first he could not analyze.

Lee, his boy, was fighting with the sticky folds, and slowly, surely, losing his own grip upon the earth!

IX

John Corliss Cranmer was by no means a coward; he stared, cried aloud, then ran indoors, seizing the first two weapons which came to hand—a shotgun and hunting knife which lay in sheath in a cartridged belt across hook of the hall-tree. The knife was ten inches in length and razor-keen.

Crammer rushed out again. He saw an indecent fluid something—which as yet he had not had time to classify—lumped into a six-foot-high center before his very eyes! It looked like one of

30

the micro-organisms he had studied! One grown to frightful dimensions. An amoeba!

There, some minutes suffocated in the rubbery folds—yet still apparent beneath the glistening ooze of this monster—were two bodies.

They were dead. He knew it. Nevertheless he attacked the flowing, senseless monster with his knife. Shot would do no good. And he found that even the deep, terrific slashes made by his knife closed together in a moment and healed. The monster was invulnerable to ordinary attack!

A pair of *pseudopods* sought out his ankles, attempting to bring him low. Both of these he severed—and escaped. Why did he try? He did not know. The two whom he had sought to rescue were dead, buried under folds of this horrid thing he knew to be his own discovery and fabrication.

Then it was that revulsion and insanity came upon him.

There ended the story of John Corliss Cranmer, save for one hastily scribbled paragraph—evidently written at the time Rori had seen him atop the wall.

May we not supply with assurance the intervening steps?

Cranmer was known to have purchased a whole pen of hogs a day or two following the tragedy. These animals were never seen again. During the time the wall was being constructed is it not reasonable to assume that he fed the giant organism within—to keep it quiet? His scientist brain must have visualized clearly the havoc and horror which could be wrought by the loathsome thing if it ever were driven by hunger to flow away from the Lodge and prey upon the countryside!

With the wall once in place, he evidently figured that starvation or some other means which he could supply would kill the thing. One of the means had been made by setting fire to several piles of the disgorged timbers; probably this had no effect whatever.

The amoeba was to accomplish still more destruction. In the throes of hunger it threw its gigantic, formless strength against the house walls *from the inside;* then every edible morsel within was assimilated, the logs, rafters and other fragments being worked out through the contractile vacuole.

During some of its last struggles, undoubtedly, the side wall of brick was weakened—not to collapse, however, until the giant amoeba no longer could take advantage of the breach. In final death lassitude, the amoeba stretched itself out in a thin layer over the ground. There it succumbed, though there is no means of estimating how long a time intervened.

The last paragraph in Cranmer's notebook, scrawled so badly that it is possible some words I have not deciphered correctly, reads as follows:

> In my work I have found the means of creating a monster. The unnatural thing, in turn, has destroyed my work and those whom I held dear. It is in vain that I assure myself of innocence of spirit. Mine is the crime of presumption. Now, as expiation—worthless though that may be—I give myself...

It is better not to think of that last leap, and the struggle of an insane man in the grip of the dying monster.

Editor and pulp writer Anthony M. Rud (1893-1942) is perhaps best known as the author of the first story in the first issue of the world's foremost magazine of the supernatural, Weird Tales. "Ooze" has been called "something of a modern classic in horror fiction." But he was also editor of the critically respected pulp, Adventure, from October 1927 to February 1930. The author of many competent pulp stories of all types, Rud is the creator of detective Jigger Masters and the author of several detective-borderline science fiction novels including The Stuffed Men (Macaulay, 1935).

Coven

Manly Wade Wellman

*...They pledge themselves to frequent the midnight
assemblies. These conventicles or covens were bands or
companies of witches, composed of men and women,
apparently under the discipline of an officer...*

—History of Witchcraft and Demonology,
Montague Summers

Chapter I
The Cursed Damozel

Wasn't Shiloh supposed to be named after an angel or a devil? Angels and devils were both there, sorting the two armies through for who should live and who should die, who go to heaven and who go to hell. We Southerners won the first day and part of the second, even after they'd killed General Albert Sidney Johnston. When I say he was about as great as General Lee, I expect to be believed. When we fell back, Bedford Forrest sent some of us to save a field piece that Bragg's artillery left behind. But the Yankees got there fustest with the mostest men. They carried off the gun, and two or three of us Tennessee cavalry with it.

They were bivouacking on the field—sundown, April 7, 1862. I was marched far back. Passing a headquarters, I saw a fateful little man with a big cigar—General Grant. With him was a taller, red-whiskered man, who was crying. Someone said he was Sherman, but Sherman never seemed to me like a man who would cry over any sorrow, his own or another's.

This introduction is jumbled. So was my mind at the time. I must

33

have looked forlorn, a skinny gray-clad trooper plundered of saber, carbine, and horse. One of the big blue cavalrymen who escorted the prisoners leaned down from his saddle and rubbed the heel of his hand on my feebly fuzzy cheek.

"Little Johnny Reb's growing some nice black whiskers to surprise his sweetheart," he said, laughing.

"I haven't got a sweetheart," I snapped, trying to sound like a big soldier. But he laughed the louder.

"Hear that, boys?" he hailed the others of the escort. "This little feller never had a sweetheart." They mingled their cackles with his, and I wished I'd not spoken. They repeated my words again and again, tagging on sneers and merriments. I frowned, and tried not to cry. This was at dusk, the saddest time of day. We'd been marched back for miles, to some sort of reserve concentration in a tiny town.

"We've robbed the cradle for sure," the big blue cavalryman was saying to friends he met. "This little shaver—no sweetheart, he says!"

A new gale of laughter from towering captors all around me. It hushed suddenly at a stern voice:

"Bring that prisoner to me."

He rolled out from between two sheds, as heavily and smoothly as a gun-limber. He was a short, thick man in a dragoon jacket and one of those little peaked Yankee caps. There was just enough light to show me his big beard and the sergeant's stripes on his sleeve.

"Bring him along," he ordered again. "March the others to the stockade."

A moment later, he and I stood alone in the gloom. "What's your name?" he asked.

"High Private Cole Wickett," I replied. A prisoner could say that much. If he asked about my regiment, or the conditions of the army—But he didn't. His next question was: "How old are you?"

"Fifteen next birthday." Again no reason to lie, though I'd told the recruiting sergeant eighteen.

"Fourteen years, and some months," the big man figured it out. "Come with me."

He put a hand the size of a hay-fork on my shoulder, and steered me into a back yard full of soldiers playing cards by firelight. He paused, and scolded them for gambling. Any sergeant in Forrest's command who had tried that would have been hooted at, maybe struck at—we Confederates respected God and General Johnston and Bedford Forrest, and scorned everyone else. But these men put away the cards and said, "Yes sir," as if he had been an officer. He marched me on into the house beyond the yard, and sat me in a chair in what had been the kitchen.

There he left me. I could hear him talking to someone in the next room. There was a window through which I might have climbed. But it was dark, and I was tired, hungry, sick, and not yet fifteen. I couldn't have fought my way back through Grant, Sherman, and the rest of the Yankees. I waited where I was until the sergeant opened the door and said, "Come in here, Wickett."

The front room was lighted by one candle, stuck in its own grease on a table. There sat a tall, gray officer with a chaplain's cross for insignia. He was eating supper—bread, bacon, and coffee. My eyes must have been wolfish, for he asked if I'd have some. I took enough to make a sandwich, and thanked him kindly. Then the chaplain said, "My boy, is it true what Sergeant Jaeger heard? That you're only a child, and never had a sweetheart?"

I stuck my chin out and stood up straight. The Yankees must be worse than all our southern editors and speech-makers claimed, if even a preacher among them made jokes about such things. "Sir," I said, keeping my voice deep in my chest, "it's none of your business."

"But it is my business," he replied solemnly, "and the business of many people. Upon your answer, Cole, depends an effort to help some folk out of awful trouble—northern and southern both—and to right a terrible wrong. Now will you reply?"

"I don't know what you mean," I returned, "but I never even thought much about girls. What's wrong with that?"

"Nothing's wrong with it," answered the big sergeant named Jaeger. "You should be proud to say that thing, Wickett, if it's really true."

"Sergeant," I sputtered, "I'm a southern gentleman. If you and I were alone, with horses and sabers, I'd teach you to respect my words."

His face grew as dark as his beard, and he said, "Respect your elders and betters, youngster. So says the Bible."

"The catechism, not the Bible, Sergeant," corrected the chaplain. "Cole, it's only that we must be dead sure." He pushed a black-bound book across the table toward me. "This is the Bible. Do you believe in the sanctity of an oath?"

"My word's good, sir, sworn on the Bible or not," I told him, but I put my hand on the book. "Must I swear something?"

"Only that you told the truth about never having a sweetheart," he said, and I did so. The chaplain put away the book, and looked at

Sergeant Jaeger.

"Something tells me that we have the help we needed, and couldn't be sure of in our own forces," he said. "Take care of this boy, for we're lost without him."

He went out. Sergeant Jaeger faced me. He was no taller than I, even then, but about twice as broad.

"Since you're a man of your word, will you give your parole?" he asked.

I swallowed the last bite of bacon, and shook my head. "I'll escape," I announced, "as soon as there's light enough."

"Will you give me your parole until sunrise?" he almost pleaded.

Wondering, I gave it. He put his hand on my shoulder again, steered me to a narrow stairway and up to a little room the size of a pantry. There was a cot with a gray blanket, Union army issue, on it.

"Sleep here," he said. "No, no questions—I won't answer them. Be ready for orders at an hour before dawn."

He left me. I took off my tunic and boots, and stretched out on the cot. Still puzzling over things, I went to sleep.

I woke to the touch of a hand, cold as a washrag, on my brow. Somehow there was light enough for see a woman standing there. She wore a frosty white dress and veil, like a bride's. Her face was still whiter.

I saw a straight, narrow-cut nose, a mouth that must be very red to be so darkly alive, and eyes that glowed green. Perhaps the eyes gave the light. I sat up, embarrassed.

"I was told to sleep here, ma'am," I said. "Is this your house?"

"Yes," she whispered, "it is my house." She sat on the edge of the cot. Her hand moved from my face to the shoulder. Her grip was as strong as Sergeant Jaeger's. "Your name is Cole Wickett. You are a brave soldier, but you never had a sweetheart."

I was tired of hearing about it. I said nothing, and she went on:

"I will be your sweetheart." And she put her arms around me.

She was beautiful, more than anyone I had ever seen. But when she came that close I felt a horrible sick fear. Perhaps it was the smell of deadness, as of a week-old battlefield. Or all of them.

I wriggled loose and jumped off the cot. She laughed, a little gurgle like water in a cave.

"Do not be afraid, Cole. Stand where you are."

She, too, rose. She was taller than I. Her eyes fixed mine, and I could not move. If you want to know how I felt, stare for a while at some spot on the wall or floor. After a moment, you'll have trouble looking away. It's called hypnotism, or something. She came near again, and this time I did not shrink when she put her hands on my shoulders.

"Now," she said.

Then Sergeant Jaeger opened the door, took one look, and began to say something, very rapidly and roughly. It sounded like Bible verses: "In the beginning was the Word, and the Word was with God—"

The woman shrieked, high and ear-tingling, like a bat. She let go of me.

She was gone. It was like a light being blown out, or a magic-lantern image switched from a screen.

I stared stupidly, like a country idiot. Jaeger cleared his throat, and tugged his beard. "That was close," he said.

"Who was she?" I asked, and the words had a hard time forming in my throat.

"Somebody whose call we'll return," he put me off gruffly. "She thought she'd destroy the one power we're counting on. It's time to strike back."

I followed him outside. The night was black, but the early-morning stars had wheeled up into heaven. We passed two different sentries, and came through the sleeping streets of the little town to a church, either ruined or shell-smashed. Beyond was a burying ground, grown up in weeds and walled around with stone. At the broken-down gate stood the chaplain. He held the bridle of a chunky black stallion colt, not quite full grown.

"I can vouch for the beast," he greeted Sergeant Jaeger. "It is sad that we watch our animals so much more carefully than our own children."

"This night I almost failed on my own duty of watching," replied Jaeger in a tired voice. To me he said, "Crawl out of those clothes. Don't stare. Do as I say."

By this time there had been so much strangeness and mystery that I did not argue. I shucked my uniform, and the pre-dawn air was cold on my bare skin. The chaplain motioned for me to mount. I did, and he led the colt into the burying ground.

There were wreaths and wrappings of mist. Through them I saw pale, worn-out tombstones. We tramped over them. It wasn't polite nor decent, but I saw that the chaplain and the sergeant—he came behind, carrying some shovels and a mattock—meant business. I kept my mouth closed. Riding the colt, I was steered across that burying ground, and across again.

In the middle of the second crossing, the colt planted his hooves and balked.

Jaeger, bringing up the rear, struck with the handle of a shovel. The colt stood firm. The chaplain tugged in front, Jaeger flogged behind. The colt trembled and snorted, but he did not move.

The chaplain pointed. A grave-mound, a little naked wen of dirt among the weeds, showed just in front of the planted hooves.

"Your book tells the truth," he said, strangely cheerful. "Here is a tomb he will not cross."

"Get down, Wickett," commanded Jaeger. "Dress, and help dig."

I hurried to the gate, threw on my clothes anyhow, and returned. The chaplain was scraping with a shovel. Jaeger swung a mattock. I grabbed another spade and joined in.

As the first moment of gray dawn was upon us, we struck a coffin lid. Jaeger scraped earth from it. "Get back!" he grunted, and I did so; but not before he heaved up the lid with his mattock.

Inside lay the woman who had come to my cot, in her bridal dress.

"The stake," said the chaplain, and passed down a sharp stick like a picket-pin. I judged it was of hawthorn, cut from a hedge some-where. "Strike to the heart," went on the chaplain, "while I strike at the throat."

He suited action to word, driving down the blade of his shovel. At the same moment Jaeger made a strong digging thrust with the stick. I heard again the bat-squeaking; and then, was made faint by a horrid stink of rottenness.

Jaeger slammed down the lid—I heard it fall—and scrambled out of the grave. He and the chaplain began tumbling clods into the hole.

Jaeger looked at me over his shoulder, haggard but triumphant.

"I give you back your parole," he panted. "Jump on that colt and clear out. To the west there'll be none of our troops. If you ever tell what was done here, nobody will believe you!"

I needed no second permission.

Chapter II
The Flying Horned One

I remembered that adventure, strangest moment of all my war-boyhood, on a late night in the fall of 1876.

The wagon track I walked was frozen to rutted concrete. Wind as cold as fear rustled the tall dead grass and the naked twigs of roadside thickets. A round moon reminded me of a pancake, and I tried not to think of that or anything else to eat. It had been long since I had eaten.

The black beard prophesied me by a long-vanished Yankee captor hung thick on my jowls. I was gaunt, big-boned, seam-faced. My clothes were torn, dirty, inadequate—overall pants, a frayed jumper, a hickory shirt that was little more than the traditional "button and frill," outworn cowhide brogans, no hat. I warmed my knuckly hands under my armpits, and blew out steamy breath.

A man, hungry and weary and unsheltered, might die tonight. I wondered, without much dread, if I were at the end of my sorry trail. Other Southern veterans had died, from sheer want, after surviving the heartbreak of war and defeat. In 1865, after my becoming sergeant and finally lieutenant under Bedford Forrest, the general surrender on all hands had failed to include me. I had been detached somewhere, and had gone home. There was no home—Kilpatrick's cavalry had burned the place in '64, and I found only the graves of my mother and sister. They had died of sickness, as my father had died of a minie ball at Chattanooga. After that the black "Reconstruction" period. I had been gambler, Ku Klux raider, jailbird, chicken thief, swamp trapper. And now a tramp.

Up ahead were lights, two houses fairly close together. I knew that I was near the Missouri-Arkansas border. A loosely joined community hereabouts was called Welcome Rock. Would those lights welcome me?

As I faced them, I saw the moon clear. Something winged slowly across it.

What I saw seems unreal to you, as the sight then seemed unreal to me. That winged shape must have been larger than any creature that flies; I made certain of that later.

At the moment, I saw only how black it was, with a body and legs half-human, and great bat-wings through which the moon shone as through umbrella cloth.

I told myself sagely that hunger showed me a vision.

The thing flopped around and across the moon again. I saw its ball-shaped head, with curved horns. Then it swooped downward. Suddenly I heard the voices of men.

One laughed, another cursed. The third cried pitifully. From somewhere beyond me came strength, fury, decision. I ran heavily forward, my broken shoes heavy and clumsy. I saw the three at a distance. One was strung up by his hands to a tree's bare branch, the other two were flogging him with sticks.

I passed under other trees to approach. The crisscross of boughs shut away sight of whatever fluttered overhead. The captive's face showed white as curd, and the floggers seemed black. Running, I stooped and grabbed up a stone the size of my fist. When I straightened, I made out horns on the black skulls, horns like those of the flying thing. Somebody jeered: "You told on us. Now you beg us. But we—"

The two floggers were aware of me, and dropped their sticks.

"Knife," said one, and the other drew a blade from under his coat. I threw my stone, and it struck the knife-holder's black horned brow with a sound like an axe on wood. The knife dropped, and its owner sprawled upon it. I charged in after my rock.

The other man stood absolutely still. His outline could stand for a symbol of frightened surprise. He was mumbling words in an unknown tongue:

"Mirathe saepy Satonich yetmye—but it *won't work!*"

From the moonlit sky came whickering, like a bad horse in terror. Then I was upon the mumbler.

We struggled and strove. His gabble of strange sounds had failed to do something or other. Now he saved his breath, and fought with more strength than mine. I found myself hugged and crushed in his long, hard arms, and remembered a country wrestling trick. I feigned limpness, and when he unconsciously slacked his grip, I slid down out of it. Catching him around the knees, I threw him heavily. Then I fell with all my weight upon him, clutching at his throat.

Overhead the whickering rose shrill and shaky, and grew faint. The man I fought thrust my hands from his windpipe. I now saw that the blackness of his face, and the horns to either side, were a mask. He was wheezing, "If I get away quick, will that suit you?"

I tried to gouge his eye through a slit in the mask, but with a sudden effort he tore clear from me. Rising, he seized and dragged away the man my rock had struck down.

My strength and fury were ebbing, and I waited on one knee, watching the two flee among the brush. I glanced up. The flier was also gone.

The man who hung in bonds began to babble brokenly:

"You're free from cursing...free from cursing..."

The knife dropped by one of the masked pair still lay on the frozen ground. I picked it up and went to the man. Cords were noosed over his thumbs, drawing him up to the branch so that his toes barely touched ground. The shirt was torn from his back, which showed a shocking mass of gore.

I cut him down, and he collapsed in my arms like a wet coat.

Then spoke a challenging voice I remembered from long ago, "What are you doing to him?"

I had breath left only to say: "Help!"

"I heard the noise of fighting, and came at once." A thick body approached in the half-light. "Bring him to my cabin."

I glanced upward, and the newcomer did likewise. "Oh, then you saw the Flying Horned One? He must have fled when I came."

"He fled before that," I said, for I had recovered a little wind. My words seemed to make the thick man start and stare, but he made no rejoinder. We got the poor flogged wretch between us and dragged him across a field to the nearest lighted house. The moon showed me a dwelling, small but well built of adzed logs, with the chinks plastered and whitewashed. On the threshold the man we helped was able to speak again:

"This is the preacher's place. I want baptism."

"I baptized you once before," growled the burly man from the other side of him. "Once is enough, even when you backslide."

"What he wants is doctoring, not baptizing," I put in. "His back's all cut to hash."

It was all of that. But the answer was still: "Baptize me."

We helped him in. "I don't think it will hurt you," said the burly one, and as we came into the light of a kerosene lamp I saw whose voice I remembered.

This was the Yankee Sergeant Jaeger, whom I had last seen nearly fifteen years before, spading dirt over a woman who had seemingly died twice. He wore rough country boots and pants, but a white shirt and a string tie. He set the poor fellow in a splint-bottomed chair, where I steadied him, then went to the kitchen and returned with his hand wet. He laid the wet hand on the rumpled hair.

"Peter, I baptize thee in the name of the Father, the Son—"

At his touch the tortured form relaxed, the eyes seemed to close softly in slumber. Jaeger looked across at me.

"You're a stranger to the Welcome Rock country. Or are you?"

"A stranger here, but not to you," I replied. "I'm Cole Wickett, formerly with General Forrest—at your service, Sergeant."

His eyes fixed me. He tugged his beard, which I saw had begun to thread through with gray. He opened his hard mouth twice before speaking.

"It is the same," he said then, more to himself than to me. "A strong weapon twice placed in the hands of the righteous."

The man we had saved sank almost out of the chair, and I caught him. But he was dead, and no wonder, for the beating had been terrific.

Jaeger laid him out on a strip of carpet, and caught a blanket from a cot to cover him.

"Poor Peter Dole," he muttered. "He backslid from one congregation without rebuke. When he tried backsliding from his new fellowship, it was his destruction."

I told what had happened outside in full. Jaeger did not seem particularly surprised about the bat-winged monster or the men with masks. He only said, "God grant that the baptism Peter asked for will bring him peace in the grave."

"What is this mystery, Sergeant Jaeger?" I demanded.

He waved the title away. "I am done with war. I am the Reverend Mr. Jaeger now, a poor man of God, striving with adversaries worse than any your rebel army marshalled against me—Wickett, you make a dark hour bright."

"More mystery," I reminded him. "I want explanations."

He studied me, wisely and calculatingly. "If I'm not mistaken, you are hungrier now than when we met before. Wait."

He left me alone with the blanketed corpse of Peter Dole, and I heard him busy in the kitchen. He came back with a tin plate on which were cold biscuits, sardines from a tin, and some sort of preserves.

He also brought a cup, old Union army issue, filled with hot black coffee.

"Eat," he bade me, "while I enlighten you."

Chapter III
The Night Side of Preaching

"I repeat," began Jaeger, as I gobbled, "that your second appearance to me is in the nature of an act of Providence. How could you meet my need so aptly twice, with years and a continent in which to be lost? Probabilities against it are millions to one. Yet you've come, Cole Wickett, and with your help I'll blunt the claws of demons."

I scalded my throat with the coffee.

"You promised me the story," I reminded.

"It will be short. You remember the digging up of a grave. The woman you saw was not dead, nor alive. She was a vampire."

That word is better known now, but I appreciated its meaning with difficulty. Jaeger's voice grew sharp:

"You must believe me. You were close to a fearful fate, and to me you owe life and soul—when I defended you from that monster. Let me read from this book."

He took it from a shelf above the table that served him for desk. It was old and musty, with a faded title in German. "The work of the German, Dom Augustin Calmet," he explained, and read from the cover: "'A Treatise on the Appearance of Spirits, Vampires, and so on.' Written a century ago. And here," leafing through it, "is the reference you will need. I'll translate, through my German is rusty."

He cleared his throat and read: "'They select a pure young lad, and mount him naked on a stallion colt that has never stumbled, and is coal-black with no white hair. The stallion is ridden in and out among the graves, and the grave which he will not cross, despite hard blows, is where the vampire is buried.'"

He closed the book. "You begin to see what service you rendered. That part of the country was plagued by what seemed consumption or fever—strong people sickening and dying. Only I, and that wise chaplain, saw that their lives were sapped by a vampire. Other cases have occurred in this country—in Connecticut before the war, and in Rhode Island only two years ago. Men would have scoffed at our claim, and so we acted secretly."

I accepted the honesty, if not the accuracy, of his tale. "You speak," I said, "as if I am doing you a similar service."

"You can if you choose. I saw little of your struggle this night, but enough to know that enchantment cannot touch you."

My eyes were on the blanket-draped corpse as I said, "You think that one victory begets another."

"I do." He leaned forward eagerly, the old book in his hands. "You survived one peril of the unknown. Like one who survives a sickness, you have some immunity."

I let that hang, too. "You speak as if another combat of the sort is coming."

"Again you anticipate me. The combat has now begun—here in the Welcome Rock country, from which I thought to stamp all evil worship."

The story he then told me seems to be fairly well known, at least in that community, which once was called Fearful Rock. Leaving the Union army, he came there as a frontier preacher without pay. Vestiges of an ancient and evil influence clung around a ruined house, and stories about it caused settlers to stay away. After his efforts to exorcise the apparent malevolent spirit, several farmers homesteaded nearby, and the name of the district was changed. Recently, he and the men of his little congregation had built a church.

"That started things again," he said, and I must have looked my utter stupid amazement, for he smiled sadly.

"If you study the lore of demon-worship, as I have studied it, you would know that the deluded fools must have a church at which to aim their blasphemies. Look at the history of the defilers of the North Berwick Church in Scotland. Look at the story of the Salem witches in a minister's pasture."

"Those are only legends," I suggested, but he shook his head.

"They are true. And the truth is manifest here. I am being crusaded against. Stop and think—I defeated evil beings on their own dunghill. They were overthrown and chased out. But their black hearts, if they have hearts, yearn back to here. This place is their Unholy of Unholies."

"I see," I replied, wondering if I did. Then I glanced again at the blanket-covered thing on the carpet. Jaeger saw the direction of my glance.

"I'm coming to poor Peter Dole. It was last Sunday—five days ago. I came early to my little church. The lock was broken, the Bible tipped from the pulpit, various kinds of filth on the benches and in the aisles, and on the walls some charcoal writing. It is not fit to repeat to you, but I recognized the hand."

"Bad boys?"

"Bad men. I cleaned up the mess, and made a change in my text and sermon. I preached from Twelfth of Revelation, 'The devil is come unto you, having great wrath; for he knoweth that he hath but a short time.' I stressed the second clause of the observation."

"'He hath but a short time,'" I repeated.

"Yes. I spoke of the outrage, and said that the enemy gained no victory, but only shame. I read a little further into Revelation, the part where certain people are made to hide among rocks to escape the just wrath of heaven. Then I said that I knew who had written on the walls." He eyed my empty cup. "More coffee? No?"

I shook my head. He continued.

"Peter Dole came to me after the benediction. It was he whose writing I had recognized. Terrified, he confessed some things I had already made sure of—his membership as a very humble figure in a coven."

I shook my head, to show that I did not know what a coven was.

"It's an old-country word. Scotch, maybe. It means a gathering of thirteen witches or wizards or devil-worshippers, twelve rank-and-file, and a chief devil. Maybe that's where we got the unluckiness of the number thirteen. Peter was of the twelve rank-and-file, and he pleaded for mercy. I referred him to the Lord, and asked who were his mates. He said he'd pray courage into himself to tell me. Tonight he must have been coming to see me. And his comrades beat him to death."

"One of his comrades has wings, then," I said.

Jaeger tugged his beard thoughtfully.

"I have seen that shape against the full moon before this. Full moon-time is their meeting time, as with the underground cults of old Greece and Rome. The full moon makes wolves howl, and turns weak minds mad. I don't like the full moon. Anyway, that creature is the chief devil of which I spoke."

"Chief devil?" I repeated. "I thought that probably—"

"That probably some human leader dressed up for the part?" he finished for me. "Not here, at least. Hark!"

I, too, heard what his ear had caught—the flip-flop of great membranes, and the faraway chatter of strange inhuman jaws.

Then a knock at the door, sharp and furtive.

With shame I remember how I flinched and looked for a way out. Jaeger rose, flipped open a drawer in his work-table, and took out a big cap-and-ball revolver. He walked heavily toward the door.

Pausing with his hand on the knob, he spoke clearly:

"If you seek trouble, your search ends here. Too long have I borne with the ungodly, meekly turning my other cheek. Vengeance is mine, sayeth the Lord, I will repay."

He opened the door, took one look, and lowered his weapon. A girl came stumbling in.

She wore a dark dress of coarse wool, very full-skirted and high-necked, with edging of white at throat and cuffs. Her brown hair was disarrayed, under a knitted shawl. Her face was cream-white, set with bright, scared eyes.

"Please," she said, out of breath, "they shouted that I'd find my father with you." She swallowed, and her lips quivered. "Badly hurt, they said."

"Sit down, Susan," bade Jaeger. "He is here, but no more in pain or terror."

She saw the body then, seemed to recognize it through the blanket. Sitting down, as Jaeger had told her, she grew one shade whiter, but calm.

"I will not cry," she promised us. "I would even be glad, if I thought the curse was gone from him—"

"Then be glad, Susan," rejoined Jaeger, "for he repented and died a believer."

He turned his gaze to me. "Now will be proven, or not proven, my thought that you have strength against wickedness. For the gates of hell are open, and our enemies close in about us."

The girl Susan and I both turned toward him. He continued, with an impatient note in his voice.

"How can mankind defend himself when he does not take thought? This is Satan's one night of the year, the wizard's Christmas."

Chapter IV
The Gathering of the Vultures

In the outer night rose again the whickering cry, that rose into a shrill yearning whine. Jaeger cocked his bearded head sidewise. "The flying horned one summons his faithful. This is their day, and midnight will be their hour. Shakespeare knew that, and passed the word on to us—'The time of night when Troy was set on fire.'"

I looked at a little old clock of dark wood, set on a bracket. "It is past eleven now. Have you time to tell me what you mean by the witches' Christmas?"

"Briefly, this: In ancient heathen times a festival of scorn was held, from which grew the Christian Hallowe'en—"

"But this is the middle of November!" I protested.

"Witches are simple folk. They reckon by full moons. We have one tonight, and they've crept out of their dens to do what mischief their hearts, and their demon, tells them. Beginning at my house."

He fixed his eyes on the girl. She had been sitting silent and tense, staring straight before her. "Susan," he said gently, "they sent you to find your father's body. Did they send you for any other purpose? If so—"

She rose, and lifted her hands. She spoke, slowly and questioningly, as though reciting an unfamiliar lesson:

"Mirathe saepy Satonich—"

I started and opened my mouth, to tell her where I had heard those words, earlier in the night. But Jaeger signed me to keep silent. Susan was not chanting understandably.

"Stand still, stand still! No more than a tree or a rock can you depart! This by the four elements, the seven unspoken numbers, the innumerable stars in the sky! This by the name of—of—"

Abruptly she sat down, as if utterly weary. "I can't!" she sobbed. "I can't say that name!"

Jaeger smiled, beautifully for all his broad shagginess, and stepped across to her side. He laid his hand on her head. "No decent person can, child," he comforted her softly. "They failed in the plot when they chose you for a tool."

She looked up, and faint color had come to her cheeks. Her eyes and lips had regained steadiness. She appeared to be wakened and calmed from a nightmare.

"I'll guess what happened," he went on. "Those who told you that your father was here also gave you a message to deliver. They spoke the words for you to repeat, making passes before your eyes—thus, eh?"

Slowly he drew his open hand through the air, as if stroking invisible fur. Susan nodded, and bit her lip.

"Several names for that," Jaeger commented to me over his shoulder. "Mesmerism, animal magnetism, hypnotism. Most occult dabblers know a little of it, would God they did not! But I had no fear of Susan, even when I saw that she was entranced. In the book of James Braid I read that nobody will do things when hyponotized that he would not do in his right mind; and, whatever her father's sad delusions, Susan is healthy and good."

Susan began to weep. "I would never have hurt you, Mr. Jaeger," she managed to protest.

"Certainly not." He touched her head again, comfortingly. "That spell was to make us both stand like posts, while the prowlers came and did what they pleased with us.

"Even had she said it in full, however, it would not work. It already failed on you, Wickett. For myself, I was silently saying the counter-charm, from this book."

He again produced a volume from his shelf, this time a sort of pamphlet in gray paper. On its cover was the title:

Pow-Wows, or Long Lost Friend

And, underneath, the picture of an owl. Jaeger flipped it open—I saw the page number, 69—and began to patter nimbly:

"Like unto the cup and the wine—may we be guarded in daytime and nighttime—that no wild beast may tear us, no weapons wound us, no false tongues injure us—and no witchcraft or enchantment harm us. Amen."

I took it that such was the counter-spell he mentioned, and thought it odd that a minister should use such a device. But scant time for philosophy was left us. Outside voices began to laugh.

I say voices, not men. To this day I do not know just what sort of throats uttered that merriment. At the time it seemed to me that human beings were trying to sound like beasts, or beasts were trying to sound like human beings. The blending of beast and human was imperfect, and horrid to hear. Jaeger laid down the little book on the table, and again took up his revolver.

"Wickett," he said softly, "there is a window where you can watch the door. Take your post there. Watch. If they enter—and they probably will—stand still, as if the charm had worked. Because we can trap them so, as they meant to trap us."

He had no more time to prepare me, for outside there came a new chorus, this time of rhythmic recital:

"I strolled through a red forest, and in the red forest was a red church. In the red church stood a red altar, and upon the red altar lay a red knife."

A breathless moment of silence. Then a single booming voice, strangely accented, as if it echoed in a deformed mouth:

"Take the red knife and cut red bread!"

Jaeger sniffed. "Their sacrament ritual," he muttered. "A vile blasphemy. The window, Wickett."

He jerked his bearded chin toward an alcove by the door, and I moved into it. The window there looked upon the entrance from one side. Beneath the sill hung an old Chicopee saber, such as the Yankees once carried, and such as the Southern cavalry filched from enemy dead or captives. I started to draw it.

"No," Jaeger warned. "Only stay near, and seize it when they least expect. They will expect Susan to put out the light before they venture any nearer."

He bent toward the lamp, and blew strongly down its glass chimney. Its flame went out, and we were left in a sort of bluish gloom. I could barely see Jaeger's thick body stiffen into a statue, and I imitated him, my eyes on the window.

"Move only when I do," cautioned Jaeger softly.

Outside rose more racket. Those who besieged us were plainly trying to put fire into their own hearts.

"Hola noa massa!" spoke the strange booming voice. And back came a chorus intonation:

"Janna, janna! Hoa, hoa! Sabbat, sabbat! Moloch, Lucifer, Asteroth!"

Those, I fancied, were the names of pagan gods and devils. As the last syllable died away, something came into view beyond the window glass.

With the house dark, the moon made sufficient pale radiance outside. It showed me what was approaching the door.

It was a black low shape, greened here and there as light struck it, like an expanse of old worn broadcloth. My first impression was of a monstrous flood of filthy liquid.

Then I saw that it was indeed a creeping creature, not more in solid bulk than a big man, but with outspread wings like ribbed blankets. It paused at the squared section of log that served for doorstep, and straightened up from its crouch. I could not have looked away for wealth or hope of salvation.

This was the same thing I had earlier seen flapping across the face of the moon. Now it stood upon two flat slabs of feet, like charred shingles. Its legs were long and lean, and seemed to bend backward, cricket fashion. The deep chest thrust forward prowlike—the breastbone must have been like a bird's, a protruding blade from which great muscles branched to employ those wings. For the batlike membranes would measure twenty feet and more from tip to tip, and hung from two long lumpy arms. The thing had hands, or what might resemble hands. From them sprouted the wingribs downward, and the gaunt, sharp fingers outward.

But of face I saw nothing for all the moonlight, only an owlish roundness of skull, and two curved horns that gleamed like polished jet, and narrow green eyes like the eyes of a meat-eating animal.

It started to lift a flat foot to the step, then paused. It bent, and I knew that it had a mouth, for it blew upon Jaeger's lock, then whickered. The door opened slowly, as if pushed by invisible hands. The entity turned and moved away.

"Enter," it boomed to whatever companions lurked behind. "Do as you have been commanded, and do it well."

I froze to immobility in my alcove. A moment later, the horde outside made a concerted rush across the threshold. With them came the ugliest and rottenest of pale lights.

Chapter V
The Rout of the Witches

I knew an instant of terror more complete and sickening than any that had been mine in the war, a worse chill than at Murfreesboro, Selma, or Shiloh itself. Then the terror departed from me, and left me almost serenely strong and confident. For those who came in were only men.

They were murderous men, perhaps. They possessed ugly powers—witness that light in which they seemed to be dipped, and the chivvying commands from that being called the Flying Horned One. They were men joined for a steadfast purpose of evil. They did not simply lack ideals, morals, or character, but adhered to ideals, morals, and character antithetic to all I honored. They had a belief, even a form of travestied worship, that claimed them as ever pure religion claimed saints or martyrs. They had come to execute horrors upon me.

But their master had stayed outside. These, his followers, were no more than men, and as such had but muscles with which to attack, vital organs in which to receive wounds. I asked no lesser opponents than such.

Jaeger had spoken of twelve members to the coven, under rule of the Flying Horned One. The death of Peter Dole, the pitiful renegade, would leave only eleven. I think that that many came in now, and the light seemed to burst from the uplifted hand of the tallest. But my second glance showed me that the hand was not his. It was a five-fingered candle or taper, fixed by the wristlike base upon a tin plate, and each of the fingers sprouted a kindled wick.

I had lost sight, though not thought, of Susan. She stood near Jaeger, and came forward. One of the throng whooped in laughter—his voice was muffled by his mask and thickened by alcohol—and confronted her.

"She did it, good girl! She bound them!" He turned upon the motionless form of Jaeger. "Why aren't you preaching, Parson? Walloping the pulpit and quoting chapter and verse? Pretty quiet and stiff, ain't you?"

He drew a straight dagger like the one drawn against me at the scene of the flogging.

"Take the red knife," he quoted unsteadily, "and cut red bread!"

"Wait," interposed the tall man who held the five-fingered light. "There's something to do first. There lies some dead clay under the blanket yonder. I'd guess it for what's left of Dirt Fire, known to men as Peter Dole."

Dirt Fire. Dirt Fire—I had heard somewhere of how witches, upon joining the circle, were baptized mockingly to new names. That had befallen Peter Dole, and he had asked for a second baptism to clear his soul of the horror he felt. The tall one passed his tin plate, with the light, to a pudgy figure who must have been a woman, masked and in men's rough riding clothes. Then he took a step toward Susan and towered over her.

"You've served us well," he spoke. "Our coven is one short. You will fill the emptiness."

There was no asking of her whether she wanted to. Perhaps some quick instruction by Jaeger had prepared her for this. In any case, she voiced neither acceptance nor refusal. She only faced the tall masked man, silently and gravely.

"Thirteen we shall be, counting our master," intoned the tall one. "Susan Dole, say after me the words I now repeat."

He lifted a hand, and made the stroking gesture in air that Jaeger had called "hypnotic." Susan drew herself up. The spell seemed to be catching hold of her on the instant.

Just then, Jaeger made a little twitching motion with the right hand that had hung quietly at its side. That hand held his revolver, unnoticed by the invaders. Fire spurted, powder exploded. The tall hypnotist seemed to somersault sidewise, and banged down on the floor to lie without a quiver.

I had been like a hound on leash all this while, forcing myself to wait for the cue of Jaeger's first move. Now, before the sharp echo of the revolver-shot died in that room, I had flung out my left hand and snatched the saber from its fastenings by the sill. My right hand brought it from the sheath with a loud rasp of metal. I gathered my legs under me and leaped at the man with the drawn dagger.

He knew I was coming, somehow or other. For he turned, trying to fend me off with that straight blade he had meant for Jaeger. My first axelike chop broke his steel close to the hilt. My second assault, a drawing slice, severed muscles, arteries, and tendons at junction of neck and shoulder. Down he went at my knee, the gushing blood all black and shiny in that pallid light. I stepped across him, and into the melee that had sprung into being around Jaeger.

No less than myself, those invaders must have been keyed up to expectation of violence. When Jaeger's first shot felled their comrade, they threw themselves upon the sender of that shot. A big mask-wearer came in under the revolver muzzle, stood up under a terrific blow with the barrel, and grappled Jaeger. Others seized him by the arms, beard, throat, legs. They were pulling him down, as dogs pull down a bear. The pudgy one who held the five-fingered light stood apart, drawing another of those straight daggers. The look of the hand that held the dagger convinced me more than ever that here was a woman in men's garments.

Coming upon the press, I slid my saber-point into the back of the big fellow whose arms were around Jaeger. He subsided, coughing and struggling, and I cleared my weapon in time to face another who quit his assault on Jaeger to leap at me. He tried to avoid my slash, and I smote his jaw with the curved guard that enclosed my knuckles. He sprawled upon a comrade, and both fell.

Then Jaeger, fighting partially free, fired two more shots. One of his attackers fell limply, and another flopped away, screaming and cursing by the names of gods I did not recognize.

The light-holder now gave tongue in a shrill warning:

"Betrayed, we're betrayed! Run! Get away!"

Those who could respond did so. Jaeger fired yet again, his fourth bullet. The last of those who fled was down, floundering awkwardly to crawl across the hewn log outside the door. Two of the others caught the squirming body and dragged it clear. We were suddenly alone.

"Don't close that door," said Jaeger from the dimness that fell again—for the five-fingered light had been knocked down and extinguished. "I doubt if we need to be fenced in from them." He was kindling his own kerosene lamp, that gave a healthier radiance. "Count the dead, Wickett."

I did so, noting that all wore coats or jackets turned inside out. Two had perished by my saber, two more by Jaeger's bullets, while a third whom he had shot died even as I bent over him. The man I uppercut with the saber-hilt was still alive and breathing heavily, but quite unconscious. I reckoned the one dragged away must be badly hurt, if not also dying.

"We killed or wounded seven," was my report. Jaeger had led Susan to one side, where she might not look. Then he went from one body to the other, pulling away their horned masks of dingy black cloth. At the sight of each face he grunted his recognition.

"All of them are my neighbors," he announced, "and all of them in my congregation, or pretending to be. Look Wickett! This one is a woman—she and that first man you sabered were husband and wife. I would have spared her had I known her sex. But here is one who seems to be awakening."

The single survivor sat up. He fingered his bruised chin, wagging it tenderly. His face, unmasked, looked long and sharp and vicious. His small, dark eyes burned as they fixed upon Susan.

"She tricked us," he accused, spitting blood.

"It was I who tricked you," corrected Jaeger. "Stand up, Splain. But make any sudden move, and I will fire one of the two bullets still in this revolver." He held it up significantly.

The captive stood up. Like the others, he wore his coat inside out. "My name isn't Splain any more," he stated, with a show of defiance. "Now I'm called—"

"Spare us what foolish name your devil master gave you," interrupted Jaeger sharply. "I know most of that stupid ritual, that you think so frightening—another baptism, another book of prayer, another submission to mastery. I will call you Splain, and to that name you will answer, if you hope for mercy. Take off that coat, and put it on properly."

"You can't make me," flared Splain.

Jaeger pocketed the revolver, caught Splain by a shoulder, and shook him like a rug in a high wind. Splain squealed, cursed, and fumbled inside his coat. But Jaeger pinned his wrists, gave it a wrench, and a knife fell to the floor.

"I've seen this kind of knife before," I said, picking it up.

"Yes, several like it," agreed Jaeger. He had shaken the resistance out of Splain, had roughly dragged the reversed coat from him, and was now turning it back as it should go. "Get into this, Splain...Yes, so. Clothing turned inside out was an invulnerability charm as long ago as the Egyptian pharaohs, but it did not protect you. Wickett, I judge that it is a magic dagger, so-called, that you hold. Potent against all enemies that are not prepared."

"It looks homemade," I ventured, examining the weapon.

"Of course. Each wizard must make his own knife, hand-forging it of metal never before used. The blade is inscribed? In strange characters? I thought so."

We picked up four other knives, including the one I had broken, from the floor. Jaeger gathered them on a table, also the plate with the extinguished five-finger taper.

"A poor imitation," he said of this last object. "The hand of glory, cut from a hanged murderer's arm, is supposed to shed light and strike victims numb. Having no hanged murderer convenient, these made a dummy of wax. It failed against us as other charms have failed."

He smiled grimly at Splain. "Had the blades been simple and honest, your friends might have killed us. But they were enchanted—and useless. Get out, Splain."

"Out?" repeated the other stupidly.

"Yes. Seek that monster you call your lord, who thought a poor minister of God could not plan and fight a battle. Tell him that I prophesy his defeat. Six of the eleven he sent against us have died. The souls and bodies of the remainder are his responsibility. I shall require them at his hands. You obey?"

"Yes, Parson," grumbled Splain. He shambled toward the door.

Green fire suddenly played about him, like many little lightnings, or some display of fireworks. Splain shuddered, sagged, crumpled. He, too, was dead, the seventh to perish on the floor of Jaeger's front room.

Jaeger looked at him, at me. Then he whistled in his beard.

"So much for a defeated wizard," he commented pithily. "In some way the Flying Horned One knew of Splain's failure, and he has no use for failures."

He had produced his revolver once more. Flipping the cylinder clear, he drew the two charges remaining. Then he carefully loaded the gun afresh. From a box in the table drawer he took the bullets, pale and gleaming.

"Those look like silver," I said.

"They are silver. The sovereign weapon against wicked creatures which are more and less than human."

"You are going to shoot at the Flying Horned One?"

"No, Wickett," said the Reverend Mr. Jaeger, and put the weapon into my hand. "You are."

Chapter VI
The Five Silver Bullets

Jaeger's talk about the influence called hypnotism came back to my mind later, when I found myself outside in the chill moonglow, the revolver in my right hand, moving with quick stealth toward a distant sound of mouthy misery.

Of me he had made a champion, in this frontier strife of angels good and bad. Reiterating his insistence that my share in that uncanny adventure after Shiloh had made me somewhat immune to evil magic, he had given me the revolver and sent me forth. Where? And to do what? My head was clearing now, as after too much drink. I began to ponder the recent events with something of disgusted wonder at my own readiness to mix into what was surely no business of mine.

After all, I was strange in this Welcome Rock country. I had had no idea of staying more than the night through. I had no practical interest in any quarrels there, even quarrels incited by demons. But from the first I had taken a hand—charging those who flogged Peter Cole, wielding a saber in the parson's parlor, and now stepping forth, gun in hand, to seek and battle the Flying Horned One.

I told myself that I was a fool. I entertained the thought of finding the through trail and tramping away from Welcome Rock. There were silver bullets in the gun. They might have some cash value to buy me breakfast, miles away—

The cries grew louder. They rose from beyond one of the leafless thickets that banded the country. From that point also came a musty glow of the green cold light. I heard a voice:

"No! We did our best! Don't!"

Something struck, hard and heavy. The voice broke away from the words into a scream of agony.

As at the flogging earlier that night, I quickened my pace to a run. I was fully prepared to meddle yet again.

Beyond two or three belts of trees I came in sight of a round cleared space. Away off to one side rose the dark pinnacle that once had been called Fearful Rock, in whose shadow had been done strange matters. I lurked inside the thicket, watching what happened in the open.

There were gathered my late adversaries, only four of them now. They were wailing, posturing and wriggling, as though blows fell upon them. But it was well away from them that the punishment was dealt. There stood the Flying Horned One, or perhaps he hovered— in any case his feet touched the ground, and his wings may have fluttered slightly to hold him erect. From him came the unpleasant light. He was striking again and again with a stick, at dark objects that lay limp on the ground.

"No! No!" the voices begged him. "Strike no more, master!"

He ceased the blows, and flourished the stick at them. "You have had enough?" he demanded, in that uncouth horselike voice of his.

They assured him, tearfully, that they had.

"Then obey. Go back and kill—"

"We have no powers, no powers!" cried the plump woman who had held the five-fingered candle.

Her misshapen ruler made an impatient fluttering gesture with his umbrella wings. "This, I think, is your coat," he said, and touched with the point of his stick one of the dark objects on the ground. I saw then that these objects were garments, cloaks or coats. The woman squealed and clasped her hands.

"Don't beat on me again!" she sobbed.

To my mind came one of the most familiar legends about witches, the one about hurting at a distance. The wax image or portrait pierced with needles, the hair or nail-clipping burnt—yes, and the discarded garment beaten. I was seeing such a thing done.

"Abiam, dabiam, fabiam," babbled the monster over his stick. It was a conjuration of some sort, I guessed; indeed, Jaeger told me later that a similar spell is included in Albertus Magnus. "True you speak," he continued. "But you are bad servants." I saw his long green eyes glitter. "Perhaps I should discard you and get others. You who summoned me among you, step forward."

A fragile, oldish man came away from the others. His mask had been torn, probably in the fight, and his skin showed corpse-pale through the rent.

"I did according to the law and the books," he quavered. "If we have served you badly, it was because we did not know how to serve. Teach us."

The Flying Horned One put his armlike upper limbs, that bore the wings, akimbo. The membranes drooped around him like an ugly living shawl. "You never asked if I wished to leave my own world," he charged fiercely. "You did not wait to think if I was happy there or not. You hauled me in among strange things and thoughts. You talk about serving me, but you meant that I should serve you. Huh? Deny it if you will!"

They did not deny it. I gathered that he referred to some ceremony which had brought him into existence among them. Of such things, too, I had heard.

Again he addressed the thin oldster. "Do as you did when you summoned me."

There was a moment of scared silence. Then, "You mean the circle, master? And the pentacle?"

"You will be sorry if I command you twice," said the Flying Horned One.

The magic-maker hopped and fluttered like a frightened rabbit to obey. Stooping, with his dagger in hand, he traced on the ground a figure like a shallow-pointed star, about three yards across. As he did so he mumbled words, apparently one for each point. "Gaba," he said loud enough for me to hear, and again, "Tetragrammaton." The other words I did not catch. Having finished the star, he traced a circle outside it. His comrades all moved back, but the winged monster hovered near, in some eagerness.

"Shall I say the rest?" quavered the circle-tracer.

"Not unless you wish to bring me a brother among you," replied the Flying Horned One, and it was plain that his hearers had no such wish. "Say only the first part."

There came forth a flood of gibberish, spoken by the old man with both forefingers uplifted. The others joined in briefly at the end, chanting as if at prayer. I saw the lines that the knife had marked suddenly grow more plain and hot-looking—the star was outlined as in rosy brightness, like a figure of heated wire; and the circle gleamed blue-green, like a tracing of phosphorus.

"Look!" commanded the winged master, in a voice that made my flesh change position on my bones. "Is it—"

"The door!" hoarsely finished the magician. "It is ready to be opened unto us."

"Yes," agreed the Flying Horned One. "Opened unto you. Speak on."

The magician fronted his glowing diagram. His words became spaced and cadenced, like verse from some ponderous tragedy:

"Fear is stronger than love!

"Serve those above with joy! Serve those below with terror!

"For those above, a sacrifice of one white sheep! For those below, a sacrifice of two black sheep!

"For those above, a sacrifice of one white slave! For those below, a sacrifice of two black slaves!"

"The door opens," the others intoned.

It was more like a wall, dark and gloom-clotted, that showed itself in the center of the star-circle diagram. From it rose, lazily, a thin little veil of vapor.

"Enough," decreed the Flying Horned One, and suddenly shot out his two upper talons to seize the shoulders of the magician.

I heard a thin choking squeal for mercy. The Flying Horned One lowered his wings about the man he had grasped, and I could only guess what happened to that man under their jagged shadow. It was sufficiently horrible, I make no doubt. Lifting the revolver, I fired my first shot.

It missed its mark, for I heard it strike a tree-trunk beyond. The three companions of the magician heard my shot and turned toward its sound. Not so the monster who ruled them, for he extended his wings and with a single beat of them rose into the air. In all four of his talons he gripped the limp form of the magician. I am sure that I saw blood on that form—dark wetness, anyway. Two great flops carried the victim above the diagram and its inner opening. The talons let go, and the body fell into the hole, away from sight.

"Ohhh!" intoned the others, as if it were part of the ritual. Probably they were entranced, half delirious, unable to see their peril. Their lord flew back at and among them.

"In after him," he grunted, and seized two of them by their necks.

I fired a second shot, more carefully. It tore a hole through one of those wing membranes. For a moment I saw the tear, quite large and ragged, and moonlight through it. Then the Flying Horned One had dashed his two captives at the hole, one after the other. They vanished. I could swear that the hole gulped at and seized them, like a hungry, knowing mouth.

I came into the open, firing twice more. But my hand trembled, and both bullets went wide. This revolver, with which Jaeger had killed so coolly and capably at our earlier fight, was doing very little for me. Then I ran close. The Flying Horned One had seized the last of his worshippers, the fat woman, and twitched her in front of him as I fired a fifth time.

She caught my bullet, and whether it inflicted a slight or serious wound I cannot say. The Flying Horned One whinnied, and tossed her after the others. She, too, was vanished. I faced the dark winged silhouette, with not a dozen yards between us.

"You, too, have power," the inhuman voice addressed me levelly. "Power, but not wit. Do not use the weapon again, it is empty."

That much was truth. Jaeger had loaded it with five charges, the hammer being down on an empty chamber. I poised the gun to use as a club, and came slowly forward. The winged form moved to meet me.

"You have escaped," and the voice was scarcely more than a whisper. "Nothing that I said, or my slaves did, harmed you. Man, have you lived in more worlds than one, like me?"

I made no reply. I could think of none. Two talons reached out to clutch at me.

Then we struggled and fought. He tore at my face and at my chest, as though he would rend my flesh away. I struck with my fists and the clubbed revolver, but made no impression. His substance did not seem to have any true resistance, yet I knew that he had strength and weight.

"At my leisure, in another place—I will examine you," he told me, and heaved me toward the glowing diagram.

I grabbed him close to the elbow-joints, and we both fell heavily toward the black hole.

I struck the ground first, and there was a flash of fire, real or imaginary. Too, there was a little breathless shriek, out of the dark face of my adversary. Suddenly all weight and grip was gone from me.

I sat up. The diagram was no more than knife-edges in the moonlight. The hole—there was no hole any more, only hard earth. Of the Flying Horned One was nothing to be seen.

Jaeger, then, had been right. Power to resist evil magic kept me safe. Endeavoring to carry me away, the Flying Horned One had fallen alone into the hole and had, so to speak, pulled the hole in after him.

Rising, I wondered if I should consider myself the victor.

Chapter VII
The Grave-Digging

The morning sun was warm, invigoratingly so. Jaeger and I strove, with grubbing hoe and shovel, at earth that was no longer frozen to stony hardness.

"Make the grave wide, but not too shallow," he directed as he toiled. "Seven must go into it. I wonder if I can spare blankets enough to wrap them all."

"Will nobody ask questions?" I demanded. "Have they no friends or families?"

"Their friends and families will know that fate overtook them, but not in what form," replied Jaeger. "If no corpse shows above earth, I will not be required to explain anything. That is the way of the law hereabouts, and it is well. Wrestlings with demons do not court publicity."

I reflected that, after all, here was a wild and unwatched country. It was no more than four or five years since many more persons had been killed in Kansas by the Bender family, and the detection had come only by the slimmest of chances. Jaeger seemed confident that the matter was as good as closed.

"I shall read a prayer for them all." He took up the subject again. "God knows that few men have needed prayers more, but I do not despair of their souls. They were only misled, not wicked of their own wish."

I wiped my face on my sleeve. "Didn't they flog Peter Dole to death?" I reminded. "Didn't they come to kill us? Didn't—"

"All at the bidding of the Flying Horned One. He had bound them in a spell. But he is gone, and I doubt if he ever comes again to Welcome Rock." Jaeger was speaking triumphantly. "His reception was calculated to daunt even a demon."

"Demon," I repeated. "Mr. Jaeger, tell me now, simply and shortly, what sort of a person a demon is?"

"No sort of person. For a demon is not born on Earth, nor does it die there. It comes from another place."

"From hell, yes."

"Perhaps from the place we think of as hell. What that place is like I cannot tell you, nor could any other man—not even if the Flying Horned One's betrayed servants returned to life. For we live and behave in but one sphere, with no conception of others. Yet, if another sphere could touch ours by accident or purpose, and beings come from it to us—"

He paused, and let the rest of the explanation grow in my own mind.

I considered the bizarre possibility. We of this life are two-legged things with blood in our veins, appetites to satisfy, hopes and duties to impel our actions. Basic concepts of nature as we know her make us all brothers. This is what we call the universe, this tiny handful of objects experienced through our few senses and imaginations.

But another universe, wherein not only beings and viewpoints and constructions are different, but the very elements of them—had that spawned the Flying Horned One?

Perhaps his very appearance, strange though it seemed, was only his effort to conform with a new state of afairs. Perhaps his original impulses had been influenced by the worship paid him, and by the expectations of the worshippers. Perhaps he had thought of himself as neither good nor evil, but doing something which partook of neither quality. He might have been the least proper item by which to judge that stranger universe.

But I had no desire to visit such a place, or to encounter others of its creatures.

"Of morals to be drawn from our experience, there are perhaps a thousand," Jaeger resumed. "One, however, I shall build into a sermon. My text shall be, 'He that increaseth knowledge increaseth sorrow.'"

"From Ecclesiastes," I said.

"What I shall say is that a fascinating study can sometimes do more harm than good, especially to the careless. What hopes must that poor fellow have had, who drew a diagram and clumsily performed a ceremony he could not understand—thereby opening a trapdoor to another sphere and admitting the Flying Horned One to ours!"

"He went to the Flying Horned One's sphere, and his knowledge is painfully increased," I reminded.

"Can you say for certain to what sphere they went? Perhaps they have blundered into yet another manner of living, bringing strangeness and pain with them."

We had finished our digging. Jaeger looked toward the house.

"Smoke is coming up the chimney. Susan has made some sort of breakfast for us. After that, to bury the dead."

"And after that?" I prompted. "I am too tired to move on just yet."

Jaeger smiled.

"Why move on at all? There are empty acres here. Nobody will discourage a young man who wants to settle down, work, and rebuild his fortune. If you are lonely, notice that Susan Dole is beautiful and helpful."

But I had already noticed that.

An entertaining, prolific writer in almost all fields, big, burly, courteous Manly Wade Wellman (1906–1986) is best remembered for his science fiction and supernatural stories. Born in Portuguese West Africa, Wellman was brought to the U.S. at the age of six. After earning a B.A. at Wichita State University in 1926 and a B.Lit. at Columbia in 1927, the former football player and bouncer quit his reporting job to become a professional writer. One of his first sales was to **Weird Tales,** *a major market for decades; Wellman was to sell them more than a quarter-million words. Perhaps his best novel from the pulp magazine years was* **Twice in Time** *(Avalon, 1957), about a time traveler who goes back to Leonardo da Vinci's Florence and finds no trace of him. In the mystery field, Wellman won First Prize in the first (1946)* **Ellery Queen's Mystery Magazine** *Contest for "A Star for a Warrior," with William Faulkner taking second place. His work in hardcovers includes mysteries, young adult books, and a biography of the Confederate general Wade Hampton,* **Giant in Gray** *(Scribner's, 1949). He is best known for his creation of John the Ballader, who finds and destroys supernatural evil in the mountains of the South, in* **Who Fears the Devil?** *(Arkham House, 1963). A huge collection of his supernatural fiction,* **Worse Things Waiting** *(Carcosa House, 1973), won the World Fantasy Award for him; a second equally huge volume,* **Lonely Vigils,** *followed in 1982. Wellman spent the last third of his life in North Carolina, where he died a few months after an illness necessitated the amputation of both his legs.*

THE LEGEND OF JOE LEE

JOHN D. MACDONALD

"Tonight," Sergeant Lazeer said, "we get him for sure."

We were in a dank office in the Afaloosa County Courthouse in the flat wetlands of south central Florida. I had come over from Lauderdale on the half chance of a human interest story that would tie in with the series we were doing on the teenage war against the square world of the adult.

He called me over to the table where he had the county map spread out. The two other troopers moved in beside me.

"It's a full moon night and he'll be out for sure," Lazeer said, "and what we're fixing to do is bottle him on just the right stretch, where he got no way off it, no old back-country roads he knows like the shape of his own fist. And here we got it." He put brackets at either end of a string-straight road.

Trooper McCullum said softly, "That there, Mister, is an eighteen-mile straight, and we cruised it slow, and you turn off it, you're in the deep ditch and the black mud and the 'gator water."

Lazeer said, "We stake out both ends, hide back good with lights out. We got radio contact, so when he comes, whistling in either end,

62

we got him bottled."

He looked up at me as though expecting an opinion, and I said, "I don't know a thing about roadblocks, Sergeant, but it looks as if you could trap him."

"You ride with me, Mister, and we'll get you a story."

"There's one thing you haven't explained, Sergeant. You said you know who the boy is. Why don't you just pick him up at home?"

The other trooper, Frank Gaiders, said, "Because that fool kid ain't been home since he started this crazy business five, six months ago. His name is Joe Lee Cuddard, from over to Lasco City. His folks don't know where he is, and don't much care, him and that Farris girl he was running with, so we figure the pair of them is off in the piney woods someplace, holed up in some abandoned shack, coming out at night for kicks, making fools of us."

"Up till now, boy," Lazeer said. "Up till tonight. Tonight is the end."

"But when you've met up with him on the highway," I asked, "you haven't been able to catch him?"

The three big, weathered men looked at each other with slow, sad amusement, and McCullum sighed, "I come the closest. The way these cars are beefed up as interceptors, they can do a dead honest hundred and twenty. I saw him across the flats, booming to where the two road forks come together up ahead, so I floored it and I was flat out when the roads joined, and not over fifty yards behind him. In two minutes he had me by a mile, and in four minutes it was near two, and then he was gone. That comes to a hundred and fifty, my guess."

I showed my astonishment. "What the hell does he drive?"

Lazeer opened the table drawer and fumbled around in it and pulled out a tattered copy of a hot-rodder magazine. He opened it to a page where readers had sent in pictures of their cars. It didn't look like anything I had ever seen. Most of it seemed to be bare frame, with a big chromed engine. There was a teardrop-shaped passenger compartment mounted between the big rear wheels, bigger than the front wheels, and there was a tail-fin arrangement that swept up and out and then curved back so that the high rear ends of the fins almost met.

"That engine," Frank Gaiders said, "it's a '61 Pontiac, the big one he bought wrecked and fixed up, with blowers and special cams and every damn thing. Put the rest of it together himself. You can see in the letter there, he calls it a C.M. Special. C.M. is for Clarissa May, that Farris girl he took off with. I saw that thing just one time, oh, seven, eight months ago, right after he got it all finished. We got this magazine from his daddy. I saw it at the Amoco gas in Lasco City. You could near give it a ticket standing still. 'Strawberry flake paint' it says in the letter. Damnedest thing, bright strawberry with little like gold flakes in it, then covered with maybe seventeen coats of lacquer, all rubbed down so you look down into that paint like it was six inches deep. Headlights all the hell over the front of it and big taillights all over the back, and shiny pipes sticking out. Near two year he worked on it. Big racing flats like the drag-strip kids use over to the airport."

I looked at the coarse-screen picture of the boy standing beside the car, hands on his hips, looking very young, very ordinary, slightly self-conscious.

"It wouldn't spoil anything for you, would it," I asked, "if I went and talked to his people, just for background?"

"Long as you say nothing about what we're fixing to do," Lazeer said. "Just be back by eight-thirty this evening."

Lasco City was a big brave name for a hamlet of about five hundred. They told me at the sundries store to take the west road and the Cuddard place was a half-mile on the left, name on the mailbox. It was a shacky place, chickens in the dusty yard, fence sagging. Leo Cuddard was home from work and I found him out in back, unloading cinder block from an ancient pickup. He was stripped to the waist, a lean, sallow man who looked undernourished and exhausted. But the muscles in his spare back writhed and knotted when he lifted the blocks. He had pale hair and pale eyes and a narrow mouth. He would not look directly at me. He grunted and kept on working as I introduced myself and stated my business.

Finally he straightened and wiped his forehead with his narrow arm. When those pale eyes stared at me, for some reason it made me remember the grisly reputation Florida troops acquired in the Civil War. Tireless, deadly, merciless.

"That boy warn't no help to me, Mister, but he warn't no trouble neither. The onliest thing on his mind was that car. I didn't hold with it, but I didn't put down no foot. He fixed up that old shed there to work in, and he needed something, he went out and earned up the money to buy it. They was a crowd of them around most times, helpin' him, boys workin' and gals watchin'. Them tight-pants girls. Have radios on batteries set around so as they could twisty dance while them boys hammered that metal out. When I worked around and overheared 'em, I swear I couldn't make out more'n one word from seven. What he done was take that car to some national show, for prizes and such. But one day he just took off, like they do nowadays."

"Do you hear from him at all?"

He grinned. "I don't hear from him, but I sure God hear about him."

"How about brothers and sisters?"

"They's just one sister, older, up to Waycross, Georgia, married to an electrician, and me and his stepmother."

As if on cue, a girl came out onto the small back porch. She couldn't have been more than eighteen. Advanced pregnancy bulged the front of her cotton dress. Her voice was a shrill, penetrating whine. "Leo? Leo, honey, that can-opener thing just now busted clean off the wall."

"Mind if I take a look at that shed?"

"You help yourself, Mister."

The shed was astonishingly neat. The boy had rigged up drop-lights. There was a pale blue pegboard wall hung with shining tools. On closer inspection I could see that rust was beginning to fleck the tools. On the workbench were technical journals and hot-rodder magazines. I looked at the improvised engine hoist, at the neat shelves of paint and lubricant.

The Farris place was nearer the center of the village. Some of them were having their evening meal. There were six adults as near as I could judge, and perhaps a dozen children from toddlers on up to tall, lanky boys. Clarissa May's mother came out onto the front porch to talk to me, explaining that her husband drove an interstate truck from the cooperative and he was away for the next few days. Mrs. Farris was grossly fat, but with delicate features, an indication of the beauty she must have once had. The rocking chair creaked under her weight and she fanned herself with a newspaper.

"I can tell you, it like to broke our hearts the way Clarissa May done us. If'n I told LeRoy once, I told him a thousand times, no good would ever come of her messin' with that Cuddard boy. His daddy is trashy. Ever so often they take him in for drunk and put him on the county road gang sixty or ninety days, and that Stubbins child he married, she's next door to feeble-witted. But children get to a certain size and know everything and turn their backs on you like an enemy. You write this up nice and in it put the message her momma and daddy want her home bad, and maybe she'll see it and come on in. You know what the Good Book says about sharper'n a sarpent's tooth. I pray to the good Lord they had the sense to drive that fool car up to Georgia and get married up at least. Him nineteen and her seventeen. The young ones are going clean out of hand these times. One night racing through this county the way they do, showing off, that Cuddard boy is going to kill hisself and my child, too."

"Was she hard to control in other ways, Mrs. Farris?"

"No sir, she was neat and good and pretty and quiet, and she had the good marks. It was just about Joe Lee Cuddard she turned mulish. I think I would have let LeRoy whale that out of her if it hadn't been for her trouble.

"You're easier on a young one when there's no way of knowing how long she could be with you. Doc Mathis, he had us taking her over to the Miami clinic. Sometimes they kept her and sometimes they didn't, and she'd get behind in her school and then catch up fast. Many times we taken her over there. She's got the sick blood and it takes her poorly. She should be right here, where's help to care for her in the bad spells. It was October last year, we were over to the church bingo, LeRoy and me, and Clarissa May been resting up in her bed a few days, and that wild boy come in and taking her off in that snorty car, the little ones couldn't stop him. When I think of her out there...poorly and all..."

At a little after nine we were in position. I was with Sergeant Lazeer at the west end of that eighteen-mile stretch of State Road 21. The patrol car was backed into a narrow dirt road, lights out. Gaiders and McCullum were similarly situated at the east end of the trap. We were smeared with insect repellent, and we had used spray on the backs of each other's shirts where the mosquitoes were biting through the thin fabric.

Lazeer had repeated his instructions over the radio, and we composed ourselves to wait. "Not much travel on the road this time of year," Lazeer said. "But some tourists come through at the wrong time, they could mess this up. We just got to hope that don't happen."

"Can you block the road with just one car at each end?"

"If he comes through from the other end, I move up quick and put it crosswise where he can't get past, and Frank has a place like that at the other end. Crosswise with the lights and the dome blinker on, but we both are going to stand clear because maybe he can stop it and maybe he can't. But whichever way he comes, we got to have the free car run close herd so he can't get time to turn around when he sees he's bottled."

Lazeer turned out to be a lot more talkative than I had anticipated. He had been in law enforcement for twenty years and had some violent stories. I sensed he was feeding them to me, waiting for me to suggest I write a book about him. From time to time we would get out of the car and move around a little.

"Sergeant, you're pretty sure you've picked the right time and place?"

"He runs on the nights the moon is big. Three or four nights out of the month. He doesn't run the main highways, just these back-country roads—the long straight paved stretches where he can really wind that thing up. Lord God, he goes through towns like a rocket. From reports we got, he runs the whole night through, and this is one way he comes, one way or the other, maybe two, three times before moonset. We got to get him. He's got folks laughing at us."

I sat in the car half-listening to Lazeer tell a tale of blood and horror. I could hear choruses of swamp toads mingling with the whine of insects close to my ears, looking for a biting place. A couple of times I had heard the bass throb of a 'gator.

Suddenly Lazeer stopped and I sensed his tenseness. He leaned forward, head cocked. And then, mingled with the wet country shrilling, and then overriding it, I heard the oncoming high-pitched snarl of high combustion.

"Hear it once and you don't forget it," Lazeer said, and unhooked the mike from the dash and got through to McCullum and Gaiders. "He's coming through this end, boys. Get yourself set."

He hung up and in the next instant the C.M. Special went by. It was a resonant howl that stirred echoes inside the inner ear. It was a tearing, bursting rush of wind that rattled fronds and turned leaves over. It was a dark shape in moonlight, slamming by, the howl diminishing as the wind of passage died.

Lazeer plunged the patrol car out onto the road in a screeching turn, and as we straightened out, gathering speed, he yelled to me, "Damn fool runs without lights when the moon is bright enough."

As had been planned, we ran without lights, too, to keep Joe Lee from smelling the trap until it was too late. I tightened my seat belt and peered in the moonlit road. Lazeer had estimated we could make it to the far end in ten minutes or a little less. The world was like a photographic negative—white world and black trees and brush, and no shades of gray. As we came quickly up to speed, the heavy sedan began to feel strangely light. It toe-danced, tender and capricious, the wind roared louder than the engine sound. I kept wondering what would happen if Joe Lee stopped dead up there in darkness. I kept staring ahead for the murderous bulk of his vehicle.

Soon I could see the distant red wink of the other sedan, and then the bright cone where the headlights shone off the shoulder into the heavy brush. When my eyes adjusted to that brightness, I could no longer see the road. We came down on them with dreadful speed. Lazeer suddenly snapped our lights on, touched the siren. We were going to see Joe Lee trying to back and turn around on the narrow paved road, and we were going to block him and end the night games.

We saw nothing. Lazeer pumped the brakes. He cursed. We came to a stop ten feet from the side of the other patrol car. McCullum and Gaiders came out of the shadows. Lazeer and I undid our seat belts and got out of the car.

"We didn't see nothing and we didn't hear a thing," Frank Gaiders said.

Lazeer summed it up. "Okay, then. I was running without lights, too. Maybe the first glimpse he got of your flasher, he cramps it over onto the left shoulder, tucks it over as far as he dares. I could go by without seeing him. He backs around and goes back the way he came, laughing hisself sick. There's the second chance he tried that and took it too far, and he's wedged in a ditch. Then there's the third chance he lost it. He could have dropped a wheel off onto the shoulder and tripped hisself and gone flying three hundred feet into the swamp. So what we do, we go back there slow. I'll go first and keep my spotlight on the right, and you keep yours on the left. Look for that car and for places where he could have busted through."

At the speed Lazeer drove, it took over a half-hour to traverse the eighteen-mile stretch. He pulled off at the road where we had waited. He seemed very depressed, yet at the same time amused.

They talked, then he drove me to the courthouse where my car was parked. He said, "We'll work out something tighter and I'll give you a call. You might as well be in at the end."

I drove sedately back to Lauderdale.

Several days later, just before noon on a bright Sunday, Lazeer phoned me at my apartment and said, "You want to be in on the finish of this thing, you better do some hustling and leave right now."

"In a manner of speaking." He sounded sad and wry. "He dumped that machine into a canal off Route 27 about twelve miles south of Okeelanta. The wrecker'll be winching it out any time now. The diver says he and the gals are still in it. It's been on the radio news. Diver read the tag, and it's his. Last year's. He didn't trouble hisself getting a new one."

I wasted no time driving to the scene. I certainly had no trouble identifying it. There were at least a hundred cars pulled off on both sides of the highway. A traffic-control officer tried to wave me on by, but when I showed him my press card and told him Lazeer had phoned me, he had me turn in and park beside a patrol car near the center of activity.

I spotted Lazeer on the canal bank and went over to him. A big man in face mask, swim fins, and air tank was preparing to go down with the wrecker hook.

Lazeer greeted me and said, "It pulled loose the first time, so he's going to try to get it around the rear axle this time. It's in twenty feet of water, right side up, in the black mud."

"Did he lose control?"

"Hard to say. What happened, early this morning a fellow was goofing around in a little airplane, flying low, parallel to the canal, the water like a mirror, and he seen something down in there so he came around and looked again, then he found a way to mark the spot, opposite those three trees away over there, so he came into his home field and phoned it in, and we had that diver down by nine this morning. I got here about ten."

"I guess this isn't the way you wanted it to end, Sergeant."

"It sure God isn't. It was a contest between him and me, and I wanted to get him my own way. But I guess it's a good thing he's off the night roads."

I looked around. The red and white wrecker was positioned and braced. Ambulance attendants were leaning against their vehicle, smoking and chatting. Sunday traffic slowed and was waved on by.

"I guess you could say his team showed up," Lazeer said.

Only then did I realize the strangeness of most of the waiting vehicles. The cars were from a half-dozen counties, according to the tag numbers. There were many big, gaudy, curious monsters not unlike the C.M. Special in basic layout, but quite different in design. They seemed like a visitation of Martian beasts. There were dirty fenderless sedans from the thirties with modern power plants under the hoods, and big rude racing numbers painted on the side doors. There were other cars which looked normal at first glance, but then seemed to squat oddly low, lines clean and sleek where the Detroit chrome had been taken off, the holes leaded up.

The cars and the kids were of another race. Groups of them

formed, broke up, and re-formed. Radios brought in a dozen stations. They drank Cokes and perched in dense flocks on open convertibles. They wandered from car to car. It had a strange carnival flavor, yet more ceremonial. From time to time somebody would start one of the car engines, rev it up to a bursting roar, and let it die away.

All the girls had long burnished hair and tidy blouses or sun tops and a stillness in their faces, a curious confidence of total acceptance which seemed at odds with the frivolous and provocative tightness of their short shorts, stretch pants, jeans. All the boys were lean, their hairdos carefully ornate, their shoulders high and square, and they moved with the lazy grace of young jungle cats. Some of the couples danced indolently, staring into each other's eyes with a frozen and formal intensity, never touching, bright hair swinging, girls' hips pumping in the stylized ceremonial twist.

Along the line I found a larger group. A boy was strumming slow chords on a guitar, a girl making sharp and erratic fill-in rhythm on a set of bongos. Another boy, in nasal and whining voice, seemed to improvise lyrics as he sang them. "C.M. Special, let it get out and *go/* C.M. Special, let it way out and *go/*Iron runs fast and the moon runs slow."

The circle watched and listened with a contained intensity.

Then I heard the winch whining. It seemed to grow louder as, one by one, the other sounds stopped. The kids began moving toward the wrecker. They formed a big, silent semicircle. The taut, woven cable, coming in very slowly, stretched down at an angle through the sun glitter on the black-brown water.

The snore of a passing truck covered the winch noise for a moment.

"Coming good now," a man said.

First you could see an underwater band of silver, close to the dropoff near the bank. Then the first edges of the big sweeping fins broke the surface, then the broad rear bumper, then the rich curves of the strawberry paint. Where it wasn't clotted with wet weed or stained with mud, the paint glowed rich and new and brilliant. There was a slow sound from the kids, a sigh, a murmur, a shifting.

As it came up farther, the dark water began to spurt from it, and as the water level inside dropped, I saw, through a smeared window, the two huddled masses, the slumped boy and girl, side by side, still belted in.

I wanted to see no more. Lazeer was busy, and I got into my car and backed out and went home and mixed a drink.

I started work on it at about three-thirty that afternoon. It would be a feature for the following Sunday. I worked right on through until two in the morning. It was only two thousand words, but it was very tricky and I wanted to get it just right. I had to serve two masters. I had to give lip service to the editorial bias that this sort of thing was wrong, yet at the same time I wanted to capture, for my own sake, the flavor of legend. These kids were making a special world we could not share. They were putting all their skills and dreams and energies to work composing the artifacts of a subculture, power, beauty, speed, skill, and rebellion. Our culture was giving them damned little, so they were fighting for a world of their own, with its own customs, legends, and feats of valor, its own music, its own ethics and morality.

I took it in Monday morning and left it on Si Walther's desk, with the hope that if it were published intact, it might become a classic. I called it "The Little War of Joe Lee Cuddard."

I didn't hear from Si until just before noon. He came out and dropped it on my desk. "Sorry," he said.

"What's the matter with it?"

"Hell, it's a very nice bit. But we don't publish fiction. You should have checked it out better, Marty, like you usually do. The examiner says those kids have been in the bottom of that canal for maybe eight months. I had Sam check her out through the clinic. She was damn near terminal eight months ago. What probably happened, the boy went to see her and found her so bad off he got scared and decided to rush her to Miami. She was still in her pajamas, with a sweater over them. That way it's a human-interest bit. I had Helen do it. It's page one this afternoon, boxed."

I took my worthless story, tore it in half, and dropped it into the wastebasket. Sergeant Lazeer's bad guess about the identity of his moonlight road runner had made me look like an incompetent jackass. I vowed to check all facts, get all names right, and never again indulge in glowing, strawberry-flake prose.

Three weeks later I got a phone call from Sergeant Lazeer.

He said, "I guess you figured out we got some boy coming in from out of county to fun us these moonlight nights."

"Yes, I did."

"I'm right sorry about you wasting that time and effort when we were thinking we were after Joe Lee Cuddard. We're having some bright moonlight about now, and it'll run full tomorrow night. You want to come over, we can show you some fun, because I got a plan that's dead sure. We tried it last night, but there was just one flaw, and he got away through a road we didn't know about. Tomorrow he won't get that chance to melt away."

I remembered the snarl of that engine, the glimpse of a dark shape, the great wind of passage. Suddenly the backs of my hands prickled. I remembered the emptiness of that stretch of road when we searched it. Could there have been that much pride and passion, labor and love and hope, that Clarissa May and Joe Lee could forever ride the night roads of their home county, balling through the silver moonlight? And what curious message had assembled all those kids from six counties so quickly?

"You there? You still there?"

"Sorry, I was trying to remember my schedule. I don't think I can make it."

"Well, we'll get him for sure this time."

"Best of luck, Sergeant."

"Six cars this time. Barricades. And a spotter plane. He hasn't got a chance if he comes into the net."

I guess I should have gone. Maybe hearing it again, glimpsing the dark shape, feeling the stir of the night wind, would have convinced me of its reality. They didn't get him, of course. But they came so close, so very close. But they left just enough room between a heavy barricade and a live-oak tree, an almost impossibly narrow place to slam through. But thread it he did, and rocket back onto the hard-top and plunge off, leaving the fading, dying contralto drone.

Sergeant Lazeer is grimly readying next month's trap. He says it is the final one. Thus far, all he has captured are the two little marks, a streak of paint on the rough edge of a timber sawhorse, another nudge of paint on the trunk of the oak. Strawberry red. Flecked with gold.

*P*opular *and prolific, John D. MacDonald (1916-1986) was the author of more than sixty paperback original novels and a growing number of hardcover blockbuster best-sellers, some, like* **Condominium** *(1977), being made into movies. He is best known as the creator of Travis McGee, a husky Robin Hood type who recovers stolen property from thieves and restores it to the owners for a percentage. Born in Sharon, Pennsylvania, MacDonald earned an M.B.A. from Harvard in 1939 and then served in the O.S.S. during World War II, leaving with the rank of Lt. Colonel. Returning from the war, he began a new career in writing. One of the few remaining writers to get basic training in* *the pulp magazines, MacDonald wrote almost every type of story imaginable, including such science fiction novels as **Wine of the Dreamers** (Greenberg, 1951) and **The Girl, the Gold Watch, and Everything** (Fawcett, 1962). Most of his work is in the detective-crime field. Filled with social comment, it is harsh, violent, and often centered around the crimes of big business and the appalling human cost of the "anything-for-a-buck" philosophy. In 1972 he received the Mystery Writers of America's Grand Master Award for lifetime achievement.*

The Wait
Kit Reed

Penetrating a windshield blotched with decalcomanias of every tourist attraction from Luray Caverns to Silver Springs, Miriam read the road sign.

"It's Babylon, Georgia, Momma. Can't we stop?"

"Sure, sweetie. Anything you want to do." The little, round, brindle woman took off her sunglasses. "After all, it's your trip."

"I know, Momma, I know. All I want is a popsicle, not the Grand Tour."

"Don't be fresh."

They were on their way home again, after Miriam's graduation trip through the South. (Momma had planned it for years, and had taken two months off, right in the middle of the summer, too, and they'd left right afer high school commencement ceremonies. "Mr. Margulies said I could have the whole summer, because I've been with him and Mr. Kent for so long," she had said. "Isn't it wonderful to be going somewhere together, dear?" Miriam had sighed, thinking of her crowd meeting in drugstores and in movies and eating melted ice cream in the park all through the good, hot summer. "Yes," she'd said.)

Today they'd gotten off 301, somehow, and had driven dusty Georgia miles without seeing another car or another person, except for a Negro driving a tractor down the softening asphalt road, and two kids walking into a seemingly deserted candy store. Now they drove slowly into a town, empty because it was two o'clock and the sun was shimmering in the streets. They *had* to stop, Miriam knew, on the pretext of wanting something cold to drink. They had to reassure themselves that there were other people in the town, in Georgia, in the world.

In the sleeping square, a man lay. He raised himself on his elbows when he saw the car, and beckoned to Miriam, grinning.

"Momma, see *that* place. Would you mind if I worked in a place like *that?*" They drove past the drugstore, a chrome palace with big front windows.

"Oh, Miriam, don't start that again. How many times do I have to tell you, I don't *want* you working in a drugstore when we get back." Her mother made a pass at a parking place, drove once again around the square. "What do you think I sent you to high school for? I want you to go to Katie Gibbs this summer, and get a good job in the fall. What kind of boyfriends do you think you can meet jerking sodas? You know, I don't want you to work for the rest of your life. All you have to do is get a good job, and you'll meet some nice boy, maybe from your office, and get married, and never have to work again." She parked the car and got out, fanning herself. They stood under the trees, arguing.

"Momma, even if I *did* want to meet your nice people, I wouldn't have a thing to wear." The girl settled into the groove of the old argument. "I want some pretty clothes and I want to get a car. I know a place where you only have to pay forty dollars a month. I'll be getting thirty-five a week at the drugstore—"

"And spending it all on yourself, I suppose. How many times do I have to explain, nice people don't work in places like that. Here I've supported you, fed you, dressed you, ever since your father died, and now, when I want you to have a *nice* future, you want to throw it out of the window for a couple of fancy dresses." Her lips quivered. "Here I am practically dead on my feet, giving you a nice trip, and a chance to learn typing and shorthand and have a nice future—"

"Oh, Momma." The girl kicked at the sidewalk and sighed. She said the thing that would stop the argument. "I'm sorry. I'll like it, I guess, when I get started."

Round, soft, jiggling, and determined, her mother moved ahead of her, trotting in too-high heels, skirting the square. "The main thing, sweetie, is to be a *good* girl. If boys see you behind a soda fountain, there're liable to get the wrong idea. They may think they can get away with something, and try to take advantage..."

In the square across the street, lying on a pallet in the sun, a young boy watched them. He called out.

"...Don't pay any attention to him," the mother said. "...And if boys know you're a *good* girl, one day you'll meet one who will want to marry you. Maybe a big businessman, or a banker if you have a good steno job. But if he thinks he can take advantage," her eyes were suddenly crafty, "he'll never marry you. You just pay attention. Don't ever let boys get away with anything. Like when you're on a date, do you ever—"

"Oh, Momma," Miriam cried, insulted.

"I'm sorry, sweetie, but I do so want you to be a *good* girl. Are you listening to me, Miriam?"

"Momma, that lady seems to be calling me. That one lying over there in the park. What do you suppose she wants?"

"I don't know. Well, don't just stand there. She looks like a *nice* woman. Go over and see if you can help her. Guess she's sunbathing, but it *does* look funny, almost like she's in bed. Ask her, Mirry. Go *on!*"

"Will you move me into the shade?" The woman, obviously one of the leading matrons of the town, was lying on a thin mattress. The shadow of the tree she was under had shifted with the sun, leaving her in the heat.

Awkwardly, Miriam tugged at the ends of the thin mattress, got it into the shade.

"And my water and medicine bottle too, please?"

"Yes ma'am. Is there anything the matter, ma'am?"

"Well." The woman ticked the familiar recital off on her fingers: "It started with cramps and—you know—lady-trouble. Thing is, now my head burns all the time and I've got a pain in my left side, not burning, you know, but just sort of tingling."

"Oh, that's too bad."

"Well, has your mother there ever had that kind of trouble? What did the doctor prescribe? What would *you* do for my kind of trouble? Do you know anybody who's had anything like it? That pain, it starts up around my ribs, and goes down, sort of zigzag..."

Miriam bolted.

"Momma, I've changed my mind. I don't want a popsicle. Let's get out of here, please. Momma?"

"If you don't mind, sweetie, I want a coke." Her mother dropped on a bench. "I don't feel so good. My head..."

They went into the drugstore. Behind the chrome and plate glass, it was like every drugstore they'd seen in every small town along the east coast, cool and dim and a little dingy in the back. They sat at one of the small, round wooden tables, and a dispirited waitress brought them their order.

"What did Stanny and Bernice say when you told them you were going on a big tour." Miriam's mother slurped at her coke, breathing hard.

"Oh, they thought it was all right."

"Well, I certainly hope you tell them all about it when we get back. It's not every young girl gets a chance to see all the historical monuments. I bet Bernice has never been to Manassas."

"I guess not, Momma."

"I guess Stanny and that Mrs. Fyle will be pretty impressed when you get back and tell 'em where all we've been. I bet that Mrs. Fyle could never get Toby to go anywhere with her. Of course, they've never been as close as we've been."

"I guess not, Momma." The girl sucked and sucked at the bottom half of her popsicle, to keep it from dripping on her dress.

In the back of the store, a young woman in dirty white shorts held onto her little son's hand and talked to the waitress. The baby, about two, sat on the floor in gray, dusty diapers.

"You're birthday's coming pretty soon, isn't it?" She dropped the baby's hand.

"Yeah. Oh, you ought to see my white dress. Golly, Anne, hope I won't have to Wait too long. Anne, what was it like?"

The young woman looked away from her, with the veiled face of the married, who do not talk about such things.

"Myla went last week, and she only had to stay for a couple of days. Don't tell anybody, because of course she's going to marry Harry next week, but she wishes she could see Him again..."

The young woman moved a foot, accidentally hit the baby. He snuffled and she helped him onto her lap, gurgling at him. In the front of the store, Miriam heard the baby and jumped. "Momma, come *on*. We'll never get to Richmond by night. We've already lost our way twice!" Her mother, dabbling her straws in the ice at the bottom of her paper cup, roused herself. They dropped two nickels on the counter and left.

They skirted the square again, ignoring the three people who lay on the grass motioning and calling to them with a sudden urgency. Miriam got into the car.

"Momma, come *on!* Momma!" Her mother was still standing at the door by the driver's seat, hanging on to the handle. Miriam slid across the front seat to open the door for her. She gave the handle an impatient twist and then started as she saw her mother's upper body and face slip past the window in a slow fall to the pavement. "Oh, I knew we never should have come!" It was an agonized, vexed groan. Redfaced and furious, she got out of the car, ran around to help her mother.

On their pallets in the park, the sick people perked up. Men and women were coming from everywhere. Cars pulled up and stopped and more people came. Kneeling on the pavement, Miriam managed to tug her mother into a prone position. She fanned her, and talked to her, and when she saw she wasn't going to wake up or move, she looked at the faces above her in sudden terror.

"Oh, please help me. We're alone here. She'll be all right, I think, once we get her inside. She's never fainted before. Please, someone get a doctor." The faces looked interested, but nobody moved. Almost crying, Miriam said, "Oh, no, never mind. Just help me get her to the car. If she isn't all right in a few miles, I'll take her to a a doctor." Then, frantically, "I just want to get out of here!"

"Why, honey, you don't need to do that. Don't you worry." A shambling, balding pleasant man in his forties knelt beside her and put his hand on her shoulder. "We'll have her diagnosed and started on a cure in no time. Can you tell me what's been her trouble?"

"Not so far, Doctor."

"I'm not a doctor, honey."

"Not so far," she said dazedly, "except she's been awfully hot." (Two women in the background nodded at each other knowingly.) "I thought it was the weather, but I guess it's fever." (The crowd was waiting.) "And she has an open place on her foot—got it while we were sightseeing in Tennessee."

"Well, honey, maybe we'd better look at it." The shoe came off and when it did, the men and women moved even closer, clucking and whispering about the wet, raw sore.

"If we could just get back to Queens," Miriam said. "If we could just get home, I know everything would be all right."

"Why, we'll have her diagnosed before you know it." The shambling man got up from his knees. "Anybody here had anything like this recently?" The men and women conferred in whispers.

"Well," one man said, "Harry Parkins's daughter had a fever like that; turned out to be pneumonia, but she never had nothin' like that on her foot. I reckon she ought to have antibiotics for that fever."

"Why, I had somethin' like that on my arm." A woman amputee was talking. "Wouldn't go away and wouldn't go away. Said I woulda died, if they hadn't of done this." She waved the stump.

"We don't want to do anything like that yet. Might not even be the same thing," the bald man said. "Anybody else?"

"Might be tetanus."

"Could be typhoid, but I don't think so."

"Bet it's some sort of staphlococcus infection."

"Well," the bald man said, "since we don't seem to be able to prescribe just now, guess we'd better put her on the square. Call your friends when you get home tonight, folks, and see if any of them know about it; if not, we'll just have to depend on tourists."

"All right, Herman."

"G'bye, Herman."

"See ya, Herman."

"G'bye."

The mother, who had come to during the dialogue and listened with terrified fascination, gulped a potion and a glass of water the druggist had brought from across the street. From the furniture store came the messenger boy with a thin mattress. Someone else brought a couple of sheets, and the remainder of the crowd carried her into the square and put her down not far from the woman who had the lady-trouble.

When Miriam last saw her mother, she was talking drowsily to the woman, almost ready to let the drug take her completely.

Frightened but glad to be away from the smell of sickness, Miriam followed Herman Clark down a side street. "You can come home with me, honey," he said. "I've got a daughter just about your age, and you'll be well taken care of until that mother of yours gets well." Miriam smiled, reassured, used to following her elders. "Guess you're wondering about our little system," Clark said, hustling her into his car. "What with specialization and all, doctors got so they were knowin' so little, askin' so much, chargin' so much. Here in Babylon, we found we don't really need 'em. Practically everybody in this town has been sick one way or another, and what with the way women like to talk about their operations, we've learned a lot about treatment. We don't need doctors any more. We just benefit by other people's experience."

"Experience?" None of this was real, Miriam was sure, but Clark had the authoritative air of a long-time parent, and she knew parents were always right.

"Why, yes. If you had chicken pox, and were out where everybody in town could see you, pretty soon somebody'd come along who had had it. They'd tell you what you had, and tell you what they did to get rid of it. Wouldn't even have to pay a doctor to write the prescription. Why, I used Silas Lapham's old nerve tonic on my wife when she had her bad spell. She's fine now; didn't cost us a cent except for the tonic. This way, if you're sick, we put you in the square, and you stay there until somebody happens by who's had your symptoms; then you just try his cure. Usually works fine. If not, somebody else'll be by. Course, we can't let any of the sick folks leave the square until they're well; don't want anybody else catchin' it."

"How long will it take?"

"Well, we'll try some of the stuff Maysie Campbell used—and Gilyard Pinckney's penicillin prescription. If that doesn't work, we may have to wait till a tourist happens through."

"But what makes the tourists ask and suggest?"

"Have to. It's the law. You come on home with me, honey, and we'll try to get your mother well."

Miriam met Clark's wife and Clark's family. For the first week, she wouldn't unpack her suitcases. She was sure they'd be leaving soon, if she could just hold out. They tried Asa Whitleaf's tonic on her mother, and doctored her foot with the salve Harmon Johnson gave his youngest when she had boils. They gave her Gilyard Pinckney's penicillin prescription. "She doesn't seem much better," Miriam said to Clark one day. "Maybe if I could get her to Richmond or Atlanta to the hospital—"

"We couldn't let her out of Babylon until she's well, honey. Might carry it to other cities. Besides, if we cure her, she won't send county health nurses back, trying to change our methods. And it might be bad for her to travel. You'll get to like it here, hon."

That night Miriam unpacked. Monday she got a job clerking in the dime store.

"You're the new one, huh?" The girl behind the jewelry counter moved over to her, friendly, interested. "You Waited yet? No, I guess not. You look too young yet."

"No, I've never waited on people. This is my first job," Miriam said confidentially.

"I didn't mean *that* kind of wait," the girl said with some scorn. Then, seemingly irrelevantly, "You're from a pretty big town, I hear. Probably already laid with boys and everything. Won't have to Wait."

"What do you mean? I never have. Never! I'm a *good* girl!" Almost sobbing, Miriam ran back to the manager's office. She was put in the candy department, several counters away. That night she stayed up late with a road map and a flashlight, figuring, figuring.

The next day, the *No Visitors* sign was taken down from the tree in the park, and Miriam went to see her mother.

"I feel terrible, sweetie, you having to work in the dime store while I'm out here under these nice trees. Now you just remember all I told you, and don't let any of these town boys get fresh with you. Just because you have to work in the dime store doesn't mean you aren't a nice girl, and as soon as I can I'm going to get you out of that job. Oh, I *wish* I was up and around."

"Poor Momma." Miriam smoothed the sheets and put a pile of movie magazines down by her mother's pillow. "How can you stand lying out here all day?"

"It isn't so bad, really. And y'know, that Whitleaf woman seems to know a little something about my trouble. I haven't really felt right since you were nine."

"Momma, I think we ought to get out of here. Things aren't right—"

"People certainly are being nice. Why, two of the ladies brought me some broth this morning."

Miriam felt like grabbing her mother and shaking her until she was willing to pick up her bedclothes and run with her. She kissed her goodbye and went back to the dime store. Over their lunch, two of the counter girls were talking.

"I go next week. I want to marry Harry Phibbs soon, so I sure hope I won't be there too long. Sometimes it's three years."

"Oh, you're pretty, Donna. You won't have too long to Wait."

"I'm kind of scared. Wonder what it'll be like."

"Yeah, wonder what it's like. I envy you."

Chilled for some reason, Miriam hurried past them to her counter, and began carefully arranging marshmallow candies in the counter display.

That night, she walked to the edge of the town, along the road she and her mother had come in on. Ahead in the road, she saw two gaunt men standing, just where the dusty sign marked the city limits. She was afraid to go near them, and almost ran back to town, frightened, thinking. She loitered outside the bus station for some time, wondering how much a ticket out of the place would cost her. But of course she couldn't desert her mother. She was investigating the family car, still parked by the square, when Tommy Clark came up to her. "Time to go home, isn't it?" he asked, and they walked together back to his father's house.

"Momma, did you know it's almost impossible to get out of this town?" Miriam was at her mother's side, a week later.

"Don't get upset, sweetie. I know it's tough on you, having to work in the dime store, but that won't be forever. Why don't you look around for a little nicer job, dear?"

"Momma, I don't *mean* that. I want to go home! Look, I've got an idea. I'll get the car keys from your bag here, and tonight, just before they move you all into the courthouse to sleep, we'll run for the car and get away."

"Dear," her mother sighed gently. "You know I can't move."

"Oh, Mother, can't you *try?*"

"When I'm a little stronger, dear, then maybe we'll try. The Pinckney woman is coming tomorrow with her daughter's herb tea. That should pep me up a lot. Listen, why don't you arrange to be down here? She has the best-looking son!—Miriam, you come right back here and kiss me goodbye."

Tommy Clark had started meeting Miriam for lunch. They'd taken in one movie together, walking home hand in hand in an incredible pink dusk. On the second date, Tommy had tried to kiss her, but she'd said, "Oh, Tommy, I don't know the Babylon rules," because she knew it wasn't good to kiss a boy she didn't know very well. Handing Tommy half her peanut-butter sandwich, Miriam said, "Can we go to the ball game tonight? The American Legion's playing."

"Not tonight, kid. It's Margy's turn to go."

"What do you mean, turn to go?"

"Oh." Tommy blushed. "You know."

That afternoon, right after she finished work, Tommy picked her up and they went to the party given for Herman Clark's oldest daughter. Radiant, Margy was dressed in white. It was her eighteenth birthday. At the end of the party, just when it began to get dark, Margy and her mother left the house. "I'll bring some stuff out in the truck tomorrow morning, honey," Clark said. "Take care of yourself." "Goodbye." "G'bye." "Happy Waitin', Margy!"

"Tommy, where is Margy going?" Something about the party and something in Margy's eyes frightened Miriam.

"Oh, you know. Where they all go. But don't worry." Tommy took her hand. "She'll be back soon. She's pretty."

In the park the next day, Miriam whispered in her mother's ear, "Momma, it's been almost a month now. Please, please, we *have* to go! Won't you please try to go with me?" She knelt next to her, talking urgently. "The car's been taken. I went back to check it over last night, and it was gone. But I sort of think, if we could get out on the highway, we could get a ride. Momma, we've got to get out of here." Her mother sighed a little, and stretched. "You always said you never wanted me to be a bad girl, didn't you, Momma?"

The older woman's eyes narrowed.

"You aren't letting that Clark boy take advantage—"

"No, Momma. No. That's not it at all. I just think I've heard something horrible. I don't even want to talk about it. It's some sort of law. Oh, Momma, please. I'm scared."

"Now, sweetie, you know there's nothing to worry about. Pour me a little water, won't you, dear? You know, I think they're going to cure me yet. Helva Smythe and Margaret Box have been coming in to see me every day, and they've brought some penicillin pills in hot milk that I think are really doing me some good."

"But Momma, I'm scared."

"Now, dear, I've seen you going past with that nice Clark boy. The Clarks are a good family, and you're lucky to be staying with them. You just play your cards right, and remember: be a good girl."

"Momma, we've got to get out."

"You just calm down, young lady. Now go back and be nice to that Tommy Clark. Helva Smythe says he's going to own his daddy's business someday. You might bring him out here to see me tomorrow."

"Momma!"

"I've decided. They're making me better, and we're going to stay here until I'm well. People may not pay you much attention in a big city, but you're really somebody in a small town." She smoothed her blankets complacently, and settled down to sleep.

That night, Miriam sat with Tommy Clark in his front porch swing. They'd started talking a lot to each other, about everything. "...so I guess I'll have to go into the business," Tommy was saying. "I'd kind of like to go to Wesleyan or Clemson or something, but Dad says I'll be better off right here, in business with him. Why won't they ever let us do what we want to do?"

"I don't know, Tommy. Mine wants me to go to Katharine Gibbs— that's a secretarial school in New York—and get a typing job this fall."

"You won't like that much, will you?"

"Uh-uh. Except now, I'm kind of anxious to get back up there— you know, get out of this town."

"You don't like it here?" Tommy's face clouded. "You don't like me?"

"Oh, Tommy, I like you fine. But I'm pretty grown up now and I'd like to get back to New York and start in on a job. Why, I got out of high school last month."

"No kidding. You only look about fifteen."

"Aw, I do not. I'll be eighteen next week—Oh, I didn't want to tell you. I don't want your folks to have to do anything about my birthday. Promise you won't tell them."

"You'll be eighteen, huh. Ready for the Wait yourself. Boy, I sure wish *I* didn't know you!"

"Tommy! What do you mean? Don't you like me?"

"That's just the point. I *do* like you. A lot. If I were a stranger, I could break your Wait."

"Wait? What kind of wait?"

"Oh"—he blushed—"you know."

A week later, after a frustrating visit with her mother in the park, Miriam came home to the Clarks' and dragged herself up to her room. Even her mother had forgotten her birthday. She wanted to fling herself on her pillow and sob until supper. She dropped on the bed, got up uneasily. A white, filmy, fullskirted dress hung on the closet door. She was frightened. Herman Clark and his wife bustled into the room, wishing her happy birthday. "This dress is for you." "You shouldn't have," she cried. Clark's wife shooed him out, and helped Miriam dress. She started downstairs with the yards of white chiffon whispering and billowing about her ankles.

Nobody else at her birthday party was particularly dressed up. Some of the older women in the neighborhood watched Tommy help Miriam cut the cake, moist-eyed. "She hardly seems old enough—" "Doubt if she'll have long to Wait." "Pretty little thing, wonder if Tommy likes her?" "Bet Herman Clark's son wished *he* didn't know her," they said. Uneasily, Miriam talked to them all, tried to laugh, choked down a little ice cream and cake.

"G'bye, kid," Tommy said, and squeezed her hand. It was just beginning to get dark out.

"Where are you going, Tommy?"

"Nowhere, silly. I'll see you in a couple of weeks. May want to talk to you about something, if things turn out."

The men had slipped, one by one, from the room. Shadows were getting longer, but nobody in the birthday-party room had thought to turn on the lights. The women gathered around Miriam. Mrs. Clark, eyes shining, came close to her. "And here's the best birthday present of all," she said, holding out a big ball of brilliant blue string. Miriam looked at her, not understanding. She tried to stammer a thank-you. "Now, dear, come with me," Clark's wife said. Frightened, Miriam tried to bolt from the room. Clark's wife and Helva Smythe caught her by the arms, and gently led her out of the house, down the gray street. "I'm going to see if we can get you staked out near Margy," she said. They started off into the August twilight.

When they came to the field, Miriam first thought the women were still busy at a late harvest, but she saw that the maidens, scores of them, were just sitting on little boxes at intervals in the seemingly endless field. There were people in the bushes at the field's edge; Miriam saw them. Every once in a while one of the men would start off, following one of the brilliantly colored strings toward the woman who sat at the end of it, in a white dress, waiting. Frightened, Miriam turned to Mrs. Clark. "Why am I here? Why? Mrs. Clark, explain!"

"Poor child's a little nervous. I guess we all were, when it happened to us," Clark's wife said to Helva Smythe. "It's all right, dear, you just stand here at the edge and watch for a little while, until you get used to the idea. Remember, the man must be a stranger. We'll be out with the truck with food for you and Margy during visitors' time Sunday. That's right. And when you go out there, try to stake out near Margy. It'll make the Wait nicer for you."

"*What* wait?"

"The Wait of the Virgins, dear. Goodbye."

Dazed, Miriam stood at the edge of the great, domed field, watching the little world crisscrossed by hundreds of colored cords. She moved a little closer, trying to hide her cord under her skirts, trying not to look like one of them. Two men started toward her, one handsome, one unshaven and hideous, but when they saw she had not yet entered the field, they dropped back, waiting. Sitting near her, she saw one of the dime-store clerks, who had quit her job two weeks back and had suddenly disappeared. She was fidgeting nervously, casting hot eyes at a young man ranging the edge of the field. As Miriam watched, the young man strode up to her cord, without speaking, threw money into her lap. Smiling, the dime-store girl stood up, and the two went off into the bushes. The girl nearest Miriam, a harelip with incredibly ugly skin, looked up from the half-finished sweater she was knitting.

"Well, there goes another one," she said to Miriam. "Pretty ones always go first. I reckon one day there won't be any pretty ones here, and then I'll go." She shook out her yarn. "This is my fortieth sweater." Not understanding, Miriam shrank away from the ugly girl. "I'd even be glad for old Fats there," she was saying. She pointed to a lewd-eyed old man hovering near. "Trouble is, even old Fats goes for the pretty ones. Heh! You ought to see it, when he goes up to one of them high-school queens. Heh! Law says they can't say no!" Choking with curiosity, stiff, trembling, Miriam edged up to the girl.

"Where...where do they go?"

The harelip looked at her suspiciously. Her white dress, tattered and no longer white, stank. "Why, you really don't know, do you?" She pointed to a place near them, where the bushes swayed. "To lay with them. It's the law."

"Momma! Mommamommamomma!" With her dress whipping at her legs, Miriam ran into the square. It was just before the time when the sick were taken to sleep in the hall of the courthouse.

"Why, dear, how pretty you look!" the mother said. Then, archly, "They always say, wear white when you want a man to propose."

"Momma, we've got to get out of here." Miriam was crying for breath.

"I thought we went all over that."

"Momma, you always said you wanted me to be a good girl. Not ever to let any man take advan—"

"Why, dear, of course I did."

"Momma, don't you see! You've got to help me—we've got to get out of here, or somebody *I don't even know*...Oh, Momma, please. I'll help you walk. I saw you practicing the other day, with Mrs. Pinckney helping you."

"Now, dear, you just sit down here and explain to me. Be calm."

"Momma, *listen!* There's something every girl has to do when she's eighteen. You know how they don't use doctors here, for anything?" Embarrassed, she hesitated. "Well, you remember when Violet got married, and she went to Dr. Dix for a checkup?"

"Yes, dear—now calm down, and tell Momma."

"Well, it's a sort of a *checkup*, don't you see, only it's like graduating from high school too, and it's how they...see whether you're any good."

"What on earth are you trying to tell me?"

"Momma, you have to go to this field, and sit there and sit there until a man throws money in your lap. *Then you have to go into the bushes and lie with a stranger!*" Hysterical, Miriam got to her feet, started tugging at the mattress.

"You just calm down. Calm down!"

"But, Mother, I want to do like you told me. I want to be good!"

Vaguely, her mother started talking. "You said you were dating that nice Clark boy? His father is a real-estate salesman. Good business, dear. Just think, you might not even have to work—"

"Oh, Momma!"

"And when I get well, I could come live with you. They've very good to me here—it's the first time I've found people who really *cared* what was wrong with me. And if you were married to that nice, solid boy, who seems to have such a *good* job with his father, why we could have a lovely house together, the three of us."

"Momma, we've got to get *out* of here. I can't do it. I just *can't*." The girl had thrown herself on the grass again.

Furious, her mother lashed out at her. "Miriam. Miriam Elise Holland. I've fed you and dressed you and paid for you and taken care of you ever since your father died. And you've always been selfish, selfish, selfish. Can't you ever do anything for me? First I want you to go to secretarial school, to get a nice opening, and meet nice people, and you don't want to do that. Then you get a chance to settle in a good town, with a *nice* family, but you don't even want that. You only think about yourself. Here I have a chance to get well at last, and settle down in a really nice town, where good families live, and see you married to the right kind of boy." Rising to her elbows, she glared at the girl. "Can't you ever do anything for *me?*"

"Momma, Momma, you don't *understand!*"

"I've known about the Wait since the first week we came here." The woman leaned back on her pillow. "Now pour me a glass of water and go back and do whatever Mrs. Clark tells you."

"*Mother!*"

Sobbing, stumbling, Miriam ran out of the square. First she started toward the edge of town, running. She got to the edge of the highway, where the road signs were, and saw the two shabby, shambling men, apparently in quiet evening conversation by the street post. She doubled back and started across a neatly plowed field. Behind her, she saw the Pinckney boys. In front of her, the Campbells and the Dodges started across the field. When she turned back toward town, trembling, they walked past her, ignoring her, on some business of their own. It was getting dark.

She wandered the fields for most of the night. Each one was blocked by a Campbell or a Smythe or a Pinckney; the big men carried rifles and flashlights, and called out cheerfully to each other when they met, and talked about a wild fox hunt. She crept into the

Clarks' place when it was just beginning to get light out and locked herself in her room. No one in the family paid attention to her storming and crying as she paced the length and width of the room.

That night, still in the bedraggled, torn white dress, Miriam came out of the bedroom and down the stairs. She stopped in front of the hall mirror to put on lipstick and repair her hair. She tugged at the raveled sleeves of the white chiffon top. She started for the place where the virgins Wait. At the field's edge, Miriam stopped, shuddered as she saw the man called old Fats watching her. A few yards away she saw another man, young, lithe, with bright hair, waiting. She sighed as she watched one woman, with a tall, loose boy in jeans, leave the field and start for the woods.

She tied her string to a stake at the edge of the great, domed field. Threading her way among the many bright-colored strings, past waiting girls in white, she came to a stop in a likely-looking place and took her seat.

B orn in California, Lillian Craig "Kit" Reed (1932-   ) is a 1954 graduate of the College of Notre Dame of Maryland; a former reporter (twice winner of the New England Newspaperwoman of the Year Award, 1954 and 1958); a wife, mother, and feminist advocate; and the author of some dozen books, including such novels as **Tiger Rag** *and* **Magic Time.** *She was awarded a Guggenheim Fellowship in 1964. She is probably best known for the science fiction stories that largely began her career, such as the often reprinted "Food Farm" and "Golden Acres," suggesting how the future may deal with the problems of today.*

FAST-TRAIN IKE

JESSE STUART

"Ooooo-ooouh-uh," the whistle screams. The black smoke rolls in great puffs—clouds with their sides puffing out and bursting into ash-colored and cream-colored swirls. "Ooooooooooo-ooouh," and the smoke falls in a stream back across the engine top like a rabbit laying its ears back and taking through the brush—back from the tall stack like smoke sucking groundward from the rock chimney at home when there's going to be fallen-weather. See the engine coming like a bench-legged bull—stout as a bull, mad as a bull, and charging against the wind—right down the track—two streaks of rust—red in the sunlight of August among the ragweeds and the rotted crossties. "Ooooooo-ooouh," and huffety-huffety-puffety-puffety and the bench-legged bull slows down for Fast-Train Ike's red handkerchief. Any bull will stop for red. People stick their heads out the window and look—look at the hills on each side the track—the old worn-out Kentucky hills and the sprouts and briars and the cinders along the track—the piles of rotted crossties—the dewberry briars among them—vining and crawling and running around over the company's premises without their permission.

"Ah," says Conductor Harry. (Everybody knows Conductor Harry on the O.L.S., the Old Line Special. He's been on this train for forty-nine years.) "I thought you wasn't going to ride this train any more. The way you've been acting ever since I've been on this road—w'y you've given us more trouble than any man that's ever gone to town with us. Keep the passengers scared to death the way you go on—" And Conductor Harry helps Fast-Train Ike on the train—a tall man with a long nose—with curly locks of uncut hair—hair that is going to seed—a man with a slow walk—a take-your-time walk—a man with big hands that dangle from pipe-stem arms. A mouth that is always about to say something and seldom ever does. Fast-Train walks into the last coach and takes his seat. People on the train draw their heads in at the window and quit looking at the old worn-out Kentucky hills, the saw-briars, the dewberries—and the sassafras sprouts on the hills. Women sitting by their men whisper in their ears and point to Fast-Train Ike. He is something for them all to look at—not a man in forty miles dressed like him. "Got the old time dress that man has. Big high stiff collars and the necktie outside. Tie pin big as a goose egg. That hat was the kind Grandpa wore—look at that suit won't you—wrinkled and old-fashioned—" And the train starts just as Fast-Train Ike sits down and picks up the paper. It leaves the station like a bench-legged bull. Mad because it had to stop for old Fast-Train Ike. Goes out huffety-puffety-huffety-puffety—mad, pawing and scraping—scraping and pawing—and belching hot cinders from his belly—mad as a bull right down the two streaks of rust. "Ooooooooooo—oooooooooo—wooooo—wooooooooooouh-uh—woooooo—uh—uh." And the clouds of smoke boil from the long stack—the big bull's-eye right up in front looks through the long dark tunnel ahead—one tunnel and then another—right down two streaks of rust over the rotted oak ties and the burnt-top ragweeds—down, down, down—down the grade. People on the train going somewhere. Going from the hills to the town—laughing, laughing—talking and looking out at the windows at the worn-out hills with sulphur blood streaming from their pierced sides where the railroad gets its coal—stumps on the hills where the railroad hauls its logs.

"W'y," says Conductor Harry, "we got that crazy old bachelor Fast-Train Ike back there on the train. Never was a man in this country like him. Have trouble every time he gets on the train. Raises cain and gets all the women scared. Says the train is going to wreck and kill him. Yet he's rid this train ever since I have been here—forty-nine years last April—seems to me like he's never changed his suit—I know he's always wore that big tie pin and read the paper. People know him for miles around. That's why they call him Fast-Train Ike. Just because he's afraid of the train. Brakeman Charlie, keep your eye on him. Watch for him to take one of his tantrums. When he does—warn me. He'll have one when the sun goes down and it starts getting dark."

"Mama, will that old Fast-Train Ike hurt you? I heard he would, Mama—he's so ugly. Mama, I'm afraid of him—" "Honey, Fast-Train Ike won't hurt you. He's been riding this train ever since I have. That's been thirty years. He's never hurt anybody yet." And the train moves on—a little bench-legged, one-eyed bull, with its square eye in the top of its head—right down the track a-charging over the ragweeds— over the rotted crossties and the two streaks of rust—charging against the wind—going to town down the grade—down the grade to town. Sunset, but the one-eyed engine looks straight ahead for a tunnel—a dark hole in the earth and under—under the big rocks and the hills— one eye to see the bridges and there are so many of them across the rivers—bridges and trestles where the sawbriars climb all over the company's premises.

Ah, babies crying on the train. Men talking about coal in these hills, gold in the hills that the Indians left and silver among thse hills—men talking about women—and women taking care of their babies and their men—women talking to each other about other women— getting acquainted on the train—laughing—laughing—talking as the wind blows past the coaches outside—the three passenger coaches and the mail car. Over the hills to a destiny—and the wind zooms in the rusty telephone wires and through the sawbriars along the right-of-way—along the track—coaches lumbering, lumbering, lumbering over the two streaks of rust—train going into the night following two streaks of rust—into holes under the hills and across rivers. See the sunset against an August Kentucky hill—a great blotch of blood above the trees. A blotch of blood that is growing darker—and the night is coming—night in Kentucky and the whippoorwills in the oaks—the zoom of the night winds among the rusted wires and the sawbriars— the people talking to each other—the laugh, the cry, the endless chatter—and all going to some destiny and some end.

"W'y they tell me that old Fast-Train Ike's got a whole pot full of money. W'y I've heard he wasn't crazy only on some things. Just afraid of a train. You know you've seen people crazy in some ways. There's a lot of ways to be crazy now—you know that. He can't be crazy and make all the money he's made. W'y the man has to be smart—" "Ssssssssss—he'll hear you talking about him. Leave him alone," says Conductor Harry, "long as he's contented with the paper. About the time he finishes reading the paper and sees dark against the window—and feels the train plunging into the darkness—then he takes his spell—God, and a lot of people on this train won't know about him. It takes too much time to go around and whisper it to people about it. It takes too long to explain to people. And when he starts hollering it'll scare all the women to death. They'll be lunging and plunging through these coaches like rabbits in front of a ferret in a hole. Maybe we'll have to stop the train. I'll run for representative next time myself and get to Frankfort to pass a law that no nut can ride a train. We need more laws about fools and nuts. I'll tell you the world is crazy or that man is one. We need more laws against men like him. I can't tell him to stay off the train. If I could have he'd not have been on this train in the past forty-nine years. So, sssshhhhhhhhh—don't bother him. For God's sake. Let him read the paper."

Fast-Train Ike turns the pages slowly and scans the gray pages—up and down and his eyes peep over the big-rimmed spectacles that cover his eyes. His Adam's apple moves in and out as he works his head. He reads the paper—and the train still huffety-puffety-huffety-puffety like a bench-legged bull a-running over to the other side of the pasture to fight another bull—right down the two streaks of rust now—plunging and lunging into the night. Kentucky's night winds try to follow the train. Hear them zoom among the rusted wires and the sawbriars—Hear them sweep across the hills—Hear them sweep into the night—mocking the voices inside the coaches—voices of women talking to each other and about their children, their loved ones, their homes, husbands and the women about them. Men meeting on the train and drinking—smoking together the fragrant weed—getting to be friends the first night. "I tell you if you never saw a fellow and you take a drink together—or a good smoke on a train—you'll wake up friends the next day. That's why Kentucky is one of the best states in this United States. We furnish the good whiskey to drink—Government booze—or mountain white mule. Just about anything you want." And it brings friendship between men and tides men over sorrows, trials and tribulations. It's a tonic—a medicine. And the fragrant weed is good to partake of—good to see the swirls of clouds go away from your lips when you are riding over the hills on a train—sitting on a good seat—riding a train into the night. And Kentucky grows the fragrant weed—great fields of it under the Kentucky sun—great fields of burley—great broad leaves flapping for men on the train to partake of in their pipes of peace—riding, riding, riding over two streaks of rust to some certain destiny with a nut on the train and only a few people knowing he is a nut when it comes to riding a train. And if you could hear the endless chatter here—if you could see the red moon on the low hills and hear the rumble and the tumble of the coaches in the night—the zoom of the wind in the rusted wires and the briars—and the moan of the engine's whistle— ah, if you were only here as we speed over the rough earth on a one-eyed train to some destiny—over the rivers, under the hills, over the hills and around the hills and up the valleys—speeding, speeding behind a mad bench-legged bull that stops for a red handkerchief and to get a drink of water—a bull mad and hot and blowing cinders from his belly into the night—red hot lumps into the night—when over our heads the red moon rides and the stars twinkle over the Kentucky earth.

"I told you," says Fast-Train Ike—"I told you didn't I—what the world is the matter you put me on this tail-end coach—Didn't I walk back there on the little porch—didn't I walk back there—come nigh as a pea walking off the train—and what do you think would have happened to me the way this train is going—tearing out down over these hills. Didn't I tell you once I didn't want to ride on the last coach. I want to be safer—ah, if I had any other way to get out of these hills—I'd never ride your train—ah, you low-down scamp of a conductor. You ought to be fired—think no more of your passengers than you do. Put me on the last coach—W'y this train is going to kill me. I am going to die on a train. How many times have I told you— how many times have you listened? Have you ever once believed me? Listen, you will believe me—when I die you'll see that I die in a train wreck. Take my suitcase in another car. Get it—don't wait for someone else—carry it yourself. It's not going to hurt your hands."

"Stay off'n this train from now on," says Conductor Harry. "You have been more trouble to me than all the other passengers on this road. I've had them to get too much licker—want the winder raised—and I couldn't raise it quick enough—they've pulled their pistols and shot them out—vomited out the winders—paid me like gentlemen for the glass and said they's sorry but they were in a hurry and had to act—but you—you are the worst I ever saw—You stay off this train—I'd have this train stopped for a minute and put you off into the night—" "What's the matter Conductor—what's the matter—something wrong with the train—" "Oh, no, my good woman—just this nut here—He's afraid of a train. Says he's going to die on a train—" "Yes, but I had a dream last night—a bad dream about a train. I dreamed it wrecked—yes I did—honest—and it all comes back—a train wreck—God, but I can see it all now—I can see it—a train wreck." And she screams. "Oh, it's going to happen," says

Fast-Train Ike, "it's going to happen. I've been forewarned fifty years ago. People think I'm crazy but it's going to happen. You all get prepared for we've got several more rivers to cross before we get to town—" "What did you say?" says the big red-faced woman with the little girl on her lap—"I said," says Fast-Train Ike, "that this train is going to wreck. Get prepared for we've just a few more rivers to cross before we get to town. That is what I said, Lady." "Why don't you get prepared yourself if you know the train is going to wreck?" "Lady, I've been prepared for fifty years. Ever since I've had the dream— ever since I got the vision—ever since I've been forewarned. I've always taken my time about things. That's why I never married. I knew it was a matter of time when I'd have to leave my sweet little wife and my children—So, I just didn't bother about marrying. I knew I'd have to ride this train if I stayed among my hills—and I knew I was going to stay—for I've drunk water from the same well for fifty-eight years. Pap drunk it from this same well his lifetime. Why should I quit drinking it because I'm to die in a train wreck. Why should I leave my happy home—ah, why should I—got to go one time. Just as well be in a train wreck as any other way—only I want to hit on the dirt of a soft cushion—I don't want to be ground to sausage or squeezed between the walls of one of these coaches. I want to get out of it with my natural body not changed a particle. That's me, Lady—I know that train is going to wreck. That's why I come from the other coach in here—"

"Train's a-going to wreck—ah, train is going to wreck—"

"Who said the train was going to wreck—ah, ah—that fellow huh—well that fellar's not all there—now who knows the app'inted time like that—who knows—w'y that fellar is a nut. He oughtn't be allowed to ride a train with respectable people. Look how he's dressed with that high collar—it's fifty years behind time—" "Well, you old Bib-Belly you—you—you can talk about his collar if you please—but it's better than what you got on—a homemade shirt without a sign of a collar—He looks a devil of a sight better than you—And there can be a train wreck. Guess I had a dream last night. Guess I dreamed of a train wreck. I know I would rather believe what I dreamed and what he said as to believe the things you say— you old Big-Belly fun-maker you. Keep your tongue inside your toothless gums and you'll have enough to do—" "Quiet, quiet please—quiet—quiet—please—I've a few words to say. Who said this train would wreck?" says Conductor Harry—"who says it will wreck?" "I," says Frast-Train Ike, "I say it will wreck—" "W'y this fellow," says Conductor Harry, "ought to be in the asylum. He's not all there. You people can see that. Had me to move him from the last coach up here. I tell you this fellow is not all there. You've seen 'em like that. I've been moving him from the back coach and giving him a newspaper to read or to look at the pictures for the past forty-nine years to keep him quiet on this train. Wish the Kentucky Legislature would make a law to keep nuts off'n the passenger trains. Sight what a conductor has to go through with—got my coattail cut off two or three times and a gallon jug busted over my head—three or four bottles busted around my temples—and have been vomited over a half-dozen times—yet, can't get any help from the Kentucky Legislature. The man is a nut—that's all—a nut—you all can see that—now this train is not going to wreck. Set in your seats and keep quiet. You are running me crazy—"

"I told you," says the Big-Bellied man to the woman with the red face. "I told you the man was a nut. He's not all there. How does he know so much about the train's business—the Lord's business. You know if it is the Lord's will to wreck this train he's not going to tell a lot of people about his business and let them know as much as the Lord knows himself. That's a evident fact. It wouldn't do for the Lord to let everybody know when they were going to die. It would be giving them a chance they already ought to have taken. Warn them like a rabbit before you shoot it—w'y have the whole bunch a-screaming—w'y they wouldn't even be patronizing the train. The Lord would be interfering with Business too. It don't make sense—" And the red-faced woman says: "I'll just show you how to make sense—talking about the Lord and the poor man over there and all—making me out of a liar about the dream I had—I'll let you have this umberell right between the eyes—"

"Ah," says Conductor Harry, "no fighting on this train. I'll stop the train and have you both put off. That's what I'll do. I'll have that old codger put off over there for starting all of this fracas on the train too. That nut over there started it all. Wish we'd a never stopped back there at that flagstation and got him—"

"You can't have me put off," says Fast-Train Ike, "for I know the Law. You say I'm a nut. I can prove to you after this night I am a smart man. This train is going to wreck. I have come up here in this coach so I can have it easier. You can just say what you please. I haven't lived all these years for nothing. Guess I got a little sense—You can't even stop the train now. The train is running away—It's going I tell you—I can see it—something the matter with the pistons and the brakes won't hold—going, going, going, going—down—down—down—all of you not right with the Lord had better pray. I know I'm a goner. I'm ready—Don't need to pray—I'm ready—I know I'm a goner—I've been looking for this since I was a child. I'm getting cold right now as a beef hung out in the October wind to cool—I know it's not long off—"

And the scream of the whistle—under the red moon on the low hills—the gray smoke in long streamers in the wind—running, running, running—lunging, plunging through the night. The wind zooms along the rusty telephone wires—the wind follows the train—the wind can't catch the train—a train running downgrade on two streaks of rust—running, running—rolling—and the whistle screaming—"Boys, something wrong with the O.L.S.— something wrong with the Old Line Special—never stopped for a station—went right past—Jim Henly out there at Salt Center to flag her and she come batting it right out'n the tunnel and right down the track—Jim just did clear the track as she passed with the whistle down and the people with their heads out the winders screaming like a bunch of wild geese lost at night—something is wrong I tell you—something bad the matter—smoke just streamed back like a rabbit's ears laid back when it's running from buckshot. You'll hear about all this tomorrow—maybe tonight. That track can't hold a train running that fast—people just tumbling over one another in the coaches—could get a snake's eye full of them when they passed—and of all the hollering—hollering—"

And the red moon in the Kentucky sky—red moon over the low August hills and the wheat and corn thereon—the ripe wheat—the growing corn—over the scars on the hills where the sulphur blood runs from the bowels of the Kentucky earth. If you could see the O.L.S. running away like a mad bull down the beaten path of a century with both ears laid back—mad because it's had to work overhours—It's had to work too long—it ought to be retired and a new bull—bench-legged, take its place—and throw up new white hot cinders from its belly into the night. Work an old bull to death— no wonder it wants to run away—gets something wrong with the pistons and has all the people screaming to the moon with their heads out'n the windows—out into the night air—under a million cold stars twinkling in the August heavens—no wonder—no wonder. You might think I'm crazy but the old bench-legged engine ought to be retired—one-eyed and that big tall stack—w'y it's as old-fashioned as Fast-Train Ike's collar—and the track needs a rest— rails that have held up loads for a century—"Just take a rail out when it breaks. That's all." And the great night—nothing we can do about it—and the wind—following the train and humming a song—very nice of the wind—nothing really we can do about that—nor the wheat on the hills—nor the red moon in the sky—nothing, nothing we can do about the whole affair.

"I told you you couldn't stop this train. I told you it was running away. I could tell it would happen soon as I got on the train. Pull your cord fifty times and you can't stop this train. It's gone—gone down the two streaks of rust. That's the reason I read the paper so long tonight—went over the pictures and all the print—even to the funnies—something not funny to me. But I read them tonight and shed tears. Saddest part of the paper anymore—pull one hundred times on the cord. I know what you are trying to do—stop the train—you can't stop the train—it's running away. I knew after I got on the train it was my last ride. I'm taking my last look at my hills—it's in the night too—in the moonlight. Wish I could see them in the daytime. Lord have mercy on these hills when I am gone and keep the coal picks out'n their bellies and the axes out'n the trees. Wish I could see the trees again—and the sawbriars and the old piles of crossties along the tracks. W'y if I'd a stepped off'n that train when I got on—w'y I'd a broken my neck—I know it just as same as I know this train is going to wreck—pull you old Conductor—pull two hundred times on that cord for it to stop—it won't stop until it wrecks—can't you feel the speed coming on? I can just feel it. Hear the engine whistle past these cars. Hear the wheels clashing on the weasly rails—hear it—rush, rush-rushing into the night—I'm getting cold as a cucumber—I'd be all right if I could just see the hills one more time. Pull your cord a thousand times and the train won't stop—swing on the cord like a squirrel in the grapevines. Swing on it you polecat you—we are going down, down, down—down the grade through a tunnel—Oh—I've been over this road so much I can feel the curves on every mile—I know just about where the train will wreck—just about at the next river. Don't know whether you all will come out alive or not—but know I'm a goner. I'll tell you that right now—pull you polecat—pull ten thousand times on that cord and the train won't stop—"

People are tumbling through the coaches—running and praying—babies are screaming—"Oh, you Big-Belly—pray—you—yes, you—pray. Now you see don't you—You'll believe in dreams won't you—You'll believe in prayer won't you. Oh, you old Big-Belly you—look how you treated that poor man. He'll never get off this train alive either—and you—a thing like you will be alive—you'll get off—you ought to die—" says the red-faced woman with the little girl in her arms—and the mingling of curses and prayer from the lips of the women—all, all, all, and laughter from the lips of youth—from the fun-loving youth—just another adventure—all going some place—down the two streaks of rust and the moon in the sky—down through the night—down, down, down—to where and to what destiny? To the city at the end of the road? To what city—yes—and the runaway bull keeps snorting across the pasture of hills and through the holes in the ground like a rabbit—people on the train—a living mass of creatures with minds flashing with excitement and life like lightning on a storm-clouded night when the greyhound sky is filled with leaping dog-clouds—gaunt and trim across the sky—ah, this night and the screams and the prayer—and the night—all across Kentucky—under a Kentucky moon—all something people won't believe—that old man—shivering in the cold—and it is not cold—it is an August night on the train—and the moon can see it—the wind can feel it—a night in old Kentucky and a trainload of people headed for a destiny—maybe a hole in the hill—just some place—some afraid and some glad of excitement—some laughing—some crying with excitement—some crying with fear—rock-rock—screech—screech—whistle-screaming, screaming, screaming—"Oooowoo—woooooo-wooouh—uh—uh—uh wooooowouh—woooouh—uh—uhwooooowouh—woooooooooo—uh—uh—uh woooooooooowouh—woooooooouh—uh—uh—uh—uh ooooooo—wooooooooooouh-uh—Screech—rickety-pickety-nickety—splutter—flutter—mutter—apple-butter—Wooooooo-uh-uh-uh—wooooo—uh-uh-uh—wooooo (Hold her, Newt—she's headed for the barn. Let her rare. Let her rip. Let her tear. Let her splutter. Let her splash. Let her derail—let her crash. Let her jar. Let her scold. Let her crash in a dark hole. Let her ride the rails. Let her never. Make it across a river. Whooopppee! Hold her, Newt—she's headed for the barn. Hold her, Pappie, by the old crumpled horn. She's got some life as sure as you're born. Woooooooooo-Wooooooouh-uh—woooooooooo—uh, uh—wooooooo—Shut up children and hush up your crying. Get you a new Pappie on the old Special Line. Woooooooo—uhhhhhhhhh—wooooooo."

"Stay quiet, you people. Get your seats. Set down. You are going to wreck the train by first piling on one side and then t'other. Set down before we do wreck. Is this a dream? Am I crazy? What is the matter? Am I in the clouds? Am I floating through space? Is old Fast-Train Ike on this train? Have I lost my mind? Am I dreaming—hit me some-body? Wake me up—" "Hit you hell—you never had any mind—

98

You'll find out about this train—can't you feel it leaping through the air—it's a matter of minutes—maybe seconds until you'll be cold as a piece of icicle or dead as a mackerel. Just stand up there and holler and let 'em run wild on your train. You are some conductor—you are—You ought to have been fired off this road forty-nine years ago—are you dreaming? Yes, you've always been dreaming—never any other way. Wish I could see my hills in the sunlight. A matter of minutes now—take it easy you all. Maybe it will be a quiet wreck—Just the same it's going to wreck."

"Woooooooooooooo—Woooooooooooooo—uh—uh—uh—woooooooooooo!" "Be ready—felt it jump then—too much speed for the train on these rails. The river is close. I feel it is close—prepare to meet the wreck and the eternity. Get my suitcase up there Big-Boy—I'm standing between the coaches so I can get a soft ride into eternity." Big-Boy hands Fast-Train Ike his suitcase. He is shaking like a man with the first chills of the 1917 influenza. "Rickety-pickety-jickety-mickety-wickety-split—whooppee—whooppee—let her wreck, by heck—down in the gravel up to her neck—whooppee—Woooooooooooo —Woooooooooooooo."

"Bye-bye boys. If I'm all that's gone don't break this great O.L.S. by suing for a lot of money. Let 'em keep it and fix the track with it and dig out the tunnels. I've had a good stay with you and the rest of my stay wouldn't be worth all the money you'd sue for. To the O.L.S. with the compliments of Fast-Train Ike—the smartest man that ever rode these rails by-hell. Sleep tight and don't let the bedbugs bite—" And Fast-Train Ike walks out between the coaches. "Woooooooooooooooooooooo—uh,uh—uh—woooooooooooooooo—woooooooooooooo—rip—rip—uppety-fluffy—muffety-tuffety—over and over—and roll and roll—people together—on the floor—what of the weather forevermore—a dream it seems—uppety—cuppety—juppety—duppety—whooppee! Hold her, Newt—she's headed for the barn. Didn't I say get her by the old crumpled horn—over the river and through the woods to Grandpa's wedding day—snow on the ground is white instead of gray—and have you a word to say—whow-pow-let her rip. Let her tear. Don't give a damn. For, I don't care. Rickety too-toot she shot right through that hardwood door. W'y he's my man—but he done me W—R—O—N—G. She's my train—but she's done me W—R—O—N—G. Wow—brickbats—snakes and cats—wow and my friend—the end—lumber, number—splinter—hot-as-hell-cinder comes up from the belly. Like a bowl of jelly—red as a coal. God bless our soul—Like the old cucumber—maybe he's cold."

Train crumpled on the trestle—the big bull—bench-legged with legs broken—Derailed on the trestle and the people pouring out of the windows. Walking the trestle to the land—right over the river—cars just a-hanging and not a one over. "Lucky wreck," says Conductor Harry—"a wonder we hadn't all been killed. Get 'em all safe to the bank—all off the train and the trestle. Run through the cars boys and see that they are all out. I can't find anymore—maybe it is a dream and I am fooled. Maybe it's the Lord's will that we got out safe—ah, let me see where's old Fast-Train Ike—ah, let me see—go see if you can find him—He's not in the crowd is he boys—?" "I told you," says the red-faced woman, "guess you'll believe in dreams from now on. I believe in dreams. Had a dream last night about this wreck. Looked it up in the dream book and it said I'd be in a wreck. Now I guess you see, old Fat-Belly—You ought to be in hell with your back broke. But you are the kind that would get out of a wreck—"

Steam flying from the engine—Engineer out all right—limping a little—out standing by the fire kicked out of his firebox—out in the moonlight—and the brakeman's lantern waving to and fro—over the wrecked rails—bent up among the ragweeds like big rusted wires. Steam in the air—white mist going to the red Kentucky moon over the low hills in August—what a night—what a night—what a ride. What a ride—people screaming in the moonlight. Children lost from their mothers—people crawled out of the cars like ants out of a dead stump. Like ants crawling out of a dead black snake the carrion crows killed and just ate his pecked-in skull and left the rest for the ants. Train looks like a snake in the moonlight—only a blunt-tailed copperhead instead of a long pretty-tailed black-snake. And the ants come out from the ribs—ants alive—cursing, praying, screaming—laughing, splashing, dashing—screaming for their children. All alive and all safe? Ah, no—where is Fast-Train Ike? Gone—where is he—Crushed under the train—squeezed between the sides of a coach—? Ah, no—Where is he then—who knows? "Why he's dead," says the red-faced woman. "I know he is dead for he said he'd not get out alive. That was one man I've met in my life—met only for a matter of hours—that told the truth. That man is dead. W'y didn't he say the train would wreck at the river—wrecked right on the trestle. Didn't he try to tell that Conductor what was going to happen? And he said he was a nut—He'll pay for the words he said to that man. That man—Fast-Train Ike—is in a diferent world by now."

"One man gone—Fast-Train Ike is not with us," says the Conductor—"we've checked everyplace for him. Can see under the cars—they're just derailed—He's not there. He's not hiding in the coaches and pretending he's dead I don't guess—might be in one of the toilets. Didn't look there. Go back and look, Brakeman Charlie, and see if he's hiding in the toilet on one of the coaches if the doors aren't sprung and you can get them open." All night—and the people, shook with excitement, were hauled away. Men came to straighten up the wreck. Men came to lay new rails and put in new crossties and do something with the engine and the coaches. People talked and laughed and shouted—prayed, cried—ran through the fields like wild rabbits—proud to be away from the train. What a night there at the river—what a wreck—people will tell it down for a hundred years to generations unborn about the man with the high collar—they'll speak about old Fast-Train Ike. But where is he now and the people hunting for him—hunting for his bones—his ground-up dust! Where is he now? Will we have to wait until daylight to find him? Did he go through the thin air like some spirit—run out and take wings and fly through the skies to Heaven? Just where is he? W'y he took his suitcase—it can't be found. Went through all the toilets. He's not hiding there. Just where is he? Do you reckon he jumped off before the train hit and took across the field? Or, just what has happened to him? "You are a bunch of fools," says the red-faced woman—"all of you—a bunch of fools—a bunch of stinking polecats. Didn't he say he'd be a goner if all the rest come out alive? What did he tell you? Didn't he say that he'd rather go through space and have an easy seat than to be ground up in sausage meat for the ants—or be squeezed to death between the sides of a coach—Why can't you believe him? His prophecy has all come true so far—and why isn't the rest of it true— you bunch of hypocrite-polecats. Stand there—will you—look for him. He's here someplace. Is there any water in that river or has it gone dry enough so the fish won't have drinking water like a lot of other Kentucky rivers do every summer—if there's water down there he's in it. He wanted a soft ride and a soft seat in eternity, you know. That's where he is—down there in that water."

"There's a deep hole right under the trestle. Water for the fish. Rest of the river above the trestle and below the trestle is dry. It's a deep hole below. You know Kentucky is not Kentucky any more without we have nine-tenths of our rivers dry in the summer during crop-time." The winds hum lonesome through the wires—And the winds sweep off the cries of the babies, the prayers of the women and the curses of the men—the moans and groans of them all. It is the wind—and the flutter of the leaves—and the red moon in the sky. It's going down through—See it going down, down, down—morning will soon be here—what a night, what a night in old Kentucky—ah, huh—the barking of the dog—the four-o'clock crowing of the cock—and the streaks of light in the east. The smell of cinder smoke—and the ooze of piston steam—the tired bull has been stabbed. Good for him when he tries running away one every hundred years. See the big black monster humped up there stabbed—throat cut and his back broken. Can't run away on two streaks of rust—that's it. Just can't do it when the odds are five to one with the wind—and ten to one with the night—fifty to one with destiny. Morning and the people gone and new faces coming to the wreck. New people come and kick scrap iron a hundred years old—scrap iron that has been serviceable—sides and flanks of the precious bull—why should they do it after all the years of service? Ought to give a medal—make it a Colonel instead of kicking the thighs and the ribs—the elbows and the shins. Ought to be hunting for Fast-Train Ike instead of pranking around the fire—around the cinder bed and the last breaths of steam.

"Come down to the deep hole under the trestle," says Section Foreman Press Kelley—he won the turkey last Thanksgiving for having the best section on the O.L.S. Devilish nigh worked the water out'n his men to get it. But he got the turkey. "W'y," says he, his red fce showing in the morning August sun—his flat nose that looked like it was battered with a slab of steel and burned to a red crisp by the heat from the tee rails—"W'y the way to find a man in that hole is to take a pole and split the end of it—a hickory will do—and put it down in the hole and twist it around—if he's in there you'll more than likely twist his coattail or the pants' legs—or the seat of the pants—maybe the sleeve—maybe the hair. So cut me one, Dave."

Dave cuts the pole—poor little Dave runs around like a cricket. He trims the hickory pole—splits the tip of it in tiny withes to twist with.

He puts it in the water and twists—and the people watch from the bank. "Not quite. Thought that was him. Musta been a mud turtle or a stump." "Found something. Feels like a coattail—" Twist—twist—twist—a heave—"Help me Dave—Help me—pull—Get holt there." And they pull—and again they pull—up to the muddy surface—it is a man—it is Fast-Train Ike—His color just like it was before he left the train—His face about the same—on up and he holds the suitcase with a death grip like he's traveling someplace. Taking his old suit—his suitcase and his tiepin.

"What did I tell you," says the red-faced woman on the bank. "Didn't I tell you that you'd find him here in this water? He wanted a soft seat—a quick ride and he got it—Ah, that crazy Conductor that you call Harry—He's a nut. Think of this man. He prophesied it all—and it's come true—wouldn't even sue the railroad. Said his compliments to them. Take the money and build a better track. Poor old Fast-Train Ike—he's riding on a different train now." And she shouts and screams as they pull him from the water—his long gangly frame with the wet suit sticking close to his flanks and his ribs.

"One thing about this wreck," says Conductor Harry, "we won't have that Fast-Train Ike on any more trains scaring everybody to death about a wreck. The wreck is over—it's worth it to get rid of him. Seems like the Lord just takes 'em out like that. He's had old Fast-Train Ike spotted ever since I been on this road and He just got his work caught up last night. He got him. It'll save me a lot of worry—it'll give me joy to know he's riding on some other man's train and not one where I'm conductor. Just to tell you the truth I'm glad to get rid of him. I won't have to run for a member of the Kentucky Legislature and be up to have my rep probed and my character peeled with rocks. That's what I was going to do until the Lord interfered and took Fast-Train Ike home. It's strange the way things come out in the end. But they do. You just wait and see—but that night—ah, last night—what a night—what a time—in all my life that was the worst I ever put over my head."

Dave gets between the tall man's legs. He gets a leg under each arm. Hiram Pratt gets him by an arm. Judd Sluss gets him by an arm. They start around the deep hole—around among the poison vines—his clothes wet and dripping—the suitcase still in his hand. The crowd follows—the red-faced woman, Conductor Harry, Brakeman Charlie—a whole crowd of children and nearby people who have come to see the train wreck. They whisper to each other about the long dead man. "W'y the glass in the door is out," says Conductor Harry, "he went right through the door." "Don't know whether he tried to jump off, or whether the train just bumped him through the door. Guess he could tell you if he could speak." Right up the railroad bank they carry him. "Lord," says Judd Sluss, "he's heavy as any old soggy crosstie I ever took from under the tee rails. Honest, his arm's a load for me." "What about me back here with both legs," says Dave, "a-trying to get up this bank." "W'y we're a-pulling you up the hill with your load," says Hiram Pratt, "heavier than a switch tie." Up the bank a past the rotted crossties, past the sawbriars. The sun is hot and the sunrays dance on the old rusted rails and the wrecked train—all heaped up on the spread-out, bent-up rails. The big black horses hitched to the dead-wagon chomp the bits and the foam flies from their thick, gummy rubber lips.

"Heave on him, boys," says Section Foreman Press Kelley, "heave-oh—heave-oh," and they heave the wet-stiff body holding to the suit-case up in the dead wagon. "Got a death grip on that suitcase," says Section Foreman Press Kelley. "They tell me a death grip is harder to come undone than a hangman's knot. Just like he's holding to that suitcase and traveling on." "Glad he's on some other road than the O.L.S.," says Conductor Harry. "Hope he don't give the new conductor as much trouble as he's give me. Worried me for forty-nine years. Every time he got on the train. My worries are over, for the rest of my years on this road will be spent in peace."

*A novelist and poet of power and charm, Jesse Stuart (1907-1984) was born in a log cabin near Riverton in the Kentucky mountains, the scene of most of his books. Working his way through Lincoln Memorial University (B.A. 1929), he returned home to become high school principal and county school superintendent during the bad Depression years. He later received honorary doctoral degrees in literature from the University of Kentucky, Marietta College, and Baylor University. His book of poems, **Man with a Bull-Tongue Plow** (1934), brought him fame; a best-selling novel, **Taps for Private Tussie** (1943), brought fortune. Service in the Naval Reserve was followed by time spent traveling and teaching overseas. In 1971 a stroke confined the burly six-footer to a wheelchair. His work is known for celebrating traditional family values without being narrow-minded. Other titles include the story collection **Head o' W-Hollow** (1936); and the novel **Foretaste of Glory** (1941), in which the people of a small Kentucky town mistake the Aurora Borealis for the Last Judgment—and react accordingly.*

Dark Melody of Madness

Cornell Woolrich

At four in the morning, a scarecrow of a man staggers dazedly into the New Orleans Police Headquarters building. Behind him at the curb a lacquered Bugatti purrs like a drowsy cat, the finest car that ever stood out there. He weaves his way through the anteroom, deserted at that early hour, and goes in through the open doorway beyond. The sleepy desk-sergeant looks up; an idle detective scanning yesterday's *Times-Picayune* on the two hind legs of a chair tipped back against the wall raises his head; and as the funnel of light from the cone-shaped reflector overhead plays up their visitor like flashlight powder, their mouths drop open and their eyes bat a couple of times. The two front legs of the detective's chair come down with a thump. The sergeant braces himself, eager, friendly, with the heels of both hands on his desk-top and his elbows up in the air. A patrolman comes in from the back room, wiping a drink of water from his mouth. His jaw also hangs when he sees who's there. He sidles nearer the detective and says behind the back of his hand, "That's Eddie Bloch, ain't it?"

The detective doesn't take the trouble to answer. It's like telling him what his own name is. The three stare at the figure under the light, interested, respectful, almost admiring. There is nothing professional in their scrutiny, they are not the police studying a suspect; they are nobodies looking at a celebrity. They take in the rumpled tuxedo, the twig of gardenia that has shed its petals, the tie hanging open in two loose ends. His topcoat was slung across his arm originally; now it trails along the dusty station-house floor behind him. He gives his hat the final, tortured push that dislodges it. It drops and rolls away behind him. The policeman picks it up and brushes it off—he never was a bootlicker in his life, but this man is Eddie Bloch.

Still it's his face, more than who he is or how he's dressed, that would draw stares anywhere. It's the face of a dead man—the face of a dead man on a living body. The shadowy shape of the skull seems to peer through the transparent skin; you can make out its bone-structure as though an X-ray were outlining it. The eyes are stunned, shocked, haunted gleams, set in a vast purple hollow that bisects the face like a mask. No amount of drink or dissipation could do this to anyone, only long illness and the foreknowledge of death. You see faces like that looking up at you from hospital-cots when all hope has been abandoned—when the grave is already waiting.

Yet strangely enough, they knew who he was just now. Instant recognition of who he was came first—realization of the shape he's in comes after that, more slowly. Possibly it's because all three of them have been called on to identify corpses in the morgue in their day. Their minds are trained along those lines. And this man's face is known to hundreds of people. Not that he has ever broken or even fractured the most trivial law, but he has spread happiness around him, set a million feet to dancing in his time.

The desk-sergeant's expression changes. The patrolman mutters under his breath to the detective, "Looks like he just came out of a bad smashup with his car." "More like a drinking-bout, to me," answers the detective. They are simple men, capable within their limitations, but those are the only explanations they can find for what they now see before them.

The desk-sergeant speaks. "Mr. Eddie Bloch, am I right?" He extends his hand across the desk in greeting.

The man can hardly stand up. He nods, he doesn't take the hand.

"Is there anything wrong, Mr. Bloch? Is there anything we can do for you?" The detective and the patrolman come over closer. "Run in and get him a drink of water, Latour," the sergeant says anxiously. "Have an accident, Mr. Bloch? Been held up?"

The man steadies himself with one arm against the edge of the sergeant's desk. The detective extends an arm behind him, in case he should fall backwards. He keeps fumbling, continually fumbling in his clothes. The tuxedo-jacket swims on him as his movements shift it around. He is down to about a hundred pounds in weight, they notice. Out comes a gun, and he doesn't even have the strength to lift it up. He pushes it and it skids across the desk-top, then spins around and points back at him.

He speaks, and if the unburied dead ever spoke this is the voice they'd use. "I've killed a man. Just now. A little while ago. At half-past three."

They're completely floored. They almost don't know how to handle the situation for a minute. They deal with killers every day, but killers have to be gone out after and dragged in. And when fame and wealth enter into it, as they do once in a great while, fancy lawyers and protective barriers spring up to hedge the killers in on all sides. This man is one of the ten idols of America, or was until just lately. People like him don't kill people. They don't come in out of nowhere at four in the morning and stand before a simple desk-sergeant and a simple detective, stripped to their naked souls, shorn of all resemblance to humanity, almost.

There's silence in the room for a minute, a silence you could cut with a knife. Then he speaks again, in agony. "I tell you I've killed a man! Don't stand there looking at me like that! I've killed a man!"

The sergeant speaks, gently, sympathetically. "What's the matter, Mr. Bloch, been working too hard?" He comes out from behind the desk. "Come on inside with us. You stay here, Latour, and look after the telephone."

And when they've accompanied him to a back room: "Get him a chair, Humphries. Here, drink some of this water, Mr. Bloch. Now what's it all about?" The sergeant has brought the gun along with him. He passes it before his nose, then breaks it open. He looks at the detective. "He's used it, all right."

"Was it an accident, Mr. Bloch?" the detective suggests respectfully. The man in the chair shakes his head. He's started to shiver all over, although the New Orleans night is warm and mellow. "Who'd you do it to? Who was it?" the sergeant puts in.

"I don't know his name," Bloch mumbles. "I never have. They call him Papa Benjamin."

His two interrogators exchange a puzzled look. "Sounds like—" The detective doesn't finish it. Instead he turns to the seated figure and asks almost perfunctorily: "He was a white man, of course?"

"He was colored," is the unexpected answer.

The thing gets more crazy, more inexplicable, at every step. How should a man like Eddie Bloch, one of the country's best-known band-leaders, who used to earn a thousand dollars every week for playing at Maxim's, come to kill a nameless colored man—and then be put into this condition by it? These two men have never seen anything like it in their time; they have subjected suspects to forty-eight-hour grillings and yet compared to him now those suspects were fresh as daisies when they got through with them.

He has said it was no accident and he has said it was no hold-up. They shower questions at him, not to confuse him but rather to try to help him pull himself together. "What did he do, forget his place? Talk back to you? Become insolent?" This is in *those* days, remember.

The man's head goes from side to side like a pendulum.

"Did you go out of your mind for a minute? Is that how it was?"

Again a nodded no.

The man's condition has suggested one explanation to the detective's mind. He looks around to make sure the patrolman outside isn't listening. Then very discreetly: "Are you a needle-user, Mr. Bloch? Was he your source?"

The man looks up at them. "I've never touched a thing I shouldn't. A doctor will tell you that in a minute."

"Did he have something on you? Was it blackmail?"

Bloch fumbles some more in his clothes; again they dance around on his skeletonized frame. Suddenly he takes out a cube of money, as thick as it is wide, more money than these two men have ever seen before in their lives. "There's three thousand dollars there," he says simply and tosses it down like he did the gun. "I took it with me tonight, tried to give it to him. He could have had twice as much, three times as much, if he'd said the word, if he'd only let up on me. He wouldn't take it. That was when I had to kill him. That was all there was left for me to do."

"What was he doing to you?" They both say it together.

"He was killing me." He holds out his arm and shoots his cuff. The wristbone is about the size of the sergeant's own thumb-joint. The expensive platinum wristwatch that encircles it has been pulled in to the last possible notch and yet it still hangs almost like a bracelet. "See? I'm down to 102. When my shirt's off, my heart's so close to the surface you can see the skin right over it move like a pulse with each beat."

They draw back a little, almost they wish he hadn't come in here. That he had headed for some other precinct instead. From the very beginning they have sensed something here that is over their heads, that isn't to be found in any of the instruction-books. Now they come out with it. "How?" Humphries asks. "How was he killing you?"

There's a flare of torment from the man. "Don't you suppose I would have told you long ago, if I could! Don't you suppose I would have come in here weeks ago, months ago, and demanded protection, asked to be saved—if I could have told you what it was? If you would have believed me?"

"We'll believe you, Mr. Bloch," the sergeant says soothingly. "We'll believe anything. Just tell us—"

But Bloch in turn shoots a question at them, for the first time since he has come in. "Answer me! Do you believe in anything you can't see, can't hear, can't touch—?"

"Radio," the sergeant suggests not very brightly, but Humphries answers more frankly: "No."

The man slumps down again in his chair, shrugs apathetically. "If you don't, how can I expect you to believe me? I've been to the biggest doctors, biggest scientists in the world—they wouldn't believe me. How can I expect you to? You'll simply say I'm cracked, and let it go at that. I don't want to spend the rest of my life in an asylum—" He breaks off and sobs. "And yet it's true, it's true!"

They've gotten into such a maze that Humphries decides it's about time to snap out of it. He asks the one simple question that should have been asked long ago, and the hell with all this mumbo-jumbo. "Are you sure you killed him?" The man is broken physically and he's about ready to crack mentally too. The whole thing may be an hallucination.

"I know I did. I'm sure of it," the man answers calmly. "I'm already beginning to feel a little better. I felt it the minute he was gone."

If he is, he doesn't show it. The sergeant catches Humphries's eye and meaningfully taps his forehead in a sly gesture.

"Suppose you take us there and show us," Humphries suggests. "Can you do that? Where'd it happen, at Maxim's?"

"I told you he was colored," Bloch answers reproachfully. Maxim's is tony. "It was in the Vieux Carré. I can show you where, but I can't drive any more. It was all I could do to get down here with my car."

"I'll put Desjardins on it with you," the sergeant says and calls through the door to the patrolman: "Ring Dij and tell him to meet Humphries at the corner of Canal and Royal right away!" He turns and looks at the huddle on the chair. "Buy him a bracer on the way. It don't look like he'll last till he gets there."

The man flushes a little—it would be a blush if he had any blood left in him. "I can't touch alcohol any more. I'm on my last legs. It goes right through me like—" He hangs his head, then raises it again.

"But I'll get better now, little by little, now that he's—"

The sergeant takes Humphries out of earshot. "Pushover for a padded cell. If it's on the up-and-up, and not just a pipe dream, call me right back. I'll get the commissioner on the wire."

"At this hour of the night?"

The sergeant motions toward the chair with his head. "He's Eddie Bloch, isn't he?"

Humphries takes him under the elbow, pries him up from the chair. Not roughly, but just briskly, energetically. Now that things are at last getting under way, he knows where he's at; he can handle them. He'll still be considerate, but he's businesslike now; he's into his routine. "All right, come on, Mr. Bloch, let's get up there."

"Not a scratch goes down on the blotter until I'm sure what I'm doing," the sergeant calls after Humphries. "I don't want this whole town down on my neck tomorrow morning."

Humphries almost has to hold him up on the way out and into the car. "This it?" he says. "Wow!" He just touches it with his nail and they're off like velvet. "How'd you ever get this into the Vieux Carré without knocking over the houses?"

Two gleams deep in the skull jogging against the upholstery, dimmer than the dashboard lights, are the only sign that there's life beside him. "Used to park it blocks away—go on foot."

."Oh, you went there more than once?"

"Wouldn't you—to beg for your life?"

More of that screwy stuff, Humphries thinks disgustedly. Why should a man like Eddie Bloch, star of the mike and the dance-floor, go to some colored man in the slums and beg for his life?

Royal Street comes whistling along. He swerves in toward the curb, shoves the door out, sees Desjardins land on the running-board with one foot. Then he veers out into the middle again without even having stopped. Desjardins moves in on the other side of Bloch, finishes dressing by knotting his necktie and buttoning his vest. "Where'd you get the Aquitania?" he wants to know, and then, with a look beside him: "Holy Kreisler, Eddie Bloch! We used to hear you every night on my Emerson—"

"Matter?" Humphries squelches. "Got a talking-jag?"

"Turn," says a hollow sound between them and three wheels take the Bugatti around into North Rampart Street. "Have to leave it here," he says a little later, and they get out. Congo Square, the old stamping-ground of the slaves.

"Help him," Humphries tells his mate tersely, and they each brace him by an elbow.

Staggering between them with the uneven gait of a punch-drunk pug, quick and then slow by turns, he leads them down a ways, and then suddenly cuts left into an alley that isn't there at all until you're smack in front of it. It's just a crack between two houses, noisome as a sewer. They have to break into Indian file to get through at all. But Bloch can't fall down; the walls almost scrape both his shoulders at once. One's in front, one behind him.

"You packed?" Humphries calls over his head to Desjardins, up front.

"Catch cold without it," the other's voice comes back out of the gloom.

A slit of orange shows up suddenly from under a window-sill and a shapely coffee-colored elbow scrapes the ribs of the three as they squirm by. "This far 'nough, honey," a liquid voice murmurs.

"Bad girl, wash y'mouth out with soap," the unromantic Humphries warns over his shoulder without even looking around. The sliver of light vanishes as quickly as it came.

The passage widens out in places into mouldering courtyards dating back to French or Spanish colonial days, and once it goes under an archway and becomes a tunnel for a short distance. Desjardins cracks his head and swears with talent and abandon.

"Y'left out—" the rearguard remarks drily.

"Here," pants Bloch weakly, and stops suddenly at a patch of blackness in the wall. Humphries washes it with his torch and crumbling mildewed stone steps show up inside it. Then he motions Bloch in, but the man hangs back, slips a notch or two lower down against the opposite wall that supports him. "Let me stay down here! Don't make me go up there again," he pleads. "I don't think I can make it any more. I'm afraid to go back in there."

"Oh, no!" Humphries says with quiet determination. "You're showing us," and scoops him away from the wall with his arm. Again, as before, he isn't rough about it, just businesslike. Dij keeps the lead, watering the place with his own torch. Humphries trains his on the band-leader's forty-dollar custom-made patent-leather shoes jerking frightenedly upward before him. The stone steps turn to wood ones splintered with usage. They have to step over a huddled drunk, empty bottle cradled in his arms. "Don't light a match," Dij warns, pinching his nose, "or there'll be an explosion."

"Grow up," snaps Humphries. The Cajun's a good dick, but can't he realize the man in the middle is roasting in hellfire? This is no time—

"In here is where I did it. I closed the door again after me." Bloch's skull-face is all silver with his life-sweat as one of their torches flicks past it.

Humphries shoves open the sagging mahogany panel that was first hung up when a Louis was still king of France and owned this town. The light of a lamp far across a still, dim room flares up and dances crazily in the draught. They come in and look.

There's an old broken-down bed, filthy with rags. Across it there's a motionless figure, head hanging down toward the floor. Dij cups his hand under it and lifts it. It comes up limply toward him, like a small basketball. It bounces down again when he lets it go—even seems to bob slightly for a second or two after. It's an old, old colored man, up in his eighties, even beyond. There's a dark spot, darker than the wizened skin, just under one bleared eye and another in the thin fringe of white wool that circles the back of the skull.

Humphries doesn't wait to see any more. He turns, flips out and down, and all the way back to wherever the nearest telephone can be found, to let headquarters know that it's true after all and they can rouse the police commissioner. "Keep him there with you, Dij," his voice trails back from the inky stairwell, "and no quizzing. Pull in your horns till we get our orders!" The scarecrow with them tries to stumble after him and get out of the place, groaning, "Don't leave me here! Don't make me stay here—!"

"I wouldn't quiz you on my own, Mr. Bloch," Dij tries to reassure him, nonchalantly sitting down on the edge of the bed next to the corpse and retying his shoelace. "I'll never forget it was your playing 'Love in Bloom' on the air one night in Baton Rouge two years ago gave me the courage to propose to my wife—"

But the Commissioner would, and does, in his office a couple hours later. He's anything but eager about it, too. They've tried to shunt him, Bloch, off their hands in every possible legal way open to them. No go. He sticks to them like flypaper. The old colored man *didn't* try to attack him, or rob him, or blackmail him, or kidnap him, or anything else. The gun didn't go off accidentally, and he didn't fire it on the spur of the moment either, without thinking twice, or in a flare of anger. The Commissioner almost beats his own head against the desk in his exasperation as he reiterates over and over: "But why? Why? Why?" And for the umpteenth time, he gets the same indigestible answer: "Because he was killing me."

"Then you admit he did lay hands on you?" The first time the poor Commissioner asked this, he said it with a spark of hope. But this is the tenth or twelfth and the spark died out long ago.

"He never once came near me. I was the one looked him up each time to plead him. Commissioner Oliver, tonight I went down on my knees to that old man and dragged myself around the floor of that dirty room after him, on my *bended knees,* like a sick cat—begging, crawling to him, offering him three thousand, ten, any amount, finally offering him my own gun, asking him to shoot me with it, to get it over with quickly, to be kind to me, not to drag it out by inches any longer! No, not even that little bit of mercy! Then I shot—and now I'm going to get better, now I'm going to live—"

He's too weak to cry; crying takes strength. The Commissioner's hair is about ready to stand on end. "Stop it, Mr. Bloch, stop it!" he shouts, and he steps over and grabs him by the shoulder in defense of his own nerves, and can almost feel the shoulder-bone cutting his hand. He takes his hand away again in a hurry. "I'm going to have you examined by an alienist!"

The bundle of bones rears from the chair. "You can't do that! You can't take my mind from me! Send to my hotel—I've got a trunkful of reports on my condition! I've been to the biggest minds in Europe! Can you produce anyone that would dare go against the findings of Buckholtz in Vienna, Reynolds in London? They had me under observation for months at a time! I'm not even on the borderline of insanity, not even a genius or musically talented. I don't even write my own numbers, I'm mediocre, uninspired—in other words completely normal. I'm saner than you are at this minute, Mr. Oliver. My body's gone, my soul's gone, and all I've got left is my mind, but you can't take that from me!"

The Commissioner's face is beet-red. He's about ready for a stroke, but he speaks softly, persuasively. "An eighty-odd-year-old colored man who is so feeble he can't even go upstairs half the time, who has to have his food pulleyed up to him through the window in a basket, is killing—whom? A white stumble-bum his own age? No-o-o, Mr. Eddie Bloch, the premier bandsman of America, who can name his own price in any town, who's heard every night in all our homes, who has about everything a man can want—that's who!"

He peers close, until their eyes are on a level. His voice is just a silky whisper. "Tell me just one thing, Mr. Bloch." Then like the explosion of a giant firecracker, "How?" He roars it out, booms it out.

There's a long-drawn intake of breath from Eddie Bloch. "By thinking thought-waves of death that reach me through the air."

The poor Commissioner practically goes all to pieces on his own rug. "And you don't need a medical exam!" he wheezes weakly.

There's a flutter, the popping of buttons, and Eddie Bloch's coat, his vest, his shirt, undershirt, land one after another on the floor around his chair. He turns. "Look at my back! You can count every vertebra thought the skin!" He turns back again. "Look at my ribs. Look at the pulsing where there's not enough skin left to cover my heart!"

Oliver shuts his eyes and turns toward the window. He's in a particularly unpleasant spot. New Orleans, out there, is stirring, and when it hears about this, he's going to be the most unpopular man in town. On the other hand, if he doesn't see the thing through now that it's gone this far he's guilty of a dereliction of duty, malfeasance in office.

Bloch, slowly dressing, knows what he's thinking. "You want to get rid of me, don't you? You're trying to think of a way of covering this thing up. You're afraid to bring me up before the Grand Jury on account of your own reputation, aren't you?" His voice rises to a scream of panic. "Well, I want protection! I don't want to go out there again—to my death! I won't accept bail! If you turn me loose now, even on my own cognizance, you may be as guilty of my death as he is. How do I know my bullet stopped the thing? How does any of us know what becomes of the mind after death? Maybe his thoughts will still reach me, still try to get me. I tell you I want to be locked up, I want people around me day and night, I want to be where I'm safe—!"

"Shh, for God's sake, Mr. Bloch! They'll think I'm beating you up—" The Commissioner drops his arms to his sides and heaves a gigantic sigh. "That settles it! I'll book you all right. You want that and you're going to get it! I'll book you for the murder of one Papa Benjamin, even if they laugh me out of office for it!"

For the first time since the whole thing has started, he casts a look of real anger, ill will, at Eddie Bloch. He seizes a chair, swirls it around, and bangs it down in front of the man. He puts his foot on it and pokes his finger almost in Bloch's eye. "I'm not two-faced. I'm not going to lock you up nice and cozy and then soft-pedal the whole thing. If it's coming out at all, then all of it's coming out. Now start in! Tell me everything I want to know, and what I want to know is—everything!"

The strains of 'Goodnight Ladies' die away; the dancers leave the floor, the lights start going out, and Eddie Bloch throws down his baton and mops the back of his neck with a handkerchief. He weighs about two hundred pounds, is in the pink, and is a good-looking brute. But his face is sour right now, dissatisfied. His outfit starts to case its instruments right and left, and Judy Jarvis steps up on the platform, in her street clothes, ready to go home. She's

Eddie's torch singer, and also his wife. "Coming, Eddie? Let's get out of here." She looks a little disgusted herself. "I didn't get a hand tonight, not even after my rumba number. Must be staling. If I wasn't your wife, I'd be out of a job, I guess."

Eddie pats her shoulder. "It isn't you, honey. It's us, we're beginning to stink. Notice how the attendance has been dropping the past few weeks? There were more waiters than customers tonight. I'll be hearing from the owner any minute now. He has the right to cancel my contract if the intake drops below five grand."

A waiter comes up to the edge of the platform. "Mr. Graham'd like to see you in his office before you go home, Mr. Bloch."

Eddie and Judy look at each other. "This is it now, Judy. You go back to the hotel. Don't wait for me. G'night, boys." Eddie Bloch calls for his hat and knocks at the manager's office.

Graham rustles a lot of accounts together. "We took in forty-five hundred this week, Eddie. They can get the same ginger ale and sandwiches any place, but they'll go where the band has something to give 'em. I notice the few that do come in don't even get up from the table any more when you tap your baton. Now, what's wrong?"

Eddie punches his hat a couple of times. "Don't ask me. I'm getting the latest orchestrations from Broadway sent to me hot off the griddle. We sweat our bald heads off rehearsing—"

Graham swivels his cigar. "Don't forget that jazz originated here in the South, you can't show this town anything. They want something new."

"When do I scram?" Eddie asks, smiling with the southwest corner of his mouth.

"Finish the week out. See if you can do something about it by Monday. If not, I'll have to wire St. Louis to get Kruger's crew. I'm sorry, Eddie."

"That's all right," broad-minded Eddie says. "You're not running a charity bazaar."

Eddie goes out into the dark danceroom. His crew has gone. The tables are stacked. A couple of old colored crones are down on hands and knees slopping water around on the parquet. Eddie steps up on the platform a minute to get some orchestrations he left on the piano. He feels something crunch under his shoe, reaches down, picks up a severed chicken's claw lying there with a strip of red rag tied around it. How the hell did it get up there? If it had been under one of the tables, he'd have thought some diner had dropped it. He flushes a little. D'ye mean to say he and the boys were so rotten tonight that somebody deliberately threw it at them while they were playing?

One of the scrubwomen looks up. The next moment, she and her mate are on their feet, edging nearer, eyes big as saucers, until they get close enough to see what it is he's holding. Then there's a double yowl of fright, a tin pail goes rolling across the floor, and no two stout people, white or colored, ever got out of a place in such a hurry before. The door nearly comes off its hinges, and Eddie can hear their cackling all the way down the quiet street outside until it fades away into the night. "For gosh sake!" thinks the bewildered Eddie. "They must be using the wrong brand of gin." He tosses the object out onto the floor and goes back to the piano for his music scores. A sheet or two has slipped down behind it and he squats to collect them. That way the piano hides him.

The door opens again and he sees Johnny Staats (traps and percussion) come in in quite a hurry. He thought Staats was home in bed by now. Staats is feeling himself all over like he was rehearsing the shim-sham and he's scanning the ground as he goes along. Then suddenly he pounces—and it's on that very scrap of garbage Eddie just now threw away! And as he straightens up with it, his breath comes out in such a sigh of relief that Eddie can hear it all the way across the still room. All this keeps him from hailing Staats as he was going to a minute ago and suggesting a cup of java. But— "Superstitious," thinks broad-minded Eddie. "It's his good luck charm, that's all, like some people carry a rabbit's foot. I'm a little that way myself, never walk under a ladder—"

Then again, why should those two women go into hysterics when they lamp the same object? And Eddie recalls now that some of the boys have always suspected Staats has colored blood, and tried to tell him so years ago when Staats first came in with them, but he wouldn't listen to them.

Staats slinks out again as noiselessly as he came in, and Eddie decides he'll catch up with him and kid him about his chicken-claw on their way home together. (They all roost in the same hotel.) So he takes his music-sheets, some of which are blank, and he leaves. Staats is way down the street—in the *wrong direction,* away from the hotel! Eddie hesitates for just a minute, and then he starts after Staats on a vague impulse, just to see where he's going—just to see what he's up to. Maybe the fright of the scrubwomen and the way Staats pounced on that chicken-claw just now have built up to this, without Eddie's really knowing it.

And how many times afterwards he's going to pray to his God that he'd never turned down that other way this night—away from his hotel, his Judy, his boys—away from the sunlight and the white man's world. Such a little thing to decide to do, and afterwards no turning back—ever.

He keeps Staats in sight, and they hit the Vieux Carré. That's all right. There are a lot of quaint places here a guy might like to drop in. Or maybe he has some Creole sweetie tucked away, and Eddie thinks: I'm lower than a ditch to spy like this. But then suddenly right before his eyes, halfway up the narrow lane he's turned into—there isn't any Staats any more! And no door opened and closed again either. Then when Eddie gets up to where it was, he sees the crevice between the old houses, hidden by an angle in the walls. So that's where he went! Eddie almost has a peeve on by now at all this hocus-pocus. He slips in himself and feels his way along. He stops every once in a while and can hear Staats's quiet footfall somewhere way up in front. Then goes on again. Once or twice the passage spreads out a little and lets a little green-blue moonlight partway down the walls. Then later, there's a little flare of orange light from under a window and an elbow jogs him in the appendix. "You'd be happier here. Doan go the rest of the way," a soft voice breathes. A prophecy if he only knew it!

But hardboiled Eddie just says: "G'wan to bed, y'dirty stay-up!" out of the corner of his mouth, and the light vanishes. Next a tunnel and he bangs the top of his head and his eyes water. But at the other end of it, Staats has finally come to a halt in a patch of clear light and seems to be looking up at a window or something, so Eddie stays where he is, inside the tunnel, and folds the lapels of his black jacket up over his white shirtfront so it won't show.

Staats just stands there for a spell, with Eddie holding his breath inside the tunnel, and then finally he gives a peculiar, dismal whistle. There's nothing carefree or casual about it. It's a hollow swampland sound, not easy to get without practice. Then he just stands there waiting, until without warning another figure joins him in the gloom. Eddie strains his eyes. A huge Negro roustabout. Something passes from Staats's hand to his—the chicken-claw possibly—then they go in, into the house Staats has been facing. Eddie can hear the soft shuffle of feet going upstairs on the inside, and the groaning, squeaking of an old decayed door—and then silence.

He edges forward to the mouth of the tunnel and peers up. No light shows from any window; the house appears to be untenanted, deserted.

Eddie hangs onto his coat collar with one hand and strokes his chin with the other. He doesn't know just what to do. The vague impulse that has brought him this far after Staats begins to peter out now. Staats has some funny associates—something funny is going on in this out-of-the-way place at this unearthly hour of the morning—but after all, a man's private life is his own. He wonders what made him do this, he wouldn't want anyone to know he did it. He'll turn around and go back to his hotel now and get some shut-eye; he's got to think up some novelty for his routine at Maxim's between now and Monday or he'll be out on his ear.

Then just as one heel is off the ground to take the turn that will start him back, a vague, muffled wailing starts from somewhere inside that house. It's toned down to a mere echo. It has to go through thick doors and wide, empty rooms and down a deep, hollow stairwell before it gets to him. Oh, some sort of revival meeting, is it? So Staats has got religion, has he? But what a place to come and get it in!

A throbbing like a faraway engine in a machine shop underscores the wailing, and every once in a while a *boom* like distant thunder across the bayou tops the whole works. It goes: *Boom-putta-putta-boom-putta-putta-boom!* And the wailing, way up high at the moon: *Eeyah-eeyah-eeyah...*

Eddie's professional instincts suddenly come alive. He tries it out, beats time to it with his arm as if he were holding a baton. His fingers snap like a whip. "My God, that's grand! That's gorgeous! Just what I need! I gotta get up there!" So a chicken-foot does it, eh?

He turns and runs back, through the tunnel, through the courtyards, all the way back where he came from, stooping here, stopping there, lighting matches recklessly and throwing them away as he goes. Out in the Vieux Carré again, the refuse hasn't been collected. He spots a can at the corner of two lanes, topples it over. The smell rises to heaven, but he wades into it ankle-deep like any levee-rat, digs into the stuff with both forearms, scattering it right and left. He's lucky, finds a verminous carcass, tears off a claw, wipes it on some newspaper. Then he starts back. Wait a minute! The red rag, red strip around it! He feels himself all over, digs into all his pockets. Nothing that color. Have to do without it, but maybe it won't work without it. He turns and hurries back through the slit between the old houses, doesn't care how much noise he makes. The flash of light from Old Faithful, the jogging elbow. Eddie stoops, he suddenly snatches in at the red kimono sleeve, his hand comes away with a strip of it. Bad language, words that even Eddie doesn't know. A five-spot stops it on the syllable, and Eddie's already way down the passage. If only they haven't quit until he can get back there!

They haven't. It was vague, smothered when he went away; it's louder, more persistent, more frenzied now. He doesn't bother about giving the whistle, probably couldn't imitate it exactly anyhow. He dives into the black smudge that is the entrance to the house, feels greasy stone steps under him, takes one or two and then suddenly his collar is four sizes too small for him, gripped by a big ham of a hand at the back. A sharp something that might be anything from a pocket-knife blade to the business edge of a razor is creasing his throat just below the apple and drawing a preliminary drop or two of blood.

"Here it is, I've got it here!" gasps Eddie. What kind of religion is this, anyway? The sharp thing stays, but the hand lets go his collar and feels for the chicken claw. Then the sharp thing goes away too, but probably not very far away.

"Whyfor you didn't give the signal?"

Eddie's windpipe gives him the answer. "Sick here, couldn't."

"Light up, lemme see yo' face." Eddie strikes a match and holds it. "Yo' face has never been here before."

Eddie gestures upward. "My friend—up there—he'll tell you!"

"Mr. Johnny yo' friend? He ax you to come?"

Eddie thinks quickly. The chicken claw might carry more weight than Staats. "That told me to come."

"Papa Benjamin sen' you that?"

"Certainly," says Eddie stoutly. Probably their deacon, but it's a hell of a way to—The match stings his fingers and he whips it out. Blackness and a moment's uncertainty that might end either way. But a lot of savoir-faire, a thousand years of survival instincts, are backing Eddie up. "You'll make me late. Papa Benjamin wouldn't like that!"

He gropes his way on up in the pitch blackness, thinking any minute he'll feel his back slashed to ribbons. But it's better than standing still and having it happen, and to back out now would bring it on twice as quickly. However, it works, nothing happens.

"Fust thing y'know, all N'yorleans be comin' by," growls the watchman sulkily, and flounders down on the staircase with a sound like a tired seal. There is some other crack about "darkies lookin' lak pinks," and then a sigh.

But Eddie's already up on the landing above and so close to the *boom-putta boom* now it drowns out every other sound. The whole framework of the decrepit house seems to shake with it. The door's closed but the thread of orange that outlines it shows it up to him. Behind there. He leans against it, shoves a little. It gives. The squealings and the grindings it emits are lost in the torrent of noise that comes rushing out. He sees plenty, and what he sees only makes him want to see all the more. Something tells him the best thing to do is slip in quietly and close it behind him before he's noticed, rather than stay there peeping in from the outside. Little Snowdrop might always come upstairs in back of him and catch him there. So he widens it just a little more, oozes in, and kicks it shut behind him with his heel—and immediately gets as far away from it as he can. Evidently no one has seen him.

Now, it's a big shadowy room and it's choked with people. It's lit by a single oil-lamp and a hell of a whole lot of candles, which may have shone out brightly against the darkness outside but are pretty dim once you get inside with them. The long flickering shadows thrown on all the walls by those cavorting in the center are almost as much of a protection to Eddie, as he crouches back amidst them, as the darkness outside would be. He's been around, and a single look is enough to tell him that whatever else it is, it's no revival meeting. At first, he takes it for just a gin or rent party with the lid off, but it isn't that either. There's no gin there, and there's no pairing off of couples in the dancing—rather it's a roomful of devils lifted bodily up out of hell. Plenty of them have passed out cold on the floor all around him and the others keep stepping over them as they prance back and forth, only they don't always step over but sometimes *on*—on prostrate faces and chests and outstretched arms and hands. Then there are others who have gone off into a sort of still trance, seated on the floor with their backs to the wall, some of them rocking back and forth, some just staring glassy-eyed, foam drooling from their mouths. Eddie quickly slips down among them on his haunches and gets busy. He too starts rocking back and forth and pounding the flooring beisde him with his knuckles, but he's not in any trance, he's getting a swell new number for his repertoire at Maxim's. A sheet of blank score paper is partly hidden under his body, and he keeps dropping one hand down to it every minute jotting down musical notes with the stub of pencil in his fingers. "Key of A," he guesses. "I can decide that when I instrument it. Mi-re-do, mi-re-do. Then over again. Hope I didn't miss any of it."

Boom-putta-putta-boom! Young and old, black and tawny, fat and thin, naked and clothed, they pass from right to left, from left to right, in two concentric circles, while the candle flames dance crazily and the shadows leap up and down on the walls. The hub of it all, within the innermost circle of dancers, is an old, old man, black skin and bones, only glimpsed now and then in a space between the packed bodies that surround him. An animal-pelt is banded about his middle; he wears a horrible juju mask over his face—a death's head. On one side of him, a squatting woman clacks two gourds together endlessly, that's the "putta" of Eddie's rhythm; on the other, another beats a drum, that's the "boom." In one upraised hand he holds a squalling fowl, wings beating the air; in the other a sharp-bladed knife. Something flashes in the air, but the dancers mercifully get between Eddie and the sight of it. Next glimpse he has, the fowl isn't flapping any more. It's hanging limply down and veins of blood are trickling down the old man's shrivelled forearm.

"That part don't go into my show," Eddie thinks facetiously. The horrible old man has dropped the knife; he squeezes the lifeblood from the dead bird with both hands now, still holding it in mid-air. He sprinkles the drops on those that cavort around him, flexing and unflexing his bony fingers in a nauseating travesty of the ceremony of baptism.

Drops spatter here and there about the room, on the walls. One lands near Eddie and he edges back. Revolting things go on all around him. He sees some of the crazed dancers drop to their hands and knees and bend low over these red polka-dots, licking them up from the floor with their tongues. Then they go about the room on all fours like animals, looking for others.

"Think I'll go," Eddie says to himself, tasting last night's supper all over again. "They ought to have the cops on them."

He maneuvers the score-sheet, filled now, out from under him and into his side-pocket; then he starts drawing his feet in toward him preparatory to standing up and slipping out of this hell-hole. Meanwhile a second fowl, black this time (the first was white), a squeaking suckling pig, and a puppy dog have gone the way of the first fowl. Nor do the carcasses go to waste when the old man has dropped them. Eddie sees things happening on the floor, in between the stomping feet of the dancers, and he guesses enough not to look twice.

Then suddenly, already reared a half-inch above the floor on his way up, he wonders where the wailing went. And the clacking of the gourds and the boom of the drum and the shuffling of the feet. He blinks, and everything has frozen still in the room around him. Not a move, not a sound. Straight out from the old man's gnarled shoulder stretches a bony arm, the end dipped in red, pointing like an arrow at Eddie. Eddie sinks down again that half-inch. He couldn't hold that position very long, and something tells him he's not leaving right away after all.

"White man," says a bated breath, and they all start moving in on him. A gesture of the old man sweeps them into motionlessness again.

A cracked voice comes through the grinning mouth of the juju mask, rimmed with canine teeth. "Whut you do here?"

Eddie taps his pockets mentally. He has about fifty on him. Will that be enough to buy his way out? He has an uneasy feeling however that none of this lot is as interested in money as they should be—at least not right now. Before he has a chance to try it out, another voice speaks up. "I know this man, paploi. Let me find out."

Johnny Staats came in here tuxedoed, hair slicked back, a cog in New Orleans's night-life. Now he's barefooted, coatless, shirtless—a tousled scarecrow. A drop of blood has caught him squarely on the forehead and been traced, by his own finger or someone else's, into a red line from temple to temple. A chicken feather or two clings to his upper lip. Eddie saw him dancing with the rest, groveling on the floor. His scalp crawls with repugnance as the man comes over and squats down before him. The rest of them hold back, tense, poised, ready to pounce.

The two men talk in low, hoarse voices. "It's your only way, Eddie. I can't save you—"

"Why, I'm in the very heart of New Orleans! They wouldn't dare!" But sweat oozes out on Eddie's face just the same. He's no fool. Sure the police will come and sure they'll mop this place up. But what will they find? His own remains along with those of the fowls, the pig, and the dog.

"You'd better hurry up, Eddie. I can't hold them back much longer. Unless you do, you'll never get out of this place alive and you may as well know it! If I tried to stop them, I'd go too. You know what this is, don't you? This is voodoo!"

"I knew that five minutes after I was in the room." And Eddie thinks to himself, "You son-of-a-so-and-so! You better ask Mombo-jombo to get you a new job starting in tomorrow night!" Then he grins internally and, clown to the very end, says with a straight face: "Sure I'll join. What d'ye suppose I came here for anyway?"

Knowing what he knows now, Staats is the last one he'd tell about the glorious new number he's going to get out of this, the notes for which are nestled in his inside pocket right now. And he might even get more dope out of the initiation ceremonies if he pretends to go through with them. A song or dance for Judy to do with maybe a green spot focussed on her. Lastly, there's no use denying there *are* too many razors, knives, and the like, in the room to hope to get out and all the way back where he started from without a scratch.

Staats's face is grave, though. "Now don't kid about this thing. If you knew what I know about it, there's a lot more to it than there seems to be. If you're sincere, honest about it, all right. If not, it might be better to get cut to pieces right now than to tamper with it."

"Never more serious in my life," says Eddie. And deep down inside he's braying like a jackass.

Staats turns to the old man. "His spirit wishes to join our spirits."

The papaloi burns some feathers and entrails at one of the candle-flames. Not a sound in the room. The majority of them squat down all at once. "It came out all right," Staats breathes. "He reads them. The spirits are willing."

"So far so good," Eddie thinks. "I've fooled the guts and feathers."

The papaloi is pointing at him now. "Let him go now and be silent," the voice behind the mask cackles. Then a second time he says it, and a third, with a long pause between.

Eddie looks hopefully at Staats. "Then I can go after all, as long as I don't tell anyone what I've seen?"

Staats shakes his head grimly. "Just part of the ritual. If you went now, you'd eat something that disagreed with you tomorrow and be dead before the day was over."

More sacrificial slaughtering, and the drum and gourds and wailing start over again, but very low and subdued now as at the beginning. A bowl of blood is prepared and Eddie is raised to his feet and led forward, Staats on one side of him, an anonymous colored man on the other. The papaloi dips his already caked hand into the bowl and traces a mark on Eddie's forehead. The chanting and wailing grow louder behind him. The dancing begins again. He's in the middle of all of them. He's an island of sanity in a sea of jungle frenzy. The bowl is being held up before his face. He tries to draw back, his sponsors grip him firmly by the arms. "Drink!" whispers Staats. "Drink—or they'll kill you where you stand!"

Even at this stage of the game, there's still a wisecrack left in Eddie, though he keeps it to himself. He takes a deep breath. "Here's where I get my vitamin A for today!"

Staats shows up at orchestra rehearsal next morning to find somebody else at drums and percussion. He doesn't say much when Eddie shoves a two-week check at him, spits on the floor at his feet, and growls: "Beat it, you filthy—"

Staats only murmurs: "So you're crossing them? I wouldn't want to be in your shoes for all the fame and money in this world, guy!"

"If you mean that bad dream the other night," says Eddie, "I haven't told anybody and I don't intend to. Why, I'd be laughed at. I'm on remembering what I can use of it. I'm a white man, see? The jungle is just trees to me; the Congo, just a river; the night-time, just a time for electric lights." He whips out a couple of C's. "Hand 'em these for me, will ya, and tell 'em I've paid up my dues from now until doomsay and I don't want any receipt. And if they try putting rough-on-rats in my orange juice, they'll find themselves stomping in a chain-gang!"

The C's fall where Eddie spat. "You're one of us. You think you're pink? Blood tells. You wouldn't have gone there—you couldn't have stood that induction—if you were. Look at your fingernails sometime. Look in a mirror at the whites of your eyes. Goodbye, dead man."

Eddie says goodbye to him, too. He knocks out three of his teeth, breaks the bridge of his nose, and rolls all over the floor on top of him. But he can't wipe out that wise, knowing smile that shows even through the gush of blood.

They pull Eddie off, pull him up, pull him together. Staats staggers away, smiling at what he knows. Eddie, heaving like a bellows, turns to his crew. "All right, boys. All together now!" *Boom-putt-putta-boom-putta-putta-boom!*

Graham shoots five C's on promotion and all New Orleans jams its way into Maxim's that Saturday night. They're standing on each other's shoulders and hanging from the chandeliers to get a look. "First time in America, the original *Voodoo Chant,*" yowl the three sheets on every billboard in town. And when Eddie taps his baton, the lights go down and a nasty green flood lights the platform from below and you can hear a pin drop. "Good evening, folks. This is Eddie Bloch and his Five Chips, playing to you from Maxim's. You're about to hear for the first time on the air the Voodoo Chant, the age-old ceremonial rhythm no white man has ever been permitted to listen to before. I can assure you this is an accurate transcription; not a note has been changed." Then very softly and far away it begins: *Boom-putta-putta-boom!*

Judy's going to dance and wail to it, she's standing there on the steps leading up to the platform, waiting to go on. She's powdered orange, dressed in feathers, and has a small artificial bird fastened to one wrist and a thin knife in her other hand. She catches his eye, he looks over at her, and he sees she wants to tell him something. Still waving his baton he edges sideways until he's within earshot.

"Eddie, don't! Stop them! Call it off, will you? I'm worried about you!"

"Too late now," he answers under cover of the music. "We've started already. What're you scared of?"

She passes him a crumpled piece of paper. "I found this under your dressing-room door when I came out just now. It sounds like a warning. There's somebody doesn't want you to play that number!"

Still swinging with his right hand, Eddie unrolls the thing under his left thumb and reads it:

You can summon the spirits but can you dismiss them again? Think well.

He crumples it up again and tosses it away. "Staats trying to scare me because I canned him."

"It was tied to a little bunch of black feathers," she tries to tell him. "I wouldn't have paid any attention, but my maid pleaded with me not to dance this when she saw it. Then she ran out on me—"

"We're on the air," he reminds her between his teeth. "Are you with me or aren't you?" And he eases back center again. Louder and louder the beat grows, just like it did two nights ago. Judy swirls on in a green spot and begins the unearthly wail Eddie's coached her to do.

A waiter drops a tray of drinks in the silence of the room out there, and when the headwaiter goes to bawl him out he's nowhere to be found. He has quit cold and a whole row of tables has been left without their orders. "Well, I'll be—!" says the captain and scratches his head.

Eddie's facing the crew, his back to Judy, and as he vibrates to the rhythm, some pin or other that he's forgotten to take out of his shirt suddenly catches him and strikes into him. It's a little below the collar, just between the shoulder blades. He jumps a little, but doesn't feel it any more after that...

Judy squalls, tears her tonsils out, screeches words that neither he nor she knows the meaning of but that he managed to set down on paper phonetically the other night. Her little body goes through all the contortions, tamed down of course, that that she-devil greased with lard and wearing only earrings performed that night. She stabs the bird with her fake knife and sprinkles imaginary blood in the air. Nothing like this has ever been seen before. And in the silence that suddenly lands when it's through, you can count twenty. That's how it's gotten under everyone's skin.

Then the noise begins. It goes over like an avalanche. But just the same, more people are ordering strong drinks all at once than has ever happened before in the place, and the matron in the women's restroom has her hands full of hysterical sob-sisters.

"Try to get away from me, just try!" Graham tells Eddie at curfew time. "I'll have a new contract, gilt-edged, ready for you in the morning. We've already got six-grand worth of reservations on our hands for the coming week—one of 'em by telegram all the way from Shreveport!"

Success! Eddie and Judy taxi back to their rooms at the hotel, tired but happy. "It'll be good for years. We can use it for our signature on the air, like Whiteman does the Rhapsody."

She goes into the bedroom first, snaps on the lights, calls to him a minute later: "Come here and look at this—the cutest little souvenir!" He finds her holding a wax doll, finger high, in her hands. "Why it's you, Eddie, look! Small as it is it has your features! Well isn't that the clev—!"

He takes it away from her and squints at it. It's himself all right. It's rigged out in two tiny patches of black cloth for a tuxedo, and the eyes and hair and features are inked onto the wax.

"Where'd you find it?"

"It was in your bed, up against the pillow."

He's fixing to grin about it, until he happens to turn it over. In the back, just a little below the collar, between the shoulder-blades, a short but venomous-looking black pin is sticking.

He goes a little white for a minute. He knows who it's from now and what it's trying to tell him. But that isn't what makes him change color. He's just remembered something. He throws off his coat, yanks at his collar, turns his back to her. "Judy, look down there, will you? I felt a pin stick me while we were doing that number. Put your hand down. Feel anything?"

"No, there's nothing there," she tells him.

"Musta dropped out."

"It couldn't have," she says. "Your belt-line's so tight it almost cuts into you. There couldn't have been anything there or it'd still be there now. You must have imagined it."

"Listen, I know a pin when I feel one. Any mark on my back, any scratch between the shoulders?"

"Not a thing."

"Tired, I guess. Nervous." He goes over to the open window and pitches the little doll out into the night with all his strength. Damn coincidence, that's all it was. To think otherwise would be to give them their inning. But he wonders what makes him feel so tired just the same—Judy did all the exercising, not he—yet he's felt all in ever since that number tonight.

Out go the lights and she drops off to sleep right with them. He lies very quiet for a while. A little later he gets up, goes into the bathroom where the lights are whitest of all, and stands there looking at himself close to the glass. "Look at your fingernails sometime; look at the whites of your eyes," Staats said. Eddie does. There's a bluish, purplish tinge to his nails that he never noticed before. The whites of his eyes are faintly yellow.

It's warm in New Orleans that night but he shivers a little as he stands there. He doesn't sleep any more that night...

In the morning, his back aches as if he were sixty. But he knows that's from not closing his eyes all night, and not from any magic pins.

"Oh my God!" Judy says, from the other side of the bed. "Look what you've done to him!" She shows him the second page of the *Picayune*. "John Staats, until recently a member of Eddie Bloch's orchestra, committed suicide late yesterday afternoon in full view of dozens of people by rowing himself out into Lake Pontchartrain and jumping overboard. He was alone in the boat at the time. The body was recovered half an hour later."

"I didn't do that," says Eddie grimly. "I've got a rough idea what did, though." Late yesterday afternoon. The night was coming on, and he couldn't face what was coming to him for sponsoring Eddie for giving them all away. Late yesterday afternoon—that meant *he* hadn't left that warning at the dressing-room or left that death-sentence on the bed. He'd been dead himself by then—not black, not white, just yellow.

Eddie waits until Judy's in her shower, then he phones the morgue. "About Johnny Staats. He worked for me until yesterday, so if nobody's claimed the body send it to a funeral parlor at my exp—"

"Somebody's already claimed the remains, Mr. Bloch. First thing this morning. Just waited until the examiner had established suicide beyond a doubt. Some colored organization, old friends of his it seems—"

Judy comes in and remarks: "You look all green in the face."

Eddie thinks: I wouldn't care if he was my worst enemy, I can't let that happen to him! What horrors are going to take place tonight somewhere under the moon? He wouldn't even put cannibalism beyond them. The phone's right at his fingertips, and yet he can't denounce them to the police without involving himself, admitting that he was there, took part at least once. Once that comes out, bang! goes his reputation. He'll never be able to live it down—especially now that he's played the Voodoo Chant and identified himself with it in the minds of the public.

So instead, alone in his room again, he calls the best-known private agency in New Orleans. "I want a bodyguard. Just for tonight. Have him meet me at closing-time at Maxim's. Armed, of course."

It's Sunday and the banks are closed, but his credit's good anywhere. He raises a G in cash. He arranges with a reliable crematorium for a body to be taken charge of late tonight or early in the morning. He'll notify them just where to call for it. Yes, of course! He'll produce the proper authorization from the police. Poor Johnny Staats couldn't get away from "them" in life, but he's going to get away from them in death, all right. That's the least anyone could do for him.

Graham slaps a sawbuck-cover on that night, more to give the waiters room to move around in than anything else, and still the place is choked to the roof. This Voodoo number is a natural, a wow.

But Eddie's back is ready to cave in, while he stands there jogging with his stick. It's all he can do to hold himself straight.

When the racket and the shuffling is over for the night, the private dick is there waiting for him. "Lee is the name."

"Okay, Lee, come with me." They go outside and get in Eddie's Bugatti. They whiz down to the Vieux, scrounge to a stop in the middle of Congo Square, which will still be Congo Square when its official name of Beauregard is forgotten.

"This way," says Eddie, and his bodyguard squirms through the alley after him.

"'Lo, suga' pie," says the elbow-pusher, and for once, to her own surprise as much as anyone else's, gets a tumble.

"'Lo, Eglantine," Eddie's bodyguard remarks in passing. "So you moved?"

They stop in front of the house on the other side of the tunnel. "Now here's what," says Eddie. "We're going to be stopped halfway up these stairs in here by a big lout. Your job is to clean him, tap him if you want, I don't care. I'm going into a room up there, you're going to wait for me at the door. You're here to see that I get out of that room again. We may have to carry the body of a friend of mine down to the street between us. I don't know. It depends on whether it's in the house or not. Got it?"

"Got it."

"Light up. Keep your torch trained over my shouder."

A big, lowering figure looms over them, blocking the narrow stairs, arms and legs spread-eagle in a gesture of malignant embrace, teeth showing, flashing steel in hand. Lee jams Eddie roughly to one side and shoves up past him. "Drop that, boy!" Lee says with slurring indifference, but then he doesn't wait to see if the order's carried out or not. After all, a weapon was raised to two white men. He fires three times, from two feet away and considerably below the obstacle, hits where he aimed to. The bullets shatter both kneecaps and the elbow joint of the arm holding the knife.

"Be a cripple for life now," he remarks with quiet satisfaction. "I'll put him out of his pain." So he crashes the butt of the gun down on the skull of the writhing colossus, in a long arc like the overhead pitch of a baseball. The noise of the shots goes booming up the narrow stairwell to the roof, to mushroom out there in a vast rolling echo.

"Come on, hurry up," says Eddie, "before they have a chance to do away with—"

He lopes on up past the prostrate form, Lee at his heels. "Stand there. Better reload while you're waiting. If I call your name for Pete's sake don't count ten before you come in to me!"

There's a scurrying back and forth and an excited but subdued jabbering going on on the other side of the door. Eddie swings it wide and crashes it closed behind him, leaving Lee on the outside. They all stand rooted to the spot when they see him. The papaloi is there and about six others, not so many as on the night of Eddie's initiation. Probably the rest are waiting outside the city somewhere, in some secret spot, wherever the actual burial, or burning, or— feasting—is to take place.

Papa Benjamin has no juju mask on this time, no animal pelt. There are no gourds in the room, no drum, no transfixed figures ranged against the wall. They were about to move on elsewhere; he just got here in time. Maybe they were waiting for the dark of the moon. The ordinary kitchen chair on which the papaloi was to be carried on their shoulders stands prepared, padded with rags. A row of baskets covered with sacking is ranged along the back wall.

"Where is the body of John Staats?" raps out Eddie. "You claimed it, took it away from the morgue this morning." His eyes are on those baskets, on the bleared razor he catches sight of lying on the floor near them.

"Better far," cackles the old man, "that you had followed him. The mark of doom is on yo' even now—" A growl goes up all around.

"Lee," grates Eddie, "in here!" Lee stands next to him, gun in hand. "Cover me while I take a look around."

"All of you over in that corner there," growls Lee, and kicks viciously at one who is too slow in moving. They huddle there, cower there, glaring. Eddie makes straight for those baskets, whips the covering off the first one. Charcoal. The next. Coffee beans. The next.

Rice. And so on.

Just small baskets that Negro women balance on their heads to sell at the marketplace. He looks at Papa Benjamin, takes out the wad of money he's brought with him. "Where've you got him? Where's he buried? Take us there, show us where it is."

Not a sound, just burning, shriveling hate in waves that you can almost feel. He looks at that razor blade lying there, bleared, not bloody, just matted, dulled, with shreds and threads of something clinging to it. Kicks it away with his foot. "Not here, I guess," he mutters to Lee and moves toward the door.

"What do we do now, boss?" his henchman wants to know.

"Get the hell out of here I guess, where we can breathe some air," Eddie says, and moves on out to the stairs.

Lee is the sort of man who will get what he can out of any situation, no matter what it is. Before he follows Eddie out, he goes over to one of the baskets, stuffs an orange in each coat-pocket, and then prods and pries among them to select a particularly nice one for eating on the spot. There's a thud and the orange goes rolling across the floor like a volleyball. "Mr. Bloch!" he shouts hoarsely. "I've found—him!" And he looks pretty sick.

A deep breath goes up from the corner where the Negroes are. Eddie just stands and stares, and leans back weakly for a minute against the doorpost. From out the layers of oranges in the basket, the five fingers of a hand thrust upward, a hand that ends abruptly, cleanly at the wrist.

"His signet," says Eddie weakly, "there on the little finger—I know it."

"Say the word! Should I shoot?" Lee wants to know.

Eddie shakes his head. "They didn't—he committed suicide. Let's do what we have to—and get out of here!"

Lee turns over one basket after the other. The stuff in them spills and sifts and rolls out upon the floor. But in each there's something else. Bloodless, pallid as fish-flesh. That razor, those shreds clinging to it, Eddie knows now what it was used for. They take one basket, they line it with a verminous blanket from the bed. Then with their bare hands they fill it with what they have found, and close the ends of the blanket over the top of it, and carry it between them out of the room and down the pitch-black stairs, Lee going down backwards with his gun in one hand to cover them from the rear. Lee's swearing like a fiend. Eddie's trying not to think what the purpose, the destination of all those baskets was. The watchman is still out on the stairs, with a concussion.

Back through the lane they struggle and finally put their burden down in the before-dawn stillness of Congo Square. Eddie goes up against a wall and is heartily sick. Then he comes back again and says: "The head—did you notice—?"

"No, we didn't," Lee answers. "Stay here, I'll go back for it. I'm armed. I could stand anything now, after what I just been through."

Lee's gone about five minutes. When he comes back, he's in his shirt, coatless. His coat's rolled up under one arm in a bulky bulge. He bends over the basket, lifts the blanket, replaces it again, and when he straightens up, the bulge in his folded coat is gone. Then he throws the coat away, kicks it away on the ground. "Hidden away in a cupboard," he mutters. "Had to shoot one of 'em through the palm of the hand before they'd come clean. What were they up to?"

"Practice cannibalism maybe, I don't know. I'd rather not think."

"I brought your money back. It didn't seem to square you with them."

Eddie shoves it back at him. "Pay for your suit and your time."

"Aren't you going to tip off the squareheads?"

"I told you he jumped in the lake. I have a copy of the examiner's report in my pocket."

"I know, but isn't there some ordinance against dissecting a body without permission?"

"I can't afford to get mixed up with them, Lee. It would kill my career. We've got what we went there for. Now just forget everything you saw."

The hearse from the crematorium contacts them there in Congo Square. The covered basket's taken on, and what's left of Johnny Staats heads away for a better finish than was coming to him.

"G'night, boss," says Lee. "Anytime you need any other little thing—"

"No," says Eddie. "I'm getting out of New Orleans." His hand is like ice when they shake.

He does. He hands Graham back his contract, and a split week later he's playing New York's newest, in the frantic Fifties. With a white valet. The Chant, of course, is still featured. He has to; it's his chief asset, his biggest draw. It introduces him and signs him off, and in between Judy always dances it for a high-spot. But he can't get rid of that backache that started the night he first played it. First he goes and tries having his back baked for a couple of hours a day under a violet-ray lamp. No improvement.

Then he has himself examined by the biggest specialist in New York. "Nothing there," says the big shot. "Absolutely nothing the matter with you: liver, kidneys, blood—everything perfect. It must be all in your own mind."

"You're losing weight, Eddie," Judy says. "You look bad, darling." His bathroom scales tell him the same thing. Down five pounds a week, sometimes seven, never up an ounce. More experts, X-rays this time, blood analysis, gland treatments, everything from soup to nuts. Nothing doing. And the dull ache, the lassitude, spreads slowly, first to one arm, then to the other.

He takes specimens of everything he eats, not just one day, but every day for weeks, and has them chemically analyzed. Nothing. And he doesn't have to be told that anyway. He knows that even in New Orleans, way back in the beginning, nothing was ever put into his food. Judy ate from the same tray, drank from the same coffeepot he did. Nightly she dances herself into a lather, and yet she's the picture of health.

So that leaves nothing but his mind, just as they all say. "But I don't believe it!" he tells himself. "I don't believe that just sticking pins into a wax doll can hurt me—me or anyone!"

So it isn't his mind at all, but some other mind back there in New Orleans, some other mind *thinking,* wishing, ordering him dead, night and day.

"But it can't be done!" says Eddie. "There's no such thing!"

And yet it's being done; it's happening right under his own eyes. Which leaves only one answer. If going three thousand miles away on dry land didn't help, then going three thousand miles away across the ocean will do the trick. So London next, and the Kit-Kat Club. Down, down, down go the bathroom scales, a little bit each week. The pains spread downward into his thighs. His ribs start showing up here and there. He's dying on his feet. He finds it more comfortable now to walk with a stick—not to be swanky, not to be English—to rest as he goes along. His shoulders ache each night just from waving that lightweight baton at his crew. He has a music-stand built for himself to lean on, keeps it in front of his body, out of sight of the audience while he's conducting, and droops over it. Sometimes he finishes up a number with his head lower than his shoulders, as though he has a rubber spine.

Finally he goes to Reynolds, famous the world over, the biggest alienist in England. "I want to know whether I'm sane or insane." He's under observation for weeks, months; they put him through every known test, and plenty of unknown ones, mental, physical, metabolic. They flash lights in front of his face and watch the pupils of his eyes; they contract to pinheads. They touch the back of his throat with sandpaper; he nearly chokes. They strap him to a chair that goes around and around and does somersaults at so many revolutions per minute, then ask him to walk across the room; he staggers.

Reynolds take plenty of pounds, hands him a report thick as a telephone book, sums it up for him. "You are as normal, Mr. Bloch, as anyone I have ever handled. You're so well-balanced you haven't even got the extra little touch of imagination most actors and musicians have." So it's not his own mind, it's coming from the outside, is it?

The whole thing from beginning to end has taken eighteen months. Trying to out-distance death, with death gaining on him slowly but surely all the time. He's emaciated. There's only one thing left to do now, while he's still able to crawl aboard a ship—that's to get back where the whole thing started. New York, London, Paris, haven't been able to save him. His only salvation, now, lies in the hands of a decrepit colored man skulking in the Vieux Carré of New Orleans.

He drags himself there, to that same half-ruined house, without a bodyguard, not caring now whether they kill him or not, almost wishing they would and get it over with. But that would be too easy an out, it seems. The colossus Lee crippled that night shuffles out to him between two sticks, recognizes him, breathes undying hate into his face, but doesn't lift a finger to harm him. The spirits are doing the job better than he could ever hope to. Their mark is on this man, woe betide anyone who comes between them and their hellish satisfaction. Eddie Bloch totters up the stairs unopposed, his back as safe from a knife as if he wore steel armor. Behind him the guard sprawls upon the stairs to lubricate his long-awaited hour of satisfaction with rum—and oblivion.

He finds the old man alone there in the room.

"Take it off me," says Eddie brokenly. "Give me my life back—I'll do anything, anything you say!"

"What has been done cannot be undone. Do you think the spirits of the earth and of the air, of fire and water, know the meaning of forgiveness?"

"Intercede for me, then. You brought it about. Here's money, I'll give you twice as much, all I earn, all I ever hope to earn—"

"You have desecrated the obiah. Death has been on you from that night. All over the world and in the air above the earth you have mocked the spirits with the chant that summons them. Nightly your wife dances it. The only reason she has not shared your doom is that she does not know the meaning of what she does. You do. You were here among us."

Eddie goes down on his knees, scrapes along the floor after the old man, tries to tug at the garments he wears. "Kill me right now, then, and be done with it. I can't stand any more—" He bought the gun only that day, was going to do it himself at first, but found he couldn't. A minute ago he pleaded for his life, now he's pleading for death. "It's loaded, all you have to do is shoot. Look! I'll close my eyes—I'll write a note and sign it, that I did it myself—"

He tries to thrust it into the witch-doctor's hand, tries to close the bony, shriveled fingers around it, tries to point it at himself. The old man throws it down, away from him. Cackles gleefully, "Death will come, but differently—slowly, oh, so slowly!"

Eddie just lies there flat on his face, sobbing drily. The old man spits, kicks at him weakly. He pulls himself up somehow, stumbles toward the door. He isn't even strong enough to get it open at the first try. It's that little thing that brings it on. Something touches his foot, he looks, stoops for the gun, turns. Thought is quick but the old man's mind is even quicker. Almost before the thought is there, the old man knows what's coming. In a flash, scuttling like a crab, he has shifted around to the other side of the bed, to put something between them. Instantly the situation's reversed, the fear has left Eddie and is on the old man now. He's lost the aggressive. For a minute only, but that minute is all Eddie needs. His mind beams out like a diamond, like a lighthouse through a fog. The gun roars, jolting his weakened body down to his shoes. The old man falls flat across the bed, his head too far over, dangling down over the side of it like an overripe pear. The bed frame sways gently with his weight for a minute, and then it's over...

Eddie stands there, still off balance from the kickback. So it was as easy as all that! Where's all his magic now? Strength, willpower flood back through him as if a faucet was suddenly turned on. The little smoke there was can't get out of the sealed-up room, it hangs there in thin layers. Suddenly he's shaking his fist at the dead thing on the bed. "I'm gonna live now! I'm gonna live, see?" He gets the door open, sways with it for a minute. Then he's feeling his way down the stairs, past the unconscious guard, mumbling it over and over but low, "Gonna live now, gonna live!"

The Commissioner mops his face as if he were in the steam room of a Turkish bath. He exhales like an oxygen tank. "Judas, Joseph, and Mary, Mr. Bloch, what a story! Wish I hadn't asked you; I won't sleep tonight." Even after the accused has been led from the room, it takes him some time to get over it. The upper right-hand drawer of his desk helps some—just two fingers. So does opening the windows and letting in a lot of sunshine.

Finally he picks up the phone and gets down to business. "Who've you got out there that's absolutely without a nerve in his body? I mean a guy with so little feeling he could sit on a hatpin and turn it into a paperclip. Oh yeah, that Cajun, Desjardins, I know him. He's the one goes around striking parlor-matches off the soles of stiffs. Well, send him in here."

"No, stay outside," wheezes Papa Benjamin through the partly open door to his envoy. "I'se communin' with the obiah and yo' unclean, been drunk all last night and today. Deliver the summons. Reach yo' hand in to me, once fo' every token, yo' knows how many to take."

The crippled Negro thrusts his huge hand through the aperture, and from behind the door the papaloi places a severed chicken claw in his upturned palm. A claw bound with a red rag. The messenger disposes of it about his tattered clothing, thrusts his hand in for another. Twenty times the act is repeated, then he lets his arm hang stiffly at his side. The door starts closing slowly. "Papaloi," whines the figure on the outside of it, "why you hide yo' face from me, is the spirits angry?"

There's a flicker of suspicion in his yellow eyeballs in the dimness, however. Instantly the opening of the door widens. Papa Benjamin's familiar wrinkled face thrusts out at him, malignant eyes crackling like fuses. "Go!" shrills the old man, "'liver my summons. Is you want me to bring a spirit down on you?" The messenger totters back. The door slams.

The sun goes down and it's night-time in New Orleans. The moon rises, midnight chimes from St. Louis Cathedral, and hardly has the last note died away than a gruesome swampland whistle sounds outside the deathly still house. A fat Negress, basket on arm, comes trudging up the stairs a moment later, opens the door, goes in to the papaloi, closes it again, traces an invisible mark on it with her forefinger and kisses it. Then she turns and her eyes widen with surprise. Papa Benjamin is in bed, covered up to the neck with filthy rags. The familiar candles are all lit, the bowl for the blood, the sacrificial knife, the magic powders, all the paraphernalia of the ritual are laid out in readiness, but they are ranged about the bed instead of at the opposite end of the room as usual.

The old man's head, however, is held high above the encumbering rags, his beady eyes gaze back at her unflinchingly, the familiar semi-circle of white wool rings his crown, his ceremonial mask is at his side. "I am a little tired, my daughter," he tells her. His eyes stray to the tiny wax image of Eddie Bloch under the candles, hairy with pins, and hers follow them. "A doomed one, nearing his end, came here last night thinking I could be killed like other men. He shot a bullet from a gun at me. I blew my breath at it, it stopped in the air, turned around, and went back in the gun again. But it tired me to blow so hard, strained my voice a little."

A revengeful gleam lights up the woman's broad face. "And he'll die soon, papaloi?"

"Soon," cackles the wizened figure in the bed. The woman gnashes her teeth and hugs herself delightedly. She opens the top of her basket and allows a black hen to escape and flutter about the room.

When all twenty have assembled, men and women, old and young, the drum and the gourds begin to beat, the low wailing starts, the orgy gets under way. Slowly they dance around the three sides of the bed at first, then faster, faster, lashing themselves to a frenzy, tearing at their own and each other's clothes, drawing blood with knives and fingernails, eyes rolling in an ecstasy that colder races cannot know. The sacrifices, feathered and furred, that have been fastened to the two lower posts of the bed squawk and flutter and fly up and down in a barnyard panic. There is a small monkey among them tonight, clawing, biting, hiding his face in his hands like a frightened child. A bearded Negro, nude torso glistening like patent leather, seizes one of the frantic fowls, yanks it loose from its moorings, and holds it out toward the witch-doctor with both hands. "We'se thirsty, papaloi, we'se thirsty fo' the blood of ou' enemies."

The others take up the cry. "We'se hung'y, papaloi, fo' the bones of ou' enemies!"

Papa Benjamin nods his head in time to the rhythm.

"Sac'fice, papaloi, sac'fice!"

Papa Benjamin doesn't seem to hear them.

Then back go the rags in a gray wave and out comes the arm at last. Not the gnarled brown toothpick arm of Papa Benjamin, but a bulging arm thick as a piano leg, cuffed in serge, white at the wrist, ending in a regulation police revolver with the clip off. The erstwhile witch-doctor's on his feet at a bound, standing erect atop the bed, back to the wall, slowly fanning his score of human devils with the mouth of his gun, left to right, then right to left again, evenly, unhurriedly. The resonant bellow of a bull comes from his wizened slit of a mouth instead of papaloi's cracked falsetto. "Back against that wall there, all of you! Throw down them knives and jiggers!"

But they're slow to react; the swift drop from ecstasy to stupefaction can't register right away. None of them are over-bright anyway or they wouldn't be here. Mouths hang open, the wailing stops, the drums and gourds fall still, but they're still packed close about this sudden changeling in their midst, with the familiar shriveled face of Papa Benjamin and the thick-set body, business suit of a white man— too close for comfort. Blood-lust and religious mania don't know fear of a gun. It takes a cool head for that, and the only cool head in the room is the withered coconut atop the broad shoulders behind that gun. So he shoots twice, and a woman at one end of the semicircle, the drum beater, and a man at the other end, the one still holding the sacrificial fowl, drop in their tracks with a double moan. Those in the middle slowly draw back step by step across the room, all eyes on the figure reared up on the bed. An instant's carelessness, the wavering of an eye, and they'll be in on him in a body. He reaches up with his free hand and rips the dead witch-doctor's features from his face, to breathe better, see better. They dissolve into a crumpled rag before the blacks' terrified eyes, like a stocking-cap coming off someone's head—a mixture of paraffin and fibre, called moulage—a death-mask taken from the corpse's own face, reproducing even the fine lines of the skin and its natural color. Moulage. And behind them is the grinning, slightly perspiring, lantern-jawed face of Detective Jacques Desjardins, who doesn't believe in spirits unless they're under a neat little label. And outside the house sounds the twenty-first whistle of the evening, but not a swampland sound this time; a long, cold, keen blast to bring figures out of the shadows and doorways that have waited there patiently all night.

Then the door bursts inward and the police are in the room. The prisoners, two of them dangerously wounded, are pushed and carried downstairs to join the crippled door-guard, who had been in custody for the past hour, and single file, tied together with ropes, they make their way through the long tortuous alley out into Congo Place.

In the early hours of that same morning, just a little more than twenty-four hours after Eddie Bloch first staggered into Police Headquarters with his strange story, the whole thing is cooked, washed, and bottled. The Commissioner sits in his office listening attentively to Desjardins. And spread out on his desk as strange an array of amulets, wax images, bunches of feathers, balsam leaves, *ouangas* (charms of nail parings, hair clippings, dried blood, powdered roots), green mildewed coins dug up from coffins in graveyards, as that room has ever seen before. All this is State's Evidence now, to be carefully labeled and docketed for the use of the prosecuting attorney when the proper time comes. "And this," explains Desjardins, indicating a small dusty bottle, "is methylene blue, the chemist tells me. It's the only modern thing we got out of the place, found it lying forgotten with a lot of rubbish in a corner that looked like it hadn't been disturbed for years. What it was doing there or what they wanted with it I don't—"

"Wait a minute," interrupts the Commissioner eagerly. "That fits in with something poor Bloch told me last nght. He noticed a bluish color under his fingernails and a yellowness to his eyeballs, but *only* after he'd been initiated that first night. This stuff probably had something to do with it. An injection of it must have been given him that night in some way without his knowing it. Don't you get the idea? It floored him just the way they wanted it to. He mistook the signs of it for a giveaway that he had colored blood. It was the opening wedge. It broke down his disbelief, started his mental resistance to crumbling. That was all they needed, just to get a foothold in his mind. Mental suggestion did the rest, has been doing it ever since. If you ask me, they pulled the same stunt on Staats originally. I don't believe he had colored blood any more than Bloch has. And as a matter of fact the theory that it shows up in that way generations later is all the bunk anyway, they tell me."

"Well," says Dij, looking down at his own grimy nails, "if you're just going to judge by appearances that way, I'm full-blooded Zulu."

His overlord just looks at him, and if he didn't have such a poker face, one might be tempted to read admiration or at least approval into the look. "Must have been a pretty tight spot for a minute with all of them around while you put on your act."

"Nah," answers Dij. "I didn't mind."

Eddie Bloch, the murder charge against him quashed two months ago, and the population of the State Penitentiary increased only this past week by the admission of twenty-three ex-voodoo-worshippers for terms varying from two to ten years, steps up on the platform at Maxim's for a return engagement. Eddie's pale and washed-out looking, but climbing slowly back up through the hundred-and-twenties again to his former weight. The ovation he gets ought to do anyone's heart good, the way they clap and stamp and stand up and cheer. And at that, his name was kept out of the recently concluded trial. Desjardins and his mates did all the states-

138

witnessing necessary.

The theme he comes in on now is something sweet and harmless. Then a waiter comes up and hands him a request. Eddie shakes his head. "No, not in our repertoire any more." He goes on leading. Another request comes, and another. Suddenly someone shouts it out at him, and in a second the whole place has taken up the cry. "The Voodoo Chant! Give us the Voodoo Chant!"

His face gets whiter than it is already, but he turns and tries to smile at them and shake his head. They won't quit, the music can't be heard, and he has to tap a lay-off. From all over the place, like a cheering section at a football game. "We want the Voodoo Chant! We want—!"

Judy's at his side. "What's the matter with 'em anyway?" he asks. "Don't they know what that thing's done to me?"

"Play it, Eddie, don't be foolish," she urges. "Now's the time, break the spell once and for all, prove to yourself that it can't hurt you. If you don't do it now, you'll never get over the idea. It'll stay with you all your life. Go ahead. I'll dance it just like I am."

"Okay," he says.

He taps. It's been quite some time, but he can rely on his outfit. Slow and low like thunder far away, coming nearer. *Boom-putta-putta-boom!* Judy whirls out behind him, lets out the first preliminary screech. *Eeyaeeya!*

She hears a commotion in back of her and stops as suddenly as she began. Eddie Bloch's fallen flat on his face and doesn't move again after that.

They all know, somehow. There's an inertness, a finality about it that tells them. The dancers wait a minute, mill about, then melt away in a hush. Judy Jarvis doesn't scream, doesn't cry, just stands there staring, wondering. That last thought—did it come from inside his own mind just now—or outside? Was it two months on its way, from the other side of the grave, looking for him, looking for him, until it found him tonight when he played the Chant once more and laid his mind open to Africa? No policeman, no detective, no doctor, no scientist, will ever be able to tell her. Did it come from inside or from outside? All she says is: "Stand close to me, boys—real close to me, I'm afraid of the dark."

*C*alled the Poe of the Twentieth Century, Cornell Woolrich (1903–1968) had an unstable childhood, spending half of *each year with his socialite mother in his native New York City and half with his father, a civil engineer, in revolution-torn Central America. Shy, withdrawn, mother-dominated, Woolrich dropped out of Columbia University when his second novel, **Children of the Ritz** (1927), won a $10,000 First Prize in a contest sponsored by a movie studio and **College Humor** magazine, to become a full-time writer. A Hollywood marriage failed and Woolrich spent the rest of his life in hotel rooms with his mother. The Depression led him to suspense writing, first in the pulps and then in 1940 with a series of six novels beginning with **The Bride Wore Black.** The field made him famous and rich; his tense, doom-haunted stories were ideal for movies and TV (the **Alfred Hitchcock Show** ran many), and by the end of his life Woolrich was a millionaire. Someone once said that Hell is other people; Woolrich's haunted and hunted heroes knew that Hell is the self. His stories are set in a universe that is not merely indifferent but nightmarishly hostile to man. His best work is probably **Night Has a Thousand Eyes** (1945) and "Three O'Clock," a novelette called "the most powerful suspense story anyone ever wrote" (F.M. Nevins, Jr.), in which a man intending to kill his wife with a time bomb is tied and gagged by burglars and left to watch the clock tick toward explosion. A substantial part of his work was dark fantasy; the best are collected in **The Fantastic Stories of Cornell Woolrich** (Southern Illinois Univ., 1981). His best short mysteries can be found in **Nightwebs** (Harper & Row, 1971); **Angels of Darkness** (Mysterious Press, 1978); and **Darkness at Dawn** (Southern Illinois Univ., 1985).*

THE FIREPLACE

HENRY S. WHITEHEAD

When the Planter's Hotel in Jackson, Mississippi, burned to the ground in the notable fire of 1922, the loss to that section of the South could not be measured in terms of that ancient hostelry's former grandeur. The days had indeed long passed when a Virginia ham was therein stewed in no medium meaner than good white wine; and as the rambling old building was heavily insured, the owners suffered no great material loss. The real loss was the community's, in the death by fire of two of its prominent citizens, Lieutenant-Governor Frank Stacpoole and Mayor Cassius L. Turner. These gentlemen, just turning elderly, had been having a reunion in the hotel with two of their old associates, Judge Varney J. Baker of Memphis, Tennessee, and the Honorable Valdemar Peale, a prominent Georgian, from Atlanta. Thus, two other Southern cities had a share in the mourning, for Judge Baker and Mr. Peale both likewise perished in the flames. The fire took place just before Christmas on the twenty-third of December, and among the many sympathetic and regretful comments which ensued upon this holocaust was the many-times-repeated conjecture that these gentlemen had been keeping a kind of Christmas anniversary, a fact which added no little to the general feeling of regret and horror.

On the request of these prominent gentlemen, the hotel management had cleared out and furnished a second floor room with a great fireplace, a room for long used only for storage, but for which, the late mayor and lieutenant-governor had assured them, the four old cronies cherished a certain sentiment. The fire, which gained headway despite the truly desperate efforts of the occupants of the room, had its origin in the fireplace, and it was believed that the four, who were literally burned to cinders, had been trapped. The fire had started, it appeared, about half an hour before midnight, when everybody else in the hotel had retired. No other occupant of the house suffered from its effects, beyond a few incidental injuries sustained in the hurried departure at dead of night from the blazing old firetrap.

Some ten years before this regrettable incident ended the long and honorable career of this one-time famous hostelry, a certain Mr. James Callender, breaking a wearisome journey north at Jackson, turned into the hospitable vestibule of the Planter's, with a sigh of relief. He had been shut up for nine hours in the mephitic atmosphere of a soft-coal train. He was tired, hungry, thirsty, and begrimed with soot.

Two grinning negro porters deposited his ample luggage, toted from the railway station in the reasonable hope of a large emolument, promised by their patron's prosperous appearance and the imminence of the festival season of Christmas. They received their reward and left Mr. Callender in the act of signing the hotel register.

"Can you let me have number twenty-eight?" he enquired of the clerk. "That, I believe, is the room with the large fireplace, is it not? My friend, Mr. Tom Culbertson of Sweetbriar, recommended it to me in case I should be stopping here."

Number twenty-eight was fortunately vacant, and the new guest was shortly in occupation, a great fire, at his orders, roaring up the chimney, and he himself engaged in preparing for the luxury of a hot bath.

After a leisurely dinner of the sort for which the old hotel was famous, Mr. Callender first sauntered slowly through the lobby, enjoying the first fragrant whiffs of a good cigar. Then, seeing no familiar face which gave promise of a conversation, he ascended to his room, replenished the fire, and got himself ready for a solitary evening. Soon, in pajamas, bathrobe, and comfortable slippers, he settled himself in a comfortable chair at just the right distance from the fire and began to read a new book which he had brought with him. His dinner had been a late one, and it was about half-past nine when he really settled to his book. It was Arthur Machen's *House of Souls,* and Mr. Callender soon found himself absorbed in the eery ecstasy of reading for the first time a remarkable work which transcended all his previous secondhand experiences of the occult. It had, he found, anything but a soporific effect upon him. He was reading carefully, well into the book, with all his faculties alert, when he was interrupted by a knock on the door of his room.

Mr. Callender stopped reading, marked his place, and rose to open the door. He was wondering who should summon him at such an hour. He glanced at his watch on the bureau in passing and was surprised to note that it was eleven-twenty. He had been reading for nearly two hours, steadily. He opened the door, and was surprised to find no one in the corridor. He stepped through the doorway and glanced right and then left. There were, he observed, turns in both directions at short distances from his door, and Mr. Callender, whose mind was trained in the sifting of evidence, worked out an instantaneous explanation in his mind. The occupant of a double room (so he guessed) had returned late, and, mistaking the room, had knocked to apprize his fellow occupant of his return. Seeing at once that he had knocked prematurely, on the wrong door, the person had bolted around one of the corners to avoid an awkward explanation!

Mr. Callender, smiling at this whimsical idea of his, turned back into his room and shut the door behind him.

A gentleman was sitting in the place he had vacated. Mr. Callender stopped short and stared at this intruder. The man who had appropriated his comfortable chair was a few years older than himself, it appeared—say about thirty-five. He was tall, well-proportioned, and very well dressed, although there seemed to Mr. Callender's hasty scrutiny something indefinably odd about his clothes.

The two men looked at each other appraisingly for the space of a few seconds, in silence, and then abruptly Mr. Callender saw what was wrong with the other's appearance. He was dressed in the fashion of about fifteen years back, in the style of the late nineties. No one was wearing such a decisive-looking piccadilly collar, nor such a huge puff tie which concealed every vestige of the linen except the edges of the cuffs. These, on Mr. Callender's uninvited guest, were immaculate and round, and held in place by a pair of large, round, cut-cameo black buttons.

The strange gentleman, without rising, broke the silence in a well-modulated voice with a deprecatory wave of a very well-kept hand.

"I owe you an apology, sir. I trust that you will accept what amends I can make. This room has for me a peculiar interest which you will understand if you will allow me to speak further, but for the present I confine myself to asking your pardon."

This speech was delivered in so frank and pleasing a fashion that Mr. Callender could take no offense at the intrusion of the speaker.

"You are quite welcome, sir, but perhaps you will be good enough to continue, as you suggest. I confess to being mightily puzzled as to the precise manner in which you came to be here. The only way of approach is through the door, and I'll take my oath no one came through it. I heard a knock, went to the door, and there was no one there."

"I imagine I would do well to begin at the beginning," said the stranger, gravely. "The facts are somewhat unusual, as you will see when I have related them; otherwise I should hardly be here, at this time of night, and trespassing upon your good nature. That this is no mere prank I beg that you will believe."

"Proceed, sir, by all means," returned Mr. Callender, his curiosity aroused and keen. He drew up another chair and seated himself on the side of the fireplace opposite the stranger, who at once began his explanation.

"My name is Charles Bellinger, a fact which I will ask you kindly to note and keep well in mind. I come from Biloxi, down on the Gulf, and unlike yourself, I am a Southerner, a native of Mississippi. You see, sir, I know something about you, or at least who you are."

Mr. Callender inclined his head, and the stranger waved his hand again, this time as if to express acknowledgment of an introduction.

"I may as well add to this, since it explains several matters, though in itself sounding somewhat odd, that actually I am dead."

Mr. Bellinger, at this astounding statement, met Mr. Callender's facial expression of amazement with a smile clearly meant to be reassuring, and again, with a kind of unspoken eloquence, waved his expressive hand.

"Yes, sir, what I tell you is the plain truth. I passed out of this life in this room where we are sitting almost exactly sixteen years ago. My death occurred on the twenty-third of December. That will be precisely sixteen years ago the day after tomorrow. I came here tonight for the express purpose of telling you the facts, if you will bear with me and suspend your judgment as to my sanity. It was I who knocked at your door, and I passed through it, and, so to speak, through you, my dear sir!

"On the late afternoon of the day I have mentioned I arrived in this hotel in company with Mr. Frank Stacpoole, an acquaintance, who still lives here in Jackson. I met him as I got off the train, and invited him to come here with me for dinner. Being a bachelor, he made no difficulty, and just after dinner we met in the lobby another man named Turner—Cassius L. Turner, also a Jacksonian—who proposed a game of cards and offered to secure two more gentlemen to complete the party. I invited him to bring them here to my room, and Stacpoole and I came up in advance to get things ready for an evening of poker.

"Shortly afterwards Mr. Turner and the two other gentlemen arrived. One of them was named Baker, the other was Mr. Valdemar Peale, of Atlanta, Georgia. You recognize his name, I perceive, as I had expected you would. Mr. Peale is now a very prominent man. He has gone far since that time. If you happened to be better acquainted here you would know that Stacpoole and Turner are also men of very considerable prominence. Baker, who lives in Memphis, Tennessee, is likewise a well-known man in his community and state.

"Peale, it appeared, was Stacpoole's brother-in-law, a fact which I had not previously known, and all four were well acquainted with each other. I was introduced to the two newcomers and we commenced to play poker.

"Somewhat to my embarrassment, since I was both the host and the 'stranger' of the party, I won steadily from the very beginning. Mr. Peale was the heaviest loser, and although as the evening wore on he sat with compressed lips and made no comment, it was plain that he was taking his considerable losses rather hardly.

"Not long after eleven o'clock a most unfortunate incident took place. I had in no way suspected that I was not among gentlemen. I had begun, you see, by knowing only Stacpoole, and even with him my acquaintance was only casual.

"At the time I mention there began a round of jack-pots, and the second of these I opened with a pair of kings and a pair of fours. Hoping to better my hand I discarded the fours, with the odd cards, and drew to the pair of kings, hoping for a third. I was fortunate, I obtained not only the third king but with it a pair of eights. Thus, equipped with a full house, I considered my hand likely to be the best, and when, within two rounds of betting, the rest had laid down their hands, the pot lay between Peale and me. Peale, I noticed, had also thrown down three cards, and every chance indicated that I had him beaten. I forced him to call me after a long series of raises back and forth; and when he laid down his hand he was holding four fours!

"You see? He had picked up my discard.

"Wishing to give Peale the benefit of any possible doubt, I declared the matter at once, for one does not lightly accuse a gentleman of cheating at cards, especially here in the South. It was possible, though far from likely, that there had been a mistake. The dealer might for once have laid down his draw on the table, although he had consistently handed out the cards as we dealt in turn all the evening. To imply further that I regarded the matter as nothing worse than a mistake, I offered at once to allow the considerable pot, which I had really won, to lie over to the next hand.

"I had risen slightly out of my chair as I spoke, and before anyone could add a word, Peale leaned over the table and stabbed me with a bowie knife which I had not even seen him draw, so rapid was his action. He struck upwards, slantingly, and the blade, entering my body just below the ribs, cut my right lung nearly in two. I sank down limp across the table, and within a few seconds had coughed myself almost noiselessly to death.

"The actual moment of dissolution was painful to a degree. It was as if the permanent part of me, 'myself'—my soul, if you will—snapped abruptly away from that distorted thing which sprawled prone across the disordered table and which no longer moved.

"Dispassionately, then, the something which continued to be myself (though now, of course, dissociated from what had been my vehicle of expression, my body) looked on and apprehended all that followed.

"For a few moments there was utter silence. Then Turner, in a hoarse, constrained voice, whispered to Peale: 'You've done for yourself now, you unmentionable fool!'

"Peale sat in silence, the knife, which he had automatically withdrawn from the wound, still grasped in his hand, and what had been my life's blood slowly dripping from it and gradually congealing as it fell upon a disarranged pile of cards.

"Then, quite without warning, Baker took charge of the situation. He had kept very quiet and played a very conservative game throughout the evening.

"'This affair calls for careful handling,' he drawled, 'and if you will take my advice I think it can be made into a simple case of disappearance. Bellinger comes from Biloxi. He is not well known here.' Then, rising and gathering the attention of the others, he continued: 'I am going down to the hotel kitchen for a short time. While I am gone, keep the door shut, keep quiet, and clear up the room, leaving *this* (he indicated my body) where it lies. You, Stacpoole, arrange the furniture in the room as nearly as you can remember how it looked when you first came in. You, Turner, make up a big fire. You needn't begin that just yet,' he threw at Peale, who had begun nervously to cleanse the blade of his knife on a piece of newspaper; and with this cryptic remark he disappeared through the door and was gone.

"The others, who all appeared somewhat dazed, set about their appointed tasks silently. Peale, who seemed unable to leave the vicinity of the table, at which he kept throwing glances, straightened up the chairs, replaced them where they had been, and then gathered up the cards and other debris from the table, and threw these into the now blazing fire which Turner was rapidly feeding with fresh wood.

"Within a few minutes Baker returned as unobtrusively as he had left, and after carefully fastening the door and approaching the table, gathered the three others about him and produced from under his coat an awkward and hastily wrapped package of newspapers. Unfastening this he produced three heavy kitchen knives.

"I saw that Turner went white as Baker's idea dawned upon his consciousness. I now understood what Baker had meant when he told Peale to defer the cleansing of his bowie knife! It was, as plans go, a very practical scheme which he had evolved. The body—the *corpus delicti,* as I believe you gentlemen of the law call it—was an extremely awkward fact. It was a fact which had to be accounted for, unless—well, Baker had clearly perceived that *there must be no corpus delicti!*

"He held a hurried, low-voiced conversation with the others, from the immediate effect of which all, even Peale, at first drew back. I need not detail it to you. You will have already apprehended what Baker had in mind. There was the roaring fire in the fireplace. That was his means of making certain that there would remain no *corpus delicti* in that room when the others left. Without such evidence, that is, the actual body of the murdered man, there could be as you are of course well aware, no prosecution, because there would be no proof that the murder had even been committed. I should simply have 'disappeared.' He had seen all that, and the opportunity which the fireplace afforded for carrying out his plan, all at once. But the fireplace, while large, was not large enough to accommodate the body of a man intact. Hence his hurried and stealthy visit to the hotel kitchen.

"The men looked up from their conference. Peale was trembling palpably. The sweat streamed from Turner's face. Stacpoole seemed unaffected, but I did not fail to observe that the hand which he reached out for one of the great meat knives shook violently, and that he was the first to turn his head aside when Baker, himself pale and with set face, gingerly picked up from the table one of the stiffening hands...

"Within an hour and a quarter (for the fireplace drew as well then as it does tonight) there was not a vestige left of the *corpus delicti,* except the teeth.

"Baker appeared to think of everything. When the fire had pretty well burned itself out, and consumed what had been placed within it piecemeal, he remade it, and within its heart placed such charred remnants of the bones as had not been completely incinerated the first time. Eventually all the incriminating evidence had been consumed. It was as if I had never existed!

"My clothes, of course, had been burned. When the four, now haggard with their ordeal, had completed the burning process, another clearing-up and final re-arrangement of the room was undertaken. Various newspapers which they had been carrying in their coat pockets were used to cleanse the table. The knives, including Peale's, were washed and scrubbed, the water poured out and the wash-basin thoroughly scoured. No blood had got upon the carpet.

"My not inconsiderable winnings, as well as the coin and currency which had been in my possession, were then cold-bloodedly divided among these four rascals, for such I had for some time now recognized them as being. There arose then the problem of the disposal of my other belongings. There was my watch, pocket-knife, and several old seals which had belonged to my grandfather and which I had been accustomed to wear on the end of the chain in the pocket opposite that in which I carried my watch. There were my studs, scarf-pin, cuff-buttons, two rings, and lastly, my teeth. These had been laid aside at the time when Baker had carefully raked the charred but indestructible teeth out of the embers of the first fire."

At this point in the narrative, Mr. Bellinger paused and passed one of his eloquent hands through the hair on top of his head in a reflective gesture. Mr. Callender observed what he had not before clearly noted, that his guest possessed a pair of extraordinarily long, thin hands, very muscular, the hands of an artist and also of a man of determination and action. He particularly observed that the index fingers were almost if not quite as long as the middle fingers. The listener, who had been unable to make up his mind upon the question of the sanity of him who had presented this extraordinary narrative in so calm and convincing a fashion, viewed these hands indicative of so strong a character with the greatest interest. Mr. Bellinger resumed his narrative.

"There was some discussion about the disposal of all these things.

The consensus was that they must be concealed, since they could not easily be destroyed. If I had been one of those men I should have insisted upon throwing them into the river at the earliest opportunity. They could have been carried out of the room by any one of the group with the greatest ease and with no chance of detection, since altogether they took up very little room, but this simple plan seemed not to occur to them. Perhaps they had exhausted their ingenuity in the horrible task just finished and were over-anxious to depart. They decided only upon the necessity of disposal of these trinkets, and the actual disposition was haphazard. This was a method which I need not describe because I think it desirable to show them to you."

Mr. Bellinger rose and led the way to a corner of the room, closely followed by the amazed Callender. Bellinger pointed to the precise corner.

"Although I am for the present materialized," he remarked, "you will probably understand that this whole proceeding is in the nature of a severe psychic strain upon me and my resources. It is quite out of the question for me to do certain things. Managing to knock at the door took it out of me, rather, but I wished to give you as much warning of my presence as I could. Will you kindly oblige me by lifting the carpet at this point?"

Mr. Callender worked his fingers nervously under the corner of the carpet and pulled. The tacks yielded after several hard pulls, and the corner of the carpet came up, revealing a large piece of heavy tin which had been tacked down over an ancient rat-hole.

"Pull up the tin, too, if you please," requested Mr. Bellinger. The tin presented a more difficult task than had the carpet, but Mr. Callender, now thoroughly intrigued, made short work of it, though at the expense of two broken blades of his pocket-knife. At Mr. Bellinger's further direction, inserting his hand, he found and drew out a packet of cloth, which proved on examination to have been fabricated out of a trousers pocket lining. The cloth was rotted and brittle, and Mr. Callender carried it carefully over to the table and laid it down, and, emptying it out between them, checked off the various articles which Mr. Bellinger had named. The round cuff-buttons came last, and as he held these in his hand, he looked at Mr. Bellinger's wrists. Mr. Bellinger smiled and pulled down his cuffs, holding out his hands in the process, and Mr. Callender again noted carefully their peculiarities, the long, muscular fingers being especially conspicuous, thus seen under the direct light of the electric lamp. The cuff-buttons, he noted, were absolutely identical.

"Perhaps you will oblige me by putting the whole collection in your pocket," suggested Mr. Bellinger. Then, smiling, as Mr. Callender, not unnaturally, hesitated: "Take them, my dear man, take them freely. They're really mine to give, you know!"

Mr. Callender stepped over to the wardrobe where his clothes hung, and placed the packet in his coat pocket. When he returned to the vicinity of the fireplace, his guest had already resumed his seat.

"I trust," he said, "that despite the very singular—I may say, *bizarre*—character of my narrative and especially the statement with which I thought best to begin it, you will have given me your credence. It is uncommon to be confronted with the recital of such an experience as I have related to you, and it is not everybody who is—may I say privileged?—to carry on an extended conversation with a man who has been dead sixteen years!

"My object may possibly have suggested itself to you. These men have escaped all consequences of their act. They are, as I think you will not deny, four thorough rascals. They are at large and even in positions of responsibility, trust and prominence in their several communities. You are a lawyer, a man held in high esteem for your professional skill and personal integrity. I ask you, then, will you undertake to bring these men to justice? You should be able to reproduce the salient points of my story. You have seen proofs in the shape of the articles now in your coat pocket. There is the fact of my disappearance. That made a furor at the time, and has never been explained or cleared up. You have the evidence of the hotel register for my being here on that date and it would not be hard to prove that these men were in my company. But above all else, I would pin my faith for a conviction upon the mere recounting in the presence of these four, duly subpoenaed, of my story as I have told it to you. That would fasten their guilt upon them to the satisfaction of any judge and jury. They would be crying aloud for mercy and groveling in abject superstitious fear long before you had finished the account of precisely what they had done. Or, three of them could be confronted with an alleged confession made by the other. Will you undertake to right this festering wrong, Mr. Callender, and give me peace? Your professional obligation to promote justice and set wrong right should conspire with your character to cause you to agree."

"I will do so, with all my heart," replied Mr. Callender, holding out his hand.

But before the other could take it, there came another knocking on the door of the hotel room. Slightly startled, Mr. Calldner went to the door and threw it open. One of the hotel servants reminded him that he had asked to be called, and that it was the hour specified. Mr.

Callender thanked and feed the man, and turning back into the room found himself alone.

He went to the fireplace and sat down. He looked fixedly at the smoldering fire in the grate. He went over to the wardrobe and felt in his coat pocket in search of negative evidence that he had been dreaming, but his hand encountered the bag which had been the lining of a trousers pocket. He drew it out and spread a second time that morning on the table the various articles which it contained.

After an early breakfast Mr. Callender asked for permission to examine the register for the year 1896. He found that Charles Bellinger of Biloxi had registered on the afternoon of the twenty-third of December and had been assigned room twenty-eight. He had no time for further enquiries, and, thanking the obliging clerk, he hastened to the railway station and resumed his journey north.

During the journey his mind refused to occupy itself with anything except his strange experience. He reached his destination in a state of profound preoccupation.

As soon as his professional engagements allowed him the leisure to do so, he began his enquiries by having looked up the owners of those names which were deeply imprinted in his memory. He was obliged to stop there because an unprecedented quantity of new legal business claimed his more immediate attention. He was aware that this particular period in his professional career was one vital to his future, and he slaved painstakingly at the affairs of his clients. His diligence was rewarded by a series of conspicuous legal successes, and his reputation became greatly enhanced. This heavy preoccupation could not fail to dull somewhat the sharp impression which the adventure in the hotel bedroom had made upon his mind, and the contents of the trousers pocket remained locked in his safe-deposit box undisturbed while he settled the affairs of the Rockland Oil Corporation and fought through the Appellate Division the conspicuous case of *Burnet vs. De Castro, et al.*

It was in the pursuit of a vital piece of evidence in this last-named case that his duties called him South again. Having obtained the evidence, he started home, and again found it expedient to break the long journey northward, at Jackson. It was not, though, until he was actually signing the register that he noted that it was the twenty-third of December, the actual date with which Mr. Bellinger's singular narrative had been concerned.

He did not ask for any particular room this time. He felt a chill of vague apprehension, as if there awaited him an accounting for some laxity, a feeling which recalled the occasional lapses of his remote childhood. He smiled, but this whimsical idea was quickly replaced by a sombre apprehension which he could not shake off, and which emanated from the realization that the clerk by some strange fatality had again assigned him room twenty-eight—the room with the fireplace. He thought of asking for another room, but could not think of any reasonable excuse. He sighed and felt a positive sinking at the heart when he saw the figures written down at the edge of the page; but he said nothing. If he shrank from this room's occupancy, this room with its frightful secret shared by him alone of this world's company with the four guilty men who were still at large because of his failure to keep his promise, he was human enough and modern enough in his ideas to shrink still more from the imputation of oddity which his refusal of the room on no sensible grounds would inevitably suggest.

He went up to his room, and, as it was a cold night outside, ordered the fire to be made up...

When the hotel servant rapped on his door in the morning there was no answer, and after several attempts to arouse the occupant the man reported his failure at the office. Later another attempt was made, and, this proving equally ineffectual, the door was forced with the assistance of a locksmith.

Mr. Callender's body was found lying with the head in the grate. He had been, it appeared, strangled, for the marks of a pair of hands were deeply imprinted on his throat. The fingers had sunk deeply into the bluish, discolored flesh, and the coroner's jury noted the unusual circumstances when they sent out a description of the murdered confined to this peculiarity, that these marks indicated that the murderer (who was never discovered) possessed very long thin fingers, the index fingers being almost or quite as long as the middle fingers.

*P*erhaps the only high-ranking church official to be a pulp writer, the Reverend Henry St. Clair Whitehead (1882-1932) was born in Elizabeth, New Jersey. He attended Harvard College (A.B. 1904)—where he played football, receiving sports injuries that were to shorten his life—and worked as a reporter and athletic commissioner before suddenly deciding on another career in the Episcopal Church. After graduating from the Berkeley Divinity School, he held several *church posts and was sent to the Virgin Islands in 1921 as acting archdeacon. His ten years of service there inspired him to write supernatural fiction, mostly for* **Weird Tales** *and* **Adventure.** *His colorful stories of the islands are told in a solid, convincing way that adds much to their effect. They are collected in two volumes from Arkham House,* **Jumbee and Other Uncanny Tales** *(1944) and* **West India Lights** *(1946).*

BEYOND THE CLEFT

TOM REAMY

Prologue

It was born; though "born" is perhaps not the right word.

1

At 2:17 p.m. on Thursday afternoon Danny Sizemore killed and ate the Reverend Mr. Jarvis in the basement of the Church of the Nazarene in the township of Morgan's Cleft, North Carolina. Danny was fifteen years old and incapable of speech. He washed the blood from his face and hands the best he could in the rain barrel behind the parsonage. There was little he could do about the mess on his shirt and it worried him. If there was one thing the Reverend Mr. Jarvis had drilled into Danny's mist-enshrouded brain, it was cleanliness and neatness.

Still wiping at his sodden shirt, Danny started home, now and then pausing to chunk a rock in the creek. He scooted his bare feet along the road; he liked the velvety feel of the dust. He had just stopped, balancing clumsily on one leg to pluck a grassburr from his big toe, when his stomach began to churn. He leaned against the split rail fence and threw up.

He stood for a moment in confusion, pink saliva running down his chin, feeling the hollowness in him and the tingling in his puffy face.

Then he thought of the quarter and took it from his pocket to look at it. The Reverend Mr. Jarvis gave him one every week for cleaning up around the church. A quarter a week wasn't much money, even in Morgan's Cleft, but, at that, Danny was overpaid. The Reverend Mr. Jarvis used the hypothetical job as an excuse for charity even though he was reasonably sure the boy's mother wound up with the money.

His mind blank of everything but the shiny coin, Danny continued home. When he passed the Morgan's Cleft School he ignored, or perhaps was unaware of, the screams and running children.

2

At 2:17 p.m. that Thursday afternoon, the entire first, second, and third grades, under the tutelage of Miss Amelia Proxmire (a dour-faced warper of young minds) arose from their desks and devoured her.

Mrs. Edith Beatty (fourth, fifth, and sixth grades) heard Miss Proxmire's gurgling screams from her adjoining classroom. She lifted her copious bulk and waddled rapidly to investigate, but her way was blocked by Mandy Pritchard, age ten. Mrs. Beatty reached out her arm to gently remove the child from her path, but Mandy grabbed the arm and bit a bleeding chunk from it.

Mrs. Beatty, momentarily immobilized by shock, was dimly aware that some of the children in her classroom were attacking the others. She watched in fascination as Mandy bared her pink teeth for another bite. But she had had enough of this nonsense. She pulled her bleeding arm away and kicked Mandy in the shin with her heavy walking oxford. Mrs. Beatty kicked her again, in the head, opening a gash in her scalp and catapulting her underneath the front row of desks.

She waded into the mass of screaming children, pulling them apart, but she could see that little was being accomplished. As soon as she released one, the child would attack again. She calmly removed her shoe and, holding it by the toe, went to each child who seemed to be the aggressor and bashed it in the head.

There were only five of them, counting Mandy. Six of the remaining seven were hysterical and Bobby MacDonald seemed to be dead. His throat was torn open. The six still on their feet were bleeding from numerous bites and scratches. Mrs. Beatty tried to calm them but the bedlam in the hall made it impossible.

Miss Proxmire's class had erupted from her room looking for plumper prey. They found Mrs. Agnes Bledsoe (junior high) and Miss Clarissa Ogilvy (high school), accompanied by their students on their way to Miss Proxmire's room. They attacked like wolves and gained a momentary advantage because of the stunned inaction of the older children. Their attack was tenacious but not suicidal. Some of the children fought back and some of them fled. Mrs. Beatty's class had had enough and evacuated the building quickly. The entire melee rapidly moved outside with children scattering in every direction and dozens of townspeople converging on the school. The battle was brief. The three surviving teachers and the remaining children found themselves standing in the playground, numb with shock, and no one left to fight. Miss Ogilvy leaned against the johnny-stride and then slipped slowly down the pole in a faint.

There were three casualties in the school: Miss Proxmire, Bobby MacDonald, and Eloise Harper, whose ill-advised flight led her down Sandy Lane. She was overtaken by six of them.

Mrs. Beatty returned to her room to find it empty. Mandy and the four others had gone, taking Bobby MacDonald's body with them. Mrs. Beatty felt very tired and weary. Her arm hurt fiercely but she was too exhausted to do anything but clutch at it. She sat at her desk and leaned back in the chair.

3

At 2:17 that afternoon, Betty Whitman was nursing her thirteen-month-old son. She sat rocking gently, dreamily reading of Jean Harlow in a movie magazine. She jerked and gasped when the baby bit her. He had teethed early and it was happening too often. She promised herself this was the last breast feeding and went back to her magazine.

The second time he bit her she cried out. She pulled his mouth away and watched the blood gush down her side. She put the baby on the floor and stood up. She took three steps with her hand clutched to her breast and fainted. The baby looked at her a moment and began toddling toward her.

4

Mavis Sizemore was a slatternly woman of indeterminate age who managed a tenuous existence by washing and ironing for other people. Her small house, connected to the town by a narrow footbridge across Indian Creek, was as weary and woebegone as she. The back yard contained a small vegetable garden, an outhouse, a pen of disreputable-looking chickens, two scrawny pigs, and several clotheslines partially filled with drying clothes. Two black cast-iron washpots sat on kindling fires, each nearly filled with boiling water. Into one Mavis poured a can of lye and a syrup pail of cracklings left over from lard-making. She stirred the mixture with a wooden paddle and then wiped at her pewter-colored, sparrow's-nest hair with the back of her hand.

She moved wearily to a galvanized washtub and drew soapy clothes from it, scrubbed them on a rub board, and then transferred them to the other boiling pot. She punched at them with a cut-off broom handle, long ago bleached white and fuzzy, to make sure they were submerged. She left the clothes to boil and returned to the first pot, testing the contents with a chicken feather. The feather emerged blackened and curled. She added more cracklings and again stirred the thickening mixture. Her face was red and sweaty from the heat and her hands were mottled from too much lye soap and stained with bluing.

Mavis had faulty genes and in her hazy lifetime had produced eight stillbirths and Danny. She had never been married. Danny shuffled across the footbridge and came around the side of the house still lovingly engrossed with his quarter.

Her suet-colored lips began moving, making sounds at Danny. He heard them vaguely, but they meant nothing. He had long ago stopped trying to make sense of the sounds or of the woman. This was only where he went when he was sleepy or hungry. She knocked the quarter from his hand and slapped his face.

Her flesh was like putty and tasted of soap.

First Interlude

Not far from Asheville, North Carolina, an unpaved road leaves the state highway and wanders upward into the Blue Ridge. The road follows the path of least resistance; around hillsides of rhododendron; over ridges of white pine, yellow pine, and spruce; through

valleys of hemlock, laurel, and dogwood. For the most part it fol-
lows Indian Creek, a wild mountain stream which eventually flows
into the French Broad. It crosses the stream numerous times on
trestle bridges of ancient timber, and then will stray away when the
path of least resistance leads elsewhere.

The road passes through a few scattered villages and skirts an
occasional farm or logging camp. There is less and less traffic as it
penetrates deeper into the mountains. Those who live there have
little reason to enter. The road rejoins Indian Creek near the logging
town of Utley and becomes even more tentative as it passes through
the village.

From there it rises sharply for some twenty miles to pass, with the
creek, through a gap in the mountain called Morgan's Cleft. The
pass and the village beyond were named for Cleatus Morgan, leader
of the original settlers in the high valley. Once through the gap, the
road and the stream straighten and follow the approximate center
of the wide valley to the township.

Past the Church of the Nazarene, the road dwindles to little more
than a pair of wheel ruts separated by grass and wildflowers. It
divides many times along the fifteen-mile length of the valley, each
division ending at a lonely farm.

The colonials who settled here had intended to go on to Tennessee
but found themselves at a dead end. After a brief consultation with
the other families, Cleatus Morgan decided this rich and fertile val-
ley, though practically insulated from the outside world, was a defi-
nite windfall. So they settled in and prospered by their own
standards. Indian Creek, which ran pure and bright and teemed
with fish, provided power for a gristmill; the valley and surround-
ing heights were thick with Virginia deer, wild turkeys, dove, and
quail. Little was needed from the outside.

5

Orvie Morgan, direct descendant of Cleatus Morgan and heir to the
choicest farm in the valley, drove toward town with his five-year-old
son at his side. The shiny black Model A Ford, one of only five automobiles in the valley—not counting the Mercantile's Model T truck—
clattered and bounced in the wheel ruts. The tufted tops of the wild
grasses in the center flicked against the axles with small unheard
sounds. The time was 2:17 p.m. on Thursday.

Little Cleatus Morgan, this generation's proud bearer of the ancestral name, took his father's arm in his small hands. Orvie turned his head and smiled fondly at his son. The smile became a grimace of consternation when Little Cleatus's tiny sharp teeth sank in. Orvie's arm was hard-muscled but the bite still brought blood.

Orvie pushed the child away with a sharp, puzzled exclamation. Little Cleatus returned with single-minded ferocity and clamped his teeth on his father's shoulder. Orvie twisted in the seat to disengage the child. His foot pressed harder on the accelerator. The narrow tire on the front wheel struck a stone in the rut and cut sharply into the high grass. The car careened through a low growth of dogwood, flushing a flock of doves which filled the air with gray blurs and whistling wings.

Orvie pinioned his son to the seat with his bleeding arm and fought the steering wheel with one hand. But it was too late. The left front wheel spun on air. The car tipped over with maddening slowness, and slid down the embankment on its roof. The glass shattered in the windshield. The car tipped again, rolled onto its wheels, then toppled once more to land upside-down in Indian Creek.

Orvie's head twisted loosely with the movement of the water, his hair flowing like dark sea grass. Red flumes stretched farther and farther, leaving his head, shoulder, and arm and exiting through the empty windshield frame.

Little Cleatus fought like a trapped rat, tearing at his father's arm, clawing with his fingernails. Bubbles oozed from his nostrils and from between his clenched teeth. But he could not break Orvie's protective grip. Orvie drowned and, with love, took his would-be murderer with him.

6

Meridee Callahan put her hands to the small of her back and stretched. The nagging ache under her fingers eased slightly but resumed when she relaxed. She sighed and looked at her swollen abdomen. Only one more month, she thought and smiled. "I can take it if you can," she said out loud and patted her stomach.

She smoothed the chenille bedspread where she had taken a nap and looked at the clock. It was almost two and she had a lot of work still undone. Robbie had wanted old Ludie Morgan to help her out now that her time was drawing close. But, as much as Meridee hated to admit it, she simply didn't get along with her Grandaunt Ludie. The old woman meant well, she supposed, but she was bossy, meddling, gossipy, and righteous, and had enough superstitions to do the whole valley.

Meridee lifted the cuptowel and checked the bread she had put on the back of the Sunshine stove to rise. She nodded with satisfaction. She opened the door of the fire box and stirred the coals, added shavings and kindling, let it catch, and added wood. She moved the breadpans to a kitchen cabinet away from the heat. She took a mixing bowl and a pan of string beans she had picked that morning and went to sit in the shade on the front porch.

She was snapping beans when Danny Sizemore passed on his way to the church. She watched him idly and then went back inside. She dipped water from the stove reservoir into a stewer and added the beans. The stove was hot enough so she put the breadpans in the oven, then wiped the perspiration dewing on her upper lip with the cuptowel. She rolled up the door of the high closet and took a chicken leg to nibble while waiting on the bread.

Seeing Danny reminded her she should go to Mavis's and check on her washing and ironing. She knew it was only an excuse to take a walk and get out of the hot kitchen because Mavis would bring them around when she finished. That was one thing Robbie had insisted upon. She argued she was still capable of doing her own laundry, but rather gratefully gave in when he put his foot down.

Screams of terror drifted in the kitchen window from the direction of the school.

7

Robbie Callahan was the constable of Morgan's Cleft. There wasn't much for a constable to do in the valley: an occasional lost child or lost cow, a little too much corn liquor on Saturday night, an infrequent territorial dispute between farmers, a boyish prank gotten out of hand. The people were hard-working, self-reliant, and God-fearing. They didn't really need a constable. Besides, everyone knew everyone else and it was virtually impossible to get away with anything. But they needed and wanted a figure of authority: someone to organize when organization was necessary, someone to collect taxes, someone to preside at town meetings, someone to help when help was wanted.

Robbie was only twenty-six, but he had broad shoulders, long legs, sandy hair, and an easy grin, and could lick practically anybody who gave him trouble. He was well-liked and trusted and had married

Meridee Morgan three years earlier. His connection with the Morgans hadn't hurt him at election time.

But, as there wasn't much for a constable to do, and because the job paid only ten dollars a month, Robbie worked at Watson's Mercantile. He kept the accounts, went to Utley twice a week in the truck for the mail and ice and anything else needed from the outside. For all practical purposes, Robbie had been in charge of the store since old Calvin Watson began failing six years before.

The Mercantile smelled of coffee beans, licorice, cheese, dill, and leather—especially leather. He opened another crate of harness, entering it in his inventory as he hung it up: bridles, lines, traces, pads, back and hip straps, breeching, breast straps, martingales, hames, spread straps.

Frances Pritchard, who clerked for Robbie, was showing yard goods to her mother at the front of the store. Mrs. Pritchard always found it necessary to unroll every other bolt before she made up her mind. She fingered ivory silk crepe with one hand and mais chiffon mull with the other, but Frances knew her mother was only daydreaming.

"I can't make up my mind," Mrs. Pritchard said with a whine. "Which do you like best, Frances, dear?"

Frances smiled tolerantly. "The crepe is very nice, Mother, and it's two ninety-eight a yard. The mull is fifty-five and," she pushed two other bolts forward, "the chambray is nine cents a yard and the calico is ten." She cocked an eyebrow at her mother. Mrs. Pritchard sighed in resignation.

They heard a commotion from the direction of the school.

8

Edith Beatty sat at her desk looking at the huge smear of blood where Bobby MacDonald's body had been. Other smears led to the window where the body had been removed. Her brain felt like cotton. She couldn't think or reason. Her arm was numb. She held it tightly to stop the bleeding. She felt light-headed and her ears rang.

Several people came into the room. She recognized Mrs. Bledsoe and Robbie Callahan but the others were back in the deep shadows in the middle of the afternoon. Robbie leaned over her, talking to her, but she couldn't understand what he was saying. The shadows had overtaken Mrs. Bledsoe, covering her like a greasy black fog. Robbie was doing something to her arm but she couldn't tell what because of the shadows.

9

Meridee watched Morgan's Cleft through the kitchen window as she cut away the burned crust of the bread. The inside would be fine for making bread pudding, she decided. She wrapped it in a cuptowel and put it in the high closet of the stove. Not tonight; she would make pudding tomorrow. It was nearly sundown but the street was filled with milling, confused, sometimes hysterical people. Robbie would be home soon, hungry as a bear.

She made biscuits and put them in the oven and warmed up the leftover chicken. Even with the beans it didn't seem like much so she fried bacon and eggs.

She had gone to the schoolhouse with everyone else. It had all seemed unreal, like she was reading a storybook. No one could explain what had happened. Everyone stood around while the stunned children told what had taken place, trying to make sense of it all. Mrs. Beatty had passed out and was carried to Dr. Morgan's office. The bite on her arm already seemed infected. The parents of some of the missing children had gone into the woods after them; they hadn't come back yet.

A team and wagon had ripped and rattled into town. The horses had been wild with panic, rearing and screaming, their eyes round and shining, bloody froth on the bits. The wagon was empty except for sacks of oats in the bed and blood on the seat.

Robbie had sent her home when Caroline Walter ran the two miles into town carrying the body of her five-year-old Pretty. Caroline's arms were covered with bites and she screamed she had killed Pretty. They couldn't get her to say anything else. She just repeated it over and over and fought them when they tried to take Pretty from her. Then she fainted and they took her to Doc.

Meridee ate the bacon and eggs because she was so hungry and fried more for Robbie.

10

Pauly Williams felt sick to his stomach. He had a bite on his chest and another on his arm. Both throbbed and itched. Doc Morgan had swabbed them with something that stung and bandaged them. Pauly was embarrassed and ashamed. Delton Reeves was only ten years old and Pauly was twelve, but he hadn't been able to fend off Delton's ferocious attack, hadn't been able to keep Delton from biting him twice. He had never been so grateful for anything in his life as he had been when Mrs. Beatty clobbered Delton on the head with her shoe.

He scratched at the bandage on his chest, but his mother pulled his hand away. The skin around the bandage was red and the inflammation seemed to be spreading. She felt his forehead. It was hot. He had taken a fever. She pulled the covers around Pauly's neck and told him to go to sleep. She turned the lamp low, making sure the wick didn't smoke.

She went onto the front porch and looked through the moonlight toward the road that skirted the cornfield. She wished Joe Bob would get home. The chickens hadn't been fed, the eggs hadn't been gathered, and the milk still sat in the smokehouse unseparated. She had half a mind to take the lantern and do all three, but Joe Bob had told her to stay in the house with the door locked while he and the other men looked for the children.

It was hard to believe that Wayne was out there in the dark. He was only seven and had never been very strong. Pauly was the strong one. Wayne was the smart one. Thunderheads were building on the west ridge. She hoped it wouldn't rain—Wayne was sure to catch cold if it did.

She had been watching the movements of the cornstalks for several minutes before she realized what she was seeing. The tops would sway slightly as something brushed against them lower down. It was only a small area of movement. It had started at the road and crept across the field towad the creek.

She became consciously aware of it when it shifted directions and started toward the house. If we didn't have enough problems already, she though. Now the fence is down somewhere and the deer have gotten in. They loved the young corn and could mess up a field in nothing flat. But she didn't know what she could do about it. Joe Bob had forbidden her to leave the house.

The movement drew closer and paused as it reached the fence. She leaned against the porch railing and strained her eyes to see what was there, but it was too dark. She thought she saw something crawl through the fence but she wasn't sure. Yes, she had seen something. There was another one. It wasn't deer. Deer couldn't crawl through the fence like that. Besides, it was too small.

She could see nothing but dark shapes close to the ground. There must be a dozen of them, she thought. They could be bear cubs, but she didn't think there would be so many together.

She backed toward the door, beginning to be afraid. They moved toward her with such determination and purpose. She reached behind her, feeling for the handle of the screen door. One of the shapes grew suddenly taller and moved alone toward the porch. The others waited motionlessly. She pulled open the screen and slipped inside.

The single moving shape stepped into the rectangle of light cast through the open door.

"Wayne!" she cried and ran across the porch toward him. The screen door slammed behind her like a rifle shot. She stood at the top of the porch steps. She gave a little moan. He looked up at her, his clothes torn and dirty, his hair mussed, scratches on his little face and hands. She hurried down and knelt before him, throwing her arms around him, pulling him against her breast.

She saw dried blood on his neck. She pushed him from her, and held him at arm's length. Dried blood flaked from his face and stained the front of his shirt. She became aware of the other children; that they had stood up; that they were surrounding her. She rose suddenly with a frightened whimper and backed toward the porch, pulling Wayne with her.

She knew these children. She knew all of them.

Her heel caught on the edge of the step and she fell. A fierce pain shot through her elbow, numbing her whole arm. She screamed. The silent children rushed to her, covering her.

She screamed again and again. She seemed to stand outside herself watching something she couldn't believe. There was a noise like the screen door slamming. She couldn't be sure she heard it because the screams were so loud.

Delton Reeves jerked and the side of his head flew off with a little red explosion. He fell over and twisted like a rag doll. Barbara Ann Morgan clutched her hands to the front of her bloody dress, but the blood wasn't dried. It was wet and shiny.

The children ran away, scattering through the darkness like silent phantoms. A small puff of dust erupted at Wayne's feet as he ran. She pulled herself around on the steps and looked up at the porch. Pauly stood there with Joe Bob's deer rifle.

He had a satisfied look on his face.

11

Danny Sizemore walked slowly across the footbridge, looking around carefully. He had stayed inside all evening crouched at the window, watching the people running around the street. He had never seen so many in town at one time and it frightened him. So many horses and wagons and automobiles, leaving and coming back and leaving again, rattling the boards on the big bridge by the mill. People crying and yelling. Dogs barking and whining because they didn't understand what the commotion was all about. And that big fire they built in the schoolyard. But no one had crossed the footbridge. No one had come near all evening as he huddled and watched.

Now the street was empty and only a few of the houses still showed lights. And he was hungry. There had been no supper though he had sat at the table and waited. The woman had never brought it.

But another compulsion overrode the hunger, forced it deep into the mists of Danny's mind. He walked through town and down the road deeper into the valley. He didn't know where he was going but he never hesitated at a juncture of the road. When the road didn't go where he had to go, he crashed through the brush, scratching his arms on the dogwood branches, flushing startled quail, never veering from his unknown destination.

Danny's lungs burned and his puffy body trembled with fatigue. He had walked for hours but his legs kept moving. Then he was slipping and scrambling down the embankment into the creek bed. He went another hundred yards, keeping his footing with difficulty on the round smooth stones.

He saw them up ahead, working silently in the moonlight. They seemed to be excavating the high creek bank. Even the smallest among them carried rocks and armloads of dirt.

Probably for the first time in his dim existence, Danny *felt*. The feeling swelled in him, choking him, stretching his doughy flesh. He began running toward them, making a happy gurgling sound deep in his throat.

The children stopped their activity and turned to watch him silently. One of them reached down and plucked a smooth river rock from the stream. He threw it at Danny. The rock rattled on other rocks at his feet but Danny didn't notice. Others began throwing stones. Danny became gradually aware of the sharp pains growing on his body and stopped in bewilderment. The stones continued to pelt him. His arms came slowly up to protect his face.

He stood for a moment watching the children, the feeling inside him changing to a hurt far worse than any made by a stone. Then he turned and walked away. The children returned to their work. Danny looked back at them once, great tears rolling down his cheeks, but the children ignored him.

He tripped while climbing the embankment and didn't bother to get up. He lay with his face buried in the grass, choking on his sobs. It was the first time he had ever cried.

Meridee Callahan lay in the darkness beside her husband, feeling the warmth of his body. She couldn't sleep and thought from the sound of Robbie's breathing he couldn't either. She put her hand lightly on his bare chest. He turned facing her and put his arms around her, pulling her to him. She snuggled against him and felt his breath in her hair.

"You all right, hon?" he asked softly.

"Mmm-huh. I just can't go to sleep."

"Me, too." His hand slid down her arm and rested gently on her stomach. She felt his face move against hers as he smiled. "I think I felt him move."

She chuckled against his neck. "It's probably gas."

"Don't say that." Robbie sat up and put his cheek against her swollen abdomen. "Hey, you in there, my son," he whispered. "If you don't hurry up and come outa there, your old man is gonna hafta pay a visit to Mavis Sizemore."

Meridee grunted and hit him on the shoulder with her small fist. He laughed and buried his face between her breasts. Her arms went around his neck squeezing him tightly to her. They lay like that for a while, her face against his hair, which smelled of pine. He slid his hand under her gown and cupped her breast, rubbing his thumb across the nipple. She ran her fingernails lightly down his spine and the muscles on his back trembled. She stopped when she felt a warm hardness against her hip.

"Robbie?"

"Mmm?"

"Do you think…what happened to…to the children…do you think anything happened to our baby?"

He raised himself and looked into her face. "You shouldn't upset yourself with thoughts like that, Meri. Our baby will be the finest baby in the valley."

"But, how do you know…"

He put his fingers on her lips. "Now stop it," he said gently. "You're gonna worry yourself into a nervous fit about nothing. You hear me?"

She nodded. He slid his fingers to her cheek and touched his lips lightly to hers. "Now, go to sleep," he said and cuddled her in his arms.

But she didn't—not for a long time.

The Church of the Nazarene was packed. The pews were full and people stood three-deep around the sides. Even then, they weren't all inside. Others stood in the churchyard by the open windows where they could hear and still keep watch with the rifles and shotguns they held.

There was none of the running and playing which usually accompanied a town meeting. No children under the age of eleven were present, and most of those who were present were in the parsonage, which had been converted into a makeshift hospital. All who had been bitten were running high temperatures with frequent bouts of vomiting.

Robbie stood beside the lectern with papers in his hands. The silent, pinched faces stared back at him colored with hope, despair, fear, and confusion. Robbie shuffled the paper and cleared his throat. He looked tired and kept running his fingers through his tousled hair.

"Yesterday evening and this morning," he began slowly, "we contacted everybody in the valley, to tell them about this meeting and to get a head count so we would know how many people have...died and how many are missing. I have it here. Do you want me to read it or pin it on the board?"

He lifted his eyes and surveyed the people pressed into the church, but there was no response. Doc Morgan, sitting in the front pew, looked around and said quietly, "Why don't you read it, Robbie."

Robbie nodded. "Okay. These are the known dead. Orvie and Little Cleatus. They drowned when Orvie's car ran off the road into the creek." A woman began weeping softly somewhere in the rear of the room. Robbie looked up briefly and then continued. "Uh...Edith Beatty, Caroline Walker, and Joe Bob's wife died this morning from infected wounds. Everyone bitten is sick but only those three have died. Doc can answer your questions about that. The Reverend Jarvis, Mavis Sizemore, Miss Proxmire, Betty Whitman, Bobby MacDonald were...killed by the children yesterday. We found the Whitman baby in the woods this morning. He had gone nearly a mile up the valley but was dead when we found him. We also found Danny Sizemore hanging from a rafter at Mavis's place. He seems to have killed himself."

Robbie wiped the moisture from his upper lip with the side of his hand. "Pete and Prissy Morgan had been...were dead when we went by there this morning. They had six little kids—three of them not in school yet. Barbara Ann and Delton Reeves were killed when they attacked Joe Bob's wife last night. The bodies weren't there this morning but Pauly is sure they were dead. Pretty Walker was killed when she tried to kill Caroline. The Ellis baby died after falling from her crib. She apparently tried to climb out. That's eighteen we know for sure are dead." His voice was low and without emotion.

Robbie shuffled the papers without looking up. "As for the missing …the best we can figure thirty-seven children were…affected. Two of those are eleven and the rest are ten or younger. Except for the five known dead, they've all disappeared. Seven of them are under two years old; one even younger than the Ellis baby. We don't know how they managed.

"Agnes Bledsoe and her husband went by his brother's farm last night and didn't find anyone there. Calvin Watson was gone this morning. Somebody had broken in. There was no one at my…my sister's place this morning. And no one at Oss Morgan's. Oss's team came into town yesterday. There was blood on the wagon. Eloise Harper hasn't been seen since she left the schoolhouse. Able Pritchard, Will and Pansy Reeves, Gil MacDonald, Sonny Morgan, and Carroll Gilmore didn't come back last night after going to look for their kids. Counting the children, over fifty people are missing."

"What about the Sullivans?" someone asked.

Doc snorted and Robbie shook his head. "I don't know. We went up to the Hollow this morning but they wouldn't let us in."

"Took a shot at us!" Doc said with indignation.

"Must be a lotta kids up there," the same man said.

"Usta be." Doc grimaced. "Them Sullivans been inbreedin' up there in the Hollow like a bunch of pigs; ever since old Hiram Sullivan had a fallin'-out with Cleatus Morgan nearly two hundred years ago. I don't know how many of 'em survived the diphtheria that went through there in '27. I tried to vaccinate 'em but they took a shot at me then too."

"We can't worry about the Sullivans," Leo Whitman said bitterly. "I lost my wife and baby. Nearly everybody here lost somebody. We gotta figure out what to do about it. Robbie's been pussy-footin' around, not sayin' what needs to be said. Our kids have turned into wild animals, murderin' and eatin' human flesh. We need to go in and exterminate all of 'em. Like we would a pack of wolves!"

A murmur swelled from the crowd. "I don't believe what I'm hearing!" Mrs. Pritchard's voice carried over the other sounds. "You're talking about murdering our little children! My Mandy!"

"They killed your husband," Leo pointed out.

"We don't know that Able is dead!" she cried. Frances took her mother's arm and tried to calm her. Doc stood and held up his hands. When they quieted he said, "Maybe Leo's right and maybe not. That's why we're havin' this meetin'—to decide what to do. We need to find out what's going on. Maybe it will pass. Maybe it will pass and they'll come home."

"Could you shoot one of your grandkids, Doc?"

Doc looked at the floor for a moment and then shook his head. "I don't know. Joe Bob's wife wouldn't have been able to."

"We need to keep anything like that from happening again," Robbie said. "Some of you live pretty far out. You have to take care of your fields and your stock. They've already wiped out three families."

"I'll keep my shotgun with me."

"The ones who didn't come back last night had guns."

"What are we supposed to do? Lock ourselves in our houses?"

"I don't know." Robbie leaned against the lectern and wished he could sit down. He had been on horseback since dawn. "Everybody has to be aware of the situation so we can come up with something."

"I think the first thing we have to do," Doc said quietly, "is capture one of them. Ask them why they're doing this. Ask them what has happened to them."

"Capture?"

"You're talkin' about 'em as if they were animals!"

"No." Doc shook his head. "They're not animals. Animals don't think and plan. Animals can't open doors and windows and pretend to be your children so they can get close enough to kill you. If we can't stop thinking of them as our children, we may not have a chance."

14

Ludie Morgan put more wood in the stove and checked the gauge on the pressure cooker. She scalded Mason jars and sliced cucumbers to soak in lime water, humming to herself all the time.

Meridee sat at the kitchen table watching her. "You don't need to do all this, Aunt Ludie," she said with considerable awe.

"Gotta get your cannin' done. Don't want to let the garden go to waste. When those green beans and pickles are done, I'll pick a bunch of those nice green tomatoes and make chow-chow."

"I wasn't really planning to can this year. I've got enough left over from last year to feed the whole town."

"Then why plant a garden?"

"Force of habit, I guess." She looked out the window but couldn't see the church from where she sat. "How long do you think the meeting will last?"

"Lord knows. Folks get to jawin', never know when to quit. I coulda told 'em bad trouble was a-comin'."

Meridee knew she shouldn't say anything, but she did. "How did you know?"

Ludie moved air across her shiny face with a paper fan. "I know the signs. I didn't just come to town on a wagonload of watermelons. Only last week I heard a goatsucker two nights runnin'. I even found a crow's feather on my front stoop. And for the last three nights the lightnin' bugs have been so thick you could sew by the light. Them two old dogs of mine been layin' in the yard pantin' like lizards and the weather barely warm."

"What do your dogs have to do with it?"

"They could feel the evil in the air pressin' in on 'em, that's what. It's the Devil's work. You notice how the Reverend Mr. Jarvis was one of the first to go. I know the signs."

Meridee sighed but didn't argue. She looked at the pot of chicken and dumplings keeping warm on the back of the stove. She was starving. Ever since yesterday afternoon she couldn't seem to get enough to eat.

15

Robbie sat on the davenport looking up at the quilting frame suspended just below the ceiling. Meridee started on it five months ago, but hadn't worked on it lately. "My belly gets in the way," she had said. There were about a dozen people in the parlor: a few of his relatives but mostly assorted Morgans. Some were sitting anxiously and some paced nervously while others talked quietly. He hadn't been listening until he heard his name.

"What?"

"I asked how many it is now," said his seventeen-year-old cousin Travis.

"How many what?"

"How many they've killed." It wasn't necessary to explain who "they" were.

"Oh. Uh...forty-two, I think, known dead and missing."

Travis turned back to Meridee's father. "That's almost a fifth of the population."

Robbie was amazed at how calmly it was discussed now after the hysteria of those first few days. He stood up and rubbed his palms on his thighs. Doc had been in there for an hour. He went to the window, protected by bars made from wheel rims by the blacksmith, and looked out. There must be fifty people in the yard, he thought.

They had been gathering since Meridee went into labor. Her worries about the baby had spread. The entire valley wanted to know if the baby would be normal or like "them."

"Only way we could do it," Meridee's father said. "We work in groups of at least ten and half of 'em do nothin' but stand guard. It works out pretty good, but while you're helpin' someone else, your own crops ruin in the fields and they kill and eat your animals. There just aren't enough people to go around. Nearly half the farms are abandoned now, with relatives movin' in with each other for protection."

"Leo thinks the only way is to hunt 'em down and kill 'em."

"I agree, but there aren't enough men to do that and the work too. Besides, he's been out half a dozen times and hasn't seen a thing."

"They found those burrows in the creek bank."

"Yeah, but they didn't find any kids. They tried to smoke 'em out and nothin' happened. Even sent one of the dogs in but the burrow collapsed and smothered him. Doc thinks they musta moved somewhere else. What beats me is how they can eat so much."

Robbie went to the bedroom door and listened but could hear nothing. He fidgeted for a moment, then went to the kitchen for a drink of water. He had thought several times of suggesting they seek outside help, but he knew it wouldn't do any good. The people in the valley had been self-sufficient for two hundred years. It would never occur to them that they couldn't handle this alone. Also, there was a certain shame involved. How could they admit to outsiders that they were unable to handle their own children?

Robbie stepped back into the parlor when he heard the bedroom door open. Ludie stood in the doorway, her face gray. She kept rubbing her arms and not looking at him. Everyone in the room was tensely silent.

He ran into the bedroom. Doc leaned against the bassinet. He turned to Robbie and shook his head. The sheet was pulled over Meridee's face. Robbie felt the bottom of his stomach drop away. He walked slowly to the bassinet and looked in.

His daughter looked back at him and bared her teeth.

16

Leo Whitman hunkered down behind the mill wheel watching the creek. He held the deer rifle lightly across his knees. He particularly watched a clump of hemlock hugging the water on the opposite side. He thought he saw a movement there a few minutes ago but he wasn't sure. His eyes burned from too many hours of trying to see in the dark. He wanted to point out the movement to the others, but he was afraid to make a sound.

He shifted his position slightly to keep his leg from going to sleep again and then had to move a stone that dug into his hip.

There it was again: a less dark flicker among the hemlock branches. Leo raised the rifle to his shoulder and sighted on the bush. After several minutes his vision began to blur. He lowered the rifle slightly and blinked his eyes.

Then one of them stepped from behind the hemlock and into the water. It was naked but he couldn't tell from this distance whether it was a boy or girl. It began wading slowly across the stream, looking around as if smelling the air. It stopped in midstream, the water up to its chest, and stood motionless. Did it suspect it was walking into a trap?

Leo sighted on the figure and hoped none of the others would go off half-cocked. Then the child moved forward again. Others slipped silently into the water. God, Leo thought, how quietly they move. He counted eight of them, all naked. Okay, everybody, he said under his breath, wait until they all reach the bank.

But someone didn't. A rifle shot rattled through the night as the first one stepped out of the water. It was a boy, he could see now. The naked child jerked and flopped in the grass. Leo sighted on another and fired. It threshed in the water, then floated face down. Other shots peppered the water with little geysers, but there was nothing to shoot at. The children had vanished, submerged in the creek and invisible.

"Damn!" Leo yelled and ran toward the stream. He waded into the water and hurriedly dragged out the floating corpse. The others joined him. They carried the two dead children quickly away from the creek, looking anxiously over their shoulders. But there was nothing to see, not a vagrant ripple where the children had been.

"Hurry up," Leo growled. "I don't trust 'em."

They ran down the dark street toward Doc's office. They could see him standing in the lighted window watching for them. He had the door open when they got there. Doc slammed the door and lowered the bar across it as they crowded in.

"How many did you get?" Doc asked quickly.

"Two," Leo grimaced. "Some idiot fired too soon and the rest of them ducked underwater and disappeared."

"Put 'em on the table." Doc carried the lamp and held it over the bodies. There was a stunned silence as the men got their first clear look. Water puddled on the table, then dripped through the cracks to drip on the floor with soft thumps.

"My God," someone whispered.

"It's Mandy Pritchard and Wayne Williams," Leo said with dull voice. "I'm glad Joe Bob isn't here."

"Is she...?"

"Yes," Doc said slowly.

Mandy's body lay loosely on its back. The bullet had destroyed one of her breasts, but the other was large and full. Her hair was matted and grimy and showed a bald spot where Mrs. Beatty had kicked her. Her skin was darkly tanned and her abdomen swelled hugely.

"But, she's only...What? Ten?" Leo asked.

"By our reckoning, she is," Doc answered, peering close, "but I doubt if that's valid any more. You'll notice they both have a full growth of pubic hair."

"That's not all Wayne's got a full growth of," someone sniggered. "Most full-grown men wouldn't be ashamed of a pecker like that."

Doc fingered the boy's genitals. "He's fully developed all right."

"You think he's the father?"

"I don't know. He could easily be." Doc ran his hand over Wayne's stomach, pinching the cool damp skin. Then he felt Mandy's leg. "Feel their skin. It's as tough as leather. And look at their bodies. There's been a subtle change. They aren't the bodies of children any more—and Wayne seems taller, don't you think?"

There was a murmur of assent. "Now we know why they needed so much food," Doc continued.

"Why?"

"Because their bodies have been undergoing tremendous changes. Tremendous and rapid. They needed a lot of fuel for all that cell activity." He put his hand on Mandy's stomach. "I'd say she was very close to delivery."

"That's impossible," Leo blurted. "It's only been three months."

"No more impossible than the rest of it," Doc answered calmly. "But it's logical when you consider the acceleration of everything else. I imagine the baby would have been even more developed than Meri's. Probably able to take care of itself in a few weeks—maybe less."

"Then," Leo said dazed, "there'll be hundreds of them in a couple of years. In three months we've only managed to kill four. They've killed...What? Fifty or sixty of us?"

"I think that number can be increased considerably," Doc said, turning away from the bodies. "A bunch of us went by the Hollow this morning. There wasn't a soul around, nor any stock. Looked as if it had been deserted over a month. And the bluffs around the Hollow were riddled with burrows. We got outta there in a hurry."

"Do you think it's hopeless, Doc?"

"I can give you a better answer in seven and a half months."

"What?"

"Frances Pritchard is pregnant. She's the first I know of to conceive after that day."

"But Frances isn't married. Who...?"

"She moved in with Robbie after Meri died. There was no one to marry them and, I don't know, it didn't seem to matter."

Second Interlude

Not far from Asheville, North Carolina, a road leaves the state high-way and wanders upward into the Blue Ridge. It's paved now and has been since the middle Fifties. It still follows the path of least resistance although the square turns have been rounded off and the more treacherous twists have been straightened. The many bridges across Indian Creek are new—made of steel and concrete rather than splintering timbers.

There hasn't been much change in forty years. The logging camps are gone. Campgrounds and motels with cable television have sprung up with increasing frequency. The road enjoys a great deal of traffic because it eventually ends up in the Great Smoky Mountains National Park.

The villages along the way have revived with surprising vigor atfter the near death of the Depression. They were quick to discover that tourists pay much better than cows, pigs, crops, or logs. They found, rather astonishingly, the very things they were eager to cast off after the coming of electricity, television, and stereophonic sound, were just as eagerly sought by tourists.

With dumbfounded gladness they would accept money for their old polished oak iceboxes; enough money to buy new frost-free re-frigerators with automatic icemakers. Money for black cast-iron washpots bought new automatic washing machines. Homemade quilts were too valuable to put on beds. Tourists bought the quilts and the villagers happily slept under electric blankets from J.C. Penney.

The city people called it Folk Art. The villagers called it Free Enterprise.

At Utley the highway makes an unexpected turn to the southwest, going nowhere near Morgan's Cleft. The old unpaved road still goes toward the pass, following Indian Creek, to a few summer cabins and outlying farms. If you tried to follow it to Morgan's Cleft, you would find yourself in the lane to the Crenshaw farm. If you backed up and tried again, you might find it—if you looked closely. The bushes are not quite as thick, the trees are shorter, the ground is more level, and an occasional grading is still visible.

Some of the older people in Utley still remember those who fled the high valley nearly forty years ago. There weren't many—only a dozen or so—coming down the mountain in wagons and some on foot, scattered over several months. Some were hurt and died quickly from infected wounds. Those who lived moved on hastily without explanation, but the folk beyond the Cleft always were a strange lot.

17

Hollis Middleton had been to the bank that day discussing a loan. He owned a piece of very choice property that stretched from the highway to Indian Creek just in the edge of Utley. A motel there should do very nicely. But it wouldn't be just another motel. He would build a fishing veranda over the creek; the guests could fish and the motel kitchen would do the cleaning and cooking. He smiled at the idea and turned on the television set.

He yelled up the stairs for his youngest girl to turn her stereo down so he could hear the TV. He thought he detected a barely perceptible drop in the volume. He adjusted the color so Raymond Burr wouldn't look dipped in purple dye, and sat down to relax.

He groaned when he heard the dishwasher go on in the kitchen and little silver speckles began dancing across the screen. He bore his affluence with stoicism.

He heard a scream and a clatter of pots and pans from the kitchen. He arose with a sigh and went out there without too much hurry. His wife was a great screamer. She was rolling on the floor amid several pieces of her new waterless cookware. Their four-year-old grandson was wrestling with her.

Hollis shook his head and laughed. "You two sure do play rough." His grandson looked up quickly at the sound of his voice. The boy had a mouthful of flesh. Blood dribbled off his chin.

Prologue (cont.)

It grew.

Slowly and carefully, without haste or impetuosity, it grew. It had all the time in the world.

*Tom Reamy (1935-1977) is that tragic figure—the creative artist who dies just as he starts his major work. Born in Woodson, Texas, Reamy entered the science fiction field as an illustrator and later editor of fanzines (**Nickelodeon** and the Hugo Award nominee **Trumpet**), and from 1970 to 1973 did screenplays in Hollywood for small companies, two of which were produced, and at last turned to writing fiction. The horror-fantasy "Beyond the Cleft" was his first sale. Others followed, including the Nebula Award-winning novelette about a modern witch, "San Diego Lightfoot Sue" (1975); "The Detweiler Boy," combining the hardboiled detective story with the monster/mutant story; and "Waiting for Billy Star," an unforgettable combination of the love story and the ghost story. Reamy died in 1977. Almost all his short works are collected in **San Diego Lightfoot Sue** (Earthlight, 1979). One short novel in first draft form remained; it was published as **Blind Voices** by Berkley in 1978.*

THE ARM-CHAIR OF TUSTENUGGEE

WILLIAM GILMORE SIMMS

T he windy month had set in, the leaves were falling, and the light-footed hunters of Catawba set forth upon the chase. Little groups went off in every direction, and before two weeks had elapsed from the beginning of the campaign, the whole nation was broken up into parties, each under the guidance of an individual warrior. The course of the several hunting bands was taken according to the tastes and habits of these leaders. Some Indians were famous for their skill in hunting otter. These followed the course of shallow waters and swamps, and thick, dense bays. The bear hunter pushed for the canebrakes and the bee trees. The active warrior took his way towards the hills, seeking brown wolf and deer, and smiled with contempt at the more timorous. Many set forth in couples only, avoiding the clamorous of the tribe; and some few, the more surly or successful, were content to make their forward progress alone. Some of the tribe followed the course of the Catawba, even to its source. Others darted off toward the Pacolet and Broad rivers, and there were some, the most daring and swift of foot, who made nothing of a journey to the Tiger river, and the rolling mountains of Spartanburg.

There were two warriors who pursued this course. One was Conattee, and a braver and more fortunate hunter never lived. But he had a wife who was a great scold. She was the wonder and terror of the tribe, and quite as ugly as the one-eyed squaw of Tustenuggee, the Grey Demon of Enoree. The return of the husband, particularly if he brought no game, was sure to be followed by a storm of "dry thunder," which never failed to be heard at the farthest end of the village. "Now," said the young woman, who sympathized, as all proper young women will do, with the handsome husband of an ugly wife, "we know poor Conattee has come home."

The companion of Conattee was Selonee—the handsomest lad in the whole nation. He was tall and straight like a pine tree; had proved his skill and courage in several expeditions against the Chowannee red sticks, and had found no Cherokee who could circumvent him in stratagem, or conquer him in blows. His renown as a hunter was not less great. He had put to shame the best wolf-takers of the tribe, and the lodge of his father, Chifonti, was never without meat. There was no good reason why Conattee should be so intimate with Selonee; but, thrown together in sundry expeditions, they had formed an intimacy, which was neither denounced nor discouraged by the wife of the former. She who approved but few of her husband's movements, and still fewer friends, forbore all reproaches, when Selonee was his companion. She was meek, gentle, sweet-tempered, whenever the young hunter came home with her husband; and he, poor man, was consequently never so well satisfied, as when he brought Selonee along with him. It was on such occasions only that poor Conattee could regard Macourah as a tolerable personage. How he came to marry such a creature—such a termagant, and so monstrous ugly— was a mystery which none of the damsels of Catawba could elucidate, though the subject was one on which they expended no small quantity of conjecture. Conattee was quite popular among them, in spite of his bad taste, and manifest unavailableness; and their wish was universal that the Optichi-Manneyto, or Black Devil, would take the virago and leave poor Conattee some reasonable hope of being made happy by a more indulgent spouse.

II

Well, Conattee and Selonee were out of sight of the smoke of "Turkey-town," and, conscious of his freedom, the henpecked husband, by the indulgence of joke and humor, made ample amends to himself for the sober restraints which fettered him at home. Selonee joined with him in his merriment, and the resolve was mutual that they should not linger in their progress till they had thrown the Tiger river behind them. When they reached the river, they made for a cove, which lay between the parallel waters of the Pacolet, and little stream called the Thicketty, in which they had confident hopes of finding the game they desired. In former years the spot had been famous as a sheltering place for herds of wolves; and, with the impatience of a warrior waiting for his foe, the hunters prepared their strongest shafts and sharpest flints, and set their keen eyes upon the closest places of the thickets, into which they plunged fearlessly. They had not proceeded far before a single boar-wolf, of amazing size, started up in their path; and, being slightly wounded by the arrow of Selonee, darted off with a fearful howl in the direction of Conattee. But the savage was too quick. Leaping behind a tree, he avoided the rushing stroke with which the white tusks threatened him. His aim was true, and the stone blade of the shaft went quivering into the shaggy monster; who, under the pang of the last convulsion, bounded into the muddy water of Thicketty Creek. Conattee beheld him plunge furiously forward—then rest with his nostrils in the water, as the current bore him around a little elbow of the creek. Conattee stripped, threw his fringed hunting shirt on the bank, with bow and arrows, moccasins and leggings. Reserving only his knife, he plunged into the water in pursuit. Selonee gave little heed to the movements of his companion, after the first two or three vigorous strokes. Such a pursuit, as it promised no peril, called for little consideration, and Selonee amused himself by striking into a thick copse in search of other sport. There he started the she-wolf. She was lying on a bed of rushes and leaves, under the roots of a gigantic oak. Her cubs, to the number of five, lay around her, keeping a perfect silence, which she had no doubt enforced upon them until they saw him. Then the instincts could no longer be suppressed, and they joined in a short chopping bark, or cry, at the stranger, while their little eyes flashed fire, and their red jaws, thinly sprinkled with the first teeth, were gnashed together with a show of ferocious hatred to man, which marks their nature, but which, fortunately for Selonee, was too feeble at that time to make his approach to them dangerous. But the dam demanded greater consideration. With one sweep of her fore-paw she drew the young ones behind her, and began to move backward beneath the overhanging limbs of the tree, keeping her fiery eye fixed upon the hunter. It was his object to divert it, since he well knew, that with his first movement, she would probably spring upon him. Without lifting his bow, he whistled shrilly as if to his dog; and answered by a correct imitation of the bark of the Indian cur, the enemy of the wolf, and commonly his victim. The angry beast looked suddenly around as if fearing an assault upon her young ones from behind. In that moment, the arrow of Selonee was driven through her neck, and when she leaped forward to the place where he stood, he was no longer to be seen.

From a tree he had thrown between them, he watched her movements and prepared a second shaft. Before she could again turn towards him a second arrow had given her another and severer wound. Still, Selonee well knew the singular tenacity of life possessed by these fierce animals. He prudently changed his position with every shaft, and took special care to place himself in the rear of some moderately sized tree, sufficiently large to shelter him from her claws. Carrying on the war in this manner he buried five arrows in her body, and it was not until his sixth had penetrated her eye, that he deemed himself safe in a closer conflict. (It was the great boast of the Catawba warriors to grapple with the wolf, and while he yet struggled, to tear the heart from his bosom.) He placed his bow and arrows behind the tree, and taking in his left hand a chunk or fragment of a bough, while he grasped his unsheathed knife in his right, he leapt in among the cubs, and struck one of them a severe blow with the chunk. Its scream and the confusion among the rest, brought back the angry dam, and guided by their clamor, she rushed with open jaws upon the hunter. When she turned her head aside, to strike him with her sharp teeth, he thrust the pine fragment into her extended jaws, and pressing fast upon her, bore back her haunches to the earth. All this while the young ones were impotently gnawing at the heels of the warrior. But these he did not heed. The larger and fiercer combatant called for all his attention and strength to preserve the advantage he had gained. The fierce beast had sunk her teeth into the wood, and leaving it in her jaws, he seized her by the throat, and bearing her upward, to yield a plain and easy stroke at her belly, he drove the deep knife in and drew the blade upwards until resisted by the bone of the breast. While she lay writhing in the agonies of death, he tore the heart from the opening he had made, and hurled it down to the cubs, who seized it with avidity. This done, he patted and caressed them, and while they struggled for the meat, he cut a fork in the ears of each, and putting the slips in his pouch, left the young ones without further hurt, for future sport. The dam he scalped, and with this trophy in his possession, he pushed back to the place where he had left the accoutrements of Conattee, which he found undisturbed.

III

But where was Conattee? Some hours had elapsed since he had taken the river after the wolf and it was surprising to Selonee that he should have remained absent and without his clothes so long. The weather was cold and unpleasant, and it could scarce be a matter of choice with the hunter to suffer its biting bleaknesses when his garments were within reach. This reflection made Selonee apprehensive that some harm had happened to his companion. Could he have been seized with the cramp while in the stream, and drowned before he could extricate himself? Selonee reproached himself that he had not waited beside the stream until the result of Conattee's experiment was known. He went down to the bank of the river, and called aloud until the woods and waters re-echoed, again and again, with the name of Conattee. He received no other response. With a mind filled with increasing fears, Selonee plunged into the creek, and struck off for the opposite shore, at the very point at which the wolf had been about to turn when Conattee went in after him. He was soon across, and soon found the tracks of the hunter in the gray sands. He found, too, to his great delight, the traces made by the carcass of the wolf, from the blood which dropped from the reeking skin, and Selonee rejoiced in the certainty that the traces would soon lead him to his friend. But not so. He had scarcely gone fifty yards into the wood when his tracks failed him at the foot of a crooked, fallen tree; here all signs disappeared. Conattee was not only not there but had left no sort of clue by which to follow him further. This was the strangest thing of all. The footprints were distinct enough till he came to the spot where lay the crooked tree, but there he lost them. He searched the forest in every direction. Not a copse escaped his search—not a bay—not a thicket—not an island. He came back to the spot where the wolf had been skinned, faint and weary, and more sorrowful than can be well spoken. At one time he fancied his friend was drowned, at another, that he was taken prisoner by the Cherokees. But there were his tracks from the river, and there were no other tracks than his own. Besides, so far as the latter supposition was concerned, it was scarcely possible that so brave and cunning a warrior would suffer himself to be so completely entrapped and carried off by an enemy, without so much as being able to give the alarm. There were no signs of an enemy, and a singular and mournful stillness hung over the woods. Selonee called aloud, until his voice grew hoarse, and his throat sore. There was no answer, but the gibing echoes. Once more he went back to the river, once more he plunged into its bosom, and struck out for a thick green island some quarter of a mile below, to which he thought the hunger might have wandered in pursuit of other game. It was a small island, which he traversed in an hour. Finding nothing, he made his weary way back to the spot from which his friend had started on leaving him. Here he found his clothes where he had hidden them. The neighborhood of this region he traversed in like manner with the opposite—going over ground, and into places, which it was scarcely in the verge of possibility that his friend could have gone.

Midnight found him at the foot of the tree, where they had parted, exhausted but sleepless, and suffering from those apprehensions which every moment of hopeless search had necessarily helped to accumulate and strengthen. Day dawned, and his labor was renewed. The unhappy warrior went over all the ground he had traversed the night before. Once more he crossed the river, and followed, step by step, the still legible foot tracks of Conattee. But, after reaching the place where lay the fallen tree, all signs failed. Selonee looked round the crooked tree, crawled under its sprawling and twisted limbs, broke into the hollow left by its uptorn roots, and again shouted the name of Conattee, imploring him for an answer if he could hear and reply. But the echoes died away, leaving a silence that spoke more loudly to his heart than before, that his quest was hopeless. Yet he gave it not up until the day had again failed him. That night, as before, he slept on the ground. With the dawn, he again went over it, and with equally bad success. This done, he determined to return to the camp. He no longer had any spirit to pursue the sports for which he had set forth. His heart was full of sorrow, his limbs weary, and he felt none of that vigor which had given him such great renown as a brave and hunter. He tied the clothes of Conattee upon his shoulder, took his bow and arrows, and turned his eyes homeward. The next day, at noon, he reached the encampment.

IV

The hunters were in the woods, with none but squaws and papooses left in the encampment. Selonee came within sight of their back settlements, and seated himself upon a log at the edge of the forest with his back carefully turned toward the smoke of the camp. Nobody ventured to approach him while in this situation; but, at night, when the hunters came dropping in, one by one, Selonee drew nigh to them. He called them apart from the women, and told them his story.

"This is a strange tale which the wolf-chief tells us," said one of the old men, with a smile of incredulity.

"It is a true tale, father," was the reply.

"Conattee was a brave chief!"

"Very brave, father," said Selonee.

"Had he not eyes to see?"

"The great bird, that rises to the sun, had not better," was the reply.

"What painted jay was it that said Conattee was a fool?"

"The painted bird lied, that said so, my father," was the response of Selonee.

"And comes Selonee, the wolf-chief, to us, with a tale that Conattee was blind, and could not see; a coward that could not strike the she-wolf; a fool that knew not where to set down his foot; and shall we not say Selonee lies upon his brother, even as the painted bird that makes a noise in my ears. Selonee has slain Conattee with his knife. See, it is the blood of Conattee upon the war-shirt of Selonee."

"It is the blood of the she-wolf," cried the young warrior, with a natural indignation.

"Let Selonee go to the woods behind the lodges, till the chiefs say what shall be done to Selonee, because of Conattee, whom he slew."

"Selonee will go, as Emathla, the wise chief, has commanded," replied the young warrior. "He will wait behind the lodges, till the chiefs have said what is good to be done to him, and if they say that he must die because of Conattee, it is well. Selonee laughs at death. But the blood of Conattee is not upon the war-shirt of Selonee. He has said it is the blood of the wolf's mother." With these words the young chief drew forth the skin of the wolf which he had slain, together with the tips of the ears taken from the cubs, and leaving them in the place where he had sat, withdrew, without further speech, from the assembly which was about to sit in judgment upon his life.

V

The consultation that followed was close and earnest. There was scarcely any doubt in the minds of the chiefs that Conattee was slain by his companion. He had brought back with him the arms and all the clothes of the hunter. He was covered with his blood, as they thought; and the grief which filled his heart and depressed his countenance, looked, in their eyes, rather like the expression of guilt than suffering. For a long while did they consult together. Selonee had friends who were disposed to save him; but he had enemies also, as merit must have always, and these were glad to put out of their reach, a rival of whom they were jealous, and a warrior whom they feared. Unfortunately for Selonee, the laws of the nation helped the malice of his foes. These laws held him liable in his own life for that of the missing hunter; and the only indulgence that could be accorded, and which was obtained, was, that he might be allowed a single moon to find Conattee, and bring him home to his people.

"Will Selonee go seek Conattee—the windy moon is for Selonee— let him bring Conattee home to his people." Thus said the chiefs, when the young warrior was brought before them.

"Selonee would die to find Conattee," was the reply.

"He will die if he finds him not!" answered the chief Emathla.

"It is well!" calmly spoke the young warrior. "Is Selonee free to go?"

"The windy moon is for Selonee. Will he return to the lodges if he finds not Conattee?" was the inquiry of Emathla.

"Is Selonee a dog, to fly!" indignantly demanded the warrior. "Let Emathla send a warrior on the right and left of Selonee, if he trusts not what is spoken by Selonee."

"Selonee will go alone, and bring back Conattee."

VI

The confidence thus reposed in one generally esteemed a murderer and actually under sentence as such, is customary among the Indians; nor is it often abused. The loss of caste which would follow their flight from justice, is much more terrible among them than any fear of death. Their loss of caste, apart from the outlawry which follows it, is, in fact, a loss of the soul. The heaven of the great Manneyto is denied to one under outlawry of the nation, and such a person is then the known and chosen slave of the demon, Opitchi-Manneyto. It was an unnecessary insult on the part of Emathla, to ask Selonee if he would return to meet his fate. But Emathla was supposed to favor the enemies of Selonee.

With such a gloomy alternative before him, the young hunter retraced his steps to the waters where Conattee had disappeared. With a spirit no less warmly devoted to his friend, than anxious to avoid disgraceful doom, the youth spared no pains, withheld no exertion, overlooked no single spot, and omitted no art known to the hunter, to trace the fate of Conattee. But days passed of fruitless labor, and the last faint slender outlines of the moon allotted him for the search, gleamed upon his path, as he wearily traced it onward to the lodges of the tribe.

Once more he resumed his seat before the council and listened to the doom in reserve for him. When the sentence was pronounced, he untied his arrows, loosened the belt at his waist, and put a fillet of green bark around his head. Rising to his feet, he spoke thus, in language, and spirit, becoming a warrior.

"It is well. The chiefs have spoken, and the wolf-chief does not tremble. He loves the chase, but he does not weep like a woman, because it is forbidden that he go after the deer—he loves to fright the young hares of the Cherokee, but he laments not that he say ye can conquer the Cherokee without his help. Fathers, I have slain the deer and the wolf—my lodge is full of their ears. I have slain the Cherokee, till the scalps are about my knees when I walk in the cabin. I go not to the dark valley without glory—I have had the victories of gray hairs, but there is no gray hair in my own. I have no more to say—there is a deed for every arrow that is here. Bid the young men get their bows ready, let them put a broad stone upon their arrows that may go soon into the life—I will show my people how to die."

They led him forth to the place of execution—a little space behind the encampment, where a hole had been dug for his burial. While he went, he recited his victories to the youths who attended him. To each he gave an arrow and related some incident which proved his valor, either in conflict with some other warrior, or with the wild beasts of the woods. These deeds, each of them was required to remember and relate, and show the arrow given with the narrative. In this way, their traditions are preserved. When he reached the grave, he took his station before it, the executioners, with their arrows, being already placed in readiness. The whole tribe had assembled to witness the execution, the warriors and boys in the foreground, the squaws behind them. A solemn silence prevailed over the scene, and a few moments only remained to the victim; when the wife of Conattee darted forward bearing in her hands a peeled wand, with which she struck Selonee over the shoulders, exclaiming:

"Come, thou dog, thou shalt not die—thou shalt lie in the doorway of Conattee, and bring venison for his wife. Shall there be no one to bring meat to my lodge? Thou shalt do this, Selonee—thou shalt not die."

A murmur arose from the crowd at these words.

"She hath claimed Selonee for her husband, in place of Conattee—well, she had the right."

The enemies of Selonee could not object. The widow had, in fact, exercised a privilege recognized by the Indian laws almost universally; and the policy by which she was governed in the present instance, was apparent to all the village. It was evident, now that Conattee was gone, that nobody could provide for the woman who had no sons, and no male relations, and was too ugly, and too notorious a scold, to ever procure another husband so inexperienced or flexible as the one she had lost. Smartly striking Selonee on his shoulders, she repeated her command that he should rise and follow her.

"Thou wilt take this dog to thy lodge, that he may hunt thee venison?" demanded the old chief, Emathla.

"Have I not said?" shouted the scold—"Hear you not? The dog is mine—I bid him follow me."

"Is there no friendly arrow to seek my heart?" murmured the young warrior, as, rising slowly from the grave into which he had descended, he prepared to obey the laws of his nation. Even the foes of Selonee looked on him with lessened hostility, and the pity of his friends was greater now than when he stood on the precipice of death. The young women of the tribe wept bitterly as they beheld so monstrous a sacrifice. Meanwhile, the exulting hag, conscious of her control over the victim, goaded him foward with repeated strokes of her wand. She knew she was hated by the young women, and was delighted to show them a conquest. With this view she led the captive through their ranks. As they parted mournfully, to suffer the two to pass, Selonee stopped short and motioned one of the young women, looking on with eyes which gave forth an expression of desolateness. With clasped hands, and trembling as she came, the gentle maiden drew nigh.

"Was it a dream," said Selonee sorrowfully, "that told me of the love of a singing bird, and a green cabin by the trickling waters? Did I hear a voice that said to me sweetly, wait but a little, till the green corn breaks the hill, and Medoree will come to thy cabin and lie by thy side? Tell me, is this thing true, Medoree?"

"Thou sayest, Selonee—the thing is true," was the reply of the maiden, uttered in broken accents that denoted a breaking heart.

"But they will make Selonee go to the lodge of another woman—they will put Macourah into the arms of Selonee."

"Alas! Alas!"

"Wilt thou see this thing, Medoree? Can'st thou look upon it, then turn away, and going back to thy own lodge, can'st thou sing a gay song of forgetfulness as thou goest?"

The tears of the damsel flowed freely down her cheeks, and she sobbed bitterly, but said nothing.

"Take the knife from my belt, Medoree, and put its sharp tooth into my heart, ere thou sufferest this thing! Wilt thou not?"

The girl shrank back with an expression of undisguised horror. She turned from him, covering her face with her hands.

"I cannot do this thing, Selonee—I cannot stroke thy heart with the knife. Go—let the woman have thee. Medoree cannot kill thee— she will herself die."

"It is well," cried the youth, in a voice of mournful self-abandonment, as he resumed his progress toward the lodge of Ma-courah.

VII

It is now time to return to Conattee, and trace his progress from the moment he left the side of Selonee in pursuit of the wolf. We are already acquainted with his success in extricating the animal from the water, and possessing himself of its hide. He had not well done this when he heard a rushing noise in the woods above him, and fancying that there was a prospect of other game, Conattee hastened to the spot. When he reached it, however, he beheld nothing. A gigantic and deformed pine tree, crooked and most irregular in shape, lay prostrate along the ground, and formed such an intricate covering above it, that Conattee deemed it possible some beast might have made its den among the recesses of its roots. With this thought, he crawled under the spreading limbs, and searched all their intricacies. Emerging from the search, which had been fruit-less, he took a seat upon the trunk of the tree, and spreading out the wolf's hide before him, proceeded to pare away the particles of flesh which had been suffered to adhere to the skin. But he had scarcely commenced the operation, when two gigantic limbs of the fallen tree curled over his thighs and bound him to the spot. Other limbs, while he strove to move, clasped his arms and covered his shoulders. He strove to cry aloud, but his jaws were grasped before he could well open them. With his eyes, which were suffered to peer through little openings in the bark, he could see his legs encrusted by like coverings. Not a part of his own person now remained visible to himself. A bed of green velvet-like moss rested on his lap. His knees shot out a thorny excrescence: and his hands, flattened to his thighs, were enveloped in a complete casing of bark. Even his knife and wolf skin suffered in like manner, the bark having contracted them into one of those huge bulging knobs that numerously deformed the tree. With thoughts and consciousness remaining, Conattee had yet lost every faculty of action. When he tried to scream, his jaws felt the contraction of a pressure upon them, which resisted all their efforts, while an oppressive thorn growing on a vine before his face, was brought by every movement into his mouth. He was in the power of Tustenuggee, the Grey Demon of Enoree. The tree was one of the magic trees which his people entitled the "Arm-chair of Tustenuggee." In these traps the demon caught his victim, and exulted in his miseries. Here he remained until death released him; for it was not often that the power suffered his prey to escape. The only hope of Conattee was that Selonee might suspect his condition; in which event his rescue was simple and easy enough. Hew off the limbs, or bare away the bark, and the victim was uncovered in his primitive integrity. But how improbable that this discovery should be made. He had no voice to declare his bondage. He had no capacity for movement by which he might reveal the truth to his comrade's eyes. Unless some divine instinct should counsel his friend to an experiment, the poor prisoner felt that he must die in the bondage into which he had fallen. While these painful convictions were passing through his mind, he heard the distant shoutings of Selonee. In a little while he beheld the youth anxiously seeking him, following his trail to the very tree in which he was bound, crawling beneath its branches, but not sitting upon its trunk. Vainly did the poor fellow strive to utter but a few words. The effort died away like the faint sigh of some budding flower. With equal ill success did he struggle with his limbs. He was too tightly grasped, in every part, to stir in the slightest degree. He saw the search, meanwhile, which his comrade maintained, and his heart yearned in fondness for the youth. But it was with consummate horror that he saw him depart as night came on. Miserable, indeed, were his feelings that night. The voice of the Grey Demon alone kept him company, and he and his one-eyed wife goaded him the livelong night with speeches of cruel gibe and mischievous reflection:

"There is no hope for you, Conattee, till someone takes your place. Someone must sit in your lap, whom you are willing to leave behind, before you can get out of mine."

Night passed away at length, and, with the dawn, Conattee again saw Selonee appear. He remembered the words of Tustenuggee, but

188

could he consent to leave his friend behind him? Life was sweet, and great was the temptation. At one moment he almost wished Selonee would draw nigh, and seat himself. The young hunter drew nigh at that instant; but the better feelings in Conattee's heart grew strong and, striving to twist and writhe in his bondage, he manifested the noble resolution not to avail himself of his friend's position to relieve his own; and, as if the warning of Conattee had reached Selonee, the youth retraced his steps, and hurried away from the place of danger. With his final departure the hopes of the prisoner sank; and when hour after hour had gone by without any change in his condition, he gave himself up for lost. The mocks and jeers of the Grey Demon and his one-eyed squaw filled his ears all night, and brought him nothing but despair. He resigned himself to his fate with the resolution of one who however unwilling he might be to perish, had yet faced death too frequently not to yield ready defiance.

VIII

But hope had not departed from the bosom of Selonee. Perhaps the destiny which had befallen him had made him resolve the more earnestly to seek further into the fate of his friend. Macourah, hateful enough as the wife of his friend, was now doubly hateful to him as his own wife; and when, alone together, she threw her arms about the neck of the youth and solicited his endearments, a loathing sensation of disgust was coupled with the hate. Flinging away her embrace, he rushed out of the lodge, and bending his way towards the forest, soon lost sight of the encampment. Selonee was resolved never to return to the doom which had been fastened upon him, and to pursue his way into more distant and unknown forests—a self-doomed exile—unless he could restore Conattee to the nation. Steeled against those ties of love or country, which at one time had prevailed in his bosom, he now surrendered himself to friendship or despair. In Catawba, unless he restored Conattee, he could have no hope; and without Catawba he had neither hope nor love. On either hand he saw nothing but misery; but the worst form of misery lay in the lodge of Macourah. But Macourah was not the person to submit to such a determination. She was too satisfied with the exchange with which fortune had provided her, to suffer it to be lost so easily; and when Selonee darted from the cabin, she readily conjectured his determination. She hurried after him with all possible speed, little doubting that those thunders with which she had so frequently overawed Conattee, would possess an effect not less influential on his youthful successor. Macourah was gaunt as a greyhound and tough as a grey-squirrel in his thirteenth year. She did not despair of overtaking Selonee, provided she suffered him not to know she was on his trail. Having watched his first direction, she divined his aim to return to the hunting grounds where he had lost or slain his companion; and these hunting grounds were almost as well known to herself as to him. With a rapidity of movement, and a tenacity of purpose, which could only be accounted for by that wild passion which Selonee had inspired in her bosom, she followed his departing footsteps; and when, the next day, he heard her shouts behind him, he was absolutely confounded. But it was with a feeling of surprise that he heard her voice. He little dreamed that she had any real design upon himself; and believed that, to show her the evidences which led to the fate of her husband, might convince her that not only was he not the murderer, but that Conattee might not be murdered at all. He coolly awaited her approach, therefore, and proceeded to renew his statements, accompanying his narrative with the expression of the hope which he entertained of again restoring her husband to herself and the nation. But she answered his speech only with upbraidings and entreaties; and when she failed, she proceeded to thump him lustily with the wand by which she had compelled him to follow her to the lodge the day before. But Selonee was in no humor to obey the laws of the nation now; and though sorely tempted to pummel the jezebel in return, he forbore, in consideration of his friend, and contented himself with simply setting forward to elude her pursuit by an exercise of all his vigor and elasticity. Selonee was hardy as the grizzly bear, and fleeter than the wild turkey; and Macourah, virago as she was, soon discovered the difference in the chase when Selonee put forth his strength and spirit. She followed with all her pertinacity, quickened as it was by an increase of fury; but Selonee fled faster than she pursued, and every additional moment served to increase the space between them. The hunter lost her from his heels at length, and deemed himself fortunate. When he again approached the spot where his friend had so mysteriously disappeared, he renewed his search with a painful care the imprisoned Conattee all the while beheld. Once more Selonee crawled beneath those sprawling limbs and spreading arms that wrapped up the person of the warrior. Once more he emerged from the spot disappointed and hopeless, when, to the great horror of the captive, and the annoyance of Selonee, the shrill shrieks and screams of Macourah rang through the forests. Selonee dashed foward as he heard the sounds, and when Macourah reached the spot, the youth was already out of sight.

"I can go no further," cried the woman, "—a curse on him and a curse on Conattee, since in losing one I have lost both. I am too faint to follow. As for Selonee, may the one-eyed witch of Tustenuggee take him for her dog."

With this imprecation, the virago seated herself upon the inviting bed of moss which formed the lap of Conattee. This she had no sooner done, than the branches relaxed their hold upon her husband. The moment was too precious for delay, and sliding from under her with an adroitness and strength beyond her powers of prevention, and too sudden for any effort at resistance, her husband started up in full life before her, and, with the instinct of his former condition, prepared to take flight. She cried to him, but he fled faster. She strove to follow him, but the branches resumed their contracted grasp upon her limbs. The brown bark was already forming above her on every hand, and her tongue was alone free to assail him. But she had spoken but few words when the bark encased her jaws, and the ugly thorn of the vine which so distressed Conattee, had taken its place at their portals.

IX

The husband looked back but once, when the voice ceased—then, with a shivering sort of joy that his own doom had undergone a termination, he made a wide circuit and pushed on in pursuit of his friend. Great was the joy of the young warriors when they did encounter, and long and fervent was their mutual embrace. Conattee described his misfortunes, and related the manner in which he was taken; showed how the bark had encased his limbs, and how the magic had even engrossed his knife and the wolf skin. Conattee said not a word of his wife and her entrapment, and Selonee was left in the conviction that his companion owed his escape to some hidden change in the tyrannical mood of Tustenuggee, or the one-eyed woman, his wife.

"But the skin and the knife, Conattee, let us not leave them," said Selonee, "let us go back and extricate them from the tree."

Conattee showed some reluctance. He soon said, in the words of Macbeth, "I'll go no more." But Selonee, who ascribed this reluctance to very natural apprehensions of the demon, declared his readiness to undertake the adventure if Conattee would only point out the particular excrescence in which the articles were enclosed. When the husband perceived that his friend was resolute, he said, "Why should you have the risk, I myself will do it. It would be a woman-fear were I to shrink from the danger. Let us go."

The process of reasoning by which Conattee came to this determination was one that will not be hard to comprehend. If Selonee undertook the business an unlucky or misdirected stroke of his knife might sever a limb, or remove some portions of the bark which did not merit or need removal. Conattee trembled at the idea of the revelations which might follow such an unhappy result. Strengthening himself, therefore, he went forward with Selonee to the spot, and while the latter looked on, he proceeded with the excision of the swollen scab in which he had seen his wolf skin encompassed. While he performed the operation, as cautiously as if it had been the extraction of a mote from the eye of a virgin, the beldam in the tree, conscious of all his movements, maintained the most ceaseless efforts of her tongue and limbs, but without avail. Her slight breathing, which Conattee knew where to look for, denoted to his ears an overpowering but fortunately suppressed volcano within; and his heart leaped with joy when he thought that he was now safe, forever, from the tortures he had to endure so long. When he had finished the operation, he ventured upon an impertinence which spoke surprisingly for his sudden confidence. Looking up through the little aperture in the bark, from whence he had seen everything while in the same situation, he took a peep—a quick, quizzical, and taunting peep, at those eyes which he had not so dared to offend before. He drew back suddenly from the contact—so suddenly, indeed, that Selonee, who had no idea of the truth, thought he had been stung by some insect, and questioned him accordingly.

"Let us be off, Selonee," was the hurried answer, "we have nothing to wait for now."

Replied Selonee, "I had forgotten to say that your wife, Macourah, is on her way in search of you. I left her but a little behind, and thought to find her here. I suppose she is tired, however, and is resting by the way."

"Let her rest," said Conattee, "which is an indulgence much greater than any she ever accorded me. She will find me out soon enough, without making it needful that I should go in search of her. Come."

Selonee kindly suppressed the history of the transactions which had taken place in the village during the time when the hunter was supposed to be dead, but Conattee heard the facts from other quarters, and loved Selonee the better for the sympathy he had shown, not only in coming again to seek for him, but in not loving his wife

192

better than he did himself. As for the termagant Macourah, nobody but Conattee knew her fate; and he, like a wise man, kept his secret until there was no danger of rescue. Conattee found among the young squaws one that pleased him much better than the old. He had several children by her, and years and honors had alike fallen numerously upon his head, when, one day, one of his sons knocked off one of the limbs of the Chair of Tustenuggee, and to his great horror discovered the human arm which they enveloped. This led him to search farther, and limb after limb became detached until the entire but unconnected members of the old squaw became visible. The lad knocked about the fragments with little scruple, never dreaming how near was his relation to the form he treated with so little veneration. When he came home to the lodge and told his story, Selonee looked at Conattee, but said nothing. The whole truth was at once apparent to his mind. Conattee, though he still kept his secret, was seized with a sudden fit of piety, and taking his sons with him, he proceeded to the spot which he well remembered, and gathering up the bleached remains, had them carefully buried in the trenches of the tribe.

Selonee wedded the sweet girl who, though willing to die to prevent him from marrying Macourah, yet positively refused to take his life to defeat the same event. The only reason Conattee ever had for believing Selonee had not kept his secret from everybody, was that Medoree, the young wife of the latter, looked on him with a very decided coolness. "But we will see," muttered Conattee as he felt this conviction, "if Selonee will repent this confidence, since now it will never be possible to persuade her to take a seat in the Arm-chair of Tustenuggee. A wise man would have kept his secret and had no difficulty getting rid of a wicked wife."

*W*idely popular in his own time and called "the most representative man of letters save Poe produced in the South before the Civil War," William Gilmore Simms (1806-1870) is largely forgotten today, except for the short stories collected in **The Wigwam and the Cabin** (two volumes, 1845-46). Born in Charleston, South Carolina, Simms became a lawyer and newspaper editor, turning to literature when his first novel, **Martin Faber**, became an instant success in 1823. Most of his novels were historical romances of the American Revolution, in the James Fenimore Cooper tradition, but he also wrote biographies of famous American generals such as Francis Marion—the Swamp

Fox—and Nathanael Greene. Strongly supporting the Southern cause in the Civil War, he lost everything in its defeat and died in poverty. Since Simms tended to be discursive, a fault which sometimes wasted his ingenious plots, Prof. Waugh has taken the liberty of editing the story for modern tastes.

WHERE THE SUMMER ENDS
KARL EDWARD WAGNER

Along Grand Avenue they've torn the houses down, and left emptiness in their place. On one side a tangle of viaducts, railroad yards, and expressways—a scar of concrete and cinder and iron that divides black slum from student ghetto in downtown Knoxville. On the other side, ascending the ridge, shabby relics of Victorian and Edwardian elegance, slowly decaying beneath too many layers of cheap paint and soot and squalor. Most were broken into tawdry apartments—housing for the students at the university that sprawled across the next ridge. Closer to the university, sections had been razed to make room for featureless emplacements of asphalt and imitation used-brick—apartments for the wealthier students. But along Grand Avenue they tore the houses down and left only vacant weed-lots in their place.

Shouldered by the encroaching kudzu, the sidewalks still ran along one side of Grand Avenue, passing beside the tracks and the decrepit shells of disused warehouses. Across the street, against the foot of the ridge, the long blocks of empty lots rotted beneath a jungle of rampant vine—the buried house sites marked by ragged stumps of blackened timbers and low depressions of tumbled-in cellars. Discarded refrigerators and gutted hulks of television sets rusted amidst the weeds and omnipresent litter of beer cans and broken bottles. A green pall over the dismal ruin, the relentless tide of kudzu claimed Grand Avenue.

Once it had been a "grand avenue," Mercer reflected, although those years had passed long before his time. He paused on the cracked pavement to consider the forlorn row of electroliers with their antique lozenge-paned lamps that still lined this block of Grand Avenue. Only the sidewalk and the forgotten electroliers—curiously spared by vandals—remained as evidence that this kudzu-festooned wasteland had ever been an elegant downtown neighborhood.

Mercer wiped his perspiring face and shifted the half-gallon jug of cheap burgundy to his other hand. Cold beer would go better today, but Gradie liked wine. The late-afternoon sun struck a shimmering haze from the expanses of black pavement and riotous weed-lots, reminding Mercer of the whorled distortions viewed through antique windowpanes. The air was heavy with the hot stench of asphalt and decaying refuse and Knoxville's greasy smog. Like the murmur of fretful surf, afternoon traffic grumbled along the nearby expressway.

As he trudged along the skewed paving, he could smell a breath of magnolia through the urban miasma. That would be the sickly tree in the vacant lot across from Gradie's—somehow overlooked when the house there had been pulled down and the shrubbery uprooted— now poisoned by smog and strangled beneath the consuming masses of kudzu. Increasing his pace as he neared Gradie's refuge, Mercer reminded himself that he had less than twenty bucks for the rest of this month, and that there was a matter of groceries.

Traffic on the Western Avenue Viaduct snarled overhead as he passed in the gloom beneath—watchful for the winos who often huddled beneath the concrete arches. He kept his free hand stuffed in his jeans pocket over the double-barreled .357-Magnum derringer—carried habitually since a mugging a year ago. The area was deserted at this time of day, and Mercer climbed unchallenged past the railyards and along the unfrequented street to Gradie's house. Here as well, the weeds buried abandoned lots, and the kudzu was denser than he remembered from his previous visit. Trailing vines and smothered trees arcaded the sidewalk, forcing him into the street. Mercer heard a sudden rustle deep beneath the verdant tangle as he crossed to Gradie's gate, and he thought unpleasantly of the gargantuan rats he had glimpsed lying dead in gutters near here.

Gradie's house was one of the last few dwellings left standing in this waste—certainly it was the only one to be regularly inhabited. The other sagging shells of gaping windows and rotting board were almost too dilapidated even to shelter the winos and vagrants who squatted hereabouts.

The gate resisted his hand for an instant—mired over with the fast-growing kudzu that had so overwhelmed the low fence, until Mercer had no impression whether it was of wire or pickets. Chickens flopped and scattered as he shoved past the gate. A brown and yellow dog, whose ancestry might once have contained a trace of German shepherd, growled from his post beneath the wooden porch steps. A cluster of silver maples threw a moth-eaten blanket of shade over the yard. Eyes still dazzled from the glare of the pavement, Mercer needed a moment to adjust his vision to the sooty gloom within. By then Gradie was leaning the shotgun back amidst the deeper shadows of the doorway, stepping onto the low porch to greet him.

"Goddamn winos," Gradie muttered, watching Mercer's eyes.

"Much trouble with stealing?" the younger man asked.

"Some," Gradie grunted. "And the goddamn kids. Hush up that growling, Sheriff!"

He glanced protectively across the enclosed yard and its ramshackle dwelling. Beneath the trees, in crates and barrels, crude stands and disordered heaps, lying against the flimsy walls of the house, stuffed into the outbuildings: the plunder of the junk piles of another era.

It was a private junkyard of the sort found throughout any urban slum, smaller than some, perhaps a fraction more tawdry. Certainly it was as out-of-the-way as any. Mercer, who lived in the nearby student quarter, had stumbled upon it quite by accident only a few months before—during an afternoon's hike along the railroad tracks. He had gleaned two rather nice blue-green insulators and a brown-glass Coke bottle by the time he caught sight of Gradie's patch of stunted vegetables between the tracks and the house that Mercer had never noticed from the street. A closer look had disclosed the yard with its moraine of cast-off salvage, and a badly weathered sign that evidently had once read "Red's Second Hand" before a later hand had overpainted "Antiques."

A few purchases—very minor, but then Mercer had never seen another customer here—and several afternoons of digging through Gradie's trove, had spurred that sort of casual friendship that exists between collector and dealer. Mercer's interest in "collectibles" far outstripped his budget; Gradie seemed lonely, liked to talk, very much liked to drink wine. Mercer had hopes of talking the older man down to a reasonable figure on the mahogany mantel he coveted.

"I'll get some glasses." Gradie acknowledged the jug of burgundy. He disappeared into the cluttered interior. From the direction of the kitchen came a clatter and sputter of the tap.

Mercer was examining a stand of old bottles, arrayed on their warped and unpainted shelves like a row of targets balanced on a fence for execution by boys and a new .22. Gradie, two jelly glasses sloshing with burgundy, reappeared at the murkiness of the doorway, squinting blindly against the sun's glare. Mercer thought of a greying groundhog, or a narrow-eyed packrat, crawling out of its burrow—an image tinted grey and green through the shimmering curvatures of the bottles, iridescently filmed with a patina of age and cinder.

He had the thin, worn features that would have been thin and watchful as a child, would only get thinner and more watchful with the years. The limp sandy hair might have been red before the sun bleached it and the years leeched it to a yellow-grey. Gradie was tall, probably had been taller than Mercer before his stance froze into a slouch and then into a stoop, and had a dirty sparseness to his frame that called to mind the scarred mongrel dog that growled from beneath the steps. Mercer guessed he was probably no younger than fifty and probably not much older than eighty.

Reaching between two opalescent-sheened whiskey bottles, Mercer accepted a glass of wine. Distorted through the rows of bottles Gradie's face was watchful. His bright slits of colorless eyes flicked to follow the other's every motion—this through force of habit: Gradie trusted the student well enough.

"Got some more of those over by the fence." Gradie pointed. "In that box there. Got some good ones. This old boy dug them, some place in Vestal, traded the whole lot to me for that R.C. Cola thermometer you was looking at once before." The last with a slight sly smile, flicked lizard-quick across his thin lips: Mercer had argued that the price on the thermometer was too high.

Mercer grunted noncommittally, dutifully followed Gradie's gesture. There might be something in the half-collapsed box. It was a mistake to show interest in any item you really wanted, he had learned—as he had learned that Gradie's eyes were quick to discern the faintest show of interest. The too-quick reach for a certain item, the wrong inflection in a casual "How much?" might make the difference between two bits and two bucks for a dusty book or a rusted skillet. The matter of the mahogany mantelpiece wanted careful handling.

Mercer squatted beside the carton, stirring the bottles gingerly. He was heavyset, too young and too well-muscled to be called beefy. Sporadic employment on construction jobs and a more-or-less adhered-to program of workouts kept any beer gut from spilling over his wide belt, and his jeans and tank top fitted him as snugly as the older man's faded work clothes hung shapelessly. Mercer had a neatly trimmed beard and subtly receding hairline to his longish black hair that suggested an older grad student as he walked across campus, although he was still working for his bachelor's—in a major that had started out in psychology and eventually meandered into fine arts.

The bottles had been hastily washed. Crusts of cinder and dirt obscured the cracked and chipped exteriors and, within, mats of spider-web and moldy moss. A cobalt-blue bitters bottle might clean up nicely, catch the sun on the hallway window ledge, if Gradie would take less than a buck.

Mercer nudged a lavender-hued whiskey bottle. "How much for these?"

"I'll sell you those big ones for two, those little ones for one-fifty."

"I could dig them myself for free," Mercer scoffed. "These weed-lots along Grand are full of old junk heaps."

"Take anything in the box for a buck then," Gradie urged him. "Only don't go poking around those goddamn weed-lots. Under that kudzu. I wouldn't crawl into that goddamn vine for any money!"

"Snakes?" Mercer inquired politely.

Gradie shrugged, gulped the rest of his wine. "Snakes or worse. It was in the kudzu they found old Morny."

Mercer tilted his glass. In the afternoon sun the burgundy had a heady reek of hot alcohol, glinted like bright blood. "The cops ever find out who killed him?"

Gradie spat. "Who gives a damn what happens to old winos."

"When they start slicing each other up like that, the cops had damn well better do something."

"Shit!" Gradie contemplated his empty glass, glanced toward the bottle on the porch. "What do they know about knives. You cut a man if you're just fighting; you stab him if you want him dead. You don't slice a man up so there's not a whole strip of skin left on him."

II

"But it had to have been a gang of winos," Linda decided. She se-lected another yellow flower from the dried bouquet, inserted it into the bitters bottle.

"I think that red one," Mercer suggested.

"Don't you remember that poor old man they found last spring? All beaten to death in an abandoned house. And they caught the creeps who did it to him—they were a couple of his old drinking buddies, and they never did find out why."

"That was over in Lonsdale," Mercer told her. "Around here the pigs decided it was the work of hippy-dope-fiends, hassled a few street people, forgot the whole deal."

Linda trimmed an inch from the dried stalk, jabbed the red straw-flower into the narrow neck. Stretching from her bare toes, she reached the bitters bottle to the window shelf. The morning sun, spilling into the foyer of the old house, pierced the cobalt-blue glass in an azure star.

"How much did you say it cost, Jon?" She had spent an hour scrubbing at the bottle with the test tube brushes a former roommate had left behind.

"Fifty cents," Mercer lied. "I think what probably happened was that old Morny got mugged, and the rats got to him before they found his body."

"That's really nice," Linda judged. "I mean, the bottle." Freckled arms akimbo, sleeves rolled up on old blue workshirt, faded blue jeans, morning sun a nimbus through her whiskey-colored close curls, eyes two shades darker than the azure star.

Mercer remembered the half-smoked joint on the hall balustrade, struck a match. "God knows, there are rats big enough to do that to a body down under the kudzu. I'm sure it was rats that killed Midnight last spring."

"Poor old tomcat," Linda mourned. She had moved in with Mercer about a month before it happened, remembered his stony grief when their search had turned up the mutilated cat. "The city ought to clear off those weed-lots."

"All they ever do is knock down the houses," Mercer got out, between puffs. "Condemn them so you can't fix them up again. Tear them down so the winos can't crash inside."

"Wasn't that what Morny was doing? Tearing them down, I mean?"

"Sort of." Mercer coughed. "He and Gradie were partners. Gradie used to run a second-hand store back before the neighborhood had rotted much past the edges. He used to buy and sell salvage from the old houses when they started to go to seed. The last ten years or so, after the neighborhood had completely deteriorated, he started work-ing the condemned houses. Once a house is condemned, you pretty well have to pull it down, and that costs a bundle—either to the owner or, since usually it's abandoned property, to the city. Gradie would work a deal where they'd pay him something to pull a house down—not very much, but he could have whatever he could salvage.

"Gradie would go over the place with Morny, haul off anything Gradie figured was worth saving—and by the time he got the place, there usually wasn't much. Then Gradie would pay Morny maybe five or ten bucks a day to pull the place down—taking it out of whatever he'd been paid to do the job. Morny would make a show of it, spend a couple weeks tearing out scrap timber and the like. Then, when they figured they'd done enough, Morny would set fire to the shell. By the time the fire trucks got there, there'd just be a basement full of coals. Firemen would spray some water, blame it on the winos, forget about it. The house would be down, so Gradie was clear of the deal—and the kudzu would spread over the empty lot in another year."

Linda considered the roach, snuffed it out, and swallowed it. Waste not, want not. "Lucky they never burned the whole neighborhood down. Is that how Gradie got that mantel you've been talking about?"

"Probably." Mercer followed her into the front parlor. The mantel had reminded Linda that she wanted to listen to a record.

The parlor—they used it as a living room—was heavy with stale smoke and flat beer and the pungent odor of Brother Jack's barbeque. Mercer scowled at the litter of empty Rolling Rock bottles, crumpled napkins and sauce-stained rinds of bread. He ought to clean up the house today, while Linda was in a domestic mood—but that meant they'd have to tackle the kitchen, and that was an all-day job—and he'd wanted to get her to pose while the sun was right in his upstairs studio.

Linda was having problems deciding on a record. It would be one of hers, Mercer knew, and hoped it wouldn't be Dylan again. She had called his own record library one of the wildest collections of curiosa ever put on vinyl. After half a year of living together, Linda still thought resurrected radio broadcasts of *The Shadow* were a camp joke; Mercer continued to argue that Dylan couldn't sing a note. Withal, she always paid her half of the rent on time. Mercer reflected that he got along with her better than with any previous roommate, and while the house was subdivided into a three-bedroom apartment, they never advertised for a third party.

The speakers, bunched on either side of the hearth, came to life with a scratchy Fleetwood Mac album. It drew Mercer's attention once more to the ravaged fireplace. Some Philistine landlord, in the process of remodeling the dilapidated Edwardian mansion into student apartments, had ripped out the mantel and boarded over the grate with a panel of cheap plywood. In defiance of landlord and fire laws, Mercer had torn away the pane and unblocked the chimney. The fireplace was small, with a grate designed for coal fires, but Mercer found it pleasant on winter nights. The hearth was of chipped ceramic tiles of a blue and white pattern—someone had told him they were Dresden. Mercer had scraped away the grime from the tiles, found an ornate brass grille in a flea market near Seymour. It remained to replace the mantel. Behind the plywood panel, where the original mantel had stood, was an ugly smear of bare brick and lathing. And Gradie had such a mantel.

"We ought to straighten up in here," Linda told him. She was doing a sort of half-dance around the room, scooping up debris and singing a line to the record every now and then.

"I was wondering if I could get you to pose for me this morning?"

"Hell, it's too nice a day to stand around your messy old studio."

"Just for a while. While the sun's right. If I don't get my figure studies handed in by the end of the month, I'll lose my incomplete."

"Christ, you've only had all spring to finish them."

"We can run down to Gradie's afterward. You've been wanting to see the place."

"And the famous mantel."

"Perhaps if the two of us work on him?"

The studio—so Mercer dignified it—was an upstairs front room, thrust outward from the face of the house and onto the roof of the veranda, as a sort of cold-weather porch. Three-quarter-length casement windows with diamond panes had at one time swung outward on three sides, giving access onto the tiled porch roof. An enterprising landlord had blocked over the windows on either side, converting it into a small bedroom. The front wall remained a latticed expanse through which the morning sun flooded the room. Mercer had adopted it for his studio, and now Linda's houseplants bunched through his litter of canvases and drawing tables.

"Jesus, it's a nice day!"

Mercer halted his charcoal, scowled at the sheet. "You moved your shoulder again," he accused her.

"Lord, can't you hurry it?"

"Genius can never be hurried."

"Genius, my ass." Linda resumed her pose. She was lean, high-breasted, and thin-hipped, with a suggestion of freckles under her light tan. A bit taller, and she would have had a career as a fashion model. She had taken enough dance to pose quite well—did accept an occasional modeling assignment at the art school when cash was short.

"Going to be a *good* summer." It was that sort of morning.

"Of course." Mercer studied his drawing. Not particularly inspired, but then he never did like to work in charcoal. The sun picked bronze highlights through her helmet of curls, the feathery patches of her mons and axillae. Mercer's charcoal poked dark blotches at his sketch's crotch and armpits. He resisted the impulse to crumple it and start over.

Part of the problem was that she persisted in twitching to the beat of the music that echoed lazily from downstairs. She was playing that Fleetwood Mac album to death—had left the changer arm askew so that the record would repeat until someone changed it. It didn't help him concentrate—although he'd memorized the record to the point he no longer needed to listen to the words:

> *I been alone*
> *All the years*
> *So many ways to count the tears*
> *I never change*
> *I never will*
> *I'm so afraid the way I feel*
> *Days when the rain and the sun are gone*
> *Black as night*
> *Agony's torn at my heart too long*
> *So afraid*
> *Slip and I fall and I die*

When he glanced at her again, something was wrong. Linda's pose was no longer relaxed. Her body was rigid, her expression tense.

"What is it?"

She twisted her face toward the windows, brought one arm across her breasts. "Someone's watching me."

With an angry grunt, Mercer tossed aside the charcoal, shouldered through the open casement to glare down at the street.

The sidewalks were deserted. Only the usual trickle of Saturday morning traffic drifted past. Mercer continued to scowl balefully as he studied the parked cars, the vacant weed-lot across the street, the tangle of kudzu in his front yard. Nothing.

"There's nothing out there."

Linda had shrugged into a paint-specked fatigue jacket. Her eyes were worried as she joined him at the window.

"There's something. I felt all crawly all of a sudden."

The roof of the veranda cut off view on the windows from the near sidewalk, and from the far sidewalk it was impossible to see into the studio by day. Across the street, the houses directly opposite had been pulled down. The kudzu-covered lots pitched steeply across more kudzu-covered slope, to the roofs of warehouses along the rail-yard a block below. If Linda were standing directly at the window, someone on the far sidewalk might look up to see her; otherwise there was no vantage from which a curious eye could peer into the room. It was one of the room's attractions as a studio.

"See. No one's out there."

Linda made a squirming motion with her shoulders. "They walked on then," she insisted.

Mercer snorted, suspecting an excuse to cut short the session. "They'd have had to run. Don't see anyone hiding out there in the weeds, do you?"

She stared out across the tangled heaps of kudzu, waving faintly in the last of the morning's breeze. "Well, there *might* be someone hiding under all that tangle." Mercer's levity annoyed her. "Why can't the city clear off those damn jungles!"

"When enough people raise a stink, they sometimes do—or make the owners clear away the weeds. The trouble is that you can't kill kudzu once the damn vines take over a lot. Gradie and Morny used to try. The stuff grows back as fast as you cut it—impossible to get all the roots and runners. Morny used to try to burn it out—crawl under and set fire to the dead vines and debris underneath the growing surface. But he could never keep a fire going under all the green stuff, and after a few spectacular failures using gasoline on the weed-lots, they made him stick to grubbing it out by hand."

"Awful stuff!" Linda grimaced. "Some of it's started growing up the back of the house."

"I'll have to get to it before it gets started. There's islands in the TVA lakes where nothing grows but kudzu. Stuff ran wild after the reservoir was filled, smothered out everything else."

"I'm surprised it hasn't covered the whole world."

"Dies down after the frost. Besides, it's not a native vine. It's from Japan. Some genius came up with the idea of using it as an ornamental groundcover on highway cuts and such. You've seen old highway embankments where the stuff has taken over the woods behind. It's spread all over the Southeast."

"Hmmm, yeah? So who's the genius who plants the crap all over the city then?"

"Get dressed, wise-ass."

III

The afternoon was hot and sodden. The sun made the air above the pavement scintillate with heat and the thick odor of tar. In the vacant lots, the kudzu leaves drooped like half-furled umbrellas. The vines stirred somnolently in the murky haze, although the air was stagnant.

Linda had changed into a halter top and a pair of patched cutoffs. "Bet I'll get some tan today."

"And maybe get soaked," Mercer remarked. "Air's got the feel of a thunderstorm."

"Where's the clouds?"

"Just feels heavy."

"That's just the goddamn pollution."

The kudzu vines had overrun the sidewalk, forcing them into the street. Tattered strands of vine crept across the gutter into the street, their tips crushed by the infrequent traffic. Vines along Gradie's fence completely obscured the yard beyond, waved curling tendrils aimlessly upward. In weather like this, Mercer reflected, you could just about see the stuff grow.

The gate hung again at first push. Mercer shoved harder, tore through the coils of vine that clung there.

"Who's that!" The tone was harsh as a saw blade hitting a nail.

"Jon Mercer, Mr. Gradie. I've brought a friend along."

He led the way into the yard. Linda, who had heard him talk about the place, followed with eyes bright for adventure. "This is Linda Wentworth, Mr. Gradie."

Mercer's voice trailed off as Gradie stumbled out onto the porch. He had the rolling slouch of a man who could carry a lot of liquor and was carrying more liquor than he could. His khakis were the same he'd had on when Mercer last saw him, and had the stains and wrinkles that clothes get when they're slept in by someone who hasn't slept well.

Red-rimmed eyes focused on the half-gallon of burgundy Mercer carried. "Guess I was taking a little nap." Gradie's tongue was muddy. "Come on up."

"Where's Sheriff?" Mercer asked. The dog usually warned his master of trespassers.

"Run off," Gradie told him gruffly. "Let me get you a glass." He lurched back into the darkness.

"Owow!" breathed Linda in one syllable. "He looks like something you see sitting hunched over on a bench talking to a bottle in a bag."

"Old Gradie has been hitting the sauce pretty hard last few times I've been by," Mercer allowed.

"I don't think I care for any wine just now," Linda decided, as Gradie reappeared, fingers speared into three damp glasses like a bunch of mismatched bananas. "Too hot."

"Had some beer in the Frigidaire, but it's all gone."

"That's all right." She was still fascinated with the enclosed yard. "What a lovely garden!" Linda was into organic foods.

Gradie frowned at the patch of anemic vegetables, beleaguered by encroaching walls of kudzu. "It's not much, but I get a little from it. Damn kudzu is just about to take it all. It's took the whole damn neighbhorhood—everything but me. Guess they figure to starve me out once the vines crawl over my little garden patch."

"Can't you keep it hoed?"

"Hoe kudzu, miss? No damn way. The vines grow a foot between breakfast and dinner. Can't get to the roots, and it just keeps spreading till the frost; then come spring it starts all over again where the frost left it. I used to keep it back by spraying it regular with 2,4-D. But then the government took 2,4-D off the market, and I can't find nothing else to touch it."

"Herbicides kill other things than weeds," Linda told him righteously.

Gradie's laugh was bitter. "Well, you folks just look all around as you like."

"Do you have any old clothes?" Linda was fond of creating costumes.

"Got some inside there with the books." Gradie indicated a shed that shouldered against his house. "I'll unlock it."

Mercer raised a mental eyebrow as Gradie dragged open the door of the shed, then shuffled back onto the porch. The old man was more interesting in punishing the half-gallon than in watching his customers. He left Linda to poke through the dusty jumble of warped books and faded clothes, stacked and shelved and hung and heaped within the tin-roofed musty darkness.

Instead he made a desultory tour about the yard—pausing now and again to examine a heap of old hubcaps, a stack of salvaged window frames, or a clutter of plumbing and porcelain fixtures. His deviousness seemed wasted on Gradie today. The old man remained slumped in a broken-down rocker on his porch, staring at nothing. It occurred to Mercer that the loss of Sheriff was bothering Gradie. The old yellow watchdog was about his only companion after Morny's death. Mercer reminded himself to look for the dog around campus.

He ambled back to the porch. A glance into the shed caught Linda trying on an oversized slouch hat. Mercer refilled his glass, noted that Gradie had gone through half the jug in his absence. "All right if I look at some of the stuff inside?"

Gradie nodded, rocked carefully to his feet, followed him in. The doorway opened into the living room of the small frame house. The living room had long since become a warehouse and museum for all of Gradie's choice items. There were a few chairs left to sit on, but the rest of the room had been totally taken over by the treasures of a lifetime of scavenging. Gradie himself had long ago been reduced to the kitchen and back bedroom for his own living quarters.

China closets crouched on lion paws against the wall, showing their treasures behind curved-glass bellies. Paintings and prints in ornate frames crowded the spiderwebs for space along the walls. Mounted deer's heads and stuffed owls gazed fixedly from their moth-eaten poses. Threadbare Oriental carpets lay in a great mound of bright-colored sausages. Mahogany dinner chairs were stacked atop oak and walnut tables. An extravagant brass bed reared from behind a gigantic Victorian buffet. A walnut bookcase displayed choice volumes and bric-a-brac beneath a signed Tiffany lamp. Another bedroom and the dining room were virtually impenetrable with similar storage.

Not everything was for sale. Mercer studied the magnificent walnut china cabinet that Gradie reserved as a showcase for his personal museum. Surrounded by the curving glass sides, the mementos of the junk dealer's lost years of glory reposed in dustless grandeur. Faded photographs of men in uniforms, inscribed snapshots of girls with pompadours and padded-shoulder dresses. Odd items of military uniform, medals and insignia, a brittle silk square emblazoned with the Rising Sun. Gradie was proud of his wartime service in the Pacific.

There were several hara-kiri knives—so Gradie said they were—a Nambu automatic and holster, and a Samurai sword that Gradie swore was five hundred years old. Clippings and souvenirs and odd bits of memorabilia of the Pacific theater, most bearing yellowed labels with painstakingly typed legends. A fist-sized skull—obviously some species of monkey—bore the label: "Jap General's Skull."

"That general would have had a muzzle like a possum." Mercer laughed. "Did you find it in Japan?"

"Bought it during the Occupation," Gradie muttered. "From one little Nip, said it come from a mountain-devil."

Despite the heroic-sounding labels throughout the display—"Flag Taken from Captured Jap Officer"—Mercer guessed that most of the mementos had indeed been purchased while Gradie was stationed in Japan during the Occupation.

Mercer sipped his wine and let his eyes drift about the room. Aagainst one wall leaned the mahogany mantel, and he must have let his interest flicker in his eyes.

"I see you're still interested in the mantel," Gradie slurred, mercantile instincts rising through his alcoholic lethargy.

"Well, I see you haven't sold it yet."

Gradie wiped a trickle of wine from his stubbled chin. "I'll get me a hundred-fifty for that, or I'll keep it until I can get me more. Seen one like it, not half as nice, going for two hundred—place off Chapman Pike."

"They catch the tourists from Gatlinburg," Mercer sneered.

The mantel was of African mahogany, Mercer judged—darker than the reddish Philippine variety. For a miracle only a film of age-blackened lacquer obscured the natural grain—Mercer had spent untold hours stripping layers of cheap paint from the mahogany panel doors of his house.

It was solid mahogany, not a veneer. The broad panels that framed the fireplace were matched from the same log, so that their grains formed a mirror image. The mantelpiece itself was wide and sturdy, bordered by a tiny balustrade. Above that stretched a fine beveled mirror, still perfectly silvered, flanked by lozenge-shaped mirrors on either side. Ornately carved mahogany candlesticks jutted from either side of the mantelpiece, so that a candle flame would reflect against the beveled lozenges. More matched-grain panels continued ceilingward above the mirrors, framed by a second balustraded mantelshelf across the top. Mercer could just about touch it at fullest stretch.

Exquisite, and easily worth Gradie's price. Mercer might raise a hundred of it—if he gave up eating and paying rent for a month or three.

"Well, I won't argue it's a beauty," he said. "But a mantel isn't just something you can buy and take home under your arm, brush it off and stick it in your living room. You can always sell a table or a china closet—that's furniture. Thing like this mantel is only useful if you got a fireplace to match it with."

"You think so," Gradie scoffed. "Had a lady in here last spring, fine big house out in west Knoxville. Said she'd like to antique it with one of those paint kits, fasten it against a wall for a stand to display her plants. Wanted to talk me down to one twenty-five though, and I said 'no, ma'am.'"

Linda's scream ripped like tearing glass.

Mercer spun, was out the door and off the porch before he quite knew he was moving. "Linda!"

She was scrambling backward from the shed, silent now but her face ugly with panic. Stumbling, she tore a wrinkled flannel jacket from her shoulders, with revulsion threw it back into the shed.

"Rats!" She shuddered, wiping her hands on her shorts. "In there under the clothes! A great *big* one! Oh, Jesus!"

But Gradie had already burst out of his house, shoved past Mercer—who had pulled short to laugh. The shotgun was a rust-and-blue blur as he lunged past Linda. The shed door slammed to behind him.

"Oh, Jesus!"

The boom of each barrel, megaphoned by the confines of the shed, and in the finger-twitch between each blast, the shrill chitter of pain.

"Jon!"

Then the hysterical cursing from within, and a muffled stomping.

Linda, who had never gotten used to Mercer's guns, was clawing free of his reassuring arm. "Let's go! Let's go!" She was kicking at the gate, as Gradie slid back out of the shed, closing the door on his heel.

"Goddamn big rat, miss." He grinned crookedly. "But I sure done for him."

"Jon, I'm going!"

"Catch you later, Mr. Gradie," Mercer yelled, grimacing in embarrassment. "Linda's just a bit freaked."

If Gradie called after him, Mercer didn't hear. Linda was walking as fast as anyone could without breaking into a run, as close to panic as need be. He loped after her.

"Hey, Linda! Everything's cool! Wait up!"

She didn't seem to hear. Mercer cut across the corner of a weed-lot to intercept her. "Hey! Wait!"

A vine tangled his feet. With a curse, he sprawled headlong. Flinching at the fear of broken glass, he dropped to his hands and knees in the tangle of kudzu. His flailing hands slid on something bulky and foul, and a great swarm of flies choked him.

"Jon!" At his yell, Linda turned about. As he dove into the knee-deep kudzu, she forgot her own near panic and started toward him.

"I'm okay!" he shouted. "Just stay there. Wait for me."

Wiping his hands on the leaves, he heaved himself to his feet, hid the revulsion from his face. He swallowed the rush of bile and grinned.

Let her see Sheriff's flayed carcass just now, and she *would* flip out.

IV

Mercer had drawn the curtains across the casement windows, but Linda was still reluctant to pose for him. Mercer decided she had not quite recovered from her trip to Gradie's.

She sneered at the unshaded floor lamp. "You and your morning sunlight."

Mercer batted at a moth. "In the morning we'll be off for the mountains." This, the bribe for her posing. "I want to finish these damn figure studies whlie I'm in the mood."

She shivered, listened to the nocturnal insects beat against the curtained panes. Mercer thought it was stuffy, but enough of the evening breeze penetrated the cracked casements to draw her nipples taut. From the stairwell arose the scratchy echoes of the Fleetwood Mac album—Mercer wished Linda wouldn't play an album to death when she bought it.

"Why don't we move into the mountains?"

"Be nice." This sketch was worse than the one this morning.

"No." Her tone was sharp. "I'm serious."

The idea was too fanciful, and he was in no mood to argue over another of her whims tonight. "The bears would get us."

"We could fix up an old place maybe. Or put up a log cabin."

"You're been reading *Foxfire Book* too much."

"No, I mean it! Let's get out of here!"

Mercer looked up. Yes, she did seem to mean it. "I'm up for it. But it would be a bit rough for getting to class. And I don't think they just let you homestead anymore."

"Screw classes!" she groaned. "Screw this grungy old dump! Screw this dirty goddamn city!"

"I've got plans to fix this place up into a damn nice townhouse," Mercer reminded her patiently. "Thought this summer I'd open up the side windows in here—tear out this lousy sheetrock they nailed over the openings. Gradie's got his eye out for some casement windows to match the ones we've got left."

"Oh, Jesus! Why don't you just stay the hell away from Gradie's!"

"Oh, for Christ's sake!" Mercer groaned. "You freak out over a rat, and Gradie blows it away."

"It wasn't just a rat."

"It was the Easter bunny in drag."

"It had paws like a monkey."

Mercer laughed. "I told you this grass was well worth the forty bucks an ounce."

"It wasn't the grass we smoked before going over."

"Wish we didn't have to split the bag with Ron," he mused, wondering if there was any way they might raise the other twenty.

"Oh, screw you!"

Mercer adjusted a fresh sheet onto his easel, started again. This one would be "Pouting Model," or maybe "Uneasy Girl." He sketched in silence for a while. Silence, except for the patter of insects on the windows, and the tireless repetitions of the record downstairs.

"I just want to get away from here," Linda said at last.

In the darkness downstairs, the needle caught on the scratched grooves, and the stereo mindlessly repeated:

"So afraid...So afraid...So afraid...So afraid..."

By 1:00 a.m., the heat lightning was close enough to suggest a ghost of thunder, and the night breeze was gusting enough to billow the curtains. His sketches finished—at least, as far as he cared—Mercer rubbed his eyes and debated closing the windows before going to bed. If a storm came up, he'd have to get out of bed in a hurry. If he closed them and it didn't rain, it would be too muggy to sleep. Mechanically he reached for his coffee cup, frowned glumly at the drowned moth that floated there.

The phone was ringing.

Linda was in the shower. Mercer trudged downstairs and scooped up the receiver.

It was Gradie, and from his tone he hadn't been drinking milk.

"Jon, I'm sure as hell sorry about giving your little lady a fright this afternoon."

"No problem, Mr. Gradie. Linda was laughing about it by the time we got home."

"Well, that's good to hear, Jon. I'm sure glad to hear she wasn't scared bad."

"That's quite all right, Mr. Gradie."

"Just a goddamn old rat, wasn't it?"

"Just a rat, Mr. Gradie."

"Well, I'm sure glad to hear that."

"Right you are, Mr. Gradie." He started to hang up.

"Jon, what else I was wanting to talk to you about, though, was to ask you if you really wanted that mantel we was talking about today."

"Well, Mr. Gradie, I'd sure as hell like to buy it, but it's a little too rich for my pocketbook."

"Jon, you're a good old boy. I'll sell it to you for a hundred even."

"Well now, sir—that's a fair enough price, but a hundred dollars is just too much money for a fellow who has maybe ten bucks a week left to buy groceries."

"If you really want that mantel—and I'd sure like for you to have it—I'd take seventy-five for it right now tonight."

"Seventy-five?"

"I got to have it right now, tonight. Cash."

Mercer tried to think. He hadn't paid rent this month. "Mr. Gradie, it's one in the morning. I don't have seventy-five bucks in my pocket."

"How much can you raise, then?"

"I don't know. Maybe fifty."

"You bring me fifty dollars cash tonight, and take that mantel home."

"Tonight?"

"You bring it tonight. I got to have it right now."

"All right, Mr. Gradie. See you in an hour."

"You hurry now," Gradie advised him. There was a clattering fumble, and the third try he managed to hang up.

"Who was that?"

Mercer was going through his billfold. "Gradie. Drunk as a skunk. He needs liquor money, I guess. Says he'll sell me the mantel for fifty bucks."

"Is that a bargain?" She toweled her hair petulantly.

"He's been asking one-fifty. I got to give him the money tonight. How much money do you have on you?"

"Jesus, you're not going down to that place tonight?"

"By morning he may have sobered up, forgotten the whole deal."

"Oh, Jesus. You're *not* going to go down there."

Mercer was digging through the litter of his dresser for loose change. "Thirty-eight is all I've got on me. Can you loan me twelve?"

"All I've got is a ten and some change."

"How much change? There's a bunch of bottles in the kitchen—I can return them for the deposit. Who's still open?"

"Hugh's is until two. Jon, we'll be broke for the weekend. How will we get to the mountains?"

"Ron owes us twenty for his half of the ounce. I'll get it from him when I borrow his truck to haul the mantel. Monday I'll dip into the rent money—we can stall."

"You can't get his truck until morning. Ron's working graveyard tonight."

"He's off in six hours. I'll pay Gradie now and get a receipt. I'll pick up the mantel first thing."

Linda rummaged through her shoulder bag. "Just don't forget that we're going to the mountains tomorrow."

"It's probably going to rain anyway."

V

The storm was holding off as Mercer loped toward Gradie's house, but heat lightning fretted behind reefs of cloud. It was a dark night between the filtered flares of lightning, and he was very conscious that this was a bad neighborhood to be out walking with fifty dollars in your pocket. He kept one hand shoved into his jeans pocket, closed over the double-barreled derringer, and walked on the edge of the street, well away from the concealing mounds of kudzu. Once something scrambled noisily through the vines; startled, Mercer almost shot his foot off.

"Who's there!" The voice was cracked with drunken fear.

"Jon Mercer, Mr. Gradie! Jon Mercer."

"Come on into the light. You bring the money?"

"Right here." Mercer dug a crumpled wad of bills and coins from his pocket. The derringer flashed in his fist.

"Two shots, huh," Gradie observed. "Not enough to do you much good. There's too many of them."

"Just having it to show has pulled me out of a couple bad moments," Mercer explained. He dumped the money onto Gradie's shaky palm. "That's fifty. Better count it, and give me a receipt. I'll be back in the morning for the mantel."

"Take it now. I'll be gone in the morning."

Mercer glanced sharply at the other man. Gradie had never been known to leave his yard unattended for longer than a quick trip to the store. "I'll need a truck. I can't borrow the truck until in the morning."

Gradie carelessly shoved the money into a pocket, bent over a lamp-lit end table to scribble out a receipt. In the dusty glare, his face was haggard with shadowy lines. DT's, Mercer guessed: he needs money bad to buy more booze.

"This is traveling money—I'm leaving tonight," Gradie insisted. His breath was stale with wine. "Talked to an old boy who says he'll give me a good price for my stock. He's coming by in the morning. You're a good old boy, Jon—and I wanted you to have that mantel if you wanted it."

"It's two a.m.," Mercer suggested carefully. "I can be here just after seven."

"I'm leaving tonight."

Mercer swore under his breath. There was no arguing with Gradie in his present state, and by morning the old man might have forgotten the entire transaction. Selling out and leaving? Impossible. This yard was Gradie's world, his life. Once he crawled up out of this binge, he'd get over the willies and not remember a thing from the past week.

"How about if I borrow your truck?"

"I'm taking it."

"I won't be ten minutes with it." Mercer cringed to think of Gradie behind the wheel just now.

Eventually he secured Gradie's key to the aged Studebaker pickup in return for his promise to return immediately upon unloading the mantel. Together they worked the heavy mahogany piece onto the truck bed—Mercer fretting at each threatened scrape against the rusted metal.

"Care to come along to help unload?" Mercer invited. "I got a bottle at the house."

Gradie refused the bait. "I got things to do before I go. You just get back here soon as you're finished."

Grinding dry gears, Mercer edged the pickup out of the kudzu-walled yard, and clattered away into the night.

The mantel was really too heavy for the two of them to move—Mercer could handle the weight easily enough, but the bulky piece needed two people. Linda struggled gamely with her end, but the mantel scraped and scuffed as they lowered it from the truck bed and hauled it into the house. By the time they had finished, they both were sticky and exhausted from the effort.

Mercer remembered his watch. "Christ, it's two-thirty. I've got to get this heap back to Gradie."

"Why don't you wait till morning? He's probably passed out cold by now."

"I promised to get right back to him."

Linda hesitated at the doorway. "Wait a second. I'm coming."

"Thought you'd had enough of Gradie's place."

"I don't like waiting here alone this late."

"Since when?" Mercer laughed, climbing into the pickup.

"I don't like the way the kudzu crawls all up the back of the house. Something might be hiding..."

Gradie didn't pop out of his burrow when they rattled into his yard. Linda had been right, Mercer reflected—the old man was sleeping it off. With a pang of guilt, he hoped his fifty bucks wouldn't go toward extending this binge; Gradie had really looked bad tonight. Maybe he should look in on him tomorrow afternoon, get him to eat something.

"I'll just look in to see if he's okay," Mercer told her. "If he's asleep, I'll just leave the keys beside him."

"Leave them in the ignition," Linda argued. "Let's just go."

"Won't take a minute."

Linda swung down from the cab and scrambled after him. Fitful gushes of heat lightning spilled across the crowded yard—picking out the junk-laden stacks and shelves, crouched in fantastic distortions like a Daliesque vision of Hell. The darkness in between bursts was hot and oily, heavy with moisture, and the subdued rumble of thunder seemed like gargantuan breathing.

"Be lucky to make it back before this hits," Mercer grumbled.

The screen door was unlatched. Mercer pushed it open. "Mr. Gradie?" he called softly—not wishing to wake the old man, but remembering the shotgun. "Mr. Gradie? It's Jon."

Within, the table lamps shed a dusty glow across the cluttered room. Without, the sporadic glare of heat lightning popped on and off like a defective neon sign. Mercer squinted into the pools of shadow between cabinets and shelves. Bellies of curved glass, shoulders of polished mahogany smoldered in the flickering light. From the walls, glass eyes glinted watchfully from the mounted deers' heads and stuffed birds.

"Mr. Gradie?"

"Jon. Leave the keys, and let's go."

"I'd better see if he's all right."

215

Mercer started toward the rear of the house, then paused a moment. One of the glass-fronted cabinets stood open; it had been closed when he was here before. Its door snagged out into the cramped aisle-space; Mercer made to close it as he edged past. It was the walnut cabinet that housed Gradie's wartime memorabilia, and Mercer paused as he closed it because one exhibit was noticeably missing: that of the monkey-like skull that was whimsically labeled "Jap General's Skull."

"Mr. Gradie?"

"Phew!" Linda crinkled her nose. "He's got something scorching on the stove!"

Mercer turned into the kitchen. An overhead bulb glared down upon a squalid confusion of mismatched kitchen furnishings, stacks of chipped, unwashed dishes, empty cans and bottles, scattered remnants of desiccated meals. Mercer winced at the thought of having drunk from these same grimy glasses. The kitchen was deserted. On the stove an overheated saucepan boiled gouts of sour steam, but for the moment Mercer's attention was on the kitchen table.

A space had been cleared by pushing away the debris of dirty dishes and stale food. In that space reposed a possum-jawed monkey's skull, with the yellowed label: "Jap General's Skull."

There was a second skull beside it on the table. Except for a few clinging tatters of dried flesh and greenish fur—the other was bleached white by the sun—this skull was identical to Gradie's Japanese souvenir: a high-domed skull the size of a large, clenched fist, with a jutting, sharp-toothed muzzle. A baboon of sort, Mercer judged, picking it up.

A neatly typed label was affixed to the occiput: "Unknown Animal Skull. Found by Fred Morny on Grand Ave. Knoxville, Tenn. 1976."

"Someone lost a pet," Mercer mused, replacing the skull and reaching for the loose paper label that lay beside the two relics.

Linda had gone to the stove to turn off its burner. "Oh, *God!*" she said, recoiling from the steaming saucepan.

Mercer stepped across to the stove, followed her sickened gaze. The water had boiled low in the large saucepan, scorching the repellent broth in which the skull simmered. It was a third skull, baboon-like, identical to the others.

"He's *eating* rats!" Linda retched.

"No," Mercer said dully, glancing at the freshly typed label he had scooped from the table. "He's boiling off the flesh so he can exhibit the skull." For the carefully prepared label in his hand read: "Kudzu Devil Skull. Shot by Red Gradie in Yard, Knoxville, Tenn., June 1977."

"Jon, I'm going. This man's stark crazy!"

"Just let me see if he's all right," Mercer insisted. "Or go back by yourself."

"God, no!"

"He's probably in his bedroom then. Fell asleep while he was working on this...this..." Mercer wasn't sure what to call it. The old man *had* seemed a bit unhinged these last few days.

The bedroom was in the other rear corner of the house, leading off from the small dining room in between. Leaving the glare of the kitchen light, the dining room was lost in shadow. No one had dined here in years obviously, for the area was another of Gradie's storerooms—stacked and double-stacked with tables, chairs, and bulky items of furniture. Threading his way between the half-seen obstructions, Mercer gingerly approached the bedroom door—a darker blotch against the opposite wall.

"Mr. Gradie? It's Jon Mercer."

He thought he heard a weak groan from the darkness within.

"It's Jon Mercer, Mr. Gradie." He called more loudly, "I've brought your keys back. Are you all right?"

"Jon, let's *go!*"

"Shut up, damn it! I thought I heard him try to answer."

He stepped toward the doorway. An object rolled and crumpled under his foot. It was an empty shotgun shell. There was a strange sweet-sour stench that tugged at Mercer's belly, and he thought he could make out the shape of a body sprawled half out of the bed.

"Mr. Gradie?"

This time a soughing gasp, too liquid for a snore.

Mercer groped for a wall switch, located it, snapped it back and forth. No light came on.

"Mr. Gradie?"

Again a bubbling sigh.

"Get a lamp! Quick!" he told Linda.

"Let him alone, for Christ's sake!"

"Damn it, he's passed out and thrown up! He'll strangle in his own vomit if we don't help him!"

"He had a big flashlight in the kitchen!" Linda whirled to get it, anxious to get away.

Mercer cautiously made his way into the bedroom—treading with care, for broken glass crunched under his foot. The outside shades were drawn, and the room was swallowed in inky blackness, but he was certain he could pick out Gradie's comatose form lying across the bed. Then Linda was back with the flashlight.

Gradie sprawled on his back, skinny legs flung onto the floor, the rest crosswise on the unmade bed. The flashlight beam shimmered on the spreading splotches of blood that soaked the sheets and mattress. Someone had spent a lot of time with him, using a small knife—small-bladed, for if the wounds that all but flayed him had not been shallow, he could not be yet alive.

Mercer flung the flashlight beam about the bedroom. The cluttered furnishings were overturned, smashed. He recognized the charge pattern of a shotgun blast low against one wall, spattered with bits of fur and gore. The shotgun, broken open, lay on the floor; its barrel and stock were matted with bloody fur—Gradie had clubbed it when he had no chance to reload. The flashlight beam probed the blackness at the base of the corner wall, where the termite-riddled floorboards had been torn away. A trail of blood crawled into the darkness beneath.

Then Mercer crouched beside Gradie, shining the light into the tortured face. The eyes opened at the light—one eye was past seeing, the other stared dully. "That you, Jon?"

"It's Jon, Mr. Gradie. You take it easy—we're getting you to the hospital. Did you recognize who did this to you?"

Linda had already caught up the telephone from where it had fallen beneath an overturned nightstand. It seemed impossible that he had survived the blood loss, but Mercer had seen drunks run off after a gut-shot that would have killed a sober man from shock.

Gradie laughed horribly. "It was the little green men. Do you think I could have told anybody about the little green men?"

"Take it easy, Mr. Gradie."

"Jon! The phone's dead!"

"Busted in the fall. Help me carry him to the truck." Mercer prodded clumsily with a wad of torn sheets, trying to remember first aid for bleeding. Pressure points? Where? The old man was cut to tatters.

"They're little green devils," Gradie raved weakly. "And they ain't no animals—they're clever as you or me. They *live* under the kudzu. That's what the Nip was trying to tell me when he sold me the skull. Hiding down there beneath the damn vines, living off the roots and whatever they can scavenge. They nurture the goddamn stuff, he said, help spread it around, care for it just like a man looks after his garden. Winter comes, they burrow down underneath the soil and hibernate."

"Shouldn't we make a litter?"

"How? Just grab his feet."

"Let me lie! Don't you see, Jon? Kudzu was brought over here from Japan, and these damn little devils came with it. I started to put it all together when Morny found the skull—started piecing together all the little hints and suspicions. They like it here, Jon—they're taking over all the waste-lots, got more food than out in the wild, multiplying like rats over here, and nobody knows about them."

Gradie's hysterical voice was growing weaker. Mercer gave up trying to bandage the torn limbs. "Just take it easy, Mr. Gradie. We're getting you to a doctor."

"Too late for a doctor. You scared them off, but they've done for me. Just like they done for old Morny. They're smart, Jon—that's what I didn't understand in time—smart as devils. They knew that I was figuring on them—started spying on me, creeping in to see what I knew—then came to shut me up. They don't want nobody to know about them, Jon! Now they'll come after..."

Whatever else Gradie said was swallowed in the crimson froth that bubbled from his lips. The tortured body went rigid for an instant, then Mercer cradled a dead weight in his arms. Clumsily, he felt for a pulse, realized the blood was no longer flowing in weak spurts.

"I think he's gone."

"Oh God, Jon. The police will think we did this!"

"Not if we report it first. Come on! We'll take the truck."

"And just leave him here?"

"He's dead. This is a murder. Best not to disturb things any more than we have."

"Oh, God! Jon, whoever did this may still be around!"

Mercer pulled his derringer from his pocket, flicked back the safety. His chest and arms were covered with Gradie's blood, he noticed. This was not going to be pleasant when they got to the police station. Thank God the cops never patrolled this slum, or else the shotgun blasts would have brought a squad car by now.

Warily he led the way out of the house and into the yard. Wind was whipping the leaves now, and a few spatters of rain were starting to hit the pavement. The erratic light peopled each grotesque shadow with lurking murderers, and against the rush of the wind, Mercer seemed to hear a thousand stealthy assassins.

A flash of electric blue highlighted the yard.

"Jon! Look at the truck!"

All four tires were flat. Slashed.

"Get in! We'll run on the rims!"

Another glare of heat lightning.

All about them, the kudzu erupted from a hundred hidden lairs.

Mercer fired twice.

B orn in Knoxville, Tennessee, Karl Edward Wagner (1945-   ) has an impressive reputation as both author and publisher of macabre fiction. He received an M.D. from the University of North Carolina in the 1960s and began work on a Ph.D. in neurobiology when the sale of his first two books decided him on a literary career. He first gained attention with his stories of Kane, the grim and humorless swordsman of the Dark Ages, who may (or may not) be the immortal Biblical Cain, bringing death with him down through the ages. Some are collected in **The Book of Kane** (Grant, 1985). His short story "Sticks" won the August Derleth Fantasy Award in 1974 and is included in his collection **In a Lonely Place** (Warner, 1985). His publishing firm, Caroosa House, has issued four massive collections of the supernatural tales of Manly Wade Wellman, Hugh B. Cave, and E. Hoffman Price. He is currently editing **The Year's Best Horror Stories** series for DAW Publishers.

THE NIGHT OF THE PIASA

J.C. GREEN & GEORGE W. PROCTOR

Susan Avery gripped the sides of the toilet bowl and emptied her stomach until she wracked with dry heaves. Legs liquid and arms rubbery, she stood there, doubled over, cramping, eyes clamped tightly, trying to blot out what she had seen.

Minutes grinding like hours passed before she regained the strength to reach out and flush away what remained of her evening meal. Then she stood.

Shaking and weak, she pushed open the stall door. Somehow she managed to walk across the restroom to a row of sinks lining the opposite wall. Within her quivering insides, she felt a bit of relief. She was alone. The last thing she needed now was one of her students walking into the restroom to find her like this.

She twisted one of the faucets, cupped her hands under the water, and splashed the coldness over her flushed face. The harsh chill brought her to life, penetrating the numbness that filled body and brain.

"You were right to run," she said aloud, assuring herself.

She *was* right. She had no doubt about it now, not even a twinge of guilt. Justice had been served. A man had killed and had died in return. That she left the scene was of no consequence.

She could picture tomorrow's headlines exalting the valor of a young officer who risked his life to rid the city of a butcher—a crazy Indian gone berserk on wine or drugs.

More importantly, there would be no investigation, no questions to disturb a past she had no wish to unveil. She had been right; she ran.

Washing the bitterness of her own bile from her mouth, Susan stood and gazed into the cracked mirror above the sink. She smiled. The traces of her queasy stomach were fading. The face that smiled back at her was more than attractive, perhaps not beautiful, but more than just attractive.

Despite an almost Eurasian cast to her features, she appeared every inch "Anglo." Her own careful planning was aided by the atavistic genes of some forgotten Spanish lord who had taken an interest in the "immortal soul" of one of his forced converts. Later, he sent a pregnant squaw back to her family hogan to bear his bastard. Susan's face held no hint of that Indian blood running in her veins.

Her smile widened. Su-Ni-Ta Aguilar took ten years to bury. But the black-braided, dirty-faced girl who once chased goats through the reservation was dead. Susan Avery was alive and well.

She had earned the White Seal of Approval.

And she damn well intended to see that she kept it.

Why not? She had paid her dues. At fourteen, tribal funds sent her to an Indian school to learn the ways of the white man's world. She learned them, but not at the school with its black uniforms and scratchy muslin underwear.

She learned them on her back, held spread-eagle while five of the town's white studs repeatedly raped her.

The judge had tutored her, too. He handed down six-month probated sentences for statutory rape to each of her assailants after they testified they had bought her virginal body at five dollars a head. They went free, and she bore the label of a young Indian whore.

The name of the lesson—survival.

She learned it well. She graduated at the top of her class, which opened the way to government grants for the underprivileged, and college. But not before she spent a week's salary as a waitress in a local dive to pay the price of legally obtaining a white man's name. All it took was a court order and seventy-five dollars, and Susan Avery was born.

She learned the lesson, learned it so well that she was now in her second year of teaching at the most white, antiminority school in the Southwest. She didn't pass for white—she *was* white. Her clothes were white. Her hairstyle was white. She talked white. She laughed white. Her bed was for white lovers, men of her own choosing; men manipulated so subtly that few ever really realized she was the aggressor. And should any of them feel dependent or a bit possessive, she gracefully and amicably broke the relationship.

Susan kept but one possession of the dead Indian girl that was her past. Her eyes drifted to the silver medallion hanging around her neck, a gift from her grandfather that last day on the reservation. The jade-green stone inset at its center gave the pendant an obscurely oriental appearance. But closer inspection revealed the designs of the rabbit, crow, wolf, and thunderbird surrounding the stone. The medallion could never hint at her own heritage, so she wore it occasionally to remind her of the buried Su-Ni-Ta Aguilar, and how far she had come since that Indian girl hd died.

Her only other tie to Su-Ni-Ta was these Wednesday-night classes. Each week she left the security of her suburban apartment for the ghetto dubbed the Little Reservation by the city fathers. At the turn of the century, the district had been reserved for the rich and the elite. Time brought the blacks, then the Indians and a few Chicanos. Her class, basic American history for the adult education program, was ninety percent Amerindian.

She had never understood what prompted her to accept a position in the program, guilt or a wish to share her fortune with the people she had spent half her life trying to forget. For whatever reason, she did not want to be here tonight, not after what had happened less than an hour ago.

The door to the restroom swung inward. Two round-jowled women, fat and well past their prime, entered. Both were engrossed in a detailed discussion of the sexual attractiveness of a young English instructor. Susan caught the dark glance of their eyes in the mirror. She smiled. Immediately the two fell silent and moved to two stalls, closing the doors behind them.

Susan ran her hands over her pants suit, pressing out imagined wrinkles. Then she stood straight and stiff before the mirror. Satisfied with her appearance, she nodded to the reflection. Despite the jumbled mass of confusion still plaguing her mind and stomach, she could force herself to endure one hour in the classroom.

Just walk in and proceed as though nothing happened, she told herself.

Sucking in a deep breath, she turned, pushed open the door, and stepped into the deserted hallway.

Bells tore through the relative silence of the school. The hall filled as classrooms emptied. Bodies swarmed around her, shoving, pressing. A familiar face here and there smiled and nodded a greeting. She ignored them all. Her stomach churned violently, threatening to upheave its emptiness. In desperation, she pushed through the flowing river of people, seeking the refuge of her classroom.

Without a glance at the faces that peered at her when she entered, Susan slipped behind her desk, a barrier of authority to insulate her from the all-too-real world swarming around her. She jerked the file drawer open and ducked down, huddling there to thumb through meaningless folders that postponed facing her thirty adult students.

It didn't help. They were staring at her. Even through the desk's wood, she could feel their dark eyes coursing over her, drilling, probing, exploring, exposing the frayed edges of her sanity.

She could leave—feign sickness.

No! It's only guilt, she reprimanded herself, *guilt because I survived.* The admission brought no relief. She was sick. She *was.* And she had to escape, save herself before she was engulfed.

Another bell rang. She jerked upright, startled. The trap closed. Every eye in the room turned to her. Panic gripped her. Her stomach refused to stop its churning. *Too late,* she realized, *too late to run.*

Susan stared out, her gaze moving above their heads, trying to avoid eye contact. She swallowed, cleared her throat, but could not force a word up through the dryness of her mouth.

Then she found her voice. "A paper..."

She mumbled off, unable to remember the lesson for the night. Frantically, her eyes dropped to the top of the desk, searching for her textbook. It wasn't there. She had left it in the car during her mad rush to the restroom.

"A paper," she forced herself to begin again, "I want you to write a paper applying tonight's assignment to your own life. How history has affected you personally...both socially and economically."

There were no groans of protest. These students were not the pampered children of the white elite she taught during the day. These were frustrated adults, fighting to better themselves in a world that really didn't give a damn whether they did or not. She had not been fair in the assignment. But it took their eyes off her, letting her retreat back into her thoughts. Her gaze moved over their slumped heads and shoulders.

A face stared at her.

One lone head was turned toward her. A single young man stared up. Susan glanced away, shuffling a pile of papers stacked to one side of the desk. When her eyes chanced to rise, the young man was still there. His gaze was intimate. His black, gleaming eyes coursed over her. She could feel him mentally peeling away her clothing, leaving her naked to his caressing gaze.

She shivered, unsure whether disgust or excitement stirred her. Finding the seating chart in the top drawer of the desk, she quickly scanned it and found his name—Cully Ghant. How could she have forgotten?

She looked up again, her eyes meeting his with an iciness she had perfected to quell the most rebellious student. "Mr. Ghant, don't you think you'd best begin the assignment?"

Several heads turned toward the young man. His eyes lowered to the blank paper atop his desk.

Stupid Indian! She cursed to herself, calmly sitting behind the desk. He was pure-blood and wore his red skin like a badge. His every move spoke, "I'm Indian...red is beautiful!" Cully Ghant was chief of the dead-end tribe and the stupid bastard didn't even know it.

There was no trace of the filth and squalor of the reservation about him. His was the look of the Little Reservation—city-bred Indian, streetwise, a prowler, a scavenger. Cully Ghant would never be found at a Wounded Knee. He had learned his survival lessons too. But he didn't have the courage to become white. He hid behind false racial pride while he hungered for white power and all its material trappings. He stalked the streets, accepting the scraps thrown his way.

She felt his eyes on her again but ignored them, refusing him the satisfaction of disturbing her again. Instead, she sat there, counting the minutes and trying to forget the classroom, Cully Ghant, and the flashing blade.

The bell rang. Still she sat there, accepting the papers the students placed on her desk as they left.

Cully Ghant waited until the room emptied, then rose. He didn't walk toward her, but sauntered around the desk to invade her barrier of security. He pressed close, intimately. His eyes roved over her.

She felt naked. She shivered, unable to restrain a strange mixture of attraction and revulsion. She wanted to run...run before he moved even closer.

His hand rose.

She winced, then smiled nervously. He held a sheet of paper to her. She took it, glancing down at a sketch of the pendant she wore.

"Mr. Ghant...what is this?" she managed to ask.

"Your medallion," he said, then added, "little red sister."

"I'm not your sister, Mr. Ghant!" She crumpled the paper and tossed it into the waste paper can. "And this is not an art class!"

"*Brujo,*" he said, ignoring her anger. "You wear the stone of a *brujo.*"

She suppressed an uneasy tremble that threatened to destroy what remained of her composure. "Indian jewelry is very popular and stylish..."

"Not this," he said, cutting short her explanation. He reached out to lift the disk in his hand. The hard ripple of his knuckles brushed over the contours of her breast. Susan shivered, even more unsure of herself. She pulled away from him.

He made no attempt to veil a smile of amusement. The encounter was no accident. He let the medallion fall back.

"A trinket...I bought it in Albuquerque..." she said in a murmur, trying to ignore the warm glow where his hand had touched her, "... not even turquoise."

"Don't give me that!" He grasped her shoulders. His fingers were demanding, yet gentle, as though he could feel the trembling of her flesh beneath her blouse. "The blood of the *diablero* runs in your veins, little sister. Not even the whiteness of your skin can hide that. Only a *brujo* wears the stone of the shape-changer. The heart of the *Piasa* is passed from generation to generation—never pawned away into white hands! Never!"

She shook her head, trying to form an answer with her lips, but could not find the lies. Abruptly, he pulled her to him. She stiffened, then his hands were gone, and he stepped back.

"When you tire of your white way," he said, "I'll be waiting, little sister."

She didn't answer. She broke and ran. An echoing laughter rose within her, mocking her flight.

The alley was empty, then it wasn't. A garbage truck loomed out of the darkness, wheeling onto the street.

Susan's foot slammed the brake. Tires cried out in protest as asphalt bit into rubber. The Volkswagen lurched, shuddering to a halt. The truck rumbled by, fender missing fender by mere inches.

Unable to curse or give thanks, Susan collapsed onto the steering wheel. Her body shook uncontrollably and she sobbed. Her knuckles stood out a tortured white as she clung to the wheel in desperation. The night was too much for her. Bit by bit, it was stripping away the fabric of her sanity. It gathered around her. She felt it, a predator stalking its prey. It surrounded her, pressing closer and closer—the Little Reservation, the faces of her students, Cully Ghant, the silvery flash of the knife, the...

No! Damn it, no!

Fear and guilt gave way to anger. She shoved away from the steering wheel and sat straight in the seat. There was no room within her for fear and guilt or self-pity. She was alive; she was surviving, that was all that mattered, nothing else.

She froze. The laughter, the mocking voice was there, moving within her once again. It echoed up from the core of something dark and hidden, resounding against the wobbly foundations of her composure.

"Old man. Hey, old man, give us a drink."

"Yeah, share that bottle with us, old man."

Susan's head jerked, startled by the voices intruding from outside. Across the street two young boys, no more than thirteen or fourteen, taunted a wino squatted on the curb. With one hand, the man clutched a bottle of cheap booze to his chest. His free arm flailed the air, swatting away the hands trying to liberate his precious treasure.

"Go away, leave me alone." The man's words were slurred, thick with alcohol. "Get out of here."

The two boys laughed. The old man's protests only seemed to increase the vigor of their attack.

Susan felt it before the shadow passed over the Volkswagen. Like a cold finger, it pressed at the base of her spine, and she knew it.

It was there, that shifting, mistlike presence she had seen once before this night. Black even against the night sky, it floated over the street to hover above the man and the boys. As before, Susan could not take her eyes from the shifting form. She wanted to cry out, to warn the three, but the writhing cloud mesmerized her.

She was an observer again, removed and distant from the scene she gazed upon. The mist was different, changed. It seemed larger and dense, as though it was solidifying. In two hours could it have changed?

The cloud writhed, swirled, churned. A single tendril coiled down from its belly. It touched the boys, then the man, as if feeling, probing.

The mist dropped, cloaking itself to the wino.

A growl rumblng from the depths of his throat, the old man sprang to his feet. He gripped the neck of the bottle, holding it like a club. "Here, take your drink."

Arm and bottle lashed out. There was a fleshy thud, then the shattering of glass. One of the boys reeled back and fell to the pavement, his hand clutching his temple.

The old man spun, the broken bottle extended before him like a jagged-edged knife. In one swipe, he raked it across the throat of the remaining youth. The boy stumbled away a step or two, as if in a daze, unable to comprehend what had happened. He stared at the wino turned killer, the object of a harmless prank but a moment ago. Then the boy crumpled to the sidewalk, life flowing from the slash opening his throat.

As Susan stared, the presence lifted from the old man. Floating upward, it drifted above the buildings, soaring, and for the second time that night she heard its laughter, a sound that found resonance with the mocking voice deep within her.

The breaking of glass drew attention back to the wino. The remains of his deadly bottle glittered around his feet, silvery shards reflecting the street lamps. The old man's mouth opened. His quivering lips formed a whimpering sob that rose higher and higher to a whining cry of terror. His shaking head turned to one boy, then the other. Stumbling back a few steps, he looked up, seeing the Volkswagen. Then he ran. Screaming at the night, he ran.

Susan watched until he disappeared around a corner. It happened again. Like a woman coming out of a dream, she realized it had happened again!

Panic twisted within her. She couldn't stay here. She couldn't be caught at the scene. The police meant questions, inquiries that might unearth Su-Ni-Ta Aguilar. She wouldn't let that happen, not after all she had done to bury the Indian girl, not after all the time it had taken.

She glanced around. Except for two still bodies on the sidewalk, the street was empty. She was safe.

A piteous gasp escaped her throat.

In the rear-view mirror, she saw a man. His features were hidden in the shadows, but she saw his smile. She shuddered. It was the same smile, the same man who had shared the...

It can't be! It just can't be him, not again! But she knew she lied to herself. It was the same man who had stood in the alley outside the drive-in grocery earlier that night, watching her. *God! Oh god, he's coming toward me!*

The man behind her moved closer. She could almost see his face. His hand stretched out, beckoning her.

Susan reached out, twisting the ignition key. The Volkswagen coughed, the motor catching. Her foot floored the gas pedal as she slammed the gearshift into first. Tires squealed against the pavement. Susan Avery ran, fleeing toward the security of her suburban apartment, away from the Little Reservation, Su-Ni-Ta Aguilar, and the night.

He sat cross-legged in the dirt, huddled over a small fire of piñon pine. The day was sweltering, but he hugged a brightly colored blanket around his lean frame. His coarse gray hair was pulled back in a knot held by a silver clasp set with a huge chunk of male, blue turquoise. His face was as sun-baked and sand-blasted as the barren arroyo he stared down into.

His spoken name was Beasos Dihi, Dark Feather—his secret name was known only to himself. To his face, he was called Hasteen Chi, a term of respect. But whispers of fear behind his back named him *brujo* or *diablero*, a man who carried the secrets of forgotten days.

He was not a chanter men sought for the healing ceremonies of the soothing Night Chant, or to cleanse themselves of outside contact with the Enemy Way. Those who consulted Beasos Dihi did so only in secret and never revealed what transpired. The only ceremony he performed for the tribe was the burial rite; death was the greatest taboo of the People. Even the name of the dead could not be uttered, and the hogan that held death was always destroyed.

It was to this man Su-Ni-Ta had come, seeking his blessings before her journey into the white man's world.

Unlike the others, she carried no fear of Beasos Dihi. In the days before the reservation school, he had taught her the stories of the Changing Woman and the Hero Twins. She had learned the ways of the desert, the plant and animal lore of her people. His teaching had been given with the love and humor that befit a grandfather.

The old man held out his hand, indicating Su-Ni-Ta was to sit at his left. She did. In the old way, neither spoke for a long time, and neither looked directly at the other. Instead they gazed north, out across the desert. Here stunted juniper and greasewood fanned out to be replaced by sage and sandstone.

"You will leave the *Dinetah*," Beasos Dihi broke the silence. He used the ancient name, Land of the People, refusing to accede to the name given by the Spanish invaders.

"You have talked with my mother," she answered with a nod.

"I have spoken with those who know more than your mother."

"Have they told you I will go to the white man's school?"

"It is not the first time," he said, turning to her, "our women have been taken to the Place of Bells."

"I will not be taken to Albuquerque." Su-Ni-Ta repeated what had been said a hundred times before. "I want to go, to learn."

"To leave the old ways."

"The old ways are dying...our people are dying." She did not argue, she pleaded. "I want to live, *Tschai,* Grandfather."

"The old ways die, but the new are no better," Beasos Dihi said, staring off into the horizon. "You will go, but I will not see you return. Like the ways of the *Dineh,* my time is over. This I have seen."

Su-Ni-Ta was silent for several minutes in respect for his vision of death. Then she asked, "What do you see for me?"

"I see what is not old or new." The old man shook his head. "I see what I cannot understand, both pain and pleasure. I see what must go unspoken. Look, daughter, look at the horizon and tell me what you see."

Su-Ni-Ta gazed over the desert. Unlike her grandfather, her sight was limited to her eyes. To the left, the sun was fast sinking behind the rolling sandstone, tinting it coral and crimson. Before her, to the north, the direction of death, she could see the gathering darkness of night. But as she watched, she saw a deeper blackness boiling near the ground.

"The night brews a sandstorm for tomorrow," she said. "We will have desert grit for breakfast."

Beasos Dihi said nothing but slipped an amulet from his neck and held it out to Su-Ni-Ta. She took it, staring at the symbols of the rabbit, crow, wolf, and thunderbird cut into its shining surface. At its center was the polished jadelike stone—the heart of the *Piasa*—the soul of the thunderbird. She started a choked protest, but the old man stopped her short.

"No!" His voice was stern, containing a ferocity she had never heard before. "I have no need any more. But your need will be great. Wear it always. The time will come when it will open a path…"

His words trailed off into silence.

No more would be said, she realized. Pushing herself up from the dirt, she placed the medallion around her neck, then started back down the trail to the village.

> *"Now you go on your way alone.*
> *What you are now, we know not.*
> *To what clan you belong, we know not.*
> *From now on, you are not of this Earth."*

Beasos Dihi chanted in the quavering drone of a tribal singer. It was the Death Song of the People, but she did not know if he was singing it for himself or her.

There was no trace of sand or wind the next morning when she left for the white man's school.

His hand shifted into the frayed pocket of his jeans. It rummaged there a moment, then withdrew. His copper-brown fingers caressed the imitation mother-of-pearl handle of an oversized pocket knife. A broad-knuckled thumb tapped the spring-loaded insert near the end of the handle.

A razored blade flashed out.

Hidden at the rear of the store, Susan Avery saw the man approach the check-out counter. She hugged the shelves, clinging there like a trembling rabbit. She wanted to scream and warn the clerk. She wanted to free the terror ripping through her throat.

But her own hand clamped over her mouth, muting her cry to an inaudible sob. Unable to move, to scream, Susan stood there and stared down the aisle at the clerk and—the man with the knife.

"Hey!" The clerk's head twisted from the portable television that held her attention. Rough-hewed features marked the man edging toward the cash register as Amerindian, wino. "What the hell ya think you're doing, chief?"

The woman froze.

Her eyes dropped to the gleaming sliver of steel he gripped. Total incomprehension filled her face, a blankness erasing the lines of vanished youth that caked makeup failed to conceal.

Disconnected, removed from the small drive-in store in which she stood, Susan gazed on the scene with a sudden coolness that frightened her far more than the knife brandished by the man. Idly she found herself studying the clerk's features. The woman was in her mid-thirties, never beautiful, never even attractive.

Animation crept back into the clerk's face. Her eyes widened, dilating with fear. Her head moved from side to side in uncertain jerks, her hair trembling as if stirred by a chilling breeze. Her mouth opened. Her lips moved but produced no sound, not even a little whimper.

The man smiled and stepped behind the counter. The clerk shrank before his imposing hulk, no more than a fragile Dresden doll in the shadow of a descending sledgehammer. The man's smile broadened into a yellow, tobacco-stained grin.

About him was a presence, a sifting, shifting presence. Susan saw it—felt it—instinctively warned by the ancient blood coursing beneath the veneer of her civilized skin. Here was something familiar yet totally alien, something that linked her to the man with a bond stronger than their common heritage.

The man's arm jerked into the air—then fell!

"God...oh, God..." the clerk moaned, her eyes locked to the blade buried in her breast. "No...no...please don't..."

He wrenched the knife free. The woman winced and staggered back, her retreat barred by the counter. She slumped there.

The knife, a silver fang, lashed out, rending, cutting. Again. Again. The clerk found the full strength of her vocal cords and screamed.

Susan pushed against the shelves, trying to melt into the aspirin, laxatives, and toothpaste that packed the aisle. Terror gripped every fiber of her body. But beneath the fear lay an even greater horror. At the core of her being was a glowing pleasure, an orgasmic release of something carefully confined behind the walls of social restraint. It laughed within her. It taunted, mocking her fascination with the bestial slaughter being staged for her benefit alone.

Again and again, the man's arm jerked up and fell, jerked up and fell, like a disjointed marionette, dancing a macabre fling. A roar of canned laughter blared from the flickering television behind the two, forming a grotesque chorale.

The clerk's screams gave way to mindless sobs, and finally silence. In limp resignation, her arms fell to her side. Her eyes rolled to the ceiling. She was still.

The man thrust the lifeless body from him.

He staggered back. His chest heaved as he gulped down breaths in exhaustion. Trembling with excitement, he hovered over the dead woman, seeking some trace of movement. There was none. He twisted, vaulted over the counter, and ran into the night.

Without so much as a glance to the dead woman or the untouched cash register, Susan ran down the aisle after him. Outside, in the mercury vapor glow of the street lights, she saw him stumble across the street. Around him swirled a dark mass, boiling like a swarm of blowflies. It lifted from him and drifted upward.

The fleeing man stiffened for an instant. His head jerked around. Confusion contorted his face. He held the knife and his bloodied hands out before him. Shaking his head in disbelief, he touched the blood-sodden front of his shirt. He cried out hysterically, slinging the knife to the street. It shattered the unnatural silence of the night when it struck the pavement and careened across the asphalt into the gutter.

The man sank to his knees and doubled over. With great wracking heaves, he retched.

Susan barely noticed the convulsively shuddering man. Her gaze riveted to the writhing mist above the street. Illuminated by the frosty light of the vapor lamps, it turned in upon itself. She shivered. It made no sound, yet she knew it laughed, a laughter that chorused the taunting pleasure moving within her.

The moment no longer belonged solely to her. She could feel eyes staring at her. She shivered again. Her gaze ran up and down the empty block several times before locating the source of her uneasiness.

There, in the shadow of an alley directly across from her, stood a man. She could see the glint of his eyes, but his face remained in darkness. She felt rather than saw his smile. A thin smile twisted over her own lips. The man in the alley gave credence to the events unfolding this night.

"My God! I didn't mean it!" the man in the street cried out, pushing to his feet. He held his hands toward Susan. "Sweet Jesus, I didn't …"

The enormity of what had happened was too heavy. He gave a choked groan of despair, then turned to run down the street.

Rubber squealed against asphalt. A black-and-white squad car fishtailed around a corner. Like a spectator to a surrealistic movie, Susan watched.

The dark mist shimmered and dipped to touch the police car.

The officer within jerked, slamming the brake to the floorboard. There was no way the officer could know what had happened in the store, Susan realized, as he flung himself from the car and drew his service revolver.

An exploding cannon rent the night.

The fleeing man shuddered. His ankles collapsed under him. He fell, rolling. His twitching fingertips brushed the knife he had tossed to the gutter but moments before. Twice more the gun fired, spitting lead into a dead body.

The revolver extended before him, the officer cautiously crept up to his victim.

Susan's gaze rose to the black mist. It was no longer there. Her eyes darted along the street and found it crouched beside a fire hydrant like some feline licking the filth from its fur. Then it rose, drifting upward, melting into the night.

She glanced to the man in the alley for assurance that what she had seen was real. He was gone.

The full realization of what she had witnessed struck her. She came alive, no longer the spectator. She ran…ran.

Susan bolted upright in bed. She shivered; her whole body was drenched with sweat. Her eyes darted around for a few moments before she realized she was in her bedroom, in the safety of her own apartment. She sighed and shook her head.

Real, the dream had been so real, perhaps even more vivid than the scene she witnessed in the grocery earlier that night. She sighed again, remembering the flashing knife, the gunshots, the shattering bottle.

For an instant she considered lying down again, but she knew it would be useless. The dream would come again, haunting her.

A drink, she thought. *I need a drink.*

Grabbing her robe from the foot of the bed, she walked into the living room of the apartment. She found a bottle and a glass and poured three fingers. Huddling on the couch, hugging her knees, she downed half the drink.

She smiled. The bourbon was smooth. It warmed her stomach and flowed into her veins, soothing her frayed edges. Another drink, or three, would help bring the oblivion she sought. Tomorrow, the whole night would be no more than a faded memory, like some half-forgotten nightmare.

A knock came at the door.

She jumped. Bourbon splashed down the front of her robe. Her head twisted to the wall clock. Midnight. She expected no visitors. Her friends were not in the habit of dropping in unannounced during the middle of the night. She decided to let the door go unanswered.

The knock was louder, more demanding the second time.

She couldn't ignore it. Whoever it was might wake the whole building. Placing her drink on the coffee table, she crossed the room to flick off the lights. Only a soft glow penetrated the room from outside. She opened the door just enough to peer out. A startled gasp whimpered from her throat.

The man from the alley!

She recognized the silhouette of his body, the relaxed flex of his shoulders. He had followed her; he had followed her all the way from the Little Reservation where she left him in the street beside two dead boys. His eyes glinted in the darkness. She gasped again, staggering back into the room.

The door swung in and the looming figure invaded the sanctuary of her apartment.

"I decided not to wait, little sister." The voice was unmistakably Cully Ghant's.

"You!" Her voice was a mere whisper. She watched him lock the door behind him. "You were...tonight...you saw!"

"All of it," he said, moving to her. "And I knew."

"Knew?" She shook her head, confused and frightened.

He gave no answer, except to draw her to him. She came without protest, trembling when his mouth covered hers. Then she returned his kiss, willingly accepted his rough embrace. If sex was what he wanted, she would give it—anything to survive.

Abruptly, his arms left her. The light flared on overhead. Cully moved to the couch and sat there a few moments just staring at her. A pleased smile played over his lips. Finally he said, "Something to drink. I need something to drink."

Unquestioning, she walked to the kitchen. She passed by a six-pack of beer in favor of a bottle of wine neatly tucked away on the bottom shelf of the refrigerator. The wine was an expensive gift from an appreciative lover, and she had been saving it for a special occasion. Mindless of what she was doing, she pulled out the bottle. Instead of a crystal champagne glass, she took a large tumbler from the cupboard and filled it.

"So this is the hogan of my little *bruja,*" Cully said as she handed him the glass. He drank deeply, draining away most of the wine in one gulp. He glanced up to her. His black eyes ran over her body. "Not bad."

She stared at him, attempting to attain a superior air, yet uncertain whether he meant the apartment, the wine, or her.

"The little *bruja* is bewildered, perhaps a bit disappointed. She thinks I'm here for her body...to rape her." He grinned, amused. "Has she forgotten so much of her people? A brave will force himself on a woman taken from an enemy, but never a woman of the People."

He called himself a "brave," a man warring against an enemy. Cully Ghant would think of himself at war, Susan thought. It fit his image of the city-bred Indian, a lone brave against a world of Anglos. But if he hadn't come for her, then what did he want? Money? Blackmail?

His gaze slowly moved around the apartment. "No one would suspect to find one of the People here, let alone a *diablera.* Very expensive, very white. The perfect place for you to hide and wait."

"Hide?" What was he talking about? She was confused. Did he know something, more than what they had witnessed this night? It had to be blackmail.

"At the heart of the enemy camp, that's where I sit, at the arm of a *bruja,*" he said, either not hearing her or ignoring her question. He was taking his time about getting to the point, playing with her.

Cully sipped at his wine, then said, "My parents were an ordinary man and woman, without the sight, or *brujo* blood running through their veins. But they believed in the ways of the People. On the night I was born, my father had a dream, a vision. He saw his son sitting safely in the heart of the enemy camp beside a woman, yet that woman was a *diablera*."

"What in hell are you talking about?" What was he doing? Why was he dragging this out? She didn't understand.

"A vision a man held for his son is all I'm trying to tell you about," he said. "The same vision that has guided that son for twenty-five years. My father believed his dream foretold of greatness for his son, a brave who would serve the People at the arm of a powerful *bruja*. I've shared that belief. My whole life has been spent on the streets. I've learned them and their ways, because with that knowledge I'd be strong and ready to serve. And I've searched for that *bruja* in the face of every woman I've met, waiting to be called."

"Streetwise Cully Ghant ruled by the vision of another man." Her tone was thick with contempt. He was crazy or on drugs to ramble on like this. "Get off it. It doesn't suit you, chief. You're not that stupid. No one is. The magic in visions died when the first Spaniard set foot in the New World. That's reality, not some dream."

He glanced up at her. There was no trace of anger in his expression. "You're bruised."

She followed his gaze to the pendant around her neck and the purpling flesh beneath it. She winced, suddenly aware of the throbbing pain. Cully's embrace had been rougher than she realized. She twisted away from him, ashamed of letting him see that he had hurt her.

"I saw the look on your face after what happened in the store," he said. "I saw you watching it up there, then again on the street after class. You enjoyed it! You felt it, and you enjoyed it!"

"Saw what?" Susan pivoted back to face him, glaring challenge. Now he got to it. He wouldn't win. She wouldn't admit anything.

"The power, little sister." Cully casually took another sip of the wine. "I've been watching it. It was bred out there in the Little Reservation, conceived in the tenements. I've seen it. Anybody could have. It's been out there stalking the sewers, prowling the alleys—seeking. It found nourishment in the streets, sucking up the hate, the frustration, the guilt, the desires. I've watched it grow. I've watched it flex its muscles, test its strength. Tonight it singled us out—touched us. It revealed its full power to you and me. It chose us from all the People in the Little Reservation."

"The People, the old ways—they're dead! There's nothing left of the People except dirty blankets and tourist traps. They traded their ways for a bottle of cheap muscatel!"

"Nothing dies, little sister," he said. "It just changes, alters shape. The power flows up from the land to its people. The whites, the blacks, the browns, they forgot the land. They never recognized its force. They thought they had killed it. But from the ashes of a charred body, the spirit escaped and took a new form. We saw it. Tonight it chose us!"

"You've been chewing too many peyote buttons," Susan said with no attempt to veil her contempt. "Your mind's gone."

"My father and mother gave me the name Ishacolly. Tonight, the Wandering Wolf found his *bruja*—a *diablera* to open the door to the power." He was ignoring her sarcasm. "All you have to do is accept it, little sister, allow its strength to enter you. I will follow. I'm here to serve."

Despite herself, she shivered, remembering the man with the knife, the glowing pleasure he had released in her soul, the wino and his bottle, and her fascination as he killed the two boys.

"Just you and me, little sister. That's all it will take," Cully said. "You have the blood of a *bruja,* and you carry the stone, the heart of the *Piasa.* You're the focal point. All you have to do..."

"Oh, no! Not so fast, chief! There's no you and me. Just *me!*" Her coolness and ferocity frightened her. But her fear of this man had turned to anger. "You came here to scare me. You did it. But now it's over—one cheap thrill to a customer. That's all there is to it. I'm not on your trip, chief. I didn't see anything tonight, and there's no way you can prove I did. Now, get out, you two-bit, half-breed hustler!"

She walked across the room in quick, stiff strides, flung the door open, and stood there, trying to contain her anger.

Cully took a lingering last swig of his drink. He stretched wtih aggravating languor, then stood and sauntered to the door. He stopped a few inches from her, looking her up and down. There was no expression on his face, but she could feel his disgust.

"You saw it. It's still in your eyes, little sister. When you're ready, I'll be there, waiting." He stepped through the doorway and was gone.

Susan could not sleep. She tried but only stared at the ceiling. Even the bourbon wasn't helping. Cully Ghant refused to leave her mind. He had invaded the sanctuary of her apartment, and his presence lingered, taunting her.

Who did he think he was, trying to drag her back, trying to destroy what had taken so long to build? Su-Ni-Ta was buried. She would stay that way. Cully Ghant could keep the Little Reservation all to himself. She didn't need it.

Still she could not sleep. Pushing from the bed, she found jeans and a blouse in a closet. Quickly dressing, she left the apartment to escape into the night.

The air was clear and unseasonably warm. Caring little about her direction, she walked, leaving the lingering ghost of Cully Ghant and his dead-end tribe to slowly die behind her.

She should never have allowed him in the apartment. She should have screamed. It had been a mistake, now she had to forget it.

Turning at the end of the block, she strolled across the street to a small neighborhood park. When she first came to the city, the park had been her refuge. She came here often, hiding behind the wall of trees and shrubs, letting them blot out the buildings and streets that closed in around her. Tonight it would hide her from Cully Ghant.

The park refused to shelter her. Autumn had stripped the branches, leaving them barren. Their skeletal forms did nothing to close off the city. There was no privacy, only isolation; no smell of summer grasses and flowers, just the pungent stench of automobile exhaust. The park was a mistake. The walk was a mistake. Susan turned to retrace her steps back to the apartment.

"Hey, *chica.*"

There were four of them. They moved from the shadows of the trees.

"Hey, *guapa, guapita.*"

For a moment she froze, uncertain of what to do. That moment was all they needed. They closed around her, moving in with each beat of her heart.

They were Chicano. Even without their voices, she could tell that. Anglo, Spanish, Indian all bred within them; almost blood brothers. She recognized their common heritage, but they didn't. To them, she was white. White had cast them in the roles that they now intended to act out.

"*Bonita, venga aqui,*" the youth closest to her said with a leer. In his hand a silver blade glinted. "Easy, take it easy and everything will be all right. We won't hurt you."

A malicious chuckle came from behind her. She twisted around to stare into another leering face and a slowly swaying knife.

Suddenly hands gripped her shoulders, forcing her to her knees, to her stomach. They pulled at her, rolling her to her back. The fabric of her blouse rent under the rough grasp of their fingers.

"God, please don't, please." She begged, her arms desperately trying to hide her vulnerable, exposed body. "Money! I'll give you money!"

An open palm slapped sharply against the side of her face. Their faces blurred above her. Her temples pounded, threatening to explode.

"Afterwards, *bonita.*" One of them laughed, his hands sliding over her bare stomach to fumble with the buttons of her jeans. "Afterwards, we'll take your money."

The feel of his hands—their hands—was too much to endure. She panicked. She kicked out, her knee connecting solidly with his groin. The man howled, staggering back.

This time, a fist slammed into her cheek. Dazed and hurting, her arms flailed the air to fight off any further blows. It was useless. The next fist struck her jaw, driving her toward unconsciousness.

"Another stunt like that, pretty one," one of them said, splattering spittle over her face, "and my knife will ruin your beauty."

Helplessly, her hands dropped back to her chest. Her fingertips brushed something, something warm and hard and smooth. The crystal of her amulet—the heart of the *Piasa*—it vibrated with strength, pulsed with power.

Again the voice moved within her. No longer did it mock her. It called to her in the voice of Beasos Dihi. It opened the path. It opened its arms to her—the arms of Cully Ghant. It was the door.

"Yes!" She screamed out, accepting it when there was nothing else to accept.

Darkness flowed over her. She felt it massing around her, blotting out the faces of her assailants. It touched her, then entered her body, permeating the very core of her soul.

"Little sister!" A voice called to her.

She looked up. Cully was there. He came out of the night like his namesake. Recklessly, he pushed through her four attackers before they realized what was happening. Then he was there, lifting her to her feet, his arm around her waist for support.

The four rushed them. But it didn't matter. She stood there, no longer a part of the threatening scene. She prayed as she had never prayed in her life. She opened herself to the power that flowed within and without her.

A talon with great recurved claws ripped out from the night. It raked across one of the faces that moved toward her. The man screamed and fell back. But not before the talon opened his chest.

She heard the growls and the snapping jaws. She saw the torn throats of two men, life flowing crimson from them. Again there were the talons, the flapping of wings. The last of her assailants screamed, his voice drowned in a terrible cry of triumph. The man collapsed to the winter-brown grass. A mass of red stared up at her where his face had once been.

A warm glow of pleasure suffused her body as she surveyed the butchered corpses strewn at her feet. It was a fitting beginning. Her head twisted to the black wolf sitting on its haunches beside her. Its darkly gleaming eyes rolled to her, reflecting the same satisfaction.

Her own golden eyes glittered with newfound pride. She unfolded the expanse of her great wings, then rose into the air.

The night was hers—the first of many to come. She rose, soaring and swooping. The currents caressed her. It was glorious. It would have been enough just to float there on the winds. But there was much that had to be done this night. Tribute to be taken.

She turned her attention to the heart of the city. Its lights glared red in anticipation of the reign of carnage brought on the night winds. She lifted her fire-plumed head and again screamed a cry of triumph.

Below her, on the pavement, ran a dark, living shadow—a wolf that no longer wandered.

*T*exas born and bred like her collaborator, Ms. Green is a published poet; "Night of the Piasa" is her first work of fiction. George W. Proctor is best known for his science fiction novels (such as **Shadowman, The Fire at the Center,** and **Starwings**), but he has published many others, usually under pen names preventing full recognition of the extent of his work. When the single-hero pulp magazines (such as **The Shadow**) died, the paperback series replaced them; Proctor has done some or all of such series as **The Texans (Blood Moon)**, from Pinnacle; **V (The Texas Run),** also from Pinnacle; and currently **Chance (Riverboat Rampage)** from Avon, under the name of Clay Tanner. He is also co-editor, with Steven Utley, of the first all-Texas anthology of science fiction, **Lone Star Universe** (Heidelberg, 1976), containing his story "The Migration."

ONLY YESTERDAY

TED WHITE

He was waiting for her when she stepped down from the trolley.

The grass was dry and dead under his feet, and the crisp air made his nose run. He pulled a tissue from the packet in his overcoat pocket, blew into it, wadded it, looked around at the straight lines of the tracks, the receding trolley, the brown fields, the little half-open waiting shed in which he stood—then self-consciously shoved the used tissue back in his pocket.

The overhead wire was still singing. The girl's step on the cinders as she started across the tracks was loud and crisp. She was the only one to get off. She gave him a quizzical glance, then turned diagonally to his left to the well-worn path that cut across the fields. In the distance wooded hills rose darkly; closer—less than a quarter of a mile away—were a cluster of white-painted frame houses. The path headed in their direction.

Snuffling, he started after her.

"Ah, miss?" he called.

She stopped and turned, facing him. She was carrying a leather bag, a briefcase really, with a shoulder strap. It bulged and it looked heavy. He fought down the giddy impulse to ask her if he could carry her books.

"Yes?"

"You're—ah, Donna Albright?"

She started to nod, then shook her head. "You're half right. I'm Donna Smith."

He felt like doing something violent, like smacking his head with the palm of his hand. God, he felt tense about this. Instead he mumbled something incomprehensible and then said, "Umm, yes. That's what I meant. Donna Smith, I mean. My mistake."

He looked young; younger than he was. He'd shaved off his beard and he looked eighteen. He felt nervous and ill at ease. His stomach was knotted and he could still taste breakfast. He wondered why in hell he was doing this. God, she was pretty.

"Okay, so I'm Donna Smith. Were you waiting for me?"

Her brown hair was long, and hung in tight curls from under her cloche hat. The hat looked stupid, he thought; they always had. Her eyes were dark, and an impish smile lurked behind her lips. She was a lot prettier than the old photographs. He tried to think of something to say. He'd planned lots of things: clever, witty things. They were all evaporated by the reality of the scene.

"Uh, I wonder if I might, uh, walk with you...?" He felt himself flush. God, there it was: the schoolbooks gambit!

She laughed. "Okay. But I warn you—I have a pair of husky brothers at home." Her tone implied she didn't think they'd be necessary, though. He fell into step beside her; the path was a wide one. "But who are you, though?" she asked.

His fingers fidgeted with the tissues in his overcoat pocket. He'd worn that coat—the one he'd gotten from the Salvation Army— because it had seemed appropriate for the time. If he didn't take it off or open it, the clothes he had under it wouldn't matter. But now... well, what was he going to tell her? What *could* he tell her?

"Uh, I'm Bob," he said. The name felt clumsy on his lips, but he'd agreed not to use his real name. He remembered one of the lines he'd rehearsed. "I'm a friend of a friend, sorta..."

"Oh! Are you one of the guys Griff knows, down in Richmond?"

He started to deny it, then agreed.

"Have you been in the city? I mean, did you come out from Washington?"

"I was on an earlier trolley," he replied truthfully. The eight-mile trip had been quite an experience. The wooden-bodied car had swayed alarmingly from side to side as it took the long downstretch onto private right-of-way outside Rosslyn, across the bridge from Georgetown. The grade-schoolers, laughing and shouting back and forth up and down the aisle, had just whooped a little louder when the car hit the bend and then the upgrade again, and he'd clawed the worn seatback in front of him like the guard bar on a roller coaster. "I wanted to see the countryside," he added.

"This part of the Virginia is very pretty in the fall," Donna said, "but you missed the best part. I mean, when the trees turn colors. That was a couple of weeks ago; it's been a short fall. It's getting cold so fast. I expect we'll have snow soon. You can kind of smell it, you know?"

He snuffled again. "My sinuses," he offered in explanation. He dug another tissue from his pocket. It was half shredded; he'd been working it with his fingers. He pulled the cellophane packet and found a whole one. He blew on it. He glanced up to see Donna's large eyes staring at him, and he felt his face get hot again. Packets of pastel tissues—anachronistic? He hadn't thought.

The path dipped into a hollow, then crossed a stream gully on a wooden bridge. He felt very uncomfortable. The cold had started in his feet and worked well up his legs while he'd waited for her there at the trolley stop. Now he was chilled all over, and walking hadn't warmed his feet; it had only deadened them.

"You certainly are the strange one," Donna said.

He laughed nervously. He sure was.

"Uh, tell me: what year are you in college? You go to American U, don't you?"

She laughed. "Sophomore. I had a room with a girl in town last year, but I couldn't keep it up. It's almost as easy to come home nights. Good old AU…" Her voice trailed off almost dreamily. He realized he'd given her nothing, really, to say.

"Yeah, Griff told me about that," he said, trying to keep it going.

They reached the road. It was graveled clay, tufts of frost-killed weeds growing here and there down the center. They skirted an ice-filmed puddle. He glanced to the west. The sun was a weak, washed-out red blob half hidden in the tree line. Getting dark.

She noticed his glance. "Be home soon. You'll come in? Hot chocolate, tea, coffee?"

He agreed, grateful at the thought of something warm to drink. Then panic hit him: face her parents, her brothers? Could he?

The houses were to the left, grouped along the road about two hundred yards from where the path came out. Mott's Corners. Old Man Mott had put them up for each of his children. He followed

Donna to the right, following the road down a gentle slope. Donna kicked a rock that skittered along the worn track of the road and splashed into another puddle.

The sound of the car saved him from a final desperate attempt at conversation. He heard it before he saw it: a wheezing, rattling, four-banger with a muffler that had to be about shot. Then it appeared over the hill to their left, heading down a side road on a collision course with theirs. At first only its high square roof was visible over the tall tangled weeds of the field. The field was fenced off with two strands of rusty barbed wire, but he couldn't see that they served much of a purpose.

"Hey, there's Jimmy!" Donna said. "It's my brother Jimmy!" She jumped up and down and waved her arm at the approaching car.

The car answered with a raucous honk and then, with a clatter of gravel, made the turn at the foot of the hill onto their road. It was bearing down on them so fast that he made a hasty jump into the weeds at the side of the road.

"Hey!" Donna shouted, and the car jolted to a stop in front of them. It was a Model T, black. The top was frayed and the side curtains flapped loosely. The driver was a freckled kid with a wide grin. He had to be at least three years underage for a license.

"Hiya, Donna! How'dya like it? I got her running again! Thought I'd come over and pick ya up. You're late. Who's this?"

Jimmy. James Smith. It was hard to believe.

"This is Bob. He's a friend of Griff's. He's come out for the evening. He's half frozen, I think. I'm glad you came along." Donna introduced them, and Jimmy gave him a salute and waved them aboard.

The car had a nominal backseat, but all that was left was an old orange crate. He squatted on it and peered over the cracked leather back of the front seat as Donna settled next to her brother and Jimmy ground the gears to begin a lurching crawl backwards.

They backed to the intersection, then turned up the short hill. The color had faded from the sky. The farmland had the brown tinge of sepia-toned photographs. The world seemed very thin then: two-dimensional, attic-dry and musty. But at the same time every pothole the car struck was another jolt to his cold-deadened body, the car had an overpowering gasoline smell that cut through even his clogged sinuses, and Donna's head was so close to his face as he leaned forward that he could feel the heat of her skin. Getting schizy?

The car topped the rise, then raced wildly down the slope and up a more gradual grade. Ahead, two windows warm glows in the blackness of its tar-paper exterior, stood the Smith house.

Jimmy swerved the car across the hard ruts, over the rough ground, and halted it with a screech from its mechanical brakes within inches of the footings for the new wing.

Tall oaks hung like black skeletons over the narrow two-story house, a few tattered leaves still clinging to their branches. The house itself was only half finished; he recognized that without Donna's quick remark, "Dad and the boys've been building the house in their spare time; it's still got some to go." There was a note of pride in her voice, but the porch was only a rude platform without a roof, the north wing was just a line of trenches, and the siding wasn't on yet—thin strips of furring that followed the interior studs were all that held the tar paper over the subframe walls. There was no yard in front. Behind and to one side was the chicken house and chicken yard. But the garage hadn't been built next to it yet, and a truck garden showed its empty furrows on the other side of the house. It was a rude place. When he climbed awkwardly down from the car, he almost tripped over an engine block. Jimmy apologized. "Chevy engine," he said. "Next spring, boy..."

Dad Smith was a big man; he looked more like a lantern-jawed Swede than a mathematician whose parents were from Liverpool. He had a full head of bushy brown hair, and his high forehead was still clear of liver spots. He stuck out his bony hand and it was engulfing. "Friend of Griff's, huh?" Smith said, nodding. "How they treating Griff down there?"

"As well as you'd expect," he replied with a nervous laugh.

"I expect as long's you're here, you'll want to go up to the Ballards' for a chat?"

He shook his head, then improvised. "Actually, I didn't know Griff that well...I mean, when I said I'd be out in this neck of the woods, he said to say hi to Donna, and...Well, I didn't expect to do more than, uh, just that. Just a 'Hi,' and...well, I'm pushing my schedule a bit already, sir." Damn that Griff Ballard story, anyway! And damn Donna for going around so much with him, too. Of course, the Ballards and the Smiths were neighbors, and when she'd suggested it, he'd picked up on Griff as a likely introduction, so...

"This is my mother, Bob."

Mrs. Smith was tiny standing next to her husband. She had come from the doorway that led to the kitchen, wiping her hands slowly and carefully on her apron. When she spoke, it was with a touch of the Midwest—Iowa, he remembered—as she welcomed him and asked what he'd like to drink.

Soon he was settled in a comfortable chair, a mug of hot chocolate in his hand. A potbellied iron stove in the corner radiated a warm glow into the cozy room, and the smell of woodsmoke and occasional crackling of the burning logs was strangely nostalgia-evoking. He felt a warming tingle return to his toes.

"Where's Paul?" Donna asked, once she had him out of his coat and settled with the chocolate.

"Upstairs," Mr. Smith said, eyes twinkling. "Pitching pennies."

"Oh, Dad! Not again! Don't you have enough statistics by now?"

"I'll run up and get him," Jimmy volunteered.

So far no one had said anything about his clothes. "Pitching pennies?" he asked.

"Dad's a statistician—he's with the Bureau of Standards, in Washington," Donna said. She let the smile quirk up the corners of her mouth. It seemed to include him in their private joke; it made her delicately impish. "He's always got us doing things like that."

A clumping on the stairs heralded Paul, Jimmy right behind him.

"How goes it?" Mr. Smith asked.

"Cold," replied Paul, laconically. You could see he took after his father—the same big frame, bushy hair, lumberjack look, only thinner, younger. *He hasn't changed much.* "The longest run was thirteen heads."

"You have the register open?" his father asked. There was an opening in the ceiling over the stove for hot air to move into the upstairs rooms.

"I lose too many pennies that way." Paul's expression didn't change.

"Paul, this is Bob. He's a—a friend of Griff's," Donna said.

He pulled himself up out of the chair and offered his hand to Paul. Paul gave it a negligent shake, and him a vague nod. He seemed not at all interested in the boyfriends of his young sister.

"You make chocolate?" Paul asked. "I could use some; keep my hands warm, anyway."

Donna frowned, but went out to the kitchen.

He felt awkward, standing like that, so he returned to his seat with a strange guilty little knot tight in his stomach. *He had no business here.*

When Donna returned with another steaming mug, a calico cat followed her out. The cat stalked immediately over to him and sniffed at his shoes. He smiled, leaned over, and held out his hand. The cat gave one brief sniff, then turned tail and retreated to the kitchen.

"Don't mind Paul," Jimmy said, inclining his head toward the stairs.

Above, a door shut. "He's that way with everybody. He's going for his doctorate next spring."

"Mathematics?" he asked, surprised.

"English," Jimmy replied.

"Jimmy," Mr. Smith said, rising from his rocker. "Time for the chores." He led the way to the door, lifting down a tent of an old coat from the peg to the right of the door. A moment later, the front door slammed shut and the stove chuckled to itself in the fresh onslaught of cold air.

They were alone then, the two of them, by themselves in the sudden silence of the room. From the kitchen came the clang of a cast-iron skillet on the heavy metal top of the old wood-burning kitchen stove. Above them, floorboards creaked at odd moments.

She was staring at him. Again he asked himself, *What am I doing in this place?* But he made no move to get up.

Nervously fingering his narrow lapel, he broke the silence, saying, "I'd like to tell you some things...Totally outrageous things. You have to promise me just one thing first."

"What's that?" Her voice was soft. Their voices would not carry beyond the room.

"That you won't believe a word of it." That was weaseling, and he knew it. He wasn't supposed to be doing this. *This was forbidden.*

She giggled, and in that moment he was starkly aware of her youth. "Okay," she said. "Shoot."

What was he supposed to be? Could he just enter her life like this and leave it again, without telling her *any* of the truth? "I'm going to try to tell your fortune," he said, lying. It wouldn't be hers.

"You want to see my palm?"

He laughed. "Not that sort of fortune. I am going to close my eyes and see your aura, your fourth-dimensional aura. I am going to follow it into the future and tell you what I see for you there..." He squeezed shut his eyes; they felt dry and stinging. He paused. He felt as though his voice might break.

"Well?" She leaned forward eagerly. "What do you see?"

"I see you meeting a tall man with black hair," he said. "You're going to marry him."

She laughed. "I thought you knew Griff," she said. "He's short and blond."

He nodded. "That's true...I—I see great metal airliners with wings as big as this house, airplanes that can carry hundreds of people, scores of cars or trucks. They're flying so high overhead that the sound they make follows across the sky far behind them, they're so fast and far away. I see, I see great rockets, tall as high buildings, poised like bullets to shoot out into space and to the moon...

"I see sleek, low automobiles built of plastic and shimmering with iridescent colors, streaking along vast highways at speeds over a hundred miles an hour. I see...radios the size of cigarette packages... Phono—uh, gramophones that play hour-long records...Television sets that receive wireless broadcasts of color pictures on their own screens..."

She laughed again. "Oh, I've seen all those! The *Times-Herald* Sunday supplements are full of that sort of stuff."

She shouldn't have laughed.

"I see war," he said. His voice tore from his throat, and his expression was tight and twisted. "War, beyond any war you've dreamed. Bombs—so many bombs exploding over cities that the very air itself catches fire. And the airplanes that carry the bombs—so many hundreds of them that they blacken the sky. I see whole countries—continents, even—devastated, laid waste.

"A war to end all wars," he went on bitterly. "But more wars follow, more boys die, and the bombs get bigger, until a single bomb can wipe out a city the size of New York.

"I see populations growing unchecked, squalid slums and mass poverty and starvation, creeping over the world. I see death, and destruction—hatreds that tear this country apart by its roots. I see our cities collapsing in riots, mobs thronging the streets looting and killing, and the soldiers coming out in tanks and firing their guns at their countrymen.

"I see napalm washing liquid fire over a mother who sits in a gutter holding her dead baby—"

"*Stop!*"

He opened his eyes. She was staring at him, shocked, wide-eyed. Her cheeks glistened.

"Why? Why are you saying all these things?"

"I-I-'m sorry," he said. "I shouldn't have." His voice shook. "I told you, you weren't to believe me."

"I don't. Maybe we're in a Great Depression, like they say, but that's no reason to talk like *that.*"

"You're right," he said. She was right. He'd been warned. "It was a bum idea. Forget it."

"You made it all up." It wasn't quite a statement.

He nodded. "Yes," he said, "yes, I made it all up. I guess I get depressed sometimes. Things—like the Hoovervilles, you know." His mug was empty and cold. He got up. "I better go now."

She looked up at him. "You're very strange," she said.

You should only know.

"Thanks for the hospitality," he said. "Thank your mother for the hot chocolate, please." He pulled on his overcoat. "Say goodbye for me to Jimmy, Paul..."

"Bob—" She put her hands on his and looked up at him. He couldn't keep his eyes from hers. "I...You *were* making it all up?"

He felt disoriented and distant. He seemed to be staring down a long tunnel into her eyes, while somewhere else, in another place, her hands were warm and soft and alive on his.

"I'll close my eyes once more," he said. "Ahh...I see you, married, happy, in a sunlit yard beside a red-brick house. It's close by here; your father will give you the land to build on." Only her hands held him from swaying in the darkness that engulfed him. "I see no wars, only sunshine, for you," he said. It was the truth—as far as it went. He owed her at least that much.

"I believe you," she said.

The stars were cold and hard and bright, and the frosty air cut his throat. Underfoot, frozen crass crunched. Woodenly, his whole body feeling at once adrenalated and drained, Donald Albright followed the almost-familiar rutted road back down the hill. He did not see where he was walking. He could still smell her hair, still feel her soft handclasp. Wherever he looked, her dark eyes seemed to stare back at him. She was so young, so pretty, so...innocent. He began to shake with had dry sobs.

Mother, he thought. *Why did you have to die? Before I could even know you—?*

*S*cience fiction editor and author *Theodore Edward White (1938-) worked his way up from fanzine contributions (winning the Hugo Award for Best Fan Writer 1968) to editorial posts. Assistant editor of* **Fantasy and Science Fiction** *from 1963 to 1968, he is perhaps best known now for guiding* **Amazing Stories,** *the world's first science fiction magazine, through financially perilous times to its present more stable position, stressing high-quality (often avant-garde) writing, by authors such as Philip K. Dick, Ursula K. LeGuin, and Roger Zelazny. His novels include* **Phoenix Prime** *(Lancer, 1966), a fast-moving adventure about a* *psionic superman, and **By Furies Possessed** (1970), about earth-lings possessed by alien parasitic beings. Other titles include two anthologies, **The Best from Amazing Stories** and **The Best from Fantastic**, released from Manor in 1973.*

CRY HAVOC

DAVIS GRUBB

In 1923 the family Pollixfen migrated from Eire to settle in the small Ohio River town of Glory, West Virginia. Sean Pollixfen was a big florid boast of a man of common heritage. His wife, Deirdre, was a lady of gentle breeding; raised in a Georgian townhouse in Dublin's Sackville Street, she deplored Sean's harsh upbringing of their only child—ten-year-old Benjamin Michael.

The Pollixfen house was a rambling one-story structure with a great blue front door and slate flagstones set level with its threshold. Their nearest neighbor was a man named Hugger who dwelt a good three blocks up Liberty Avenue.

When the Thing began, it was an autumn night at supper. Benjy abruptly laid down his knife and fork and tilted his ear, harking. "But for what?" Sean asked him.

"I was listening for the auguries of the War that's coming, sor."

"Wisht, now, boyo!" cried Sean. "'Tis 1932. The Great War ended fourteen years ago this November. And surely there's not another one in sight."

Sean paused, reminiscing, smiling.

"Still, somehow I'd favor another War," he said. "I'm proud to be wearing the sleeve of this good linen jacket pinned up to me left shoulder. I lost that hook at First Ypres. Yet, despite that, it was a Glory."

Benjy made no reply, though a moment later he left the table, went to the bathroom, and threw up his supper.

Next morning at eight two men pulled up in a truck out front. Moments later they had laboriously borne a huge pine crate to the flagstone threshold and rang the bell. Sean, on his way to his Position at the Firm, answered their ring.

"Is this here the residence of Master Benjamin Michael Pollixfen?"

"It is that," Sean replied, rapping the crate with his malacca cane. "'Tis another gift for me boy Benjy from his Uncle Liam in Kilronan. He's always sending the lad a grand present, no matter what the occasion!"

That night when they had finished supper, Sean went to Benjy's room. He stared at the great crate's contents, all ranked round the room so thick that one could scarce walk among them. There were 5,000 miniature lead soldiers—Boche, French, and English. There was every manner of ammunition and instrument of warfare, from caissons and howitzers to hangars and tarmac for the landing fields of the miniature aircraft of all varieties and types—from Gotha bombers for the Boche to D.H.4's for the British and Bréguets for the French.

"Now Liam is showing good sense," Sean said. "Rocking horses were fine for you a year ago. But you're ten now, Benjy. 'Tis time you learned the lessons of Life's most glorious Game!"

Benjy stared at the little soldiers, cast and tinted down to the very wrinkle of a puttee, the drape of a trenchcoat. Moreover, no two soldiers wore the same facial expressions. Benjy could read in these faces Fear, Zest, Valor, Humdrum, Cravenness, Patriotism, and Sedition. And somehow each of them seemed waiting. But for what? For whom? Sean missed seeing these subtleties. Yet Benjy saw. Benjy knew. Aye, he knew all too well.

"They are green, dads," Benjy said. "Green as the turf of Saint Stephens Green park. The British officers are just days out of Sandhurst, the gun crews hardly a fortnight from the machine-gun school at Wisquies. They don't know the noise of a whizbang from a four-ten or a five-nine. Yet once they've been through a bloody baptism such as Hannescamps or the Somme they'll know. Aye, they'll know then."

"And what would *you* be knowing of Hannescamps or the Somme?" Sean chuckled.

Benjy made no reply.

And so the three strange weeks of it began. Benjy spent every waking hour working feverishly in the great black lot of non-arable ground beyond Deirdre's flower-and-kitchen garden. While about him all the world seemed filled with the sound of locusts sawing down the great green tree of summer.

Benjy carved out the laceries of trenches with his Swiss Army knife. He found strips of lath and split them to lay down as duck-boards. He sandbagged the trenches well in front. Beyond this he staked, on ten-penny nails, the thin barbed wire which had come on spools in the great crate. Some distance to the rear of both sides he set up his little field hospitals, and his hangars and the tarmac fields for the little fighter, reconnaissance, and bombing planes.

At the kitchen door Sean would watch the boy and listen as Benjy chanted songs that Sean and his men had sung at Locrehof Farm or Trone Woods once they'd billeted down for a night in some daub-and-wattle stable. He could fairly smell the sweet ammoniac scent of the manure of kine, lambs, and goats, and the fragrance as well of the Gold Flake and State Express cigarettes they smoked, saving only enough to barter for a bottle or two of Pichon Longueville '89 or perhaps a liter of Paul Ruinart.

Strange to relate, it had not yet begun to trouble Sean that the boy knew of these things, that he sang songs Sean had never taught him and sometimes in French which *no one* had ever taught him. As for Benjy he soon began to show the strain. Deirdre's scale in the bath-room showed that in ten days he had lost twelve pounds. He seldom finished supper. For there was that half-hour's extra twilight to work in. Sean gloated. Deirdre grieved.

"Why in Saint Brigid's blessed name don't you put an end to it?" she would plead.

"No, woman, I shan't."

"And why not then?"

"Because me boyo shall grow up to be what I wanted for meself—a soldier-poet more glorious than Rupert Brooke or the taffy Wilfred Owen."

"And then dead of their cursed war—dead before they could come to full flower of Saint Brigid's sacred gift."

"So much the better," Sean replied icily one night. "We must all die one day or another. And no man knows the hour. Death it has no clocks. Moreover, we are Pollixfens. Kin on me father's side to Eire's glory of poets—William Butler Yeats."

"But Yeats died in no war," Deirdre protested.

"Better he had," Sean said. "'Twould have increased his esteem a thousandfold."

Deirdre went off to bed weeping.

Next night in Benjy's room Sean spoke his dreams out plain.

"'Tis stark truth, old man," he said. "Real War is a rough go. But there is that Glory of Glories in it."

Benjy said nothing.

"Don't you understand me, boyo? Glory!"

"I see no Glory," said the child. "I see poor fools butchering each other for reasons kept secret from them. Oh, they give reasons. King and Country. They leave out, of course, Industry. No, dads, there are no fields of Honor. There are only insane abattoirs."

Sean colored at this, got up and strode from the boy's room. Yet a minute later, unable to contain himself, he was back.

"Now, boyo!" he cried out. "Either you shed from yourself these craven, blasphemous, and treasonable speculations or I shall leave you to grow up and learn War the hard way. As did I."

"And what might that mean, sor?"

"It means that I shall go to Al Hugger's garage and fetch home three ten-gallon tins of petrol and douse the length and breadth of your little No Man's Land of toys and then set a lucifer to it."

"That would be a most fearsome mistake, sor. For on the morning when the little armies came they were mine. Now I am Theirs. And so, poor dads, are you."

"That does it then! 'Tis petrol and a lucifer for all five thousand of the little perishers!"

Benjy smiled. Sadly.

"But 'tis no longer a skimpy five thousand now, man dear. 'Tis closer to a million. Perhaps more. Even files-on-parade could not count their hosts."

"Wisht, now! How could that be? Did Liam send you another great crate?"

"No, sor. There's been Conscription on both sides. And enlistments by the million. A fair fever of outrage infects every man and boy of the King's Realm from Land's End to Aberdeen since Lord Kitchener went down in one of his Majesty's dreadnaughts off the Dolomites. Then there's Foch and Clemenceau and Joffre. They've whipped up the zest of Frenchmen to a pitch not known since the days of Robespierre and Danton in the Terror. In Germany the Boche seethe at every word from Hindenburg or Ludendorff or Kaiser Willie."

Benjy chuckled, despite himself.

"Willie—the English King's cousin! Willie and Georgie! Lord, 'tis more of a family squabble than a War!"

He sobered then.

"No, sor," Benjy said. "Cry havoc now and let loose the dogs of War!"

Sean stared, baffled.

"Tell me, boyo. If you loathe War so, why do you go at your little War game with such zest?"

"Why, because there's twins inside me, I suppose," Benjy replied, and press him as he might, Sean could elicit no more from the boy.

Sean's face sobered. He went off with a troubled mind to Deirdre in their goosedown bed. Lying there on his back he could hear Benjy singing an old war ditty—*The Charlie Chaplain Walk.* Sean's batman, a Nottinghamshire collier, had used to sing that before the Somme. Sean was drowsy but could not sleep. Yet soon he roused up wide-waking from the drowsiness. Was it thunder he heard out yonder in the night? And that flickering light across the sill of the back window. Was it heat lightning?

He stole from Deirdre's sound-sleeping side and stared out the rear window. A river fog lay waist deep upon the land. Among the tinted autumn trees the cold sweet light of fireflies came and went as though they were stars that could not make up their minds. Yet the flashes and flames that flickered beneath the cloak of mists on the black lot were not sweet, not cold.

Sean could hear the small smart chatter of machine guns. There were the blasts of howitzers and whizbangs and mortars. Above the shallow sea of leprous white mists the Aviatiks and Sopwith Strutters swooped and dove and immelmanned in dogfights.

Far to the rear Sean could see Benjy in his peejays, standing and watching. The child's wild face was grievous and weeping. He had flung out his spindly arms as if transcendentally to appease the madness to which he bore such suffering witness.

Sean crept shivering back into his bed. He lay awake, again thinking of Liam's great gift that had come to life, proliferated, and had now taken possession of himself and Benjy.

And it went on thus. For another two weeks. Then one morning all was changed. Pale, half staggering from lack of sleep and haggard-eyed from poring over the war map thumbtacked to his play table beneath the gooseneck lamp's harsh circle of illumination, Benjy— almost faint—came down to breakfast all smiles.

"What does that Chessy cat grin on your face mean, boyo?" Sean asked.

"C'est la guerre, mon vieux, c'est la guerre!" cried Benjy. "But last night news came through—"

"*C'est la guerre* and so on," Deirdre intervened. "And what might that alien phrase mean to these poor untutored ears?"

"'Tis French," Sean said. "That's War, old man, that's War."

"But now—tomorrow night at midnight—it will be over!" Benjy cried brightly.

"Tomorrow night and midnight be damned!" Sean exclaimed. "*Tonight* at midnight it shall end! I am unable to endure another night of it, and so I have determined to end it all meself! Benjy, I swear now by the holy martyred names of the Insurrection of Easter '16—Pearse, Casement, John Connolly, and the O'Rahilly—that I shall not let this thing possess the two of us for even one night more! I shall end it with me petrol and me lucifer at midnight tonight!"

"Lord save us, dads, you mustn't talk so!" cried Benjy. "Word has been flashed to all forces up and down the lines that the cease-fire is set for tomorrow's midnight. Already the gunfire is only token. Already the men crawl fearlessly over sandbags and under the barbed wire and march boldly into the midst of No Man's Land to embrace each other. They barter toffees and jars of Bovrils and tins of chocs for marzipan and *fastnacht krapfen* and strudels and *himbeer kuchen!* They show each other sweat-and-muck-smeared snapshots of mothers, sweethearts, and children back home. Men who a day ago were at each others' throats!"

Deirdre watched and listened, helpless, baffled, appalled.

"No matter to all the sweet sticky treacle of your talk!" Sean cried. "I'll not let this madness take possession of our home! So 'tis petrol and a lucifer to the whole game tonight at the strike of twelve! And a fiery fitting end to it all!"

"Bloody ballocks to that!" shouted Benjy, outraged.

"Go to your room, boy," Sean said, struggling to control himself. "We have man's words to say. Not words for the hearing of your mum."

A moment later Sean was strutting the length and breadth of Benjy's bedroom like a bloated popinjay. His swagger stick was in his hand; it seemed to give him back some of his old lost Valor, some long mislaid or time-rotted Authority. As he walked he slapped it in vainglorious bellicosity against his thigh.

Benjy watched him solemnly, sadly. "They'll not let you do this thing," he said. He paused. "Nor shall I."

Sean whirled, glaring.

"Ah, so it has come to that then!" he barked out in the voice of a glory-gutted martinet. "'Tis they shan't and I shan't and you shan't, eh? Well, we shall see about that! I am King of this house. And I am King of all its environs!"

256

"No," Benjy said, his face above the war map tacked to his table. "You are no King. You are a King's Fool. Though lacking in a King's Fool's traditional and customary wisdom and vision."

Sean broke then. In a stride he crossed the room and slashed the boy across the face with the swagger stick.

A thin ribbon of blood coursed down from the corner of Benjy's mouth. A droplet of it splattered like a tiny crimson starfish or a mark on the map to commemorate some dreadful battle encounter.

"King I say! King!" Sean was shouting, pacing the room again. There was a livid stripe across the child's cheek where the leather had fallen. But there was even more change in Benjy's face. And even something newer, something darker in the mind behind that face. The boy smiled.

"Come then," Benjy said softly. "Let us sit a while and tell sad stories of the Death of Kings."

For the rest of the day neither child nor father spoke nor looked each other in the eye. When occasionally they would be forced to pass in a corridor, it was in the stiff-legged, ominous manner of pit-bulls circling in a small seat-encircled arena. Deirdre, sensing something dreadful between them, was helplessly distraught. For what did she know of any of it, dear gentle Deirdre?

Benjy did not appear for supper. Sean ate ravenously. When he was done he drove his car into town and came back moments later with the three ten-gallons of petrol. He ranked them neatly alongside the black lot's border.

At nine Sean and Deirdre went to bed. For three hours Sean lay staring at the bar of harvest moonlight which fell across the carpet from the window sill to the threshold of the bedroom door. Now and again half-hearted gunfire could be heard from the black lot. Soon Sean began speaking within himself a wordless colloquy. Fear had begun to steal upon him. Misgivings. He could not forget the Thing he had seen in the boy's face after the blow of the stiff, hardened leather. He could never forget the strange new timbre of the boy's voice when he spoke softly shortly after.

As the great clock in the hallway struck the chime of eleven-thirty, Sean decided to forego the whole headstrong project. What could another twenty-four hours matter? There was scarcely any War waging in the black lot, anyway. Cheered by his essentially craven decision he started, in his nightshirt, down the hallway toward Benjy's room to inform him of his change of mind.

Within ten feet of the boy's bolted door Sean came to a standstill. He listened. It was unmistakable. The tiny quacking chatter of a voice speaking from a field telephone. And Benjy's murmurous voice giving orders back. Only one phrase caught Sean's ear. And that phrase set beads of sweat glistening on his face in the pallid gaslight of the long broad hallway. The words were in French. But Sean knew French.

"On a besoin des assassins."

Sean felt a chill seize him, shaming the manhood of him. "We now have need of the assassins."

Shamed to the core of his soul, Sean fled back to the bedroom. With his one arm he turned the key in the door lock. With that same arm he fetched a ladder-back chair from against the wall and propped the top rung under the knob. Then he hastened to the bureau drawer where he kept the memorabilia of his old long-forgotten War and fetched out his BEF Webley.

The pistol was still well greased. It was loaded, the cartridge pins a little dark with verdigris but operable. Then Sean went and lay atop the quilt, shivering and clutching the silly, ineffectual pistol in his hand.

That was when he first heard them. Myriad feet; tiny footsteps and not those of small animals with clawed and padded paws. Boots. Tiny boots. The myriad scrape of microscopically small hobnails. Boots. By the thousands. By the thousands of thousands. And then abruptly above their measured, disciplined tread there burst forth suddenly the skirl of Royal Scots' Highlanders' bagpipes, the rattle of tiny drums, the piercing tweedle of little fifes, the brash impudence of German brass bands.

Deirdre still slept. Even the nights of the War in the black lot had never wakened her. It was to Sean's credit that he did not rouse her now. For, as never before in his life—not even in the inferno of First Ypres or the Somme—had he so craved the company of another mortal. A word. A touch. A look.

Abruptly, just beyond the door, there was a command followed by total silence. Sean chuckled. They were not out there. It had been a fantasy of the overwrought mind. A nightmare—a *cauchmare* as the French call it. But his tranquillity was short-lived. He heard a tiny voice in German crying orders to crank a howitzer to its proper angle of trajectory. Another shouted command. Sean sensed, with an old soldier's instinct, the yank of the lanyard. He heard the detonation, felt the hot Krupp steel barrel's recoil, saw flame flare as the shell blasted a ragged hole in the door where the lock had been.

The impact flung the door wide and sent the chair spinning across the moonlit carpet. And now, in undisciplined and furious anarchy, they swarmed across the door sill like a blanket of gray putrescent mud. Gone from them were the gay regimental colors, the spit-and-polish decorum of the morning of the great crate's arrival. Now they were muck-draped and gangrenous, unwashed and stinking of old deaths, old untended wounds. Some knuckled their way on legless stumps. Others hobbled savagely on makeshift crutches.

Sean sat up and emptied every bullet from the Webley into their midst. He might as well have sought to slaughter the sea with handfuls of flung seashells. All of them wore tiny gas masks. A shouted command and small steel cylinders on miniature wheeled platforms were trundled across the door sill and ranked before the bed. Another shout and gun crews of four men each wheeled in, to face the bed, behind the gas cylinders, ten Lewis and ten Maxim machine guns.

At a cry from the leader these now began a raking enfilade of Sean's body. He had but time to cross himself and begin a Hail Mary when the cocks of the little gas cylinders were screwed open and the first green cloud of gas reached his nostrils. Enveloped in a cloud of gas, the big man uttered one last choking scream and slid onto the carpet and into their very midst.

In a twinkling they swarmed over him like a vast shroud of living manure. They stabbed him with the needle points of their tiny bayonets, again and again. At last one of these sought out and found the big man's jugular vein. A shouted command again. The lift and fall of a bloody saber.

"All divisions—ri' tur'!"

And to a man they obeyed.

"All divisions—'orm rank!"

Again they obeyed.

"All divisions—quick 'arch!"

And with pipers skirling, drums drubbing, fifes shrilling, and brass bands blaring they went the way they had come. The siege was a *fait accompli.*

Awakened by all the gunfire and clamor at last, and at the very moment of the door's collapse, Deirdre sat up, watching throughout. First in smiling disbelief, then in fruitless attempt to persuade herself that she was dreaming it all, then in acceptance, and, at last, in horror. Now as the first wisps of the chlorine stung her nostrils she went raving and irreversibly insane, sprang from her side of the bed, and hurtled through the side window, taking screen and all, to tumble onto the turf three feet below.

In the hushed autumn street of the night Deirdre, beneath the moon and the galaxies and the cold promiscuous fireflies, fled back into the hallucination of Youth returned. She raced up and down under the tinted trees. She twirled an imaginary pink lace parasol as if doing a turn on a small stage. She chanted the Harry Lauder and Vesta Tilley ballads from the music halls of her Dublin girlhood.

Wakened by all this daft medley of unfamiliar songs, Al Hugger, the nearest neighbor, took down his old AEF Springfield rifle and came to the house to discover what calamity had befallen it.

When, at last, he stood in the bedroom doorway, he looked first at the monstrous ruin which had been Sean, humped in his blood on the carpet by the bed. Then Hugger saw the blasé and unruffled figure of Benjy, clad only in his peejays and sitting straight as the blackthorn stick of a Connaught County squire in the ladder-back chair now back against the wall. Almost all the gas had been cleared from the room by the clean river wind which coursed steadily between the two open windows.

"No one," Hugger said presently—more to himself than to the child—"shall likely ever know what happened in this room tonight. Better they don't. Yes, I hope they don't. Never. For there is something about it all—something—"

Benjy yawned. Prodigiously. He smiled hospitably at Al Hugger. He looked at the thing—like a great beached whale—on the carpet by the bedside. He yawned again.

"C'est la guerre, mon vieux, c'est la guerre," he said.

D̲avis Grubb (1919-1980) is best known for his novel **The Night of the Hunter,** *about a mad minister who hunts and tries to kill two children who block his search for hidden treasure, made into a rather sinister movie in 1955 starring Robert Mitchum and Lillian Gish. Grubb was born in Moundsville, West Virginia. Nearly all his earlier fiction is set in that state, including what is probably his major work, the massive novel* **The Voices of Glory**—*somewhat like a darker and grimmer* **Spoon River Anthology**—*in which are revealed the secret lives of the people of the fictional small town of Glory. Grubb is more than just a regional writer: his characters' trials, terrors, and triumphs are those of all humanity. In his later years Grubbs traveled more, lecturing and reading from his work, more of his fiction being set in other locales. His macabre stories are collected in two volumes,* **Twelve Tales of Suspense and the Supernatural** *(Scribner's, 1964), and* **The Siege of 813** *(Back Fork, 1978).*

FRANK D. McSHERRY, who lives in McAlester, Oklahoma, has had his mystery stories and articles published in *The Armchair Detective, The Mystery Fancier,* and a number of other periodicals. **CHARLES G. WAUGH**, Professor of Communications and Psychology at the University of Maine at Augusta, and **MARTIN H. GREENBERG**, an Editorial Consultant with "Amazing Stories," have coedited over 200 books in the science fiction and horror fields. McSherry, Waugh, and Greenberg previously collaborated on *A Treasury of American Horror Stories.*